ZOMROMCOM

"With heart-pounding action, delightfully madcap humor, and a swoony romance to *lose your head* over, Olivia Dade's *Zomromcom* is a riotously good time from start to finish. I couldn't turn the pages fast enough!"

—Jenna Levine, *USA Today* bestselling author of
My Vampire Plus-One

"Sexy, smart, and funny. . . . Set in a near future full of zombies, werewolves, and vampires, I was caught up not only in the world-building but also the journey of the two leads. . . . I loved this, and I can't wait to read whatever [Dade] writes next."

—Kimberly Lemming, *USA Today* bestselling author of
I Got Abducted by Aliens and Now I'm Trapped in a Rom-Com

"This book is wildly, joyfully hilarious and deliciously thrilling, mingling real paranormal chills with zany humor. I can't remember the last time any rom-com made me laugh out loud so often! A total win."

—Stephanie Burgis, author of *Wooing the Witch Queen*

remarkable, essential addition to the modern romance canon. A slow burn that delivers in spades."

—Rosie Danan, *USA Today* bestselling author of *The Roommate*

"Dade once again dazzles and delights readers as she delivers a heart-meltingly romantic, sensually steamy love story that also embraces body positivity and thoughtfully explores such real-life issues as clinical depression and grief. Wielding a devilishly wicked sense of wit . . . Dade deftly demonstrates her mastery of love and laughter."
—*Booklist* (starred review)

"This swoony contemporary romance is well-written and paced, but what really makes it shine are the intricate characters that Dade has brought to life."
—*Library Journal* (starred review)

"Nuanced, unflinching, and deeply romantic. Dade's fans and new readers alike will fall in love."
—*Publishers Weekly* (starred review)

"A funny and poignant triumph that defies expectation. . . . Dade has gifted readers with a thoughtful, swoonworthy, and emotionally satisfying contemporary romance."
—*BookPage* (starred review)

ZOM ROMCOM

OLIVIA ♥ DADE

BERKLEY ROMANCE
NEW YORK

BERKLEY ROMANCE
Published by Berkley
An imprint of Penguin Random House LLC
1745 Broadway, New York, NY 10019
penguinrandomhouse.com

Book design by Jenni Surasky

Library of Congress Cataloging-in-Publication Data

Names: Dade, Olivia, author.
Title: Zomromcom / Olivia Dade.
Description: First edition. | New York: Berkley Romance, 2025.
Identifiers: LCCN 2024048199 (print) | LCCN 2024048200 (ebook) |
ISBN 9780593818206 (trade paperback) | ISBN 9780593818213 (ebook)
Subjects: LCGFT: Romance fiction. | Paranormal fiction. | Novels.
Classification: LCC PS3604.A29 Z43 2025 (print) |
LCC PS3604.A29 (ebook) | DDC 813/.6—dc23/eng/20241104
LC record available at https://lccn.loc.gov/2024048199
LC ebook record available at https://lccn.loc.gov/2024048200

First Edition: August 2025

Printed in the United States of America
1st Printing

The authorized representative in the EU for product safety and compliance is
Penguin Random House Ireland, Morrison Chambers, 32 Nassau Street,
Dublin D02 YH68, Ireland, https://eu-contact.penguin.ie.

For Kat Latham, who kept me company as I drafted my first-ever paranormal romance, laughed at even my worst jokes, and urged me to write *yet more* Gaston songs. The joy of writing this book is splashed all over its pages, and that joy came from you. Thank you, my dear friend. Love you!

RULES:

1. Containment Zone access requires a valid passcard at every Wall. Unauthorized visitors are not permitted within the Zone.

2. Civilian use of drones is not permitted within the Zone.

3. Designate a safe shelter in case of emergency, preferably in a location accessible only via deep water or climbing. In your shelter, store enough food, water, and other necessities to last a week.

4. In the unlikely event of another breach, immediately enter and secure your shelter, then contact the Containment Zone Emergency Line, either via our handy app or toll-free number: 1-800-555-ZOMB. Once the sirens sound, all drawbridges will be raised and Walls Two, Three, and Four will seal shut. No exit from the Containment Zone will be possible. Shelter in place until responding troops give the all clear.

These rules originate from a joint task force composed of United States government officials and the Supernatural and Enhanced Ruling Council (SERC). If you have any questions or concerns, please contact your local official or Council member.

THE MORE WE KNOW, THE SAFER WE GROW!

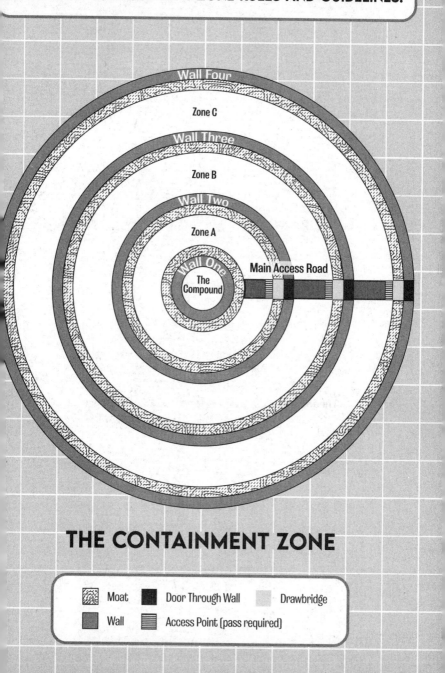

Wall Four

Zone C

Wall Three

Zone B

Wall Two

Zone A

Wall One

The Compound

Main Access Road

THE CONTAINMENT ZONE

Moat

Wall

Door Through Wall

Access Point (pass required)

Drawbridge

1

Armed with a burrito, Edie rounded her car and sprinted to intercept the zombie.

She'd prefer to be carrying the knife she brought with her on her daily zombie-scouting walks or the cleaver she sometimes used to cut her soaps. Both weapons would actually kill zombies—by cutting off their heads or carving out their hearts, two of only three ways the creatures could be slain—rather than simply sprinkling them with medium-hot corn salsa.

Too bad Chad would be a headless corpse before she could grab either weapon.

People used to picture zombies shuffling slowly toward their victims, arms outstretched as they droned about *brains, braaaaaains*, but a secret, ill-fated government experiment had proven everyone wrong. She'd seen their startling, terrifying speed for herself almost exactly twenty years before, back when she was eighteen, as she'd spotted the first gaunt, gray-pale creature racing silently on all fours toward—

Didn't matter. A burrito was what she had. Thus, a burrito she would use. Somehow. Even though the various self-defense courses she'd taken had neglected sufficient coverage of the tortilla-wielding martial arts.

Her sweet idiot of a neighbor stood on the unlit front porch of his dilapidated brick rancher as the sun dipped below the horizon and shadows stretched to swallow him. Chad wore headphones and didn't react to her shouted warning. No one else came running to help either, and no matter what happened, no one would. There were eleven homes on their cul-de-sac, and only two were currently occupied. Hers. Chad's.

She was the only one who could save him. Or at least attempt to save him.

Oh gods, she didn't want to die. But she couldn't let someone else—*anyone* else—perish while she ran to rescue herself. Not again.

The creature was only a dozen long strides away from Chad now, lunging upward and onto its hind legs in preparation for the kill, elongated teeth yellowed and sharp and bared, claws outstretched to rip Chad's head from his absurdly broad shoulders before cracking his skull open like an egg and slurping down the tasty yolk of a brain.

She skidded into the zombie's path, panting and terrified, and kicked it in the chest with every ounce of her strength and desperation.

Mistake. Big mistake. The creature stopped, true. But it stumbled maybe a half step back and to the side, that was all, while the impact numbed her entire leg and jolted her off-balance. As she struggled to stay upright, to assume a defensive stance, the zombie growled something hoarsely—

Bonjour? That couldn't be right.

—its red-rimmed eyes now fixed on . . . her. Which had been her intent, but still. Shit.

She swatted it across the snout with her foil-wrapped burrito.

Its stare narrowed, empty of anything but feral rage. As she took several hasty steps backward, the creature stalked forward, slowly now, still upright.

It could tear her to pieces whenever it wanted. It had time to play with its food.

Like her, Chad had cleared all vegetation from a sizable area surrounding his house. No attacker could approach without being seen, because even a last-second warning was better than none. But that meant the nearest climbable tree was maybe twenty, thirty feet away.

She wouldn't make it. She had to try.

Even though she probably wouldn't survive this encounter, every moment she distracted the creature would allow Chad time to finally clue in to what was happening right beside his freaking front porch and run for his life. Preferably up a ladder, where the zombie couldn't follow.

He could call the hotline then. Sound the alarm. Alert everyone else in the Containment Zone to take shelter and wait in safety until the government helicoptered in sufficient troops to remedy the breach and eradicate the zombies once and for all.

After a final shout of warning to Chad, she turned to run as the zombie bent its hind legs in preparation for a fatal pounce.

Hopefully it wouldn't hurt too much. Please, let it not hurt too much.

After only a single stride, something warm and wet sprayed across her back as the zombie's guttural snarl cut off abruptly, and an involuntary sob tore from her throat. Oh no. *No.* Poor, dim, puppy-dog-friendly Chad had attempted to rescue her and died horribly for his efforts.

Why hadn't he taken advantage of the creature's utter focus on her?

Had she really sacrificed her entire future for nothing?

If she looked back, she knew what she'd see. Tearing claws and teeth. Blood. A skull cleaved and emptied in two slurps. It was her own future spread before her, steaming in the wintry cold of a late-December dusk, since the zombie could and would still reach her before she managed to heave herself up into the nearest tree and climb high enough, no matter how hard she ran.

She looked back anyway. Then promptly tripped over something—a mole hole, maybe—and fell hard on her ass. Her miraculously intact burrito thumped onto the crabgrass beside her.

Against a dusky blue sky rapidly fading to darkness, a silhouette wavered in front of her watery stare. Someone—or something— tall, standing far too close, with thick, muscular legs braced for battle. Holding a knife, its edge dripping and dark.

Zombies couldn't use tools. Not since that last, fatal dose of serum.

Gasping, she dashed her wrist over her eyes, and he came into focus.

Chad. Not dead. Not clad in a baseball cap, faded jeans, and a Miller Lite tee. Not smiling goofily at her. Not harmless.

The zombie had leapt upon her, clearly, and she was near death herself, hallucinating in her final, semiconscious moments upon this earth. Because Chad—*just Chad, dude, last names are dumb*—was wearing an open black leather hoodie, hideous black cloven-toed shoes, and what appeared to be sheepskin under-wear. Also a bored, disdainful expression directed unmistakably at her.

That was all. That was everything.

No shirt. No pants. Not even a hint of gratitude or friend-liness.

At his feet lay the zombie, rent in two distinct pieces, both soaked in sickly yellow blood. The head to Chad's right, the body to the left, separated as neatly as any guillotine could have done. Robespierre would have been envious.

For some reason, her poor dying brain supplied a propulsive yet chilly European beat to the sight of Chad the Zombie Slayer staring down his nose at her.

With a graceful flick of his hand, he tossed aside his over-the-ear headphones. Nightfall had darkened his golden-brown hair and transformed his blue eyes into shadowed black pools. His brows were thick slashes drawn over that strong, straight nose, and his full mouth drew thin in seeming disapproval.

"You're a fool," he pronounced.

She didn't take offense. Given her current state of abject con-fusion, he might very well be correct. Although if Bro Chad had ever made such an accusation—which he never would—she'd have howled with laughter before removing the Miller Lite from his hand and pouring it over his head.

Even his voice was different now. Deeper, more clipped and supercilious, with the faintest hint of a French accent, even though she could have sworn he was one hundred percent Mid-Atlantic Bro down to his marrow.

Numbly, she took stock of herself.

When she prodded her throat, her neck felt entirely intact.

When she scanned her surroundings, she saw exactly what she'd have expected to see, excluding Euro Chad.

His ranch house, with its sagging front porch.

All the other crumbling homes arrayed on either side of their street, empty since the Breach twenty years ago. Which would now be called the First Breach, most likely, since a second had clearly occurred.

Her little brick split-level next door, its windows pitch-black, its shutters unsecured for the night. She hadn't anticipated an after-Christmas rush at the post office, and by the time she'd dealt with all her packages and hastily supervised the construction of her burrito, she'd been running far too late for comfort.

Wall Two still hunkered in the near distance, a reliable landmark and one of four thick stone barriers arrayed in concentric circles around the zombies' once-secret fireproof, bombproof underground compound. As always, the wall blocked the low-hanging moon early in the evening, along with any lights from the houses on the other side.

She patted her head. As far as she could tell, her brain remained unmasticated and still in her skull. But if she'd somehow survived intact, she didn't understand how, and she couldn't explain the appearance of Euro Chad.

Was this a dream?

The dampness from the grass had begun seeping through the thick fabric of her coveralls, though, making her butt increasingly clammy and cold. Just like it would if she were alive and conscious and not either dying horribly or thrashing through a nightmare.

She stared up at Euro Chad, trying her best to ignore the body at his feet. "Am I asleep?"

"No." He wiped his blade off on the grass, then tucked it somewhere in his hoodie. "Get up."

"Are you some kind of reaper, then, here to escort me to my afterlife? Because you don't look like one, frankly." She squinted at him, her ass still planted on the ground. "Although maybe all reapers wear sheepskin granny panties. I don't know your lives. Er, afterlives. Non-lives, whatever."

His sneer became a scowl. "These aren't granny panties. They're *fashion*."

"Look like furry granny panties to me."

Muttering something under his breath, he turned his back to her, the movement abrupt and impatient.

Her brows rose at the sight of a thong, as well as what surrounded that thong.

Say what you would about Euro Reaper Chad—both versions of him, each aggravating in his own way—but he apparently did his share of squats. Gluteus maximus indeed.

"That has to chafe," she pointed out, cautiously getting to her feet and tucking her burrito into her cross-body bag, just in case people still needed to eat in the afterlife. "Don't reapers get wedgies? Either the ass or toe variety?"

Because those aesthetic abominations on his feet and his sheepskin thong had to be freaking uncomfortable, fashionable or not.

There. She was fully upright again. Her legs still shook a little beneath her, but they were solid enough. They would carry her . . . well, wherever she needed to go next. Would Euro Reaper Chad help her cross a mystical river? Or guide her through paradisical fields of—

"We don't have time for this nonsense." Swiveling to face her once more, he claimed her hand in a firm, cool grip and began hauling her toward his front porch. "Even you must know that zombies travel as a pack. If we've seen one, we'll shortly see more. We need to seek immediate shelter before we're overrun."

"I don't understand." If she was already a goner, why worry about more zombies? "Is there some way for me to be extra super double dead?"

"You're not dead yet. But you will be if you don't *hurry*."

Shaking her head in an attempt to clear her thoughts, she stumbled after him as quickly as she could. Because if she truly was alive and conscious, Euro Non-Reaper Chad was right. She *did* need to hurry.

He hustled her through the dark front yard while she dazedly scanned the tree line of his property, searching for movement. If she had a choice, she didn't usually go out after dusk. Not because the zombies avoided daylight—in the First Breach, they'd murdered hundreds of humans under a sunlit cerulean sky—but because at nightfall the chances of spotting them in time for an escape dropped from unlikely to nearly impossible.

Which another zombie promptly proved by leaping up onto the side of the porch from the shadows below, jaw already stretched wide and aimed for her neighbor's throat, growling something that sounded very much like *bon appétit*.

Euro Non-Reaper Chad moved faster than her eyes could track. One moment, he was tugging her up the steps to his house, those impressive glutes bunching and releasing in rolling shifts of muscle that were honestly a little distracting despite the precariousness of their situation. Then, before she could blink, he'd already lunged halfway across the porch. One long-fingered hand clamped around the zombie's jaw as the creature growled and snapped at him.

The other hand tore out its heart.

Sans knife. Bare-knuckled.

He tossed the bloody organ to the wooden porch floor, released the zombie's jaw, and let the creature collapse at his feet, his face a mask of utter indifference.

The whole thing—attack, counterattack, release—took maybe three seconds.

Nauseated, she stared down at the slowing tremble of the creature's bloody heart. Her own heart, which she hoped to keep safely intact inside her chest for many decades to come, thudded faster and faster, its terrified beat echoing in her skull.

Holy fuck.

Euro Non-Reaper Chad wasn't a zombie. But he could definitely kill her just as dead.

Slowly, hoping he somehow wouldn't notice, she backed away from him and down his porch steps once more.

"Where are you going, human?"

Human. Which confirmed he . . . wasn't.

Funny, he didn't sound like he planned to murder her with his bare hands. More patronize her to death, with suffocating condescension his unknown species' weapon of choice.

She was in shock, though. She recognized that now. Tonight's terror had resurrected her worst memories from two decades before, leaving her disoriented. Her judgment couldn't be trusted, so she needed to stick with the emergency plan she and her parents had decided upon during the Battle for Containment, back when she'd been only fifteen. Back when she and the rest of the world had first learned about the zombies—and also Supernaturals and Enhanced humans, who emerged from secrecy for the first time to help common humans drive the creatures back into their compound.

If you see or hear anything that worries you, go to the attic, sweetheart, her mother had said, and lovingly tugged the end of Edie's ponytail in emphasis. *Bring the ladder up after you and lock the door. We'll have lots of snacks and drinks there, and you can camp out until we tell you everything's okay.*

Edie had frowned. *What about you and Dad? Where will you go?*

We'll come with you if we can. If we can't, we'll take care of ourselves. Your only job is to take care of you. Do you understand? Her mother had met Edie's eyes directly, searching for an honest answer. *Promise me you'll go to the attic and lock the door behind you, no matter what, Edie. Please.*

When Edie had finally, reluctantly said *I promise,* she hadn't truly understood what that promise would mean. She hadn't been able to grasp how it would feel to abandon her parents to their deaths, even when that was what they wanted, even though her life meant more to them than their own. It was unimaginable—until the moment it became her reality three years later.

But she'd survived in that fucking attic once, and she could do it again. She *would* do it again, zombies and terrifying neighbors be damned.

"I have a safe place in my house." She took another step backward, away from Definitely Not Human Chad. "I'll call the emergency number from there. I've got enough supplies to last until help comes, so don't worry about me." Her forced laugh sounded far too loud. "Not that you would. Worry about me, I mean."

He stared at her, his face hard and expressionless.

"Good luck, Chad." Against her will, her eyes drifted to the heart resting on the wooden boards of his porch. It lay still now, curls of steam rising from it like smoke. "Although maybe you don't really need luck, huh?"

He scrutinized her for another moment before lifting a broad shoulder in dismissal. "Very well."

He began to turn away. Then his head tipped to one side, and his brows drew together.

"They're close," he said abruptly. "I can hear them. Come with me."

She heard zilch. "No, really, I can—"

The next thing she knew, he was dragging her back up the steps, across the sagging porch, and through his front door, her wrist caught in his painless but inexorable grip. He flipped over a faded rug in the hall and opened a discreet hatch in the floor. A wide metal ladder descending into an inky void suddenly appeared at their feet.

"Down," he ordered. When she hesitated, his tone turned biting. "I'm waiting, human. Dither much longer and we'll both die."

He could have torn out her heart a hundred times by now if that were his goal. Then again, perhaps he simply preferred murdering at a more leisurely pace. Like the homicidal equivalent of the Slow Food movement.

Whatever. Either of the two zombies would have killed her if he hadn't intervened. She was willing to gamble that his intentions were good, or at least good enough for now.

Once she began clambering onto the ladder, he reached out to steady her, his grasp light and careful on her hips, her shoulders. "When I close and secure the hatch behind us, it'll be completely dark. Keep hold and keep descending."

Fantastic.

She began climbing down. He maneuvered onto the ladder above her, then reached for the hatch. Her palms turned damp, and she grasped the sturdy metal rungs tighter.

Thud. Thump. Click. Click. Screech.

The hatch was closed now. Closed and locked.

Absolute blackness, as advertised. She might have been in a cave, miles underground. She might have been in a coffin, buried alive.

Her chest tightened, and she couldn't seem to slow her breathing.

She halted on the ladder.

What had she done? Why had she let herself be locked into a godsdamned tomb with someone who could tear out her heart with a single thrust of his hand and twist of his wrist? And why had she done so based on his claim that he heard zombies when she hadn't heard a thing?

"Human?"

She gulped for air.

"Edie." Before her next rushed, rasping breath, he somehow managed to climb over her until he was leading the way down the ladder, a rung or two below her. He shingled his body atop hers, using it to brace her from the shoulders down. "Edie, listen."

The ladder was wide enough that he could grasp it on either side of her waist, and his hard belly pressed against her ass. For all intents and purposes, he was holding her in his arms.

Her brain promptly blue-screened. Her anxious thoughts sank beneath a tide of sheer physical awareness and pleasure, even as the chill of his half-clad frame, its solid support behind her, helped her breathe more easily.

Damn, she thought dimly. If she'd known he felt this good wrapped around her, she might have lured Bro Chad to her house with *Grand Theft Auto* and a bong freakin' *years* ago.

"Listen," he repeated, and her synapses began firing again at the insistence in his tone. "What do you hear?"

Then she caught it too. A few feet higher, through a single locked hatch . . .

Faint scratches. Grunts. Shuffling.

The half-forgotten sounds came from above this time rather than below. Still, they made her shudder. He hitched tighter against her, keeping her pinned to the ladder.

Dammit, he was right. This go-round, she wouldn't have made it to her attic in time.

With his superior hearing and because of his insistence that she accompany him to his own shelter, he'd saved her life. Again. Which she was thankful for, obviously, but also found somewhat irritating since she'd initiated this entire delightful encounter for the sole purpose of saving *him*.

When she swallowed, her spit tasted metallic. "You're sure they can't get in?"

What if the zombies had somehow evolved after the First Breach and broken through Wall One without outside assistance? The compound no longer had any real oversight or governmental presence. How would anyone even know?

"Yes." When she didn't resume her descent, he elaborated. "There are still a few functional cameras within the compound. They're monitored at all times, and nothing has changed. The creatures can't use even simple hand tools. Penetrating my hatch would require explosives."

Since the age of eighteen, she'd devoted most of her free time to researching the creatures. Their origin. Their capabilities and weaknesses. Their underground compound, which government officials had declared near impregnable, its complete destruction requiring the sort of drastic measures that would cause unacceptable damage to surrounding communities.

She'd paid special attention to the creatures' current state, studying the theories of various experts and drone footage of the zombies' very few excursions outside their compound. Not much reliable information actually existed, though. The creatures might not be smart, but they'd stopped venturing outdoors after the first few attempts resulted in missile strikes and slaughtered brethren. The military had long ago ceased sending troops inside Wall One on doomed missions. And in all her years of research, she hadn't found a single reference to operational cameras within that damn compound.

Was Definitely Not Human Chad lying to her? And if he wasn't, where exactly had he gotten his information?

He heaved an impatient sigh. "They can't climb. They can't swim. Even if they did somehow get past the hatch, they couldn't use the ladder. They'd fall into the water pit and drown. They have no chance."

According to official reports, drowning the creatures was the third and final way to slay them, so that made sense. Only—"There's a freaking *water pit* beneath us?"

"We can bypass it." The strained tolerance in his voice was rapidly leaching away, replaced by the tonal equivalent of an eye roll. "I'll guide you."

She didn't trust him, but she couldn't keep hanging on this ladder forever, and she certainly didn't intend to pop back out of that hatch and become Zombie Lunchables.

Her questions would have to wait.

Her chest expanded in a slow, deep breath, and she registered his scent for the first time. Piney and faintly sharp, like eucalyptus. It was surprisingly pleasant.

She'd always assumed her neighbor would smell like beer and noxious body spray up close. "I'm good now. You can move down."

The cool wall of strength at her back promptly disappeared, much to the displeasure of her hormones. Reluctantly, she loosened her death grip on the metal rung before her, shifted to a single-handed hold, and wiped her slick palms on the thighs of her coveralls one at a time.

She began descending again, rung by rung, matching his measured pace.

A minute passed. Two. Three. As far as she could tell, they still weren't near the end.

Her fingers hurt after a while, so she paused to shake out her left hand, then her right. As she did, she considered the heavy earth-moving equipment such an absurdly deep tunnel underground had required, how much said equipment and the labor required to use it might have cost, and what awaited her at the bottom of this oversized well.

What sort of shelter had he built down there, beyond his freaking *water pit*, and what herculean efforts had *that* construction necessitated?

He drummed his own fingers against the ladder. "Come on. Keep going."

"How deep is your damn basement, anyway?"

"Deep."

"If you're not human, what are you?" Given everything she'd seen and heard, her best guess was—

"You'll find out soon enough."

She supposed she would.

Once again, she resumed her descent into darkness, with Chad—this new, unfamiliar version of him—as her fearless, be-thonged guide.

Somewhere along the way, she forgot to be afraid.

2

At long last, Edie dropped onto blessedly solid ground beside Chad.

"Fourteen minutes. A travesty." The glow of his phone revealed a long-suffering expression. "The descent usually takes me thirty seconds."

Her hands had become claws sometime during those fourteen torturous minutes. Unzipping her bag was a challenge, as was unearthing her own cell in total darkness. No, that was the burrito ... her keys ... a tampon ... a tin of mints ...

There. The phone. And it somehow had coverage down here, which was nothing short of a miracle. The Zone's limited and crumbling infrastructure meant she frequently couldn't muster sufficient bars to place calls within the area's tall, protective walls, even aboveground.

"I suppose you can't help being a mere human, however." He seemed to consider this a generous allowance on his part. "I won't complain."

Too late.

"I salute your heroism." She tapped the Containment Zone

Emergency Line icon, something she should have done at the top of the ladder. She hadn't been thinking clearly, but that was no excuse. After putting the phone to her ear, she waited. And waited some more. "Why isn't anyone answering the fucking emergency line?"

Chad gave the world's tiniest, most uninterested shrug.

"Please state the nature of your emergency," the attendant said after an interminable delay, her voice low and smooth.

"My name is Eden Brandstrup, and I live on Cloverleaf Drive in Zone A. My neighbor and I have just been attacked by two zombies. We heard more outside our shelter, so we assume the entire pack has escaped through a breach in Wall One."

"How distressing." The attendant paused briefly, and clicking sounds filled the silence. "I'll alert the necessary parties."

"How quickly can you sound the alarm? Because everyone in Zone A is at risk until they know what's happening." No response. "Hello?"

Edie lowered her phone and looked down at it. The call had been disconnected.

Well, that was . . . startlingly abrupt. But the attendant's haste in ending the conversation made sense, upon second thought, because the sooner the woman stopped talking, the sooner she could activate the alarm. It should be starting any second now. Or maybe she needed approval from supervisors, in which case the warning sirens might not begin for another minute or two.

Either way, Edie had offered what help she could for her neighbors near and far. The rest was up to the government.

"Done." She slid the phone back into her bag. "I feel terrible for waiting so long, but hopefully our Zone A neighbors are either safely indoors for the night or visiting their families outside the Containment Zone for the holidays."

Still illuminated by his phone's blue-white glare, Definitely Not Human Chad simply looked at her.

Bro Chad had been a much better conversationalist, which was saying something.

"So . . . here we are. Your underground lair. Chad's Cave of Dreams." She turned her head, but couldn't see much. "Does your pit have electricity? Because my flashlight app will work for a while, but eventually—"

With a swipe of his forefinger against his screen, he turned on the overhead lights.

Her jaw dropped.

The place was freaking *gigantic*, with polished concrete floors stretching into the far distance and minimalist fixtures shining on them from above. An enormous kitchen gleamed to the right, all black-veined white marble and bronze, with an endless island and zero visible appliances other than a refrigerator. To the left, at least twenty feet distant from the kitchen or any other furniture, he had a seating area with chunky metal-and-wood tables positioned alongside long, low, sinuously curved cream-colored couches that belonged on a luxurious spaceship built a thousand years from now.

He watched her reaction with a faint, smug smile.

She closed her mouth. Then opened her mouth. Then closed it again.

"Wow," she finally said. "This place is *huge*. Huge and uncluttered and . . ."

"And . . . ?"

"And . . . uh . . . aggressively modern?" When he frowned down at her, she raised her hands, palms out. "Don't get me wrong. This is amazing, and my attic is basically a tiny, crowded, insufficiently insulated wooden tent, so your shelter is way, way better than mine. Just . . . damn. It's like the Guggenheim Museum and a diamond mine had a baby down here. How did I not know this place existed?"

A single golden-brown brow arched, silently chiding her obtuseness. "Because I didn't wish you to know."

Well, duh. "But I work from home. How did I not see or hear anything?"

"Most construction occurred at night, after you secured your shutters. Any necessary explosions took place in your absence."

A mysterious incident from three years ago, shortly after his arrival next door, suddenly made a lot more sense. She'd left for the post office, realized somewhere in Zone C that she'd forgotten her wallet, and driven back home. Only to experience what felt like a small earthquake in her own driveway.

She'd knocked on his door shortly thereafter to ask whether he'd noticed it too, because she couldn't find any mention of a local tremor on the internet.

"I dunno, dude." He'd offered her a bright, vapid smile and spread his hands wide in helpless confusion. "My edibles just kicked in a few minutes ago, so . . ."

"Okay." With a tiny, silent sigh and a little nod, she'd turned for home. "Sorry to bother you, Chad."

"No problemo, dude!" he'd shouted loudly enough to make her twitch. "Laters!"

"The earthquake?" she asked now.

"The explosives crew didn't notice your return in time."

"Ah." That explained it.

"Your expression of pained tolerance during our every encounter..." That small, smug smile reappeared on his stupidly handsome face. "It sparked such joy in me, I should have filmed a Marie Kondo special."

"You were fucking with me this entire time." Three years. Three damn *years*.

"Of course."

"Why?"

"Because I enjoyed it."

"I imagine you did." She raised her own brows. "But you also wanted your privacy, and playing the role of Bro Chad ensured I'd keep my distance."

He flicked a hand, indicating his vast, secret underground bunker in silent confirmation. His was not the home of someone who enjoyed neighborly socializing. Or Miller Lite, for that matter.

After a glance at the nearest masterwork of minimalist design, a bronze-edged glass console table, she returned her attention to him. "Everything here is gorgeous, obviously. But... don't you need a comfy couch and TV somewhere so you can binge-watch the newest Netflix show before it gets prematurely canceled?"

He drew himself up to his full height. "My home contains all the modern amenities."

Modern amenities, she repeated silently. A surprisingly old-fashioned phrase for someone who seemed very contemporary in his tastes. Of course, if what she suspected proved true—

"In my media room, I have a state-of-the-art television and various streaming options." He sniffed. "And my sofas feel like clouds filled with the luxurious down of a thousand denuded geese."

Apparently defensiveness brought out his eloquent side.

"I see." She disguised her snicker as a cough, smothering it against her fist. "Please forgive me. I didn't mean to insult your very nice basement or hurt your feelings. I'm extremely grateful you're sharing your shelter with me."

Which was the honest truth, for all her semi-hysterical hilarity. Only a fool would anger someone who could murder her with such terrifying ease and who was currently hiding her from ravenous zombies. She liked her brain. She'd prefer that it remain encased safely in her skull.

His lip curled. "You think you *hurt my feelings?*"

The very idea seemed to offend him further.

"Uh . . ." She scratched the tip of her nose with a ragged nail. "No. Of course not."

"I told more convincing lies in my cradle," he informed her.

"I apologize once more, then, for . . ." The gods and goddesses alone knew what had his thong in a twist now. "For implying you have feelings?"

It was her best guess.

And evidently it was wrong, because now he was outright glowering at her. "Of course I have feelings, human. I experience many emotions. Anger. Impatience. Disgust. Boredom. Schadenfreude."

Wow, his daily existence sounded *fun.*

"Not a single living creature on this planet can hurt those feelings, however. The opinion of a woman delusional enough to consider foil-wrapped foodstuffs a suitable weapon against zombies certainly means nothing to me."

Of course her opinion meant nothing to him. Why would she believe otherwise?

She lifted a shoulder. "In my defense, I got extra guac on my burrito, so it's really heavy. Top of the line as far as burrito cudgels go."

"You wish to justify your actions?" A hint of menace had entered his tone. "Because I would welcome a discussion of your stupefying idiocy earlier this evening."

She shouldn't *have* to justify her actions, since they'd been undertaken with his continued survival in mind, but if it made him happy . . .

"Sure. Get it out of your system, Euro Chad."

Shit. Evidently he'd been right. She *was* a fool. Either that or her survival instincts were broken. It was the only logical explanation for why she kept poking at him this way despite all good sense and her best intentions.

He scrutinized her with narrowed eyes, disapproval radiating from every stern line on his face. "You're always home before dark. Why not tonight?"

"Oh!" She brightened in realization. "That's why you were outside without your usual disguise, huh? You assumed I was already tucked up safe at home for the evening."

He simply stared stonily at her, waiting for her answer.

For the love of your aorta, do not roll your eyes, she instructed herself. "I had orders to drop off and boxes of supplies to sign for, and I didn't expect the post office to be so crowded right after Christmas."

Since the First Breach, mail carriers and package delivery drivers hadn't been permitted to work within the Containment Zone anymore, so all the Zone's inhabitants were obliged to venture outside the walled area for mail service. Now that her custom soapmaking business had become relatively successful, she usually drove to the post office two or three times a week. Which was fine by her, since one of her few real-life friends, Kelvin, worked there, and sometimes he had a couple minutes to chat. Not today, though.

"By the time I got out, the sun was about to set, and I had no food in my refrigerator or time to grocery shop, so I grabbed a burrito before heading home. I was just glad the Zone's entry door wasn't malfunctioning again, or else I'd have run even later." She frowned, thinking about the sequence of events. "I didn't see you when I drove up, and if you'd seen me, you wouldn't have been parading around in all your sheepskin-thonged glory. You must have come outside after I locked up the car, while I was gathering the boxes I dropped."

He would have assumed she was already home, and between the growing darkness and his headphones, he wouldn't have seen or heard her squatting beside her car, picking up her errant packages. Which she'd done, only to drop them again when she spotted the zombie sprinting toward him as he stood on his porch.

"Most likely." He leaned slightly, ominously closer. "That doesn't explain, however, why you then chose to intercept a zombie in full flight, kick him, and hit him with a burrito."

He said *burrito* the way most people might say *plague-ridden sewer rat*.

"If I'd had time to grab my knife, I'd have used that instead, obviously. But I'd forgotten it at home, so I worked with what I had." After unzipping her cross-body bag again, she produced the flattened, foil-wrapped item in question with a flourish worthy of a spokesmodel, then placed it on his console table. "Yes, it's a burrito, but I thought you would be decapitated within moments. Cut me some slack."

He thrust his face inches from hers, and the sharp scent of eucalyptus filled her lungs. "I don't give a fuck about the burrito. Even if you'd had your knife or a godsdamn *rocket launcher*, you shouldn't have interceded."

"I've taken plenty of self-defense classes. I know how to fight." Now she was the one getting defensive—no pun intended—but why wasn't he giving her any credit for her attempt to save him? Where was his gratitude? "Admit it, *dude*. My kick was a thing of beauty. I stopped a freaking zombie mid-run with one blow, and I didn't even fall."

"And then what?" He spoke the words one at a time. *And. Then. What.*

"And then *what* what?"

His voice was a whip crack. "You're an unenhanced human. You weren't wearing protective equipment. You had no nearby shelter. You were armed with a *stuffed tortilla*."

When he put it that way, her decision to put herself in the zombie's path did seem somewhat ill-considered, but—

"Explain your endgame. How were you going to stop it from ripping out your throat? How were you going to kill it?"

"Um . . ." She shifted in place, then fell silent.

His every exhalation washed coolly over her flushed face. "Tell me, Edie. Can you kick hard enough to remove a zombie's head? A zombie's heart? Are you strong enough to drag a zombie to the nearest moat and drown it without getting bitten?"

They both knew the answer to that.

"Did you think you'd survive?"

If she leaned forward another inch, she could lick his strong, straight nose. Would that distract him from this lecture? Or at least prompt him to murder her more expeditiously so she wouldn't be forced to listen to its remainder?

At this point, she'd accept either outcome.

"No. You didn't." Straightening, he sort of throttled the air with his broad hands. "Where's your sense of self-preservation, woman? And why the hells would you sacrifice yourself to save fucking *Chad*, of all the idiots in the world?"

Chad wasn't his actual name, then. Not a surprise.

"I don't want to die." She wanted that absolutely clear.

The growly sound he made did not indicate agreement.

"I don't," she insisted. "But I couldn't run away and leave *you* to die. I just . . . couldn't."

As Chad, his eyes had been the color of faded denim, as pretty as they were dull. Somewhere over the course of their conversation, that had changed. The stare scrutinizing her now was as black and sharp as obsidian. It pierced through her, pinning her in place for his pitiless inspection.

She tipped up her chin and waited, unintimidated.

He wouldn't find falsity. Didn't matter if he was a telepath or a truthseeker, and he was even now plumbing the depths of her mind. In all their encounters over the past three years, she'd never lied, which was more than he could say for himself.

He lowered his hands to his sides. "Your life means nothing to me."

For someone unconcerned with her survival, he seemed awfully invested in this conversation. A conversation they were having in his secure compound because he'd overruled her objections and dragged her through that hatch to save her life.

Another lie. Wasn't he tiring of them?

She directed a meaningful glance at herself, his home, and the nearby tunnel and ladder. Then she raised her brows at him.

He ignored the silent rebuttal. "Don't die to save me, and don't die to save anyone else. Not when they'd gladly sacrifice you to save themselves."

If that was his view of the world and its inhabitants, no wonder his limited array of emotions didn't include *joy* or *love* or even *hope*.

"And you'd do the same?"

He merely laughed in answer, the sound low and scornful. Fascinated, she watched as his irises softened from black to blue, moment by moment.

"So I shouldn't save you from harm or death even if I could?" She tipped her head, now studying him in return. "Just to clarify."

He spoke flatly. "I don't want your assistance, and I don't need it."

"Mmmm," she said with a nod. Hopefully he took that as agreement, because she wasn't promising anything.

Not that she foresaw other opportunities to test how either of them would react in an emergency, since the government—

Oh shit.

She checked her phone for alerts. Shushed him when he started to say something.

Nothing. She saw and heard *nothing*.

She turned to the Neighbor Formerly Known as Chad, grabbed the edges of his open leather hoodie, and clutched tight, her confusion and horror a growing roar in her ears.

His sneer became a frown. "What—"

"Where the fuck are the sirens?" she demanded.

3

Edie called the Containment Zone Emergency Line again.

No one answered. The line rang and rang.

While she waited for an attendant or even an automated message or voicemail option, her Neighbor Formerly Known as Chad wandered over to the kitchen, opened the refrigerator's French doors, and peered at whatever was inside. Closing the doors again, he strolled to his island—which was probably larger than many actual geographical islands—and bent over to rest his elbows on the marble countertop while he idly scrolled on his phone.

Ring. Ring. Ring. Ring. Ring. Ring.

According to the top of her screen, she still had coverage. Was the hotline simply overwhelmed by calls? Or was there something wrong with her phone in particular?

"Call the Zone hotline from your cell," she told him. "See if someone answers."

He didn't even look up. "Nah."

"What is the *matter* with you? All our neighbors—" Increasingly frantic, she strode over to the island and snatched his phone from his hand. "Fine. I'll do it myself, jackass."

He didn't resist or try to take it away from her. Instead, he simply watched as she found the correct icon and tapped it.

Ring. Ring. Ring. Ring. Ring. Ring.

Next, she tried calling the all-purpose emergency number on both phones, then Kelvin's number, and got the same endless ringing in response.

Bars or no bars, something had obviously gone wrong with the Containment Zone's lone cell tower. Was this a normal outage, born of neglect and the Zone's crumbling infrastructure? Or had the zombies somehow managed to compromise the tower? They'd been created and trained to kill werewolves, not target communications systems, and according to Not-Chad, the creatures still couldn't climb or use tools. But a random outage occurring at the exact same time as a breach seemed *very* coincidental.

Didn't matter right now. Those questions could wait until she found another way to sound the alarm and ensure her neighbors' safety.

"I assume there's internet coverage down here?" When he slanted her a look of scornful incredulity, she muttered, "Of course there is. It's a *modern amenity*. I can't make calls for some reason, but the Zone hotline must have a website where we can report a breach . . ."

When she tapped her screen to access the internet, though, she got an error message. The same thing happened on his phone.

Again, this wasn't the first time the Zone's infrastructure had failed her, and she'd already determined that the cell tower must be damaged or malfunctioning. But hadn't Not-Chad been glancing through his messages even after the phone lines stopped working?

"Why the *hells* can't I get online?" She thrust the cell back into his hands. "Fix this."

With an expression of strained tolerance, he tapped a few times on his screen. Then frowned.

"The internet's down," he said slowly.

Her glare should have turned him to ash. "Yes. I know. Do something about it."

"It's never down. I installed my own system, specifically to prevent outages." His brows drew together. "I was online just a minute ago. What the fuck?"

The overhead lights flickered and went out.

She froze, rendered silent by bewilderment and creeping dread.

They stood wordless in stygian darkness for several moments, until a faint buzzing sound heralded the return of his underground home's electricity. Not every light illuminated, but enough to see all but the most shadowy corners of the space.

"That's my generator," he said, his frown deepening. "The power's still out."

"What . . ." She spread her hands. "What the hells is happening here?"

His mouth firmed in determination. "Let me check my security system."

When he toed off his gore-stained shoes and washed his bloody hands at the kitchen sink, she did the same. Afterward, as he about-faced and marched past the seating area, she trailed behind him. A dim hallway ahead of them contained several doors, and he entered the first on the right. His media room, evidently, complete with—

Was that a softbox in the corner? And a ring light on a sturdy-looking tripod?

What in the world did Not-Chad *do* down here? Was this a sheepskin-fetish OnlyFans thing? And if so, would an irresistible combination of prurience and sheer morbid curiosity force her to subscribe to his channel?

Another sleek sofa had been placed in front of a television with a very large screen, and a computer station occupied the wall behind the off-white couch. Without a word, he strode directly to the Mac and booted it up, then sat and clicked his mouse a few times.

His wide, curved monitor lit up with footage from around his property and within his house, both the 1960s section and their current, expansive shelter far underground. Also, on the bottom right of the screen, wasn't that—

"You have no right to spy on my house!" She poked his shoulder, which had all the warmth and give of a stone statue. "What the hells, Not-Chad?"

When he didn't respond, she poked him again.

Sounding sulky, he muttered, "During construction, I needed to track your comings and goings to ensure secrecy."

"Construction is done. It's been done for a long time now, I'm guessing."

He shifted in his chair. "Criminals have claimed some abandoned buildings in the Zone. They've occasionally broken into occupied homes too."

"That explains the security system protecting *your* house, but it doesn't explain why you're filming *my* yard and all four sides of *my* house," she emphasized. "Especially when I haven't given you permission and my life ostensibly means nothing to you."

She raised her brows at him and waited.

After a long hesitation, he spoke slowly, still staring at his computer screen. "I intend to keep interlopers off my street, since I don't want anyone snooping in my house. That requires monitoring my neighbors' homes too."

She squinted at the monitor. "I don't see any houses other than ours, so—"

"Is this really the time, human? What happened to determining the cause of the outages so you can warn our neighbors?"

Okay, fair point. "Fine. But we're discussing this later."

He grunted and resumed zooming in on various images, then clicking to others.

"They haven't been able to access my electrical or communications systems," he said finally. "Whatever's happening, it isn't specific to this house."

If that was true, who the hells had managed to disable the cell tower, internet service, *and* the power grid? Had the zombies done it? If so, had someone helped them?

That had been the cause of the First Breach, of course. Back then, the thick stone walls ringing the compound had been considered entirely secure, and they'd remained unguarded and unsurveilled. A small group of militants who'd underestimated the zombies' menace after several years of safe containment had dynamited holes in Wall One and broken down the access door through Wall Two before being overrun by the very creatures they were attempting to free from captivity.

Those militants had all died horribly, along with virtually

everyone living in Zone A, including her parents. Before the human government and the Supernatural and Enhanced Ruling Council had taken joint action and sent sufficient troops to drive the zombies back into their compound, countless homeowners in Zone B had fallen too. Only sheer luck had prevented further catastrophe. If the militants had been able to set the charges for Walls Three and Four prior to meeting their grisly fates, the death toll would have been far worse.

Afterward, to prevent another such incident, the government-SERC alliance had begun conducting background checks on all current and potential Zone residents and limiting non-homeowner visitation inside the walls. The alliance had also installed deep, wide moats outside Wall One and just within Walls Two, Three, and Four. No bridge crossed the moat outside Wall One, since no one but zombies lived inside that stone barrier, and the government had long ago ceased their ill-fated attempts at either in-person surveillance or eradication. The other moats had drawbridges that lowered after the scan of a valid pass and stayed down only until the permitted vehicle had traversed the bridge and exited through the temporarily open door in the wall.

Upon word of another breach, the drawbridges would stay up and the doors would remain shut, pass or no pass, allowing no exit for Containment Zone residents. It was the price they paid for such incredibly cheap housing so close to the nation's capital, in a formerly wealthy area of Northern Virginia.

The Containment Zone had become an exclusive gated community, albeit a crumbling one where very few people actually lived. Once-thriving neighborhoods in Zones A and B had vanished in the space of three blood-smeared days, and they'd never returned. Zone C rapidly emptied too, despite remaining untouched. Humans and Supernaturals who could be killed by decapitation—shifters, vampires, trolls, and others—weren't willing to risk proximity to the creatures after such a calamitous example of how seemingly foolproof defenses could fail. Supernaturals who could survive zombie attacks—including demons, elves, and the fae—avoided the Zone as well, either because the area felt tainted by the massacre or because they wanted to live somewhere with better services and easier access.

Over the last twenty years, a mere handful of newcomers desperate for affordable housing—as well as criminals bearing forged documents, eager to take advantage of abandoned buildings and limited governmental oversight—had been permitted to join the few Zone residents too foolish, too stubborn, too poor, or too sentimental to leave. How many of those descriptors applied to Edie, she couldn't say. Most of them, probably. Maybe all of them.

Empty houses that had once cost millions began to sag. The roofs of upscale shopping complexes collapsed. Immaculately paved streets pitted and cracked.

And three years ago, Not-Chad had bought the unprepossessing house next to hers, tunneled deep beneath it, built his lair, and installed startlingly sophisticated security systems, apparently unbeknownst to anyone.

Except her now.

He pointed to one specific image on his computer monitor, the rectangle dark purple except for several dozen orangey splotches clustered in a loose grouping.

"My infrared camera." Side by side, they studied the image, and his frown deepened. "The creatures seem to be down on all fours and moving slowly."

"They must not have found anyone else yet." Otherwise, they'd be sprinting toward their victims and rising to their hind legs for the kill.

He nodded, then checked another subset of images. "Here they are on my night vision cameras. They're still searching for us. If we stay down here, they'll eventually give up and attempt to find other game."

The creatures glowed an eerie green, their eyes as bright as spotlights, the details of their gaunt, muscled frames far more visible now. The outdoor views showed them circling the property, sniffing for telltale scents, as the broken remains of his front door swung and creaked in the bitter winter wind. The interior cameras showed other members of the pack exploring the home above, flinging aside a narrow bed and swatting a closet door off its hinges to expose potential hiding places.

There were so damn many of them. Far too many for even Not-Chad to kill—with her assistance, however unwelcome—before both of them would literally lose their heads.

They were going nowhere until the pack moved on. She might be desperate to alert other Zone residents of imminent danger, but her death approximately five feet outside his home would serve no purpose and help no one.

"Other *people*," she corrected quietly. "Other people, not other game."

"Not to the zombies." He sounded dismissive. "They can't think in those terms. People are food to them, although they'd gladly slaughter Supernaturals instead of humans if given the opportunity. It's why they were created, after all."

Stung by the detached tone of his words, she turned her head to study him.

Nah, he'd said when she'd asked him to call the hotline. As if he couldn't be bothered. As if the slightest effort to aid others required more energy than he cared to expend.

Why the hells had he saved her, then?

"How about you? Do you think in those terms?" she asked. "Or is everyone else simply *other game* to you?"

He didn't answer.

His face was as smooth as his marble countertop once more, all expression gone as he checked his various security features and collected intelligence on their—his—current situation.

Finally, he straightened and turned to her. "My cameras' reach isn't foolproof. There may be stragglers I can't see, even after the bulk of the pack departs. I don't intend to leave my home until authorities give us the official all clear and I've seen no sign of zombies for at least forty-eight hours. You can stay here with me until then."

A generous offer.

She didn't understand it. Without a plausible explanation, she didn't trust it either.

"Why?" Exhaustion, hunger, and uncertainty sapped her remaining strength, and she leaned heavily against the edge of his glass work desk. "Why snatch me away from danger and lecture me about self-preservation if my life means nothing to you? Why offer me safe shelter for days or even weeks to come if the survival of others doesn't concern you?"

Whenever he offered her that one-shoulder shrug, casual and Gallic and infuriating, she wanted to smack the shit out of him.

"I noted the initial zombie's approach in time to kill it without your ill-considered assistance," he said bluntly. "Still, you believed you were saving me. You *intended* to save me. You foolishly risked your life to do so. In return, I feel obligated to provide basic assistance, at least this once."

"So you're merely fulfilling a perceived debt, then."

"Correct." How he managed to pack so much ostentatious boredom into two syllables, she'd never know.

"You don't actually care if I live or die."

"Correct."

Edie hadn't spent time around farm animals in at least three decades, but she could still identify the pungent scent of bullshit. "What if I left here tonight to warn the other Zone residents?"

It would be a suicide mission, and they both knew it.

A muscle in his jaw ticked. "I would not recommend that."

"Of course not, but would you care? Would you mourn my death?"

He silently watched her for a moment, a vein throbbing at his temple, before answering. "You told me you didn't wish to die. Was that a lie?"

"I haven't lied to you, *Chad*." Her thick sarcasm should have choked him.

"Then you won't leave before dawn."

Much as she'd love to contradict him, he was right. "If the pack moves away and the sirens don't sound during the night, I'll go at daybreak." She couldn't live with herself if she didn't at least try to alert other Zone residents and the authorities that a calamitous breach had occurred. "Thank you for your kind offer of shelter until then."

If he noted any irony in her tone, he didn't react to it. He simply nodded.

After one last glance at his monitor, he stood and left his media room. "I need to change. Wait for me in the kitchen."

He disappeared into the doorway across the hall, and she ventured back into the kitchen in search of an ice pack. Her ankle had stiffened up and was currently protesting the unanticipated evening of zombie kicking, mole hole tripping, and ladder descending.

She limped to his refrigerator, slid open his freezer drawer, and found . . . nothing. Absolutely nothing. No freezer-burned bags of corn. No microwaveable dinners. Not even a pint of Häagen-Dazs.

He reappeared at her side before she even had time to close the drawer. Somehow he'd managed to change and cross a vast expanse of concrete floor in about thirty seconds, max. Which was . . . telling, she figured.

Compared to the leather hoodie and animal-hide thong, his track pants and tight Henley were disappointingly normal, albeit ridiculously flattering. When her eyes drifted toward his rounded posterior, she whipped them upward again. She was still blinking away spots from that damn thong. Too lengthy a perusal of his ass now might entirely burn out her retinas, like staring at an eclipse.

"I don't suppose you have an ice pack tucked away somewhere else," she said.

"No." His forehead creased. "You've injured yourself?"

"My ankle isn't injured. Strained, maybe." Also twisted and jammed, but that wasn't important. Even without an ice pack, ibuprofen and a few hours off her feet should take care of the issue. "Do you have something to drink? And is there somewhere I can sit without ruining the sacrificial efforts of all those naked, shivering geese?"

She looked down at her blood-splattered, muddy coveralls

and winced. Mess didn't bother her, but gore? Yuck. Sadly, there was no point asking to borrow clean clothes. Nothing he owned would fit her generously rounded frame, on top *or* bottom.

He hesitated. "I suppose I could get some towels to put beneath you."

No doubt his towels had been woven by master towel-making craftspeople in the Alps, the glowing white of their cotton unsullied by even the merest speck of dirt.

Ah, fuck it.

"You know what? There's no need to filthify your towels. Compared to your previous outfit, I might as well be wearing a nun's habit beneath my coveralls." Without further ado, she tugged her bag over her head and set it on the countertop, then unzipped her coveralls and shoved them over her shoulders and hips and down her legs. After kicking the stained fabric into a pile beneath the island, she washed her hands thoroughly at the kitchen sink for a second time. "Got any pomegranate juice? It's my favorite."

He didn't respond.

When she turned to check on him, he was staring at her, his expression pained. Which was unfair, because she was actually wearing a bra beneath her tank top for once, and her panties were of the comfy granny variety and fully covered *her* ass cheeks. Also, they had a cute pink bubble pattern and had never served as the skin of a living creature, so . . .

"I know, I know. It's like seeing your mom in her underwear. Get over it, *Chad*." To a guy his age, no doubt her late-thirties body seemed like a cautionary tale about the dangers of gravity. Or maybe he wasn't into fat women of any age, especially those with generous bellies and thick thighs and not much in the way of T and A. His loss. "While you process your Oedipal trauma, let's find out what beverages you have in your fancy fridge. Mama's thirsty."

She swung open the French doors.

Well. Maybe he wasn't in his earlyish twenties after all. And maybe he wasn't an elf or a fae either, as she'd been theorizing all evening.

His refrigerator contained nothing but blood bags. Discreetly packaged, of course, but definitely, unmistakably blood bags.

Not-Chad—her closest neighbor, the guy with whom she was currently locked in an underground lair—was a freaking *vampire*.

4

Edie's knees weakened. She clutched the refrigerator doors tightly, unable to stop gaping at the neat rows of blood bags in front of her.

Vampires weren't somehow inherently more dangerous than elves or fae. Even the weakest representatives of all three species could kill her with ease, as desired. But idle speculation about the Supernatural status of her neighbor was different from being confronted with the reality of his superior capabilities and potential for deadly violence.

He had a fridge full of prepackaged blood. He didn't need hers.

But the realization that he could take it from her, whether she was willing or not, chilled her more thoroughly than the refrigerated air on her bare legs.

"I . . ." She swallowed hard, still staring blankly at the tidy rows of flat-bottomed bags. "I kind of knew you didn't look like a reaper. More like you just got kicked out of an exclusive, pretentious European club for surly hot dudes because you were far too surly and hot, even for your fellow members."

Her bravado-compliment-insult combo should have distracted him from her sudden nervousness. Alas.

"Human." When he yawned, he didn't bother covering his mouth. "If I wanted you dead, you'd be dead."

"How comforting." Despite her sarcasm, she relaxed a little, because he wasn't wrong.

Reports about Supernaturals—their habits, powers, vulnerabilities, cultures, and organizational structures—typically contradicted one another, leaving humans like her unsure as to what was truth and what was mere myth. There did seem to be widespread agreement in four areas concerning vampires, though.

First: Vampires, like all other Supernaturals, weren't made but born. Supernaturals weren't *supernatural* at all, in fact, but simply a different version of natural, with varying abilities depending on their species.

Second: Only the lifeblood of humans could satisfy vampiric hunger. There was no substitute. Synthetic versions sickened vamps, and animal blood left them as hungry as ever. Even fellow Supernaturals tasted like fetid rot to Not-Chad's kind. The same substance circulating in her veins kept both of them alive.

These days, humans willingly sold their blood, which was then purified and pasteurized, packaged for sale, and made available at every supermarket, convenience store, and wholesale retailer. It was all very sterile and *bloodless*, ironically, apart from the occasional vampire gone murderously rogue and . . . the flesh trade.

That was the third thing reports reliably indicated: Certain humans flocked to vampire sex workers for their reputed skill as lovers and the pleasure of their bite, while other vampires flocked to humans who offered their blood straight from the tap, so to speak. For a price.

She'd never participated in any such exchange. Her avoidance wasn't due to moral abhorrence. It wasn't even due to fear, because the whole idea was too abstract for that. Too impossible. There simply weren't very many vampires out there, just as there weren't many of any Supernatural species. Only humans procreated reliably, and only their vast numerical superiority kept them from becoming either chattel to or victims of much more powerful species.

The vampires who did exist certainly hadn't flocked to the Containment Zone, so Not-Chad was her first up-close-and-personal vampire.

Fourth and lastly: Vampires could tear out throats before their prey noticed the slightest movement.

Despite ample opportunity, Not-Chad hadn't exsanguinated her yet, though, which was encouraging. And if he didn't intend to do so in the future, as he'd just intimated, all the better.

His expression had turned thoughtful. "Killing you *would* save me from this tedious conversation, however."

"Ha-ha." Despite her anxiety, Edie knew when she was being trolled. Even though he wasn't an actual troll. "No Miller Lite in your fridge, I see. I assume you don't have any pomegranate juice either?"

He waved a hand toward the appliance's contents. "It's in the same color family."

She snorted. "I'll take that as a *no*. Fine, then. I'll wash down my burrito with water."

After opening a few empty cabinets, she found two fluted

wineglasses, claimed one, filled it at the kitchen sink, and set it on the island. Then she traversed the polished-concrete plain in search of her lost burrito. It remained where she'd abandoned it on the console table, sadly smushed but otherwise intact.

"You're . . ." He sounded horrified. "You're still going to eat that?"

Dramatically, she flattened her hand over her eyes and scanned her environs. "What? Am I missing the four-course meal your chef prepared for me?"

"You used it to *whack a zombie.*" His expression of stunned dismay transformed him into Bro Chad—whose mouth hung slightly open, always—for several entertaining moments. "Edie, *no.* Those creatures are founts of disease."

"The foil didn't rip, so it's cool." Returning to the kitchen, she reclaimed her wineglass, settled herself on a low-backed stool at the island, and unwrapped her burrito. Which was literally cool now, but fine. Needs must. "Do you have a plate? Or silverware? How about napkins?"

He was muttering to himself, elbows again propped on the island, his face in his hands.

"Did I offend you and your delicate sheepskin-thonged sensibilities? My apologies, *dude,*" she said sweetly. "Never mind. I can look for everything while you recover."

"I'm offended at *myself.*" Muffled by his palms, his voice sounded plaintive. "How is this even possible?"

Her brow furrowed. "How is *what* even possible?"

Apart from a tool to open his blood packs, his drawers proved empty, and she didn't find any plates either. No matter. She'd simply eat with her hands. Luckily, his desolate pantry contained a stack of cloth napkins, several of which she filched.

His muttering continued uninterrupted.

She sat on the stool again and picked up her burrito. "Okay, then. If you won't answer that question, here are four more: What's your actual name, Chad? How do you know about those cameras still working inside the compound? Do all vampires have fancy underground estates like yours? And if you're a vampire, why have I seen you in broad daylight?"

He raised his head, cynicism hardening his face once more.

"I mean . . ." After taking a bite, she shielded her mouth with one hand and kept talking. "You have a freaking *tan*. How does that work?"

He turned up his perfect nose. "There is such a thing as self-tanner, human."

Sounded like a dodge to her. "Is that how you got your tan, then?"

When she didn't wither under his suspicious scrutiny, he eventually sighed and relaxed a tad, his expression softening. Did that mean he was trusting her with the truth? Or had he simply come up with a plausible lie to sell her?

"My kind once avoided sunlight because darkness allowed us to feed from humans without drawing undue attention," he told her.

She chewed her burrito and listened intently, hoping he'd be honest. Hoping he'd tell her something beyond what she'd already discovered in her years of research and close scrutiny of recently declassified documents.

For millennia, people had whispered about the existence of creatures with abilities beyond normal human understanding, but without evidence, those whispers had always been discounted as the wild-eyed speculation of the gullible and overdramatic.

Until approximately thirty years ago, when a feral werewolf's attack on a hiker was caught on crystal-clear video, which the government promptly confiscated and proclaimed fake.

Publicly, anyway. As the declassified documents confirmed, that was when secret preparations began for what high-level officials considered an inevitable war for human survival against the newly discovered werewolves.

In a compound just outside the nation's capital, Project Hunter was born. The scientists recruited to the project worked around the clock for years and were encouraged to manipulate genetics, formulate proprietary serums, and do whatever they felt necessary—however untested, however ethically abhorrent—to create nonhuman supersoldiers that could track and kill werewolves or die in the attempt, with no need for further human bloodshed.

The lone werewolf the government managed to capture alive fought hard to survive the scientists' experiments, but eventually bled to death when its—her—throat was slit. With that new knowledge of their enemy's vulnerabilities, the trainers focused their efforts. The supersoldiers were taught to carry silver knives and slash at the necks of their victims, and the third iteration of the creatures seemed to be nearing optimal performance . . . until the scientists gave them a final, fatal serum and scrambled their DNA a final, fatal time.

Afterward, the supersoldiers could no longer wield tools, even a knife. They couldn't swim, climb, or reason beyond a certain animal cunning. What they could do: rip out throats with their claws and teeth, tear off their victims' heads, and eat their brains. Starting with the scientists and officials holding them captive, continuing with the previous generations of supersoldiers, and eventually moving on to the hapless world outside the compound.

Their hunger was endless, their strength and speed monstrous. They claimed countless victims. Not only common humans like herself, but the Enhanced too, those rare beneficiaries of a fickle genetic lottery, born with special abilities. Witches, warlocks, oracles, pyrokinetics, telepaths . . . no matter their talents, they all fell beneath the onslaught. As did an untold number of werewolves, vampires, trolls, and other Supernatural beings who could be killed by decapitation.

Common human opposition alone couldn't stop the zombies. For their own survival, many—but not all—Supernaturals and Enhanced humans chose to battle the creatures as well, and they did so publicly and calculatedly. The revelation of their existence had become inevitable after the discovery of their werewolf brethren, as they explained to the president and her closest advisers, and they intended to control the circumstances under which they too were discovered. By emerging into public view as they fought for common humans as well as themselves, they hoped to foster trust and forestall any future eradication efforts by the government.

And vampires like Not-Chad evidently no longer had to feed in darkness. "So before the zombies, you avoided sunlight simply because you were trying to escape human notice?"

"Yes." Tiredly, he rubbed a hand over his bristly jaw. "We had to be discreet. If our existence had become known before public opinion turned in our favor, common humans would have hunted and killed us all. But we needed human blood to survive, so we were careful to prevent witnesses to our feeding."

Wait.

She froze with the burrito poised an inch from her mouth. "Is that a roundabout way of saying you killed everyone you fed from?"

Because she didn't know how often he or other vampires had to feed, but it probably wasn't an infrequent occurrence. And if some poor soul had died for Not-Chad's every meal, dear *gods*. She couldn't even imagine how many people he'd killed over the years.

Maybe eliminating witnesses had been necessary for his species' survival. But even that reasoning didn't make the reality of repeated consequence-free murder any less horrifying.

Stomach churning, she set down her food. Goose bumps prickled along her arms and legs, and not simply because Not-Chad kept his house chillier than most humans preferred.

He glanced down at her forearms, and his brows drew together.

"No," he said hastily. "Vampires can confuse the memories of those they feed from. There was no need to kill them."

She slumped a little in relief. "So you scrambled the brains of your prey, then?"

"That's an unnecessarily dramatic way to describe a finite period of limited confusion."

"Hmmm." She thought it over. "What if you messed up and there were other witnesses?"

He drew himself stiffly upright, evidently insulted once more. Were all Supernaturals such touchy little divas, or was that only a Not-Chad thing?

"I didn't *mess up*," he pronounced firmly.

Of course. "But surely other vampires did, at least on occasion. What would happen then?"

Lips pressed together, he met her gaze steadily.

"I see." Ah yes. Back to consequence-free murder. "Better to guarantee a human's death than risk your own life."

"Of course." A flick of his wrist dismissed her implied criticism. "I told you, human: Don't die to save someone else. Not vampires, not humans, not anyone. Every single one of us would gladly sacrifice you to save ourselves."

Her personal history proved otherwise, but she didn't owe him that story. She didn't owe it to anyone. She kept it safe in her heart, a tangled bundle of love and grief, wrapped tight and buried deep.

He evidently confused her disagreement for offense. "Don't take it personally. Vampires wouldn't bother saving our own kind either. We're essentially feral cats."

"If trapped in an apartment with someone, you'd eat their face off when they died?"

"What?" His nose wrinkled as he glared at her. "No."

Touchy, touchy, touchy.

He paused. "Well, some vampires I've encountered might possibly . . ."

Yeah. Just as she thought. *Dead Roommate: It's What's for Dinner.*

"Anyway." He sort of shook himself. "I meant that we don't, as the saying goes, play well with others. In fact, violence tends to erupt when too many of us live in close proximity. Maybe because at one time, crowding would have meant not enough to eat for everyone without our presence becoming obvious."

"Feral cats often form cooperative colonies." The cheese in her burrito had solidified and turned waxy, but she chewed it thoughtfully as she considered the animal kingdom. "You're more like betta fish plopped into the same aquarium."

He scowled again. "Fish? You think we're like *fish*?"

"Very pretty fish," she said soothingly. "With frilly fins and lovely colors."

His mouth worked, but he couldn't seem to find the appropriate words in response. In the end, he simply continued glowering at her.

Since he didn't appreciate her similes, she returned to an earlier topic. "Why don't common humans like me know about the sunlight thing? Or the brain scrambling? Vampires and all the other Supernaturals and Enhanced humans have been out in the public eye for twenty years. Shouldn't we understand you better by now?"

He muttered something that sounded like *Not all Supernaturals*.

"What did you just say?" Because if she'd heard him correctly, the implications—

"I said that for all Supernaturals, too much knowledge of our abilities and vulnerabilities could prove dangerous. To maintain a certain amount of mystery, we counter any true information with total lies, so outsiders never know exactly what to believe. Also, common humans still cling to their wild imaginings from before our public emergence. That confuses the matter further, in ways we gladly encourage."

"So how do I know you're telling me the truth now?" Picking at a soggy piece of tortilla, she regarded him closely. "For that matter, how do I know you haven't already fed from me and fiddled with my mind at some point?"

His shoulder lifted in an unconcerned shrug.

"Are you? Have you?" she demanded.

"Yes, and no."

Both his face and his tone were expressionless. Impossible to read for signs of deceit.

She threw her hands in the air. "How can I be sure?"

"You can't." He sat back on his barstool, infuriatingly nonchalant. "You just have to trust me."

"You've basically told me not to trust anyone!" It was a near yell, accompanied by the near addition of the word *asshole* at the end.

He pointed at her. "Exactly. Well done, human."

Setting down her burrito, she dropped her chin to her chest, dug her knuckles into her aching temples, and tried to regain control of her temper.

For a minute, silence blanketed the austere fortress he'd built for himself.

"Do you need medicine?" When he spoke again, his voice was quiet. "I don't have any, but perhaps you carry some in your bag?"

Oh, right. Ibuprofen.

Stretching out an arm to her left, she snagged her purse and tugged it closer. The pill bottle, of course, had fallen to the bottom of the bag, so finding it took some time.

When she chanced upon her little tin of cinnamon Altoids, buried beneath her hairbrush, she looked up. "Want a mint?"

His mouth opened, then closed, and he stared at her oddly.

"That's not a hint, by the way," she told him, to clarify matters. "I just thought you'd like this flavor. It's my favorite."

His gaze flicked to the tin, then back to her.

"Or maybe you can't consume anything but blood?" That would certainly explain his refrigerator's contents. "Does human food hurt your stomach?"

He shook his head. "We can eat whatever we want. It simply has no nutritional value for us, however pleasant it might taste."

In that case, why in the world did his kitchen contain nothing but blood?

The mints rattled as she shook her tin coaxingly. "If that's true, then live a little, Not-Chad. Have a mint."

"Your container appears to be festooned with hair," he said slowly. "But thank you. That's . . . very kind."

The dented box creaked as it opened. "The hair's only on the outside. See? The mints inside are perfectly . . ." She hesitated. "Well, there's only one hair in there. Two, max."

He shuddered.

Fine. More mints for her, then. "You never answered my other questions, you know. About how you managed to get footage from inside the compound, whether all vampires have bougie underground lairs like yours, and what your real name is."

After wrestling open her bottle of ibuprofen, washing the pills down with water, and putting everything back in her purse, she ate more of her burrito and waited to discover whether Not-Chad would offer any new information, however dubious in its veracity.

He remained silent for a few moments, then sighed and gripped his nape with one broad hand. "The common human government only shares that camera footage with the highest officials from the Supernatural and Enhanced Ruling Council. At one time, I was expected to fill an open seat on SERC, and I still have connections there. Some of those connections owe me favors. Since moving to the Zone, I've allowed them to repay their debts with classified information about the creatures, including the interior footage."

She blinked at him, stunned.

He'd once been willing to serve on a council for the public good? What in the world?

SERC's creation had been another unanticipated outcome of the zombie jailbreak. As Supernatural and Enhanced groups had stepped into the spotlight and helped drive those zombies back into the underground compound, they'd coordinated with one another for the first time. Determined to address common human officials from a unified position of power, they'd formed SERC to serve as a loose governing body that could speak for its members' interests.

In the heady rush of victory following the Battle for Containment, the government had rewarded its allies by sanctioning a loose, tentative partnership with SERC. In return for the government's toleration of Supernaturals and the Enhanced, as well as prosecution of common humans who injured or killed SERC's constituents without just cause, SERC had promised that those constituents would protect common humans rather than prey upon them.

Not all humans approved of the alliance. Neither did all Supernaturals. Nevertheless, the agreement carried enough weight that a fraught, uneasy peace had taken shape and been maintained ever since.

And Mr. Trust No One had almost taken a seat on SERC? Had almost dedicated his life to maintaining peace and order—only to wind up in an underground bunker of his own, entirely alone and ostensibly unconcerned with the survival of anyone and everyone else?

Something had clearly gone very, very wrong in the interim. What the hells had happened to Not-Chad? And exactly how old *was* he, anyway?

"I don't understand," she said, setting aside his more personal revelations for another time. "Why would the government make information about and footage of the zombies classified?"

"Officials would rather not remind common human citizens of the Breach or the continued existence of creatures that could wipe out all humanity," he told her dryly. "Especially when those creatures could be eliminated in various ways if the government weren't still hopeful that future genetic tweaks might render them usable as supersoldiers again someday."

Her brow furrowed. "I thought the government didn't kill them because the only feasible weapons would cause too much damage to surrounding Zone communities."

His slight sneer was annoyingly attractive. "You believed that?"

"Not all of us are cynical assholes, *dude*." Disheartened, she slumped on her stool. "Well, the government's tactics clearly worked. When I talk to friends outside the Zone, you would think the Breach happened centuries ago and zombies didn't still exist."

"Exactly as officials would prefer."

"Would you share all that classified information and footage with me?"

"I suppose," he said, sounding mildly put-upon.

Which was weird, because . . . wasn't sharing that sort of intelligence with her, a mere common human, kind of a big deal? Shouldn't he be more *intense* about it? Or conflicted?

For that matter, why had he even agreed to do it? Everything he'd just told her might be a lie, but even he couldn't instantaneously doctor some footage and whip up a false dossier to hand over to her. Not when he'd had no clue she would enter his underground stronghold that evening.

Whatever he showed her would have to be genuine. The truth.

Even though he'd said she shouldn't trust him.

"Most vampires are wealthy." A graceful flick of his hand indicated the evidence of that wealth all around them. "We have a long time to build interest on our savings, and the rare vampires who conceive pass their fortunes down to their offspring. But ostentatious affluence can draw undue human attention. By tradition, we often hide our homes—"

"Lairs," she murmured.

"—in some fashion," he continued, ignoring her. "Sometimes underground, but not always. And to answer your final question, my first name is Gaston, although I prefer to go by—"

She nearly choked on a chunk of pork carnitas. "*Gaston?*"

Pinching the bridge of his nose, he sighed again. "Yes, yes, I know. That godsforsaken movie made my given name . . . unwieldy. I now choose to call myself—"

"Chad?"

"—Max, as Maxime is the second of my given names."

She grinned. "I can see why you prefer Max to Gaston. Still, it's a shame, since—"

"Edie," he began, his voice full of warning, but it was too late.

"—no . . . one . . . bites like Gaston," she singsonged, "drinks Miller Lites like Gaston. In a—"

"Don't make me kill you, human."

"—zombie match, nobody fights like Gaston. He has neutrals in all of his—"

"It wouldn't take any effort or cause me any regret, really. Just one lunge, et—"

"—*dec*-o-rating—"

"—voilà! No more throat."

"My, how he lies, that Gaston!"

After the echoes of her final, triumphal notes faded, he stared stonily at her. "If I told you never to sing that song again, you would no doubt misconstrue the order as defensive and the result of *hurt feelings*."

"No doubt." She raised her brows. "So I can sing it whenever I want?"

"Try it and see what happens, human." He glanced at the shadowed hallway leading to his media room and other mysterious spaces. "I have no bed for you, incidentally."

"Because you sleep in a coffin?" she asked sweetly.

His entire body stiffened in affront. "I sleep on premium memory foam so supportive and comfortable it would make astronauts weep in tormented longing."

"I see." She bit back a smile.

"I have no bed to offer you because I have one mattress, and it's *mine*," he emphasized.

Swallowing the last of her burrito, she winked at him. "Ah, that famous saying when it comes to guests: 'Mi casa es mi casa.' In that case, why don't you show me where you want me to sleep and where I can wash up before you have to leave?"

A line bisected his brow. "Leave?"

"You know." She waved an airy hand. "To round up villagers and pitchforks so you can attack the Beast's castle?"

He did his best to scowl at her, but before he turned his face away, she could have sworn she saw his lips twitch.

5

To be fair, Max's *Jetsons* couches were actually quite comfortable, and one of them was even deep enough that Edie's arm didn't hang over the edge. And his bathroom—his bathroom!

It was a wonderland. Given a sufficient number of pillows, she could easily sleep in that huge honkin' bathtub. His multi-head shower felt like a really high-end massage, the type where you paid extra for hot stones and lavender and a scalp rub or whatever, and apparently he made up for the spartan contents of his refrigerator by hoarding every expensive beauty product imaginable.

Shampoos. Conditioners. Hair masks. Face masks. Serums and powders and gels and lotions and exfoliators and primers and moisturizers and . . . essences, oh my?

He had luxury-brand makeup too. Lots of it. More than she'd ever owned. Which was interesting, since she'd never actually seen Chad/Max with anything but a bare face.

It was for the best, really. The sight of her dim-but-hot-and-far-too-young neighbor in guyliner or with a smoky eye would have caused her a great deal of turmoil as her hormones waged battle against her common sense and urged her to Mrs. Robinson that shit, pronto.

After she toweled off and stole some of his heavenly-smelling lotion for her dry hands, she reluctantly put back on her not-especially-fresh-and-turned-inside-out panties and her tank top—sans bra, since she was going to bed soon—and wandered out into the hallway.

He was sitting at his computer again, inside his media room, scanning the output from his various security cameras. She lingered in the doorway, unsure whether she wanted an update or not. There wasn't much she could do until the morning anyway, right?

The softbox in the room's corner kept niggling at her, reminding her of . . . something. "Hey, Max, why do you have a—"

"There are blankets and a pillow on the sofa. I've set a charger there for your use, and I've transferred the classified footage and information we discussed onto your phone," he said flatly, without turning around. "Once I've gone to bed, don't disturb my rest, human."

Her eventual Yelp review of his B and BBB—bed and blood-based breakfast—was going to contain a decidedly mixed evaluation of his hospitality. "What, no bedtime story?"

At that, he turned to glare at her, and she raised her hands, palms out.

"Sorry. Sorry." She leaned against the doorframe. "Thank you for letting me use your toiletries and your spare toothbrush."

When he merely grunted and returned his attention to his monitor, she gave up and headed for her makeshift bed. After arranging a blanket beneath her and plugging in the charger, she sat cross-legged on the sofa and checked her phone.

Sure enough, there were new files saved there.

She tapped the screen to open the first file and began reading. Tomorrow would arrive soon enough, and if she intended to venture outdoors to warn others about the breach, she needed to be as mentally prepared as possible.

The official reports confirmed what Max had already told her about the creatures but also gave her new insight into their capabilities and behaviors.

Continued inability to climb, swim, or use tools. Extremely limited, guttural speech, one official wrote. *French, for reasons yet to be determined.*

She hadn't hallucinated that! Hooray!

Maybe a handler or scientist in close contact with them had hailed from France? She supposed she'd never know. All the compound's employees had died long, long ago.

Subjects can go without sleep for several days at a time. Don't seem to age past peak physical fitness. When injured, don't appear to feel pain and barely bleed. All non-fatal wounds eventually heal, and creatures fight until moment of death. Only known ways to kill the subjects remain: (1) removing heart, (2) removing head, or (3) drowning. Suffocation alone is insufficient; water must be involved, and creatures must remain underwater for an extended time.

Hunt prey as a pack. Will not battle or consume creatures of their own generation, but will kill and consume the brains of all others, including members of previous cohorts and their own offspring.

For Edie, that was by far the worst revelation. The zombies were intended to be a sustainable military resource, as the documents indicated, which meant scientists had designed them to reproduce and replace any brethren killed in battle. After that last, fatal tinkering with their DNA, though, reproduction no longer served to swell their ranks. Instead, in the absence of other food sources, it sated their hunger.

They had a very short gestation period, and they fed on the brains of their own zombie progeny. Edie was trying very, very hard not to picture that.

The most recent report ended crisply and coldly:

> If the creature bites hard enough to draw blood but is interrupted before killing its victim—a rare occurrence—said victim begins exhibiting symptoms of transformation within ten minutes. No available cure. Victim must be put down for public safety.

A chill racked her body, and she shivered despite the blanket she'd tugged over her bare legs. Gods, she couldn't even imagine the horror of being savaged by such a creature and miraculously surviving the experience—only to be euthanized like a rabid dog minutes later.

"Do you require more blankets?" At some point, Max had silently returned to the kitchen, where he was studying her with one hip resting against the island. "Humans have such an inferior range of acceptable temperatures."

"No. Thank you," she said. "I just . . ."

Just feel very scared and alone.

"I just need to get some sleep." She tried to smile at him. "I'm fine."

He watched her closely, and she shivered again, for an entirely different reason.

"Don't watch the footage if you haven't already," he told her abruptly.

"What?"

He folded his arms over his chest, biceps stretching the sleeves of his Henley. "You have firsthand knowledge of how they move and attack, and the written reports will supply any other details you need to know."

"I was saving the videos for last." Putting off their eventual viewing, to be honest. Anxious that the filmed sequences would dredge up more memories from two decades ago, memories that were already far too close to the surface tonight. "You don't think I need to watch them?"

"No."

It was a firm, unequivocal answer, and she decided to accept it. With a couple of swipes, she closed the documents, then found herself returning his stare.

Her heart skittered under that heavy-lidded scrutiny, her skin blooming with heat, and she wondered if he could sense her involuntary reaction. Maybe even hear the increasingly rapid rush of blood in her veins.

Now that she knew he wasn't in his early twenties and astoundingly obtuse, the mental barrier that had stopped her from ogling her neighbor seemed to have crumbled.

In the dimly lit distance, his eyes were obsidian newly forged from molten earth, his hair a swirl of shadows and glinting gold, and her eyes traced the path her fingers wanted to follow. Through that thick hair, over that high cheekbone, along that stubble-shadowed jaw, down that strong neck, and over—

What was the weird shadow below the shoulder seam of his shirt?

"Come here," she told him.

He exhaled heavily, nostrils flaring, but crossed the concrete expanse between them with slow, deliberate steps, only to halt inches from her knees. She reached out an arm and gently tapped just above the stain, which was now unmistakable in color.

"Did you spill some of your dinner?" He'd chosen to bring a blood pack into his media room instead of eating in front of her, so it was possible, albeit unlikely. "Or are you hurt?"

His shoulder lifted, even as his brows drew together in seeming confusion. "A small puncture from the second zombie's claws. It's mostly healed already."

His black hoodie must have concealed the wound and the blood. "Is rapid healing another vampire thing?" When he nodded, she skimmed a light circle around the stain with her fingertip, his deltoid cool and firm beneath her caress. "It still hurts, though, when you get injured?"

"Yes." He made a sound low in his throat when she stopped touching him. "Edie . . ."

She pressed her forefinger to her pursed lips and laid it, feather-light, over that little patch of blood. "My mom did this. It shouldn't have made me feel better, but it always did."

She dropped her arm to her side. His throat shifted in a hard swallow as he twisted his neck to study the spot where she'd done her best to kiss his wound and make it better.

"That's not sanitary," he eventually muttered.

This time, her smile felt genuine. "No. Most good things aren't, I've found. Which is ironic, coming from a soap maker."

He smiled back at her then. Not Chad's goofy grin or Gaston's superior smirk, but an actual smile. Possibly the first he'd ever offered her.

Soft with humor and something that might have been fondness, the curve of his perfect mouth crinkled the corners of those piercing eyes and wrung the oxygen from her lungs. It crackled through her nerves and set off countless mental sirens, and she couldn't bring herself to care. Not when he was looking at her like that.

He licked his lips. Her breath caught.

Then he stepped away—one stride, two—and the earth spun back into motion.

His hand raked through his hair. "If you toss and turn all night, you'll keep me awake too. Take the bed, human, and shut the door behind you."

"And you'll sleep out here?"

She didn't completely understand his change of heart, but she wouldn't argue or question it. Not when she needed every bit of energy and strength she could muster to face what was coming tomorrow.

"Yes. So move," he ordered, and waited impatiently as she disentangled herself from the blankets, gathered her few belongings, and heaved herself to her feet. "Don't show your face again until morning. I don't like having my rest disturbed."

She rolled her eyes. "Sweet dreams to you too."

His back muscles shifted in mesmerizing ways as he bent over the sofa and began rearranging the blankets in what he clearly considered a neater, superior fashion. Tearing her gaze away took more effort than she was comfortable admitting, but she finally headed for the distant hallway. Only to halt again, unable to stop herself from asking the most crucial question of all.

"You told me so much tonight. About yourself, your species, and the zombies, and . . . I think it was the truth. I think all of it's the truth." He'd stilled, one hand braced on the back of the sofa, when she turned her head to watch him over her shoulder. "Why, Max?"

Between them, the silence stretched like taffy.

"The sort of noble fool who'd try to save Chad from his well-deserved fate?" He shook his head, still facing away from her. "She wouldn't betray anyone willingly. And even if you passed along everything I told you, it would simply be one story among many, no more or less believable than all the others."

That sounded like the beginnings of trust to her, however reluctant and tattered.

Still: "If I did betray you, you'd make me regret it, I presume."

"Obviously," he said after a moment. Oddly enough, it felt like the first lie he'd offered her in hours. "Go to sleep, Edie."

So she did, wrapped in the embrace of a mattress she'd legally marry if such a thing were possible. She sank into that premium memory foam, tugged his silky-soft sheets and ornately quilted blanket over her, and closed her eyes.

After the shocks she'd experienced that night, after the documents she'd studied and the horrors they'd revealed, she expected nightmares.

To get to her, though, any threat would have to go through him. She slept like a child in her mother's arms.

6

S tay here," Max told Edie the next morning as she popped several mints in lieu of an actual breakfast. "Only an idiot would wander outside after a breach. Besides, the zombies won't make it past the moat. They don't have a pass to let down the drawbridge and open the passage to Zone B. Even if they did have a pass, they wouldn't understand how to use it. They can't have gone far, which means *you* won't make it far before they find you."

His voice had started dispassionate and low, but it steadily rose as some indefinable emotion seeped around the edges of his words and prodded him to speak faster and faster.

Her brows lifted. "Yet they managed to break through Wall One and get across *that* moat."

His mouth tightened. He hadn't expected her to remember that little detail, apparently. "Even if they did make it across the moat to Zone B, very few people live in the Containment Zone, and everyone will have gone somewhere more congenial to visit friends and family for the holidays."

"Everyone except you and me. I wonder what that says about us."

For her, staying in the Zone had been a choice. Two friends had issued invitations, as had several distant relations, but she didn't like spending the holidays away from her parents. The house itself was what she had left of them, apart from her memories and the few possessions that hadn't been either broken or soaked in blood during the First Breach.

Max, though . . . did he have anywhere else to go, at the holidays or any other time?

He ignored her interjection. "You wouldn't be saving anyone, only endangering yourself. And surely the sirens will begin any minute now."

Neither one of them believed that. "I don't know what went wrong, but if the alarm hasn't sounded by now, I don't think it's happening. Not unless we get word to the authorities. And honestly, Max, I can't stay here much longer anyway. I need to eat, and you don't have human food."

"I can get food from your house," he said swiftly. "The pack appears to have moved on overnight, and I'm more than able to handle a stray creature or two on my own."

"I see." She smiled at Mr. Your Survival Is Immaterial to Me, imbuing her expression with all the gentle mockery his offer deserved. "Thank you, but that doesn't address the main reason I'm going."

"To help other humans."

"To help anyone who needs assistance, human or not."

"Edie." He ducked his head to make direct eye contact, unfamiliar lines bracketing his mouth. "They wouldn't help *you*."

"You don't know that."

"I do."

"Is that why you didn't want to call in the breach?" Her head tipped to the side as she studied him. "Because you don't think anyone would care about your survival, so you're returning the favor?"

"I knew someone would notify the hotline. Notably, you." His hand flicked in her direction. "But if you hadn't called, that would have been fine too. I don't care what happens to anyone else. The government and SERC will eventually notice the breach and rectify the situation. I'm more than happy to wait it out until then."

Her gaze dropped to her sneakers—which the neat freak had apparently scrubbed overnight, since they were now whiter than they'd been in years—and she frowned.

Her instincts said he didn't mean that. But he was telling her who he was, and she should believe him, even if some of his actions contradicted his words.

Maybe she truly was the lone exception to his misanthropy, temporarily tolerated only because she'd attempted to save his life and some vestigial sense of honor obliged him to help her in return. Maybe he truly was a conscienceless cipher, and she was only seeing what she wanted to see. In which case, she should leave his home no matter what, for her own safety. A sense of obligation would only carry him so far, unaided by genuine concern for her or anyone else. Soon enough, her life would mean nothing to him once more, and she'd be a fool to put herself in close proximity to such a lethal, ruthless predator.

"What?" When she didn't respond, he repeated, "What, Edie? What are you thinking?"

She swallowed. "People do sacrifice themselves for the good of others. I know that for a fact." Her eyes rose to meet the bleakness of his. "But it doesn't matter, really. I can't control what others do. I can only control what I do, and I have to look at myself in the mirror every morning and be able to live with what I see. I can't sit and wait and save myself at the expense of my neighbors' lives. I have to go."

He simply watched her, expressionless.

"Thank you for your help last night. If the phone lines start working again, please call the hotline. For me, if no one else." Disappointment stung her eyes, but she blinked the prickle away. She gave him a little nod of gratitude, of farewell, and slung her bag over her head. "Take care, Max."

He didn't respond, even with a perfunctory goodbye. His pale eyes burned into her, as blue and hot as the center of a flame, and she turned away from the scorch.

His stare followed her across the shiny concrete. She could feel it, and she rolled her shoulders to shrug off the weight of it.

When she was three steps away from the ladder, he called out her name. "*Edie.*"

Not quite a bark, not quite a plea. Not enough to stop her for long. Rather than swiveling to face him, she simply looked over her shoulder and waited.

His hands fisted at his sides. "Since moving next door, I've intercepted two would-be intruders casing your home. One last year. Another in October."

The words sounded rusty. Rough around the edges. They also sounded like the truth.

He'd helped her—potentially saved her property or even her

life—long, long before she'd attempted to save him. And he was telling her because . . .

Because he didn't want her to leave without knowing he valued at least one other person in the entire world. Her.

"I can show you the footage." He didn't sound panicked, exactly. But he certainly didn't sound dispassionate. "I saved it."

"No need. I believe you." Her lips curved, because now she'd have one last pleasant memory of him, of caring, before she met her fate. "Thank you."

Impatiently, he waved that aside. "I don't want your gratitude."

"Then what do you want?" A farewell hug? Maybe even a tiny little k—

"I want to accompany you," he announced.

Her brows slammed together in shock. *What the*— "Why?"

"Because . . ." He hesitated and shifted his weight, the muscles in his jaw working. "Because . . ."

After a few moments, she let him off the hook. He'd already revealed much more of himself over the past twenty-four hours than she would have predicted, and definitely more than was comfortable for him. His exact motivation in this instance could remain fuzzy.

He cared about her, however unwillingly. And with him at her side, she might actually survive the upcoming trek. No matter his reasoning, that was a clear win for her.

She offered him a teasing, triumphant grin. "Because you're finally acknowledging the awesomeness of my kick last night? Because you're eager to learn from me, your local warrior princess–slash–ninja?"

"Because if all humanity perishes, I'll starve," he said dryly.

"Good enough for me!" she chirped, then companionably punched his uninjured arm.

"Ow." He scowled at her, rubbing his triceps ostentatiously. "Control your bloodlust, human, and give me a minute to put together a pack."

She snickered. "Fine. I'll meet you by the ladder."

Gods, climbing up that thing was going to suck even worse than climbing down.

"I have an elevator," he told her before striding toward his bedroom.

"What?" It was an outraged squawk. "Then why didn't we use it last night?"

"We might not have made it there in time." He smiled smugly at her. "Also, I was curious how long the descent would take you. The answer: forever. A bloody *eternity*. It was sad, really."

Then he was gone, his steps swift and sure, before she could run over and punch his arm again, this time with more force.

"I've met centenarian tortoises who move faster than you did," he called through the closing bedroom door, and she aimed her middle fingers in his direction even as she laughed.

IN THE END, leaving his house took them another full hour.

Once he emerged from his room with a large backpack, they looked at a map of the Containment Zone on his phone. Without needing much discussion, they decided upon the most straightforward route: They would immediately drive to the lone access road that allowed passage over the moats and through the walls to the outside world, where they would contact the nearest authorities about the latest breach. All while avoiding a roaming pack of zombies and any straggler zombies that might be lingering nearby.

"And helping anyone in trouble along the way," she added as they studied their path.

He sighed. "If absolutely necessary."

"Also, if the sirens sound before we make it out of the Zone, we'll find safe shelter wherever we are." When he simply looked at her, as if to say *obviously*, she spread her hands. "Just making sure our priorities are aligned so we both know what to do."

The humming sound he made didn't indicate agreement, necessarily, but he didn't argue.

She looked down at herself. At some point during the night, Max had laundered her coveralls too, so they were clean and dry, and they were thick enough to prevent light scratches and abrasions. Not damage from claws and sharp teeth, however.

"Thanks for washing this, by the way." She plucked at the fraying edge of her sleeve. "It was crusty and gross."

"Yes, I know." He gave a delicate shudder.

"It's my most protective work clothing, but it doesn't shield my neck at all. Do you have anything that might? Like, a metal piece from a suit of armor or something?"

It was a valid question. Also a nosy one. While Max clearly wasn't in his early twenties after all, she had no clue how old he might actually be. If he owned an original suit of armor . . . well, she'd know more, wouldn't she?

His forehead creased in thought. "A gorget? No, unfortunately, I decided to—" He cut himself off. "No. I don't have one."

Aha! A clue at last!

"But you used to have one." She bounced on her toes.

"Because you're a super-old, immortal vampire with firsthand knowledge of armor and buboes and witch burning. And chamber pots! Oh wow, you must have used chamber pots!"

"I'm immortal, yes." Glaring at her, he drew himself up to his full height. "But not *super old*."

"So what would constitute super oldness to you, then?"

No answer.

"Did you use chamber pots or not?"

No answer.

Fine, fine. She'd let it drop if he wanted to be a spoilsport about it. "I should grab my knives from my house when we stop there for food. I know you have the one you used last night, but do you need another? I could lend you one. Or do you have another weapon of your own?"

His lips pressed together. After grumbling unintelligibly for a moment, he reached between his shoulder blades and under his newly cleaned black leather hoodie and produced . . . a sword.

A giant, shiny fucking *sword*.

Yeah, Max was totally *super old*. Daaaaamn.

"You went with the *Wonder Woman* design option for storing that sword, huh? Do you have an incredibly hot blue dress under there too?" She tilted her head, trying to get a better look beneath his hoodie. "Because if so, I want to see it."

She could only make out jeans and some sort of dark shirt, sadly. At least he'd traded in those cloven shoes for shiny but clearly well-worn boots. Much more practical and much less hideous.

He rolled his eyes at her, sheathed his sword in one swift motion, and returned to her earlier question. "Anything short of a gorget, the creatures' teeth and claws would be able to pierce.

Unless you know of a nearby armorer, human, we'll simply have to ensure we keep our necks as far from the creatures as possible."

She laughed. "I mean, that was kind of always my plan."

"How's your ankle?" He'd been silently studying how she moved all morning, and now she knew why. "Still sore? Do you need to take more medication or wrap it?"

"Good as new."

Well, more *gently used*, but that would have to be sufficient.

He narrowed his eyes at her but finally blew out a breath and nodded. Presenting her with his back, he removed half a dozen blood bags from his refrigerator and tucked them into his enormous pack. Luckily, the chill outside should keep them fresh for at least a couple of days, so he wouldn't need to sate his hunger in . . . other ways.

Although that could be interesting too, now that she considered the matter.

"Ready?" His hands were as steady as his eyes on her.

She was . . . until a sudden surge of anxiety pinned her in place. He might be immortal, but he could still be killed, and for all his bluster about ensuring his source of sustenance didn't go extinct, she knew he was only leaving his secure home for her sake.

If he died accompanying her on what he considered a stupid mission, how would that feel? Should she go it alone, as she'd originally intended?

"It's going to be dangerous," she said slowly. "Are you sure you want to risk your life for—"

"Oh for fuck's sake, come on."

Despite his impatience, his hand—planted between her

shoulder blades, hurrying her toward his bedroom and down the hall—wasn't rough or hurtful. When they reached the door at the end, he unearthed a small key. With a twist of his wrist and a quiet *click*, a library of sorts opened to them both, softly lit by stained glass lamps and decorated in blues and ornately carved honey-toned woods. *Old-fashioned* was one word that came to mind. *Cozy* and *warm* were others. The room's aesthetic emphatically rejected the minimalism and modernity of the rest of Max's home.

And he'd locked it away from her.

All his other doors had remained open, both last night and this morning. She'd had ready access to that godsforsaken ladder too, which meant he hadn't been preventing an escape. So what about this room in particular made him unwilling to allow scrutiny?

He strode across the room to reach for a thick book on a tall shelf. Something gave a decisive, muffled *thunk*, and the entire wall opened to reveal an elevator.

It was undeniably awesome. Like something from a movie. Also very over-the-top.

"Drama king," she murmured.

The narrow elevator car was lit by an intricate crystal chandelier, paneled with satiny stretches of wood, and carpeted thickly. It was also clearly meant to be a one-man—one-vampire—elevator. She stepped in anyway, curious as to whether he'd try to make the cramped space fit both of them. After entering a code on a discreet electronic panel, he half turned away from her and grabbed something small, round, and silver from a desk drawer, then shoved the object into a hoodie pocket before she could see exactly what it was.

When he squeezed into the elevator car beside her, there was no way to avoid contact. Either they plastered themselves against each other, or the door wouldn't close. Surrendering to the inevitable, she simply blew out a breath, looped her arms around his waist, and leaned into him. His entire body stiffened in her loose embrace, then gradually relaxed again.

The door closed, and the elevator began its slow ascent. She huddled closer to him.

After a few seconds, one strong hand settled on the small of her back. The other alighted on the nape of her neck and squeezed lightly.

"Claustrophobic?" he asked, his voice low and gentle.

When she shook her head, her hair rubbed against his leather-clad shoulder. "Zombie-phobic."

"I see." Something nudged the top of her head. His chin? His mouth? "Based on what I saw last night, I wouldn't have guessed that."

"I didn't have time to think." *I didn't have time to remember.* "Now I do."

The relative chill of his body seeped through his clothing and calmed her. She tended to run hot, and this hug was like cuddling up against a cool breeze made flesh. A cool breeze that filled her lungs with the scent of eucalyptus and apparently worked out quite a bit. Like, *a lot.*

They rested in each other's arms, his hand slowly sliding up and down her spine. The scent and feel of him dizzied her in the best possible way. Comforted her.

If it was her last hug on this earth, it was a good one.

"We don't have to go, Edie. One push of a button, and we can—"

"I have to go." She nuzzled her cheek against his chest, gathering strength from the soothing contact. "You don't, but I do."

He sighed, still stroking her back. "Very well."

"You're sure you want to do this?" she asked one final time, for the sake of her smarting conscience.

"I'm sure."

When the elevator halted and its door opened, he dropped his arms with another sigh, squeezed her behind him, and exited first. Another hidden mechanism let them into a part of his aboveground home she'd never seen, full of splintered furniture and other signs of thwarted, hungry rage.

He led the way to the broken front door and scanned their surroundings before stepping outside. She inhaled deeply and looked around too.

The sun was bright that morning, and she squinted a bit, her breath fogging in the frigid winter air. "I don't see any—"

And, of course, that was when two zombies leapt onto the porch and lunged toward her and Max.

Two against two. The odds could have been worse, Edie
supposed.

One of the creatures, she was leaving entirely to Max,
but he couldn't fight both at once. And he didn't need to, because
the other zombie had clearly chosen her as its prey.

She managed to dive to one side, avoiding its first fatal leap
and snapping jaws. As it whipped around, recovering its balance
and pinpointing her new location, she wrenched her cell from
the pocket of her coveralls, jacked up the volume to max, yelled
out a voice command, and tossed it halfway across the lawn onto
a small patch of snow.

Nothing happened other than a few muffled noises she
couldn't identify over the thuds and howls and grunts of Max's
battle against his own zombie. Fuck. Had she broken her phone?

He was right, damn it all. They never should have left his
fancy-ass cave.

Scrambling to her feet and whipping into her best defensive
stance, she brandished her knife and prepared to make her final

stand. The zombie in front of her crouched, its rear legs bending for another powerful leap, and—

Cardi B called everyone a *little bitch* at top volume from that tiny snowdrift, and the creature spun around in confusion at the earsplitting noise. Which was when Max, with a flash of sunlit silver and another grunt of effort, lopped off her zombie's head. Its body crumpled to the porch floor as its sickly yellow blood splattered everywhere. The head itself rolled a bit until it butted against a matching chopped-off head and rocked to a halt.

Forcing her eyes from the gruesome sight, she scanned Max for injuries as he crouched to wipe his sword on his faded welcome mat. None, as far as she could tell. Good.

"Excellent timing." She was panting, adrenaline causing her hands to shake and leaving her lightheaded. "Thank you."

"Excellent distraction," he countered. "Thank *you*."

"Cardi B bought us just enough time." She gave a halfhysterical giggle, pointing at his boots and her sneakers. "Look. Bloody shoes."

He actually grinned at her. "She's a prophet."

The way that expression transformed and warmed his face only weakened her knees further. Holding on tightly to the rail, she carefully descended his porch steps and scanned the yard again. "We'd better get moving. There could be others nearby."

His forehead creased. "Did you tweak your ankle injury when you fell?"

"Nope." With an effort, she steadied herself and crossed the lawn swiftly to reclaim her phone. "Let's go."

Together, they hustled toward her home next door, and she unlocked the front door, closed it behind them, and threw the deadbolt as quickly as she could.

"Feel free to . . ." She kicked off her shoes and glanced around, searching for something he could do to occupy himself while she got everything she needed. "Uh, whatever. I'll be as fast as I can."

As she jogged up the stairs, she tried her best not to picture him grimacing at the detritus of her life, most of which lay scattered across various dusty surfaces. She wasn't a domestic goddess and never had been. Her mom used to call her room a pigpen and bemoan Edie's habit of leaving mostly empty bottles of pomegranate juice everywhere she went, like a sticky trail of breadcrumbs.

Mom wouldn't be thrilled about the current state of their family's home. Edie wasn't thrilled either, to be fair. Under normal circumstances, she'd be living in a smaller, more manageable apartment or condo instead of a detached split-level house, but . . . circumstances hadn't been normal since she'd been eighteen. This was where her family had once lived and where her memories of them *still* lived. This was where she'd remain.

After a quick stop in the bathroom for basic toiletries, she dug through a pile of clean laundry she hadn't bothered putting away and shoved a couple more pairs of thick coveralls, some socks, and some undies into a duffel. Up in the tiny attic, she gathered her emergency collection of nonperishables, a set of plastic utensils, and her can opener and dumped it all into the increasingly heavy bag too.

A few other odds and ends later, she headed back downstairs for her knives. One of them she found in the kitchen, where she'd forgotten it on top of the small café table. The cleaver should still be in its assigned spot in her garage. Which was also her workspace and where Max had apparently gone while she was upstairs, because the door leading there was open and she couldn't see him anywhere else.

She put her shoes back on, cracked the door wider, descended the two steps to the concrete slab floor, and joined him inside. He stood in the middle of the space, turning slowly in place as he studied her setup.

Unlike the rest of her home, she kept the area strictly clean and organized. That should please him, right?

"What do you think?" They didn't have time for this, but she had to know. Stupidly, his first impression—his opinion—mattered to her. If he dismissed her work as trivial or a hobby—

"Science," he said, and nodded to the wall on her right.

Coated metal racks there contained her soapmaking supplies: safety equipment; various oils and butters; her trusty immersion blender; heat-safe bowls and measuring cups; soap cutters; silicone and birchwood molds; colorants; glitters and micas; fragrances and essential oils; fresh and dried botanicals; decorating bags and stainless-steel tips; isopropyl alcohol; and some of the many liquids she could use to dissolve her lye. Next to her supplies, she'd positioned two long, sturdy stainless-steel tables as her main work surfaces.

A quarter turn, and he tipped his head toward the wall on her left. "Art."

There, more coated metal racks contained her current inventory, including all her soaps that were in the process of curing and those still waiting to be unmolded, with a dehumidifier waiting nearby for the muggy summer months. In neat rows, she'd arranged her bar soaps alongside those shaped like cupcakes, cherry blossoms, oranges, succulents, gems, and even boba drinks. The soaps were tinted in a rainbow of colors, their combined scents heady.

Another quarter turn, and he gestured to the remaining sides of the room. "Commerce."

Against the garage door and the final wall, she'd arranged everything she required for testing, packaging, and shipping her soaps. In the corner, her desktop computer waited, with tabs open to various spreadsheets, her website—which needed some updating—and various photos to be edited. Her DSLR camera lay on a table beneath the garage's lone window—because natural daylight resulted in the best photos of her soaps—along with a few simple background papers.

She didn't have a softbox or ring light, despite sporadic guest appearances on her friends' video channels, but she was considering the purchase of both. Which was why, when she'd seen them in Max's home, she'd recognized them and wondered what exactly he did online.

Science. Art. Commerce.

In three words, he'd captured the essence of what she did and what she loved about her work. The way it combined precision, creativity, and practicality. How it allowed her to stretch herself, test her abilities, create beauty, and learn more every day.

Her supply shelving had drawn his attention again, and she smiled at his profile as she drifted to his side and reached for her cleaver.

"What's in there?" He pointed to her locked cabinet, positioned safely off the ground.

"Lye." Treated carelessly, sodium hydroxide could cause severe burns or even trigger an explosion, so she didn't fuck around with those airtight plastic containers. "AKA the reason I need gloves and goggles and face masks."

"I didn't realize everything your work involved." He wandered over to her curing racks, almost but not quite touching the soaps she'd colored and molded to resemble tiny, perfect oranges, future door prizes at the grand opening of a San Joaquin Valley farmer's market. Leaning closer, he sniffed. "Orange and . . . cloves?"

"Yep." Her cleaver felt good in her hand. Solid and familiar. She slid it into its sheath and added it to her bag. "Those are ready to go. I just don't want to package them until the last minute. And speaking of being ready to go . . ."

"These soaps are beautiful." He sounded sincere. "Before we leave, could you tell me what photo-editing software you use for your business?"

"Adobe Lightroom. Why?"

"What version?"

"I'd have to check?" She crinkled her brow at him. "Do you really think now is the best—"

"Thank you, Edie," he said with remarkable, uncharacteristic politeness.

Getting him the info he wanted—for whatever reason he wanted it—would take less time than arguing with him about how he *shouldn't* want it right now. After crossing the room to the computer, she checked the software and scrawled a note with the exact version she was currently using.

When she turned around again, he was fiddling with something in his hoodie pocket, which was also odd. Why was he so fidgety?

She passed him the paper, then led the way to the side door. "Your car or mine?"

"My SUV's tires aren't bald." His look of stern judgment tempted her to stick her tongue out at him, but she resisted. "Also, I have heated seats and emergency supplies in my trunk, including a first aid kit."

"Sold," she said, and looked both ways before exiting her garage and locking the door behind them. "Morituri te salutant."

Most of her high school Latin had disappeared over the years, but not that phrase. Which probably revealed more about her general state of mind than she cared to contemplate.

He shook his head and followed close behind her as they neared his own garage. "'Those who are about to die salute you'? That sentiment seems a bit pessimistic for you, human."

"Just checking if you know Latin." Still scanning their surroundings, she snickered. "Which you evidently do, thus raising the following questions: Were you alive during the Roman Empire? Were you BFFs with Caesar? Is Maxime short for Maximus? Did you wear short leather skirts in a gladiatorial arena and fight tigers and look really hot, all while not ruining my cherished girlhood fantasies by later throwing phones at innocent hotel clerks?"

His garage door opened with a click of his remote control, and he gestured her ahead of him, toward the passenger seat, while he jogged to the driver's side.

"Risus abundat in ore stultorum," he murmured, sliding into his leather seat and slamming the door behind him. He waited a few moments, but when she refused to give him the satisfaction of asking and concentrated instead on fastening her seat belt, he translated for her. "'Laughter is abundant in the mouth of fools.'"

"Hey!" she protested. "Rude!"

He laughed too then, and without answering even a single

one of her questions, he started the SUV and accelerated out of his garage and into the bright, dangerous unknown.

AS THEY WENDED their way through deserted, half-buckled streets to the Zone's main access road, Edie studied Max's calm, contained expression.

"I invited you to visit my workroom the first time we met." The day after he'd moved in, she'd baked a pan of cheesecake-swirl brownies and brought them over, eager to chat with her new neighbor. Hopeful they could become friends as well as mutual sources of help in an emergency. "If you were interested, why didn't you come before?"

Because he hadn't ever rung her doorbell. Not once in three years. Even when she'd given him the brownies, he'd merely accepted them with a cheerful *Whoa, thanks, dude,* then made reference to his raging case of munchies, listened to her invitation to visit, drained his Miller Lite, and crushed the can against his forehead. Only it wasn't actually empty, so beer sprayed everywhere, including all over her. After accepting his hapless apologies, she'd promptly headed home again, already knowing her neighbor wouldn't be much help in an emergency.

He hadn't bothered to return her pan in person. It had appeared, unwashed, on her doorstep a week later. Which was when she knew he wouldn't be much of a friend either.

And yet . . . here he was. Helping her in an emergency. Fresh from her workroom, which he'd surveyed with clear fascination and appreciation. Much like a friend might.

His lips thinned, and he squinted at the road ahead. "I *wasn't* interested. Not at first. And then . . ."

She waited, but he didn't finish his thought. Instead, he reached into his console for a pair of stylish oversized sunglasses, which he slid onto his nose. They made it hard for her to read his expression.

"And then . . ." she prompted.

He shifted in his seat. "Is there such a thing as soapmaking school, or are you self-taught?"

The firm set of that tempting mouth had become increasingly familiar to her, and she knew what it meant. If he didn't want to say more, he wouldn't.

"Mostly the latter. After graduating from high school, I"—*excitedly prepared to attend William and Mary, only to withdraw my acceptance after my parents died terribly while I hid in our attic*—"took online classes for business, web design, and chemistry, then started my company."

Flicking the turn signal, he smoothly braked and went right at the faded stop sign. "You make custom soaps rather than having a set stock, correct?"

Indeed she did, and she'd told him so. Three years ago.

"You remember that?" When he failed to answer her question, *again*, she sighed and addressed his. "I sell seasonal collections and a few perennial favorites on Etsy, but most of my business in recent years comes from my custom soap work. People contact me via my website, and they can either choose from a gallery of soaps I've created before or work with me to create new, one-of-a-kind small-batch soap recipes and designs. They can specify the soap's shape, along with their preferred oil and liquid mixture, colors, fragrances, internal and external swirls and decorations, botanical toppings, et cetera. Even the packaging."

"Mmmm." He tapped his forefingers against the steering wheel. "Is it difficult to make new recipes?"

"Things can get complicated, depending on the customer's choices." She tried to steer them toward recipes that would give them the outcome they wanted, but . . . "I usually have to trouble-shoot something. Specific fragrances and additives can cause discoloration or texture problems, like ricing. The design the client wants may not be possible with the oil blend they choose. There's a certain amount of experimentation and negotiation."

His lip curled. "You deal with people a lot, then."

If she'd declared slime molds to be her main customer base, he couldn't have sounded more disgusted. "Less *deal with* and more *interact with*."

For her, that was a feature of her work. Not a bug. She loved working at home and working for herself, but she missed people. She missed coworkers and neighbors and family and friends who could visit her house without needing prior permission and a special pass. Friends who *would* visit her house, full stop.

And speaking of her missing family members, there it was, whooshing by on her right: Brandstrup Arts & Crafts, her parents' former store. Once thriving and bright and cheerful, now faded and falling apart. Abandoned, like most of the Zone. Left behind, like her.

"What?" Surprisingly attentive to her shift in mood, he slowed the SUV. "What's wrong?"

She swallowed back the familiar wave of grief and shook her head.

"Did you see something?" They came to a near stop on the deserted road. "Talk to me."

Oh, sure. When he didn't want to discuss something, he just changed the subject or sealed those fine lips closed. But was she allowed to keep her own thoughts private? Nope.

"It's just my parents' old store." With a hitch of her thumb, she pointed back to the boarded-up storefront at the end of a sagging strip mall. "Keep moving."

Something about the sweep of his head as he turned to face her, the graceful twist of his neck, those stylish glasses, the way the light hit the clean, elegant line of his jaw . . . damn, it was familiar. In fact—

"Wait." She slapped the dashboard in triumph. "I know who you are."

His fingers curled tighter around the steering wheel. "What do you mean?"

She laughed in utter glee. "I know why you have that softbox and a ring light setup. I know why I keep picturing you strutting to a chilly European beat, why you were wearing such a bizarre outfit last night, and why you have so much pricy makeup in your bathroom."

"Do you?" The rumble in his low voice was a threat.

Too bad she wasn't afraid of him anymore. Maybe she should be, but nope. Once she'd cuddled up to someone and they'd rubbed her back soothingly, her prudent wariness apparently dissipated into the ether.

"I can't believe I didn't recognize you before now. I mean, Brad and Tonya are good friends of mine, and I watch all their videos."

Her head tipped to the side as she considered the matter.

Maybe she was being unfair to herself. Her neighbor Chad—rumpled, harmless, friendly, mouth-breather Chad—might have shared the same basic physical specifications as the nameless, silent founder of the cult favorite *Better Than You Beauty and Fashion* channel, but the two males looked entirely different in every other respect.

In the sunshine, Chad's uncombed hair, with its trimmed sides and floppy top, had gleamed golden. In Max's videos, whatever product he used to slick that hair back from his face had darkened it. His natural eye color hadn't been clear online either, maybe because of filters or because he wore tinted contacts to cover that distinctive shade of blue.

Her neighbor had favored faded Miller Lite tees with holes in them, either one size too big or one size too small. He'd worn baggy, ragged jeans and a vague smile. In contrast, *Better Than You Beauty and Fashion* Guy had modeled the most cutting-edge fashions and makeup trends, almost all of which would look ridiculous on anyone but him.

His videos had helped popularize bleached eyebrows and thigh-high Uggs and so much more. He either revealed his chosen outfit or demonstrated the application of his chosen makeup to the sound of that inimitable, austere electro-dance music. He never smiled. Never spoke. Didn't monetize his channel. Didn't respond to comments. All of it only added to his mystique.

On second thought, no wonder she hadn't recognized him as her sweet, goofy neighbor.

"You . . ." He spoke slowly. "You're friends with Brad and Tonya, from *Brad and Tonya Try It?*"

She nodded absently. "They saw my feather-swirl soap design a few years back. It was used for a B-list celebrity's bridal shower and went modestly viral, and they asked me for my help in recreating it. Since then, they've attempted to re-create some of my other designs too. They're awesome and funny and good people, so I'm a friend *and* a subscriber. I've seen all their videos where they try things from your channel."

Her attention wasn't really on the conversation, though.

A year or two back, when Brad and Tonya had been trying to convince Edie to appear on their channel, they'd sent samples of their most popular content to her—including a few videos inspired by and featuring clips from Max's own channel. And with only the slightest twinge of shame, Edie had downloaded several of those videos onto her phone, because *wowza* . . . and then promptly forgotten about them.

Had she ever actually looked at the downloads again? Not that she remembered.

But they should still be on her cell. No internet required.

A few swipes of her forefinger, and there they were. There *he* was.

She recognized that vast expanse of concrete flooring, although he'd carefully positioned his camera so it didn't show his furniture or any other identifiable features of his underground home. His bare, hard chest gleamed as he strode dick-first toward the camera and away again, his lace-up black boots stomping, the capacious folds of his gold lamé MC Hammer pants shimmering and fluttering, alternately molding to his strong thighs and hiding them. His eyeliner was thick and dark, his mouth lush and rosy, the sharp angles of his face emphasized by glitter and shadow and just a hint of stubbly scruff on his cheeks and chin.

He was electric. A glam god sent to enthrall humanity.

Well, until that freaking clip-on rattail came into view. Ugh.

"Please, Hammer, don't hurt 'em," she murmured.

The SUV jumped forward as her currently-rattail-free companion pressed the accelerator to the floor. "Perhaps you could set aside this fateful revelation, human, and return your attention to the task at hand."

"Perhaps not."

Despite his aggrieved grunt and the way he appeared to be strangling the steering wheel, she watched another download, then another. One of his specialties appeared to be ridiculous, uncomfortable—and ridiculously, uncomfortably sexy—underwear. Velour boxers, which she imagined would leave non-vampires drowning in their own ball sweat. Macramé bikini briefs that seemed like they would chafe painfully and that simultaneously exposed far too much and far too little. And soon, she supposed, a furry thong, accessorized by cloven-toed shoes and an open leather hoodie. He must have been dressed for his next shoot when he'd stepped outside the previous evening, his hair and makeup preparations still to come.

With his authoritative demeanor and cool confidence, he made all the looks work somehow. If she didn't know that every item on his body would either irritate the hells out of her, bankrupt her, or not be offered in her size, she'd have been whipping out her credit card.

"I only watch Brad and Tonya's content involving my channel," Max said. The streets they traveled were getting broader and somewhat better maintained as they neared the access road, and he studied them carefully as he drove. "I didn't realize they'd featured your work too."

"They've used your videos as inspiration . . . what? Half a dozen times already?" Her grin grew. "I'll never forget Brad stumbling around in those high-heeled Crocs. That face-plant into the deviled eggs platter . . ." She kissed her fingertips in appreciation. "Physical comedy is difficult. Also embarrassing, when it's accidental."

Max huffed out an amused breath, his shoulders loosening. "He's not the most graceful of souls, is he?"

"It's all part of his charm." She snorted. "I know he also regretted trying those macramé undies of yours."

At some point in the near future, she would be revisiting that particular video on a much larger screen. The bulge beneath Max's knotted bikini briefs, the shifting shadows she'd spotted through the gaps in the design . . . wow. Did he wax everything below the neck, or was lack of body hair a vampire thing? Because his skin was *very* smooth down there.

His face creased in a faint wince. "The knots are . . . unforgiving. And if there's too large a hole in the design . . ."

"Did you—" Absolutely delighted, she grabbed his arm and shook it. "Did you get your dick caught in your hand-knotted haute couture briefs, Max?"

She probably shouldn't be mentioning his dick. Or thinking about it. Or picturing it both caught in a net like a hapless carp and rising unhindered in glorious freedom.

Alas. Here she was, considering various dick-related scenarios in Technicolor detail.

"No," he stated firmly.

"Your testicles, then." Assuming vampires actually *had* testicles.

He didn't say anything as he turned onto the main access road, but something in his expression shifted. She had her answer. Also a new vision to conjure whenever she needed a good laugh.

"No . . . one . . ." She drew out the words to build anticipation.

He turned his head and whipped off his sunglasses to glare at her. "No."

". . . struts like Gaston," she sang out, with enthusiasm and joy in her heart, "injures nuts like Gaston—"

"*No.*" His brows had formed a thick, menacing line. "Human—"

"—puts sheepskin up his butt like Gaston!"

"—don't make me turn this car around."

"His macramé briefs are so *strang*-u-*la*-ting . . ."

He pinched the bridge of his nose. "I can't believe I just said that. This is a travesty."

"My, what great thighs, that Gaston!" she finished, and beamed at him. "They really are great, by the way. All firm and muscly and stuff."

"*And stuff?*" he repeated, incredulous. "Mother of gods, what—"

"Holy shit," she whispered, her attention caught by what she saw ahead of them. "Max . . ."

He slammed on the brakes, and his SUV screeched to a halt.

They'd reached the end of Zone A, and the moat and wall separating them from Zone B had come into view.

Whether or not a breach was reported, the government took no chances with such an early line of defense. The system operated on an independent, tamper-proof power grid whose workings remained mysterious even after twenty years. And unless a driver swiped a valid passcard and satisfied the facial recognition algorithm for all detected passengers, the drawbridge stayed up and the hulking door guarding the entrance through the wall remained securely shut at all times.

She'd never heard of anyone being able to sneak through the security setup, even in a vehicle's trunk or underneath its chassis. There was never a guard at the gate, or another official who could activate the mechanisms without a pass and accepted, confirmed passenger identifications, and there was no known—or even rumored—way to override the system.

Max's sunglasses tumbled from his grasp and fell to the floor. "What the fuck?"

"Yeah," she agreed, stomach churning. "What the fuck."

It shouldn't have been possible. It *wasn't* possible. But there they were.

Even though there was no other vehicle in sight, the drawbridge over the moat was down. The door through the wall was open.

Over the course of two decades, she'd seen her share of technical malfunctions on the access road. But when those malfunctions occurred, the system always—*always*—reverted to closed doors and raised bridges. It was the default state, without exception, for the safety of all.

Maybe zombies could have taken down the cell tower and power lines using sheer physical force. There was no fucking way the creatures had overridden the access road's security system, though. Not unless they'd secretly spent the last two decades becoming sophisticated hackers.

Here was the definitive proof. A terrible accident hadn't caused the breach. For a second time, horrifyingly enough—

"This was sabotage," he stated.

"Yeah," she said again, and shuddered in dread.

8

Edie ate her long-awaited, much-needed breakfast as she and Max discussed what to do next. Parked between two dumpsters, out of easy sight, they should be safe enough for a few minutes. She hoped.

"I'm not changing my mind," she told him for the dozenth time, and downed another starchy spoonful of her on-the-go meal. "But feel free to drop me off at my house so I can grab my car and go on my own."

He dragged a hand through his hair, pushing it away from his forehead. "By themselves, zombies are incredibly dangerous. But now we have to take into account whoever planned this cluster-fuck too, Edie, and they could be anywhere. *Anywhere*. We have no idea what they want or why. All we know is that they're willing to kill innocent people to get it. Which means they would kill *you* without a second thought."

"And you."

He waved that aside. "Come back to my house. Bring your"—he glanced at what she was eating and turned up his perfect nose—"whatever that is, along with the rest of your human food, and we'll hunker down until the problem is resolved."

"No."

"Do you want to be a martyr? Is that it?" His glare should have incinerated her where she sat.

"I want to be a good neighbor. A good human." When she laid a hand on his forearm, it felt like stone beneath her fingertips. "Look, you don't have to do this, Max. I've already said that a million times."

His eyes slipped shut, and he exhaled after a moment, his muscles slowly relaxing under her touch. "What is that foul concoction you're ingesting, anyway?"

"Taco in a Can. 'The world's first and best nonperishable processed taco product,' it says here." The label didn't offer much more information, other than a long list of ingredients she couldn't pronounce. Letting go of his arm, she spooned up another bite, chewed thoughtfully, and swallowed. "Honestly? It's not terrible."

"Hopefully the world's *only* nonperishable processed taco product," he muttered, opening his eyes.

"It mostly tastes like refried beans and preservatives." She lifted a shoulder. "I've had worse."

"What else did you squirrel away in here?" Without permission, he began riffling through the contents of her duffel bag. "I Can't Believe It's Not Falafel? What the fuck is that?"

"Not falafel." She pointed at him with her spoon. "I know that much."

"Pizza Jerky? I can't even *begin* to . . ." He brought the plastic wrapper closer to read the slogan. "'The party never stops with Pizza Jerky.' Dear gods."

"Grab me another pomegranate-lime juice box, would you?" When he tossed one her way, she caught it and checked the package. "Hey, look at that. It's one hundred percent juice, Judgy McJudgythong. Also, pomegranate's a superfood. Or superdrink. Whatever."

His fingernails scratched against his chin. "What, precisely, is a superfood?"

She couldn't resist. "Food that tastes super."

He groaned loudly enough that any nearby zombies were probably sprinting in their direction.

"Anyway, enough about my amazing collection of emergency foodstuffs. Let's talk about what happens next." At the thought of proceeding without him, approximately fourteen ounces of processed taco product had become a leaden lump in her stomach, but she made her voice breezy, her question casual and unconcerned. "Are you coming with me, or are you taking me back to my car?"

He didn't hesitate. "Coming with you."

Her incipient nausea eased, and a glow of warmth and relief spread like sunshine through her veins. Also a hot prickle of guilt, because he'd have stayed safe in his home, and he wouldn't have left that home if she hadn't insisted on going. But he was a grown man—grown vampire, rather—and she wasn't precisely holding him at gunpoint, so she shook off her guilt and began planning.

"All right." She drummed her fingers against the side of her can. "I see at least two potential problems directly ahead of us. First, since we don't know why the drawbridge is down, it could theoretically also go up at any time. If we were far enough along when that happened . . . it wouldn't be good."

The mechanism rose swiftly. Too swiftly for them to save themselves. The thought of trying to escape the SUV as it crashed into the water and sank into the moat's dark depths chilled her to the marrow. Alternatively, she supposed the vehicle could get flipped violently backward onto the roadway again, which was . . . not a great option either.

"The drawbridge is also very exposed to attack. I assume that's your second concern."

She nodded. "It's a bottleneck."

"But since abandoning the SUV and most of our supplies to swim across the moat isn't a good option, we don't have much of a choice but to cross the bridge."

He didn't sound frightened or even especially tense about it. Just resigned.

"Agreed. Let me finish my snack, and then we'll take our chances." After scraping out the last bite from the bottom of her can, she waved it in front of Max. "Where do you want me to put this? And please know any response similar to *where the sun don't shine* will be met with extreme prejudice."

"I would never," he said loftily. "Here."

Taking the can gingerly between two fingers, as if it were a soiled diaper, he tossed it onto the floor of the back seat.

"You're getting processed taco product on your mat," she pointed out, tucking her spoon back into her duffel and placing her empty juice box on the floor beside the can. "Doesn't that freak you out?"

"The seats and mats will already require cleaning, given the current status of our clothing and shoes."

"Ah." Now that she was paying attention, she spotted the

bloodstains. Whoops. "Since your car's already messy, does that mean I can wipe my mouth on your leather seats?"

He ignored her, his expression turning hard with purpose. "Is your seat belt low and tight across your lap?"

She tugged it a bit tighter. "Now it is."

Without another word, he put the SUV in gear and zipped out from between the dumpsters, then turned smoothly back onto the main access road. As they approached the security station, with its passcard reader and cameras and designated stopping point, his foot only pressed harder on the accelerator.

For the first time ever, she zipped past the station without halting. After a brief rumble as they passed over the seam connecting the roadway to the bridge, they were hurtling across the moat. The water sparkled on either side of them, its surface only a low barrier and an eight-foot drop away, its depths inky and glacially cold. At this speed, they'd reach Zone B in maybe ten seconds, assuming nothing went—

"*Shit*." For the second time that day, Max stomped on the brake pedal, and he flung an arm across her chest as the vehicle shuddered, skidded to a halt, and threw her violently against the unforgiving cage of her seat belt.

There were now zombies pouring through the giant open door leading to the neighboring zone, sprinting in their direction. A dozen. Two dozen. Maybe more.

That was one question answered. The pack had already made it across the moat.

"Hold on." He slammed the SUV into Reverse and began backing up as quickly as he could.

It wasn't enough. The zombies were gaining on them, racing

on all fours, gaunt flanks heaving with each panting stride, and she frantically twisted in her seat to see how far Max still had to drive before they were back on solid ground, where they could find a hiding place.

"Max, behind us!" she yelled.

Apparently not all the pack had crossed yet, because another clutch of the creatures had just rounded the security station and begun bounding toward them in full flight.

His knuckles shone white on the steering wheel, but he didn't slow down. "If they trap us on the bridge—"

"We won't have anywhere to go but the water," she finished for him.

With the accelerator pressed all the way to the floor, they barreled directly into the group of zombies behind them. The jarring impact rocked her in her seat, and the SUV's momentum tossed aside or trampled almost a dozen of the creatures before the vehicle slowed to a near halt, their bodies becoming speed bumps beneath its wheels.

She and Max panted in the sudden stillness.

"Maybe if I—" He shifted to Drive, then floored the accelerator again, but managed only a few feet of progress before the first cluster of zombies reached them and easily stopped their minimal forward momentum. "*Dammit.*"

The two parts of the pack converged on the vehicle, and the onslaught began.

The SUV shuddered, and metal screeched and glass thumped as the creatures howled and beat on the temporary shelter. Their open jaws, all sharp teeth and slavering hunger, clicked against the windshield and side windows, their features deforming as they tried to somehow press through the transparent barrier. Claws scraped and shrieked, and the interior grew dim as the swarm blocked the light. She and Max were entirely surrounded.

A buzzing began in her ears, and she couldn't catch her breath.

More creatures leapt on the rear bumper and began to climb atop the roof, stomping and smashing, frustration urging them to even greater violence.

"The glass . . ." Why wasn't it breaking?

"Bulletproof." His face had twisted into a snarl. "It may eventually crack, but it shouldn't shatter."

Get your shit together, Brandstrup, she frantically instructed herself.

The roof began to creak and indent, and she hurriedly ticked off their few remaining options. "If we leave the car and confront them on the bridge, we're dead. So we can wait here and find out whether they'll eventually crush us from above or break through the glass, or we can somehow get in the water and hope the reports are right."

"That they'll eventually drown."

She nodded. "Preferably before killing us."

And hopefully before we drown too, she allowed to remain unspoken.

"They won't give up." He kept looking down at the water and then back at her, his grim expression carving deep lines on his misleadingly youthful face. "Not unless they spot alternative prey or get attacked by someone else. Neither of which may happen soon enough."

Various scenarios played out in her imagination, flashes of chaos and death. "I don't think you can work up enough speed to make it over the bridge's barrier rail."

Funny how the SUV crashing into the water, a prospect that had terrified her only minutes before, was now the best of all possible options, and even *that* wasn't feasible. She'd laugh if she weren't too busy trying not to hyperventilate.

"Agreed." He suddenly straightened. "But what if I got us right next to it?"

She turned to him, following his train of thought without difficulty. "We can open the windows on that side only and jump into the water from there." Assuming she could squeeze through the opening. It was going to be a tight fit despite the generous window size. "Making it to the barrier rail won't be easy. Even if we somehow manage to get right up against it, zombies will be trying to reach us from the roof and every other side. But . . . it's still our best chance of survival."

"Agreed."

The roof kept caving inward, millimeter by millimeter, and she couldn't imagine the pressure that would require. "Can you even move the car with all their weight on it?"

"I suppose we'll find out." His eyes, now black with emotion, met hers as he spoke loudly enough to drown out the cacophony surrounding them. "I'll open the windows as soon as we're up against the barrier rail. Jump as far out from the bridge as possible. The water's going to be cold and dark, but the air in your lungs will float you toward the surface. Don't panic."

A loud cracking noise made her start, and she swung to look at the rear window.

His cool hands clasped her face, bringing her attention back to him. "Listen to me, Edie. Focus on your own survival. Don't waste your breath looking for me. I'll find you."

She clicked her tongue. "Bossy, bossy."

Before she could think twice, with a swarm of zombies watching and trying desperately to reach them and kill them both, she lurched forward the necessary distance to press a kiss to his cheek. It was stubbly and chilly, and she wanted to lick it for some reason, but she settled back into her seat instead.

He stared at her, unblinking.

"For luck," she explained. *And because I'm probably not going to live through this. I want something warm and bright to remember as I sink into darkness.*

"Right." After a moment, he gently drew her head forward again and nuzzled against her temple, brushing his lips over the thin, sensitive skin there. "For luck, sweet Edie."

Everything around her disappeared. Everything but him.

His gaze was intent on hers, and she mustered a shaky smile for him. His thumb lightly swept away the lone tear she hadn't managed to blink back before he let her go with a silent sigh and turned to face forward again.

Without another word, she unbuckled her seat belt, hunched over, and moved into the seat directly behind his. Kneeling on the leather, she swiftly considered her options. Her sneakers would hinder her swimming and weigh her down. If she and Max survived this desperate gambit, though, they'd probably need to run after they reached shore. She wouldn't get far on bare feet, so her shoes were staying put. She did remove her cross-body purse, however, after tucking her smaller sheathed knife safely into the cup of her bra. She also resigned herself to leaving her duffel and its delicious contents behind. Between swimming for her life in freezing water while fully clothed and fighting off zombies, she'd have neither the energy nor a free hand to wrestle with a large, heavy bag.

Max, on the other hand, slid his arms through the straps of his enormous backpack and fastened several clips across his chest to hold it in place.

She shook her head. "Show-off."

He snorted, craning his neck to see past the mass of moving bodies blocking his view of the bridge and its barrier rails. "Ready, dude?"

At the triumphant return of his Chad drawl, she had to laugh. "Ready."

He sucked in a long, hard breath, and she followed suit.

"If you die, human, I will fucking throttle you," he said to the windshield.

Then he slammed his fist on the car horn without warning. A good number of the zombies instinctively jumped back from the sudden, inexplicable, ear-splitting noise, and as soon as they did, he stomped on the gas and barreled through several creatures to reach the side of the bridge. When the SUV halted again, she was pretty sure more bodies lay crushed beneath its tires, but she couldn't let herself think about it.

She and Max were as close to the water as they could get.

The windows rolled down, and grunts and shrieks of pain and rage and effort filled her ears as she lunged forward and began her escape.

"Get out!" he shouted, and Edie did.

9

Somewhere around the time she finally managed to wriggle through the window opening and launch herself into the moat below, Edie realized Max hadn't jumped in the water too. No, that fucking dimwit was instead swinging his stupid fucking sword like a moron knight of fucking legend, keeping the thrice-damned zombies back while she made it out of the SUV.

Somewhere, a super-old French village is missing its idiot, she thought as she held her breath, leapt as far out as she could, and hit the freezing water with a painful *smack*.

It took all her will not to gasp at the chill and the shock of impact. Weighed down by her thick coveralls and shoes, she sank farther than she'd have preferred, unsure which way was up. *The air in your lungs will float you toward the surface,* he'd said, and she held on to that thought to stave off panic as she let her body drift and find its way.

With effort, she opened her eyes, and then she knew for certain which way was up—because that was where the zombies all around her came from. In twos and threes, they splashed down in the moat after her, still intent on enjoying her brain as a tasty holiday brunch offering.

Far too many creatures now surrounded her in the water. Although her lungs already felt tight, she took a moment to retrieve her knife from her bra before she began swimming for the surface. Which was good, since whenever she neared one of the zombies, it repeatedly lunged for her. Luckily, the water slowed them down, and they couldn't seem to recalibrate their attacks accordingly. The ones who got too close, she slashed at with the knife in between strokes.

The creatures didn't even try to swim. Their gaunt frames were also much less buoyant than hers, and she doubted they'd had enough forethought to take a deep breath before jumping. They sank away from her, still trying to reach her, still trying to rip out her throat, even as they slowly drowned.

Then she was swimming alone, desperately forcing herself to hold on and not take the convulsive breath hitching in her chest. Just as she was certain she couldn't stand the agonizing pressure in her lungs any longer, the surface appeared before her, sunlit and beautiful, and she flailed frantically until she could plunge upward, through the barrier, into a world filled with oxygen and the sound of something—anything—other than her laboring heartbeat.

Sucking in desperate, heaving gulps of air, she coughed and pedaled in the water to stay upright. And as soon as the sparks faded from her vision, her two-part search began. Where was the nearest safe spot to leave the water? And where the hells was Max?

The bridge was too high, obviously. She'd have to swim to one of the banks of the moat, but she had no idea which one might have a ladder or some other means of leaving the water. Also which one might still have part of the zombie pack circling and lying in wait, because those classified government reports had mentioned over a hundred creatures living in the compound, so not all of them had attacked the SUV. The rest wouldn't be far.

Didn't matter. Max would help her decide. Once she found him.

From the water, she could only see the top half of the SUV, but it appeared abandoned. At the very least, any living being in the vicinity was no longer standing. There was a good chance Max wasn't actually a living being anymore, though, after the way he—

No. He'd survived. He'd jumped into the water as they'd planned. If she let herself believe anything else, she wasn't certain she'd have the strength to swim to shore.

Was he still fighting the zombies who'd pursued him into the water? Had the weight of the backpack dragged him to the bottom of the moat? Had they ripped off his head because he'd waited too long to jump?

Had he died in defense of her?

Her raw lungs expanded with one painfully deep breath, and another, and another. Then she ducked under the glittering surface again, eyes straining against the darkness beneath her, searching for movement.

When she ran out of air, she surfaced, then lowered her head to search again.

There. A fleeting glint of gold and silver far below.

It could be a fish. It could be a shiny fallen item from Max's backpack. But it could be Max himself, his hair and sword catching a faint flicker of light, so she had to check.

Another handful of deep breaths. Every instinct screamed at

her to save herself, to swim to safety, to remain in light. Instead, she arrowed down into the murky depths of the moat once more, kicking and using a sort of clumsy breaststroke. Over and over, her hands dragged through the water in the shape of an upside-down heart, then shot through the middle, breaking the shape in two before beginning anew.

How deep was the fucking moat, anyway? Twenty feet? More? Her ears popped, and her lungs burned.

Just as she was tempted to turn back, he appeared before her, floating face down above the bottom of the moat, decapitated zombie bodies and severed zombie heads forming a gruesome circle around him. To keep her lips closed, she bit them so hard she drew blood.

He still had his own head. Maybe she could resuscitate him. She needed to get him to the surface.

The shreds of his backpack floated like seaweed, rippling slightly in the dark water, and his hands were caught in the current too. They drifted along the craggy surface below him in little sweeps, moving . . . quite a lot, actually.

If she didn't know better, she'd say they were moving with *purpose*. Like maybe he wasn't drowned after all, but rather—

Without warning, just as she reached to grab hold of his jacket or his jeans or something, *anything*, she could use to drag him upward, he jerked, turned his head, and spotted her just above him. She gasped. In joy. In relief. In shock.

In a major, major mistake, because she was at the bottom of a fucking moat.

The rest of her time in the water, she didn't remember clearly, probably because she wasn't breathing much anymore. The next thing she knew, she was lying on her side, racked by shivers and shudders as she retched and gasped and coughed foul-tasting water onto a patch of brittle crabgrass while Max alternately rubbed her back, thumped it to help her expel more of the moat's contents, and cursed at her.

"—fucking *told* you not to look for me, fucking *told you* to concentrate on your own survival, not to mention all those other times I *fucking told you* not to risk your own life to save anyone else's, including mine, and what's *the first thing you fucking do*, huh?" His chilly fingers stroked her wet hair back from her cheek. "Wait, you can't tell me, can you, Edie? Because *you fucking drowned yourself doing exactly what I told you not to do.*"

"You"—she finally managed to suck back a thimbleful of air between coughs—"tried to"—*hack hack*—"save me first"—*hack hack hack*—"you utter hypocrite. What"—she dry-heaved—"the fuck?"

His hand briefly paused in its circles on her back, but he ignored her aggrieved accusation in favor of more profane muttering.

Fine. She'd try a different question, then. "Why were you at the bottom of"—*hack hack*—"the freaking moat if you weren't drowning, *Chad*?"

The tightness in her chest had begun to ease, breath by breath, that discomfort replaced by her growing awareness of just how cold she'd become. Another few minutes out here and she could pursue a side hustle as a freelance ice sculpture.

His sigh gusted against her ear as he bent over her, and she shivered convulsively. "Those fuckers' claws ripped open my backpack, and everything fell into the water. Vampires don't need to breathe as often as humans, so once I saw you'd reached the surface safely, I went down to find my blood packs and all the other supplies. *Dude.*"

Dammit. This made two dangerous, unnecessary attempts to rescue him in less than twenty-four hours. But in her defense, her neighbor really sucked at communication.

"You could have"—*hack wheeze*—"said something," she pointed out, with what she considered laudable calm. "Told me you were all right and what you were doing."

As he helped lever her to a sitting position, he scanned the length of the bridge. "The rest of the pack might appear at any moment. I was trying to hurry."

"I thought you'd *died.*" On the verge of tears, she poked him in the chest. "I was so fucking scared, Max, and so fucking horrified that you'd drowned to protect *me.*"

The angry jut of his jaw softened, and darkness bled from his gaze, leaving his eyes a warm faded blue once more. He studied her face, then tugged a strand of her dripping hair and ducked his head. Right before he made contact, he paused, one eyebrow lifted in question. In silent answer, she closed the remaining gap between them.

She was angry, but not angry enough to deny both of them what they needed.

His lips were soft and cool, the kiss slow and deliberate. After a breathless few moments, his thumb on her chin parted her mouth and tipped her head to the exact angle he wanted. The slide of his tongue electrified her, sent sexual heat sparking down her spine, and she exhaled sharply into his mouth as his thumb brushed her earlobe.

By the time he ended the kiss, lifting his head after one last sweep of his tongue along her lower lip, incipient hypothermia wasn't the sole reason for her dazed state.

"I didn't imagine you'd be concerned." His hand, supportive on her back, stroked another soothing circle. "I apologize for your fright, my Edie. It wasn't intentionally inflicted."

Unable to speak, she simply inclined her head in acknowledgment.

I didn't imagine you'd be concerned. It was such a gut-twistingly sad statement that the remaining warmth from his kiss faded into a bone-deep chill and she almost lost her renewed battle against weeping. What the hells kind of life had he led, that he simply assumed she wouldn't care if he lived or died, even after he'd saved her own life multiple times? After everything they'd already shared?

"Your lungs sound much better." In response to her crinkled brow, he explained with exaggerated patience, "Vampire hearing. Much more sensitive than the paltry sensory capability of mere humans."

She flicked her gaze to the blue sky above. "Naturally."

That auditory sensitivity was a vulnerability as well as a strength, as he would soon discover. From now on, she intended to hum the Gaston song whenever he was within a country mile of her, in recompense for all the fun *Chad* had had at her expense.

"Are you otherwise uninjured?" He shot a glance toward the bridge once more, then returned his attention to her. "Because we need to leave soon, and my vehicle should still be drivable."

Apparently they were going to overlook his calling her *my Edie* and pretend their kiss hadn't happened, even though her lips were still tingling faintly. Which could also be due to frostbite, come to think of it.

Fine. She didn't have the mental wherewithal to puzzle out what the kiss and his choice of endearment meant or didn't mean right now. If he wanted to let the elephants in the room trumpet unacknowledged, so be it.

She nodded. "I'm fine. You're okay too?"

"I've already healed from my minor wounds." Haughty condescension soaked his every word, and he regarded her pityingly. "Just another aspect of vampires' inherent superiority to your kind."

His eyes gleamed as he watched her reaction. The corner of his mouth twitched, then stilled again.

"I'll take that as a yes," she said dryly. "Before we go, do you want to get back into the water to search more for your supplies?"

"No time." He rose to his feet in a single graceful motion and offered her his hand. "Besides, we need to get you warm. You'll be useless if you go hypothermic on me."

"Which would happen because—what was it again?" Standing with his assistance, she took a moment to regain her balance. "*Humans have such an inferior range of acceptable temperatures?*"

It wasn't a bad imitation, especially when she looked down her nose at him and sniffed loudly.

"Yes." His gusty sigh tickled her ear. "It's tragic, really."

As he clasped her arm in a gentle hold and got them walking toward the bridge, she told him, "I know why you're playing up that patronizing vampire shtick, Max. You can't fool me."

He wanted to stave off her incipient tears. To distract her from the kiss they'd shared. To amuse her. Amuse them both, maybe.

"I have no idea what you mean," he declared loftily, and helped her back to his SUV.

* * *

THE ZOMBIES HAD managed to batter through the SUV's bulletproof glass in several places and flatten part of the roof, which was both impressive and terrifying as hells. Luckily, they'd discontinued their efforts after their potential prey had leapt into the water, so her emergency supplies remained intact, and the spiderwebbed glass surrounding the windshield's holes didn't entirely obscure Max's view of the road as he drove to the nearest defensible shelter: a giant, abandoned, once-swanky mall just inside Zone B.

When she'd suggested that they keep driving straight through to Zone C, he'd ignored her. "Until you're dry and warm again, we're done. We need to get you indoors," he'd told her, and that had been that.

The sun still shone brightly above them. The heated seats were on full blast, the interior temperature set high enough to roast a turkey. Didn't matter. She couldn't stop shivering.

A frigid December wind whistled through the gaps in the windshield, her clothing didn't seem likely to dry anytime soon, and Max apparently didn't have one of those foil blankets anywhere in his damn car.

"My body temperature is naturally much lower than yours. I don't require blankets for my comfort." He ducked his head to see around a crack, an unhappy expression on his taut face. "I didn't anticipate ferrying a human passenger, so my emergency supplies are inadequate for your needs."

There was an unspoken apology in there somewhere, and she appreciated it, but her teeth were actually chattering. Like she was a freaking cartoon character, tinted blue with cold, a layer of frost slowly spreading over her clothing.

"It's f-fine." Because she hoped satisfying her curiosity would distract her from frozen misery, she asked, "Is it e-even p-possible for you to die of c-cold? Like, if y-you got s-stuck in an industrial f-freezer and b-became a vampsicle?"

"A stake through my heart will kill me. So will removing my head or"—his throat bobbed—"burning me alive. In theory, I can drown as well, but it would take a very, very long time, and I could be revived for hours afterward. Nothing else will suffice. We vampires are notoriously tough to dispatch." He directed a scowl her way, then drove onto the cracked asphalt of the mall's large, empty parking lot. "As opposed to humans, who can die far more easily in countless ways. Which is why, as noted previously, you should never, *ever*—"

"Yeah, y-yeah." She waved a shaking hand. "So f-freezing solid w-wouldn't do y-you any h-harm at all? Really?"

After circling around the side of the vast, abandoned shopping center, he wedged the SUV into yet another hiding spot between two dumpsters and put the car in Park.

His shoulder lifted. "Some temporary skin damage, perhaps. Once I got warmer, I'd simply—"

"D-defrost?" she offered innocently. "Like a chicken b-breast with freezer b-burn?"

Slowly, he turned his head to stare at her. "Do you *deliberately* choose the most insulting comparisons possible?"

"Me?" She blinked over at him, arms wrapped around her middle for warmth, and continued perfecting her imitation of him. "I w-would n-never."

"Mmmm." Shaking his head, he gathered her duffel and cross-body bag and slung them both over his shoulder, then unearthed his first aid kit. "We need to be quick and quiet, Edie. I've heard rumors about this place. If it weren't an emergency . . ." She swung her legs out from the SUV and slid down onto half-numb feet, and his mouth thinned as he watched the clumsiness of her movements. "But it is."

He didn't need to elaborate. Normally, she'd never enter an abandoned building in the Containment Zone, and neither would any other Zone resident without a death wish. Over the years, members of criminal gangs had forged identification documents and gotten accepted as residents in the Zone, where the relative lack of government oversight and media attention worked to their advantage. They'd discreetly looted where they could, then set up clandestine drug labs and stash houses in empty, derelict structures exactly like this one.

Generally, the gangs kept to themselves, as long as no one invaded their dilapidated fiefdoms. Which was precisely what she and Max were about to do, unless the mall had somehow remained entirely vacant over the past twenty years.

Highly unlikely. She might not be a cynic, but she wasn't a fool either.

Keeping his right arm free, Max wrapped his left around her shoulders and tugged her tight against his side. Not to provide warmth, because he had none to offer, but to support her and help her keep up with his rapid pace.

All possible entrances to the four-story mall had likely been smashed open by looters soon after the First Breach, including the unremarkable dented gray door near the dumpsters. A staff entrance, she guessed, now propped wide open with a concrete block, its lock disabled.

Max nudged her behind him as he entered the dim interior. The light filtering through the open door illuminated empty shelves and filthy mud-tracked linoleum, with shoeboxes scattered everywhere, their contents long gone. A stock area for a footwear store, evidently.

She kept her voice to a faint whisper. "We c-can't stay h-here."

"Agreed. We need a place zombies can't access so easily," he murmured into her ear.

Her tooth-punctured bottom lip stung when she licked it. "Yes, b-but the upper f-floors put us t-too far away from an escape r-route. We n-need to pick a s-spot on this level."

He shot her a long-suffering look. "Obviously."

In silent accord, they crept from the store's back room and emerged onto the selling floor, where they immediately ducked behind empty shoe racks and waited.

Nothing. No visible movement, no noise. No indication they weren't alone.

After a minute, they cautiously kept moving. The closer they came to the store's entrance, the brighter their surroundings got. This mall had an atrium, she suddenly remembered. A dome of glass high above the open center of the building, allowing natural light to filter into all the stores lining the edges of the structure. That sunlight, along with the lack of wind, was probably why the mall didn't feel nearly as cold as she'd feared.

Roughly twenty-two years had passed since her last visit here, but if she recalled the layout correctly . . . "There's a Pottery Barn n-nearby. Let's g-go there."

Maybe it hadn't been entirely stripped of merchandise, and they could find a chair or some bedding to dry off with. Maybe it even had some of the furniture she remembered so clearly from all her family's visits there.

His shoulder lifted a fraction. "It's as good a place as any. Which way?"

She pointed to the right. It shouldn't be far. Three storefronts away at most. But as soon as they left the shoe store, they would become easily visible to people on their level and anyone facing them on the levels above, even if they pressed right up next to the stores they were passing. And, of course, the stores themselves might not be empty.

The damp trail they left in their wake would make hiding from pursuers challenging at best, impossible at worst. They needed to make sure they weren't spotted.

Once they'd both scanned their visible surroundings a final time and listened for telltale sounds of human, zombie, or Supernatural activity nearby, they turned to each other again.

She tucked her wet hair behind her ears and inclined her head. *I'm ready.*

"Quick and quiet," he reminded her in a thread of sound.

They left their hiding spot. No one greeted their emergence from the store with shouting or gunshots, and she couldn't pinpoint any movement in response to theirs. They passed the Godiva storefront first, and she forced herself to concentrate on their stealth and safety rather than peer through the cracked glass in search of chocolate that might have been miraculously overlooked.

Then—sure enough. Pottery Barn.

The after-hours security fencing had been lowered to waist

level at some point. She had to drop to her hands and knees and crawl inside the store after Max. Who, irritatingly, had merely bent back and passed safely and gracefully beneath the barrier like he was participating in the world's least festive limbo contest.

"*Such* a sh-show-off," she breathed near-silently as she clambered back to a kneeling position and wiped her dirty palms on her wet coveralls.

He grinned down at her and offered her a hand.

Grumbling soundlessly, she took it and tried not to notice how broad it was, how secure she felt in its grasp, and how much strength he must have to lever her upright so easily.

He didn't let go as they plastered themselves against an interior wall behind a sagging shelving unit and surveyed their surroundings.

Like the other stores they'd glimpsed, this one had been ransacked over the course of many years. In the front, the only products left were a few knickknacks that hadn't even appealed to looters or transients, which was one hell of an indictment. Shadows clustered farther back in the store, obscuring what or who might be lurking there, but no doubt vampires had *superior sensory capabilities* when it came to sight as well. She'd have to trust Max to warn her if there was anything worrisome she couldn't yet see or hear.

When he pushed off the wall, she did the same. Swiftly, they moved into the rear of the store, where they would hopefully blend into those yawning shadows if anyone happened to look their way. In this area, more of the shelving remained intact, and . . .

Oh. She drifted to a stop, momentarily overcome.

"What's wrong?" he murmured, and she didn't respond. Couldn't. "Human?"

OLIVIA DADE

There it was. A sofa—*the* sofa—sturdy and unfussy in design, with rolled arms and three seats. Not the pristine gray velvet of her memory, but a stained, greasy tan color. The seat cushions were more squashed than fluffy, and the back cushions had disappeared somewhere, so the couch wouldn't be terribly comfortable for sitting anymore. When it came to sleeping on that particular model of sofa, though, she'd often removed the back cushions herself to allow more room for her shoulders and arms.

It was a good napping spot. Apparently squatters had recognized that too.

Nestling into down cushions just like these, she'd dozed off after school to the clanks and thumps and sizzles of her parents fixing dinner together, to the comfort of their low conversation and occasional laughter, to the knowledge that she wasn't and would never be alone in the world.

That certainty was a bubble, she now understood, like all security. Too fragile to last.

She missed not knowing that. She missed her family.

Max squeezed her fingers. "Edie?"

"Sorry." Blinking, she surfaced from her memories and met his searching blue gaze. "Got d-distracted for a m-moment."

Jaw working, he looked from her to the sofa, then back again.

His hand released hers. Then he picked up the entire freaking couch like it was a mere feather's weight, turned it at a wonky angle, and maneuvered it through the doorway to the store's staff-only area. As he set the furniture down, she silently shut the door behind them. Darkness enveloped the room, eased only by some light filtering down a hallway at the back of the space and to the right.

"Wait here," he said abruptly, and disappeared into the hallway before she could even blink.

She collapsed to her knees on the grimy tile floor and wondered whether anyone had either known or cared that the sofa's fabric was a water-resistant slipcover. Slowly, with trembling, numb fingers, she unzipped the first filthy, battered cushion.

The muslin surrounding the deflated down filling was somewhat yellowed, but otherwise intact and almost entirely clean. It also smelled much, much better than the tan cover, and she tossed that cover into a faraway dim corner, then repeated the process two more times. As quietly as possible, she then released some hidden Velcro fasteners and tugged off the slipcover from the couch's frame. Rising to her feet once more, she kicked the fabric into the same corner as the seat covers.

The stripped cushions might still harbor lice or fleas or bedbugs, but she honestly didn't care. As soon as she was dry, she was lying down on that sofa, resting her exhausted muscles, and letting memories warm her for a minute or two, even if her present circumstances remained too cold and volatile for true comfort.

The light emanating from the hallway dimmed and extinguished, leaving her in utter blackness.

"The door to the outside was open."

Max appeared at her side so suddenly, she let out an involuntary, squeaky yelp. A loud one. Immediately, he grabbed her elbow and drew her against the wall separating them from the customer area, nudging the door to that area slightly open.

His chest rose and fell on a soundless sigh as they waited, gazes pinned to the narrow gap. When no one and nothing came running, he raised a brow at her.

"Sorry," she whispered. "As s-soon as we're not hiding from squatters and z-zombies, we need to hang a c-cowbell around your neck. If you u-use it in one of your videos, it'll be the hottest spring a-accessory ever." She thought for a moment. "Maybe you c-can make a cowbell thong?"

When he closed the door again, she fumbled for her phone, located the flashlight app, and managed to illuminate their temporary hideout with a few shaky swipes.

"*Anyway*," he said, the word barely audible despite its aggrieved emphasis, "the door to the employee parking spaces was open. It apparently hasn't ever been forced, so it still locks. It's sturdy enough for our purposes. We can stay here while you dry off and get dressed again. Plus . . ."

With a flourish, he produced a jumbled pile of what appeared to be tablecloths.

Plucking a heap of fabric free from the stack, he flapped his jacquard offering proudly in front of her. "These were squirreled away in a low, mostly-hidden shelf in the stock room. They should make decent makeshift blankets for you, and I shook off the dust outside, so they're ready to be used."

Not all the dust, clearly.

"Thank—" Coughing noiselessly was more difficult than she'd have imagined. "Thank y-you, Max."

His brows pinched, and he patted her back until she could breathe normally again. "Don't thank me yet. Thank me after I strip you down and get you warm and dry and into a new set of those . . ." He flicked a hand at her waterlogged coveralls. "Whatever those are. Other than *unfortunate*."

"S-says the dude with the m-macramé undies."

"That wasn't a no, Edie." For all its quietness, his voice had gone low. Gravelly.

She'd never been especially modest, but right now in particular, she couldn't locate even a tiny sliver of a fuck about him seeing her naked. Her hands were shaking too hard to undress quickly, and the sooner she defrosted, the better.

When she didn't respond out loud, his palms cupped her shoulders. "If you don't want me to undress you, tell me."

"It's fine." Exhausted, she let herself slump in his grasp. "Go to t-town, vampire boy. Enjoy the sh-show."

Due to her current lack of fine motor control, her attempt at a breezy, flirty wink ended as a sort of leering squint. With both eyes.

Sighing, she allowed her lids to simply drift shut. Allowed him to fix things, even though she'd been fixing her problems entirely on her own for two decades and counting.

"Hardly a boy," he groused under his breath before getting to work.

10

With a metallic purr, the zipper of Edie's coveralls whipped open. Max's careful hands tugged her arms free of the clinging sleeves and pushed the heavy fabric down her icy legs, along with her underwear. He removed her sneakers and socks, supporting her with a steady grip on her hip as he guided her feet out of the pile of sodden clothing and onto a dry, soft tablecloth.

She hummed. "If you're n-not a boy, how o-old *are* you, th-then?"

Another grumble, this one wordless.

Her arms were up and her tank top gone before she drew another breath. The sports bra took him longer, but once he finally finessed it over her head, she was entirely naked.

In a Pottery Barn. In front of her Neighbor Formerly Known as Chad.

The realization barely had a chance to flutter through her dazed thoughts before she found herself cocooned in another tablecloth and vigorously rubbed dry. Her scalp, her neck, her back, her arms. Her palms. Between her fingers.

"I have no body heat to share," he muttered. "Friction warmth is all I can offer, which means I can't be as gentle as I'd like." A frustrated sound escaped him, and he draped yet another table-cloth over her now-dry shoulders. "You're bruised everywhere, Edie. Dammit."

He was working on her legs now, kneeling at her feet as he patted away the moisture behind her knees and chafed heat and life back into her lower limbs. Her fingertips stretched out before her, then burrowed into his icy hair and combed through the tangled strands soothingly.

"Max." When she found his temples, she rubbed them clumsily with the prickling pads of her thumbs. "It's o-okay."

He grunted, unappeased. "This has to be hurting you."

It did hurt. But it was necessary.

In lieu of a verbal response, she kept stroking his hair back from his face, carding it with her fingers. Gently, so she wouldn't tug at any knots.

An odd sound rumbled from his throat. "Do you want me to . . ."

When he didn't say more, she opened her eyes and met his. A descriptive sweep of his hand sufficed to clarify his question. He was asking whether she wanted him to dry the last wet parts of her, the trinity her high school friends had once referred to as *pits, tits, and naughty bits.*

Over the course of the last twenty-four hours, she'd begun to want those strong, capable hands on her bare skin, however she could get them there. All over her. Gripping. Guiding. Teasing. Stroking.

Drying was fine too. Drying was *great.*

But before she answered honestly, she needed to check with him. "Would that b-be okay for you? Would you mind?"

He actually laughed. It was silent, but the shaking of his shoulders was unmistakable, and mingled humor and heat had turned his eyes incandescent.

"No, sweet Edie," he murmured, his tone a caress. "I won't mind."

She raised her arms. Still kneeling, he dabbed away the moisture underneath. Then, with a roll of her shoulders, she shrugged the fabric draped over those shoulders down to her elbows.

Her breasts were bare to his sight now. Not especially large—most of her softness had settled in her belly and thighs over the years—but round and damp and crowned with chill-stiffened rosy-brown nipples. With a tap under his chin, she brought his eyes back to hers. Holding his stare, she reached down, grasped his hands, and placed them exactly where he'd been looking.

Slowly, deliberately, he cradled her breasts in his fabric-covered palms, his careful thumbs swirling the jacquard under and over the pale swells of flesh, then around her sensitive areolae. Beneath his touch, even through the cotton barrier, her skin bloomed with heat. Her goose bumps vanished as she arched her back slightly, placing herself more fully in his hands.

"Yes," she said softly. "More."

When his thumbs swept the smooth fabric over her nipples, her breath caught.

He smiled. "Such pretty breasts."

The words dragged over her skin like that soft, sweeping cloth, and she shifted her weight as the glow of warmth spread outward and kindled between her legs. Abandoning her breasts, his palms smoothed the cotton down over her generous belly, inch by inch, and blotted beneath.

She held her breath, waiting for him to move lower. Impatient for him to ease the growing ache there. Instead, he teased the backs of her thighs with fleeting little whisks of cloth and rested his cheek against her stomach. The prickle of his stubble made her shiver, but not from cold.

His nose nuzzled into her navel. She curved her palm over the back of his head, pressing him tighter to her. "Max?"

"Show me." The words were a quiet rumble, his breath a tickle of air over her belly. "If you want me, open up those thighs, Edie. Let me in."

Her grasp slid to the back of his neck and tugged him upward. "Kiss me first."

He didn't argue. He simply stood in one smooth movement, freeing a hand from the tablecloth to slide into the damp hair at her nape, while the other took firm, possessive hold of her hip. Eyes fierce and hot, he held himself still. Waited for her to come to him, just as he had the last time they'd kissed.

When she urged his head down, he didn't hesitate. He covered her mouth with his, rubbing his lips unhurriedly over her own. Sipping at her with careful, purposeful gentleness, his fingers closing tight in her hair. She opened to the leisurely slide of his tongue, and he slanted his head, gathered her closer, and licked into her with a low, pleased hum.

His mouth was cool and delicious, his incisors sharp, his kiss increasingly hungry. When he sucked the tip of her tongue, he had to swallow her faint moan.

"Sweet Edie." His lips wandered to the corner of her mouth, dragged over her cheek, and tasted the downy skin of her earlobe. "Can you stay quiet?"

She nodded, neither knowing nor caring whether she'd just answered truthfully.

"Good."

Using his grip on her hair, he slowly, painlessly tipped her head back and to the side, exposing her throat. Her jugular. He painted both with his tongue, sucking hard over her pulse, and she trembled and stroked her palms down his leather-covered back. Molded them to the swell of his ass in those dark, soaked jeans and squeezed hard, until he hissed.

He lightly bit the curve of her shoulder. Not with enough force to break her skin, but, oh, she wouldn't have minded. She'd have gladly offered him her blood as long as he kept setting her alight from the inside out, kept dizzying her with pleasure and need.

Gods and goddesses above, he was dangerous, but not for the reasons she'd once feared. He wouldn't hurt her, wouldn't force her into anything she wasn't willing to do. No, the threat was that she'd *want* to give him everything, and he'd make the taking of it pure pleasure.

His grasp on her hip disappeared, and his fist in her hair urged her head upright and her eyes to his. Holding her stare, he slid his fabric-covered hand between her legs and cupped her firmly. Held her in his palm and pressed into her until her mouth fell open on a silent gasp.

"Now that you're dry," he murmured, "let's make you slick again, my Edie."

His hand, broad and strong and steady, *rolled*, and she trembled under his touch, under his gaze. The sensation peaked and ebbed as the heel of that talented hand applied pressure in just the right spot, then eased away, only to return a moment later.

The rhythm was maddening, a taste of pleasure from a lover confident in his ability to provide it. His masterful hold fed her ache and never quite satisfied it, and she couldn't believe how close to orgasm she'd been driven when they weren't even skin-to-skin.

Then they were. The tablecloth towel dropped to the floor with a muffled sigh, and his bare, cool hand slid between her thighs and stroked. Unhurriedly. Patiently. Spreading her slickness and gliding through the heat he'd created. He pressed a long finger inside her, and her body squeezed it as he explored and caressed all the hidden spots that made her breath hitch.

"Max," she whispered as he bent his head and scraped a trail of fire along her throat. "This feels amazing. But I can't . . ."

Finally, finally, he concentrated his touch where she most wanted it. Where she could get what she needed to end this gorgeous, agonizing ache. His fingertips drifted over her clit, testing whether she liked direct pressure or—yes. Oh yes.

"There you are," he said against her jaw. "Give it to me, Edie."

He toyed with her. Lavished her with slick friction and slowly, inexorably rubbed.

Her orgasm hit her like a punch, the pleasure so sharp it neared pain. Burying her mouth against his shoulder to muffle her long, low moan, she gathered two fistfuls of leather and held on to him as she convulsed against his talented fingers and forgot everything but how fucking *good* they felt, how fucking good *she* felt.

When her knees began to buckle, he quickly covered the couch with a tablecloth and lowered her onto the cushions, following her down and claiming her mouth as he worked every last quiver of pleasure from her swollen flesh.

She kissed him back lazily, luxuriating in the aftermath of the best climax she'd had in years. Maybe ever.

Chad. Freaking *Chad*. Who knew?

When she finally slumped onto the sofa, limp and sated beneath him, he braced himself on an elbow and raised his head to study her face. The curve of his mouth was a tad smug, but his blue eyes were solemn.

She smiled at him. "That was awesome. Let's do it again sometime. About five minutes from now should be fine. But you'll have to make it quick, since I need a nap."

"Human . . ." His chin dropped to his chest, and he snorted. "Let's put you in dry clothing and go back to the SUV. I found duct tape, so we can cover the holes in my windshield. If we swaddle you in tablecloths and set the heater to max, we should be able to get you warm. You can nap while I drive."

"I feel pretty toasty right now, even without a heated seat." She wiggled her toes, which had prickled back to life around the time he'd located her clitoris. "Good work, vampire boy."

His irritated scowl at the nickname wasn't especially convincing, since he was kind of preening in self-satisfaction at the same time. "Don't call me that."

"Or . . . what?" she asked interestedly.

"Or . . ." He paused. "Or . . ."

Just as she'd thought. "Don't bother with threats. I won't believe them."

His jaw twitched in frustrated exasperation, even as his fingertips lightly skimmed her hip and paused over a bruise there. He covered the darkening blotch with his palm, frowning. "You shouldn't trust me."

"Whatever." She waved that off. "I know we have to get moving again so we can report the breach. But I need to be alert to watch your back, and I genuinely don't think I can stay functional without at least a short nap. Just let me rest here for a few minutes, Max. Please."

"But you're still chilled, Edie." His free hand chafed her upper arm, coaxing warmth back into her skin, and she wanted to purr and stretch beneath his touch like a contented cat.

"I'm warm enough for a quick snooze. And if I get too cold, I bet you could find some way to heat me up again." She waggled her brows. "If you know what I mean."

He simply looked at her.

She waggled some more. "And I think you do."

As he fought a smile, his austere expression contorted slightly.

"Or . . ." Lifting her butt from the couch, she rubbed up against him, doing her best to ignore the damp chill of soaked denim. "Since your erection is currently trying to bore a hole in my thigh, I could take you in hand and—wait. I keep forgetting to ask: How *do* vampires get erections, anyway? I would have thought there'd be blood flow issues."

His nascent smile withered into a scowl. "Vampires aren't *dead*, human. Our blood flows perfectly well. Just because it's cooler than yours and circulates more slowly doesn't mean we can't—"

"Okay, okay." She raised a hand in surrender, then slid it slowly down his chest, all the way to the snap of those formfitting, waterlogged jeans. "Forget I asked. Anyway, since we've established that your erections are chilly and sluggish but serviceable, why don't I—"

Her voice faltered as he let her feel the full weight of him, the strength, pressing her down into their makeshift bed and settling between her legs, cool and hard and ruthless.

He might be wet, but that was fine. So was she.

"*Ma bite* is far more than *serviceable*. But I want more than a few stolen minutes, fucking you with one eye on the door." His hips rolled, and her head fell back onto the cushion. "I'll have you. And when I do, I intend to give you my full attention."

She'd been wondering what drew him to her. Why he'd been catering to all her needs with so little hesitation and so much determination. Whether he considered her a mere toy, a temporary human plaything to sate his sexual hunger, or whether she'd somehow burrowed beneath his skin and slipped into his veins, arrowing toward his heart. Because with every beat of her own heart, he was making a home for himself there, and it scared the shit out of her.

Now, though, she no longer cared why he wanted her or for how long. Her fear couldn't touch her as long as *he* touched her.

"You'll drown in me, my Edie." His open mouth dragged along her flushed cheek, and his thigh pushed tight and hard between her legs. "You'll come for me until you cry."

He gripped her ass and rocked her against that swell of firm muscle, and her lips parted in a soundless moan.

If this was a fever dream, she didn't want to get better.

"Soon." With a sigh, he pushed up and off her, stood, and unzipped her duffel. "Not now."

She lay there, bereft and breathless, her damp skin prickling in the sudden chill. "What the hells, Max?"

Efficiently, he dried her off again, maneuvered her upright, and helped her step into fresh panties and coveralls, then slip on clean socks. Once she'd recovered somewhat, she slapped his hands away and did the rest herself.

"You're cranky when you're sexually frustrated," he noted, sounding amused.

She scowled at him, zipping the outfit up to her neck. "You're cranky all the time, jerkface."

"Fair enough."

When he turned away from her to gather all the dry tablecloths, he was smiling, the withholding, contrary bastard. She fought her own smile and flopped onto the couch again, wondering if she could even rest anymore with a knot of need aching deep in her belly.

Together, they tucked the makeshift blankets around her, and she bundled up another one to serve as a pillow and stuck it beneath her head.

Without a hint of modesty, he stripped to the skin, removing all his own soaked clothing as she watched avidly. There wasn't much of him she hadn't studied before, what with his furry thong and shirtless videos. The parts she hadn't seen, though . . .

Well. Maybe he wanted to use her as a convenient toy, but she'd been relying on her own toys for a while now, and he was definitely an upgrade. The luxury model.

She nestled her head more comfortably into the cloth pillow. "Below the neck, you're smooth everywhere. Like a Ken doll."

His expression of outrage was delicious.

He waved a hand, directing her attention to his semi-erect dick. "*Not* like a Ken doll, clearly."

"Hmmm." No worries. Her attention hadn't wavered from that area since he'd dropped his tablecloth. "Do you wax? Because the thought of ripping my pubic hair out by the roots . . . yeesh. No, thank you."

"It's a vampire thing," he said shortly.

"Waxing?"

As he wrapped their umpteenth tablecloth around his hips, he pinned her with another flat stare. "Very funny."

"Thank you. I thought so." Feeling loose and remarkably happy for a woman who'd likely die in an attempt to save her neighbors from a zombie attack, she decided to push her luck. "Did you find any scissors in the stock room?"

The wariness with which he regarded her was a real compliment. "Why?"

"I can make your sarong into a thong if you have a pair of shears handy," she offered sweetly. "Since that's apparently a thing for you."

He snorted again. "You just want to see my ass."

"Guilty as charged." She held out her wrists. "Cuff me, officer. Then cuddle me."

"If I must," he said with such a long-suffering sigh that she snickered.

For all his feigned reluctance, he willingly allowed himself to be tugged down and arranged to her liking. Within a few seconds, his body was spooning hers along the length of the couch, one of his tablecloth-covered biceps now her pillow, his other arm slung over her hip. A few twitches spread their makeshift blankets over both Max and herself, neck to feet.

She brought his palm to her lips and gave it a quick kiss. "Wake me up in thirty minutes, okay?"

His fingers curled into a loose fist as he exhaled. "I will."

She closed her eyes. His hand settled on her hip once more, then gradually rose to spread over her chest, between her breasts.

And no matter how many sheep leapt an imaginary fence in her mind, no matter how deep and slow she made each of her breaths, her exhausted mind kept whirling, flashes of the last twenty-four hours playing against the backs of her eyelids like the world's worst movie theater. Also the world's sexiest, depending on the flash in question.

After a few minutes, a discreet nudge of her ass against his lap told her he probably wasn't asleep either. Which was a shame for him—although she'd offered relief; if he was suffering now, that wasn't her fault—but welcome news for her.

"I think there's a Williams Sonoma next door," she whispered into the dark chill of an abandoned Pottery Barn employee breakroom. "Let's make a quick detour there before we go."

He responded immediately, his chin nudging the top of her head. "That's what you were thinking so hard about? Kitchen supplies?"

"It's *one* of the things I'm thinking about." One of the least upsetting too, which was why she was choosing to focus on it. "I need a new set of stainless-steel measuring spoons. I hope looters aren't into accurate determinations of volume." She traced over the bones of his wrist where it rested against the side of her breast. "What were you thinking about?"

He paused long enough that she didn't think he'd answer, then slowly said, "I was wondering why you don't have a soulmark. I thought I might see it when I undressed you."

"Not every human gets one." Only those with fated mates, and only if those fated mates were human as well. "I've always figured my missing mark was probably for the best. Destiny or no destiny, most potential partners would refuse to live in the Containment Zone with me."

"Mmmm." It was a noncommittal noise, full of thoughts unspoken.

He didn't need to say them aloud. She already knew the obvious response to her statement: *Couldn't you move? Why wouldn't you simply leave the Zone and live somewhere else with your mate?* But the only answers she had to offer wouldn't satisfy him, just as they hadn't satisfied anyone but her over the years. Better to change the subject entirely.

Her thumb, which had been exploring the unfamiliar, jutting terrain of his knuckles, stilled. "Is there a vampire equivalent to human soulmarks?"

Because if so, maybe he *was* simply passing time with her. Amusing himself with a mere human while he waited for the arrival of his vampire mate: an elegant, haughty creature who would match his chilly demeanor and spurn canned taco products at all costs.

She pushed his palm harder against her chest, hoping the pressure would ease the ache there.

"No." If he felt her abruptly relax against him, he didn't let on. "With few exceptions, we tend not to care deeply about anyone outside our own families. Not vampires or humans or any other species. That predilection only grows stronger over the centuries. At some point, many vampires without families dissociate entirely from the world around them, stop caring about anything at all, and simply . . . let go."

Wow, *that* didn't sound ominous. "What does *let go* mean?"

"Vampires who have detached that fully often harm either themselves or those around them." His voice sounded both exhausted and clinical. "Detachment is the leading cause of death among vampires now that most hunters have hung up their stakes."

"*Detachment*." She considered the word. How it sanitized what sounded like terrible isolation and either deep depression or psychopathy. "Is it sort of like . . . violent ennui?"

His breath ruffled the hair at the crown of her head. "Ennui's what it was called in my youth, before American vampire psychologists began studying the phenomenon."

"And your youth was . . . when?" A rumbling, openly fake snore came from behind her, and she lightly kicked his shin with her heel. "Fine. Tell me more about those *few exceptions*, then. What happens when vampires *do* care deeply about someone?"

His biceps tensed under her neck. "In defense of anyone we consider ours, we'll unleash and withstand untold violence. We either protect those we love or die in the attempt."

She winced.

Good thing she wasn't one of his *exceptions*, then. If she had her wish, no one would ever die for her safety again. And the thought of someone other than her parents protecting her was so foreign, she couldn't even imagine how it would feel. With her locked shutters and martial arts classes and daily walks scouting the neighborhood, she protected herself and others, and she neither expected nor received their protection in return. She didn't even want it.

Did she?

She swallowed over a painfully dry throat. "There's nothing for vampires in between absolute disinterest and absolute commitment? You don't ever just . . . make friends?"

"Sometimes." His voice was flat. "It's usually a mistake."

Something fragile and green inside her shriveled at that, its reaching tendrils wilting.

Of course he didn't want to be her friend. Of course he'd consider any emotional intimacy they might share during an emergency a mistake.

Still, she persevered. "What about . . ." Did she really want to know? "Have you ever had a long-term relationship with anyone?"

He took his time answering. "Once."

"A human?" This wasn't her business, but somehow she needed to know. "A Supernatural?"

"Human," he said shortly. "Enhanced."

"And?" she prompted, smothering an unexpected spark of jealousy.

"It was also a mistake."

There was a terrible finality to that statement. It thudded between them like a stone barrier.

And yet . . . she'd been wrong, hadn't she? Someone *had* been protecting her. She might not have expected her neighbor's vigilance, but he'd employed it on her behalf anyway. Not only last night, but for at least the past year, during which time he'd intercepted two different intruders on her property. Without her asking for help. Without her realizing he'd watched out for her and defended her safety. Without them so much as holding hands.

Whatever he felt for her, then, it wasn't utter indifference, and it wasn't purely sexual. Even if he considered intimacy with her—with anyone—a fool's game.

As her thoughts began to drift, she hazily wondered what to make of that conclusion. Maybe he'd lied to her about the rarity of vampire friendship and attachment. Or maybe . . . there was always the flip side of that vampiric coin. On one face, absolute disinterest.

On the other: absolute, to-the-death commitment.

Could he possibly feel that strongly about her?

She didn't see how or why he would, and she wasn't certain she wanted him to. In her weakest moments, she might long for love, but she'd rather die herself than have anyone else risk their life for hers. Including Max.

Especially Max.

She took that thought with her into slumber. Into dreams. And finally, into nightmares.

11

The familiar horror racked Edie as she perched far above the violence and cowered in fear and shame. The smell of iron choked her, howls of triumph hurt her ears, and she knew it was a dream. She'd watched this moment a thousand times in her sleep, her mind supplying the grisly details she hadn't actually witnessed in real life, so she knew what to expect and it couldn't hurt her, only—

"Edie." Cool hands drew her closer to an equally cool body. "Wake up."

The nightmare twisted, and it wasn't just her parents below her anymore.

No, she shouted, and tried to jump down from the attic, ladder or no ladder, but she kept falling endlessly, unable to look away as the zombies slaughtered everyone she—

"Shhh. You're safe." The quiet words, gentle for all their implacability, interrupted the bloodbath. "Don't cry, my Edie."

Her ears ringing, she blinked awake and scrabbled for Max's hands, his forearms, any bit of him she could snatch against herself and keep safe and whole. Her ragged nails bit deep into his skin, and she was panting as she flailed in an attempt to turn over and *see* him.

When she began to fall off the couch, he hauled her back into his embrace and against his chest, this time facing him. "Calm yourself, ma puce. I'm here. All is well."

He wrapped her in himself, and she huddled against him, trembling. One big palm cradled her nape as she pressed her face into his bare neck. The other swept up and down her spine in slow, steady strokes. She sniffled, attempting to parse her nightmarish reality and her literal nightmare, and a brief, soft pressure touched the top of her head.

After several minutes, she'd shaken off the worst of it.

"I'm sorry," she whispered, and would have curled into herself like a humiliated shrimp if he hadn't kept her stretched out against him. "I haven't had a dream like that for a while, but . . ."

He exhaled, his leg sliding against hers. "Yes. The last two days have been a challenge."

"Please." A husky feminine voice came from somewhere behind the couch. "Do tell."

Max had clearly been tempering his speed and strength for her sake, because she couldn't even follow how quickly he moved or believe how easily he moved *her*. Before she could blink, she was lying flat on the ground and hidden as fully as possible between him and the sofa, her cleaver's handle pressed into her grasp, as he stood and faced their uninvited company.

Another confrontation. More violence. Fucking *hells*.

Adrenaline flooded her veins and tasted metallic on her tongue, and she had to tighten her grip on her weapon so her fingers wouldn't tremble.

"Come no closer," he warned them—because it was more

than one person. The sounds of shuffling feet and brandished weaponry indicated a substantial gathering of people. "I don't wish to hurt you, but I will."

At that, grumbles of affront mingled with a few chuckles.

"Forgive me if I don't flee in terror," the woman said, sounding amused. "I figure a dozen armed fighters can take out one rando in a tablecloth and the woman cowering at his feet, but perhaps I'm mistaken. If so, my apologies."

Cowering.

Their intruder couldn't have pushed Edie's buttons more effectively, not even if the entire group had watched her nightmare play out live.

Max tried to stop her from scrambling to her feet, but he was hampered by the knife he held in one hand, his need to watch their unwelcome guests, and his unwillingness to hurt her. In the end, she no longer lay at his feet or remained hidden behind him. She stood at his side. As she should have from the beginning, no matter the danger.

There were, in fact, a dozen armed people ringed around the sofa, scruffy but surprisingly clean. All genders, different heights and builds and skin colors. None of them had guns, but they held their baseball bats, knives, and tire irons with the comfortable ease of long practice.

Shit.

Yeah, the two of them were goners. Unless she could sweet-talk the gang leaders and emphasize how little threat she and Max posed, but how?

When he tried to guide her behind him again, she resisted.

"*Human—*" he began under his breath, his tone vicious and

furious, the word choice a deliberate reminder of his relative invulnerability compared to her species' fragility.

"Ah, there she is." The woman—a waifish redhead with pale skin, a pixie cut, and tattoo sleeves—smiled at Edie, and it would have been charming enough to prompt a smile in return. If, that is, the redhead weren't armed with an axe. "So glad you could join the party."

"Stop playing with your food, Belinda," said a handsome Black man with a shaved head. "It's beneath you."

Edie cringed. Were they feral werewolves, or . . . ?

"That was a metaphor," a thin white guy with a luxuriant mustache and a ponytail cheerfully told them. "We're just humans. We're totally not going to eat you or anything, so don't worry. Ugh. Gross."

"Doug," the redhead chided, shaking her head. "Discretion. Please."

"But we might hurt or kill you," Doug hurried to add, waving his tire iron. "It depends."

Before Edie could ask him what, precisely, their continued survival depended upon, the Black man cleared his throat, drawing the room's attention back to him.

"As Belinda was about to tell you, outsiders aren't welcome here," he informed her and Max. "You've not only intruded upon our territory, but—"

"That's our napping couch!" Doug announced. "Austin gets really cranky without his daily nap."

The Black man pinched his forehead. "Doug. We've discussed this."

"But you *do*." Tucking his tire iron beneath his arm, the thin man peered down at the sofa's uncovered cushions. "I had no idea those were slipcovers. Amazing."

Well, there was an opening. A weird one, but so be it.

"The covers are machine washable," Edie volunteered. "The fabric is stain resistant, so they'll probably look good as new after one cycle if you presoak them."

"Huh." Doug looked intrigued.

"Also," she added quickly, before Austin or Belinda regained their threat-making mojo, "we're so sorry to have intruded. We had no idea this was your territory or your, uh"—she stifled a hysterical giggle—"napping couch. We just needed someplace to dry off and get warm before we moved on. We promise we won't go anywhere else in the mall, and we won't tell anyone we saw you here."

When Max's continued attempts to yank her behind him failed, he heaved a silent sigh and spoke. "She's telling the truth. We don't know what you're doing here. We don't *care* what you're doing here. If you'd just let us—"

"We're counterfeiters!" Doug interjected. "The best on the East Coast!"

Everyone in the room turned to stare at him. Belinda resumed shaking her head while Austin appeared to be trying to set the other man on fire with his mind.

Max's body had gone taut at her side as he braced for battle, and her frantic pulse echoed in her skull. Now that they'd unwillingly learned about the gang's activities, there was no way they'd be allowed to leave freely. Unless . . .

Okay. Last-ditch-effort time. Building empathy sometimes worked in these sorts of situations, right?

"That's fascinating!" Edie forced herself to smile at a shame-faced Doug, then at Austin and Belinda and everyone else. "I've always thought counterfeiting was an interesting blend of artistry and technology. It kind of reminds me of what I do."

"What do you do?" Perking up, Doug perched on the sofa's back and watched her curiously.

"Don't tell them," Max ordered. "Don't—"

"Tell us. Now." Belinda's axe made an ominous *whoosh*ing sound when she lifted it menacingly. "If you lie to me, I'll know, and you'll regret it."

"I'm a soap maker." Edie's throat was dust-dry, and swallowing hurt. "My job mixes art and science too."

"What the *fuck*, woman?" Max sounded like the top of his head was about to blow off. "Even if we manage to escape, they have enough information to hunt you down now."

She crinkled her nose. "I'm not a good liar."

In retrospect, she probably shouldn't have been participating in such a fraught discussion when she was exhausted, still partially frozen, and fresh from a disorienting nightmare.

"Wait," Belinda said slowly. "I know you."

"Mother*fucker*." His knife and body still poised for attack, Max glared down at Edie. "I can't believe you just told them—"

"I know *both* of you." The other woman's head tilted as she studied them, the tense readiness in her posture softening. "Wow."

"Ha! It's not just me!" Edie poked his ribs, then returned Belinda's curious stare. "Hold on. *How* do you know us? Who do you think we are?"

"We watch Brad and Tonya's channel all the time." Grinning now, Belinda tucked her axe into a leather carrying sling. "Which is where we saw you, and the reason we know about *his* channel."

Her forefinger pointed directly at Max.

"You—" His jaw worked for a moment. "You're a subscriber?"

The redhead winked at him, which was both a good sign concerning Edie's and Max's continued survival and really freaking annoying. "Ever since you modeled those tiny macramé briefs."

His shoulders relaxed a fraction. "That's my video with the most views."

"For good reason," Belinda said with emphasis.

Both Austin and Edie scowled at her.

"Now that we're all acquainted, I should take you on a tour of our headquarters. We're based at Sharper Image, since they have lots of electrical outlets. It's where we put our generator," said sweet, clueless Doug, interrupting the tense moment with yet more dangerous revelations no one had asked him to share. "And, of course, we spend a lot of time at Brookstone too."

Austin groaned faintly.

"Ah." Dismissing the momentary sting of jealousy—this was neither the time nor the place, and she had no claim on Max anyway—Edie smiled at Doug. "The massage chairs?"

"The massage chairs," he affirmed. "Want to know how counterfeiting works?"

Well, yes. But she was more invested in not getting murdered due to her unwilling acquisition of information about his gang's criminal enterprises.

"It's okay, Doug. I know you have"—she gestured toward the roomful of armed people—"um, a lot happening right now."

He frowned. "But it's so interesting. We prefer to use the basic Colombian method—"

Austin's eyes flicked to the ceiling above. "Glorious mother of the gods."

"It's fine, Austin. Her full name"—Belinda's chin tipped in Edie's direction—"is in Brad and Tonya's videos. We can easily find her address. I'm sure I can find her companion's information as well, so we don't need to kill two of our favorite content providers for knowing too much. No matter what Doug tells them." She raised her eyebrows at them, then gripped the handle of her axe. "I assume both of you realize what'll happen if you run your mouths. Correct?"

Involuntarily, Edie glanced at Doug. *Take us into your gang and tolerate us with exasperated affection?*

For the first time, Austin's expression turned severe. "Doug's a true artist and our friend. We need him. We don't need you. Understood?"

In that moment, both he and Belinda appeared more than willing to eliminate any perceived threats to their business concerns.

"Understood," Edie told him, mentally ordering all pertinent government officials *not* to conduct a random, entirely unprompted sweep of the mall in the near future.

Max simply said, "Yes."

Austin swiveled on his heel to face Doug. "We'll talk about discretion later. Again. But right now . . ." His sigh sounded heartfelt. "Go to town, man. It's okay."

Joy beamed from Doug's narrow face and quivered in his mustache.

"Let me tell you more about Colombian counterfeiting methods," he said happily. "They take advantage of the way various values of US currency share a common bill size. If you use the same paper, the bills will *feel* right, even if they're counterfeit, so we print our notes on one-dollar bills, which we turn into hundred-dollar bills using bleach and—"

Max scrubbed his free hand over his face, exhaling slowly. "Don't ask questions, Edie."

They weren't going to die. Somehow, they weren't going to die.

Jittery with the hormonal backwash of her fight-or-flight response, she nodded, clutched Max's arm, and let Doug guide them out of Pottery Barn and toward Sharper Image and Brookstone.

She hoped she got to try out the massage chairs. She could use a bit of stress relief.

SEVERAL HOURS LATER, Edie had taken Doug's impromptu tour of the gang's facilities, learned much, much more than she'd ever expected to know about the artistic precision and technology involved in creating fake money, and grown decidedly twitchy.

Counterfeiting truly did interest her on an academic level, and Doug was a total sweetheart, but she and Max should have left long, long ago. The problem: She couldn't risk upsetting Doug or offending their criminal hosts. The one time she'd launched into cautious apologies for cutting the tour short, Max's mouth had covered hers in a very firm, very purposeful kiss after about three words.

That kiss hadn't said, *I want you.* It said, *Shut the hells up, Edie.*

So she did, and here they were. Out of time.

The sun had met the horizon before Counterfeiting 101: Faking Currency for Fun and Profit wound down for the day, and only a fool would travel at night with zombies on the loose. Which was a subject Max had quietly discussed with Belinda and

Austin, all while Doug had been demonstrating to Edie how to print a yellowish watermark on a bleach-thinned dollar bill and attach a fake thread onto a second bill before the two bills got glued together to achieve the appearance and thickness of a legitimate hundred-dollar note.

It really was ingenious. She wished she could have paid more attention to the process instead of eavesdropping as Max told the lead counterfeiters what they needed to know about the breach and discussed how they could best protect themselves and their entire gang. The zombies might not have stumbled upon the mall yet, but it was only a matter of time.

When the threesome had left, along with a handful of others, to conduct a sweep of the property and secure it against possible zombie intrusion, she'd had to ask Doug to repeat himself. Which, thankfully, hadn't appeared to bother him. He seemed used to it.

Now that everyone had returned to Brookstone, Max was confirming the bargain he'd reached with Belinda and Austin. As she listened, Edie let a worn massage chair dig deep into her stiff lumbar region and basked in the warmth of an electric heater.

"As agreed, you'll let us access your shower and bathroom facilities, stay overnight in the Pottery Barn, and leave at dawn tomorrow, all in guaranteed safety." One by one, Max ticked the items off, his expression alert and unsmiling. "You'll also supply us with a towel, soap, shampoo, and a dry set of clothing that fits me adequately. Correct?"

Belinda nodded. "Correct."

"Don't—" The calf massager kicked into gear, and Edie had to pause. Damn. That thing should be freaking *bronzed*. "Don't forget the measuring spoons."

After she'd mentioned the spoons to Doug, Austin had taken a gander around Williams Sonoma and returned brandishing the exact set Edie had been hoping to find. The one with the weird measures, including two-thirds and three-quarters of a teaspoon. At which point he'd proceeded to hold the set hostage until an official agreement had been reached.

He had the nerve to grin at her, the jerk. "We won't forget them, Edie. They're a key bargaining chip for our side."

Unperturbed by the interruption, Max added, "You will also give Edie her measuring spoons. In return, we promise to remain in either the Pottery Barn or the bathroom at all times, except while en route from one location to the other. We will not share your presence or activities here with the authorities or anyone else, no matter the circumstances."

"Oh!" Doug straightened from where he'd been slumped in his own massage chair. "Edie said she'd help troubleshoot my cupcake soap once she got back home. She thinks I didn't make the trace thick enough for the frosting."

"I have no idea what that means, but okay." Belinda turned to Austin. "I meant to tell you, Max agreed to show me how to do a smoky eye in shades of red without looking like I have conjunctivitis. So let's make that an official part of our bargain too."

"Yeah, your first attempt was . . . unfortunate." Austin's face scrunched up in pained reminiscence. "Is that everything?"

Nods all around.

"Then the bargain is set." When Belinda slid her axe partway from its sling, it glinted in the glare of the work light placed in the store's corner. "As a reminder, if the agreement's terms get broken—"

"It won't be by us," Edie quickly interjected.

The other woman let her weapon settle back into place. "Excellent."

"I know!" Doug dropped his chair's remote and pointed at Edie and Max. "You should have dinner with us. We can make sushi!"

Belinda stared at him. "Really? We're feeding our intruders now?"

Doug's mustache drooped. "What's the point of making counterfeit money if we can't spend it on our friends?"

"Fine, fine. Get the sticky rice going." Austin waved a hand, then directed his attention to Max and Edie. "I assume you'll stay for dinner?"

The exact cause of Max's faintly disgruntled look wasn't clear to Edie. Maybe he'd reached his socialization limit. Maybe he'd rather not have to eat human food and continue pretending he wasn't, in fact, a super-old, superstrong vampire and thus a salient threat to the counterfeiters. Maybe he simply didn't like sushi.

It made no difference. No matter what either of them wanted, there was only one correct response to give to the armed criminal gang surrounding them.

"We'd be delighted," she answered for them both.

12

Later that night, Max shook out the first item from his bundle of borrowed clothing. Together, he and Edie contemplated a pair of gold lamé pants and the generous amount of fabric ballooning forth in the garment's thigh region.

Savagely, she bit her lip.

"They gave me MC Hammer pants." His voice was flat. "Like in my video."

The light from her phone—which Doug had insisted she charge using the generator's power—reflected against the shiny surface of the pants and illuminated the far wall. She pointed her face in that direction, quelling the irresistible urge to laugh.

Max sighed. "No wonder Austin looked entirely too pleased with himself."

Getting herself under control, she turned back. "You should be proud, Max. You're an influencer, right? And you clearly influenced someone in that gang." The fabric was slinky and cool under her outstretched fingertip. "It's very soft. Also very dry, unlike your jeans, and far less precarious than the tablecloth toga you've been wearing all afternoon."

Several counterfeiters had been watching that toga, their hungry gazes willing its folds to part and its knots to unravel. Alas, the tablecloth had proven sturdier than expected. She and Max remained the only people in that mall who'd seen him entirely naked.

To clarify, alas for the counterfeiters. Not her. She was quite pleased to have the viewing of his birthday suit remain a party of two.

"I suppose." He dug through the rest of the clothing pile, then paused. "Shit."

"Show me. Come on, Max. Share with the class."

When he held up a leather tunic with a Mandarin collar and nipple and navel cutouts, she choked on thin air and began coughing and laughing at the same time. He glared at her as he thumped her back.

"I—I'm guessing that's from your videos too," she wheezed.

He offered her zero expression. "Possibly."

"What—" She caught her breath. "What else did they give you?"

To his credit, he didn't try to dodge the question. "Velour boxers and a clip-on rattail."

When a strangled sound emerged from her straining lungs and she began cough-laughing again, he deposited their borrowed towel in her hand.

"Let's take our showers, human." Only the faintest indentation at the corner of his mouth revealed his own reluctant amusement. "Perhaps you'll be less gleeful at the misfortune of others once you're clean."

"Probably not." She wouldn't lie to him. "But you're sweet to think so."

According to Belinda, the former employees at the nearby sporting goods store had been urged to bike to work, so one bathroom in the back came equipped with a shower, not merely a sink and a toilet. Her gang used that shower, and they'd given Edie and Max access for the night too.

Together, the two of them walked over, nodding at a sleepy-looking Austin as they passed the Sharper Image. When they reached their destination, their steps echoed across the vast emptiness of the dark sporting goods store, and Edie hastened to the staff area in the rear, where the counterfeiters had rigged up some lighting. In contrast to the huge selling floor, the employee break room would accommodate a half dozen people, max, and the white-tiled bathroom with the shower was slightly claustrophobic. Its surfaces sparkled with surprising cleanliness, however—probably due to the cleaning rotation on the wall, upon which Austin had posted a sticky note reading "THIS MEANS YOU TOO, CODY"—and thank goodness for that. Edie had no desire to contract a fungal infection even as she scrubbed away all traces of moat water.

Max was quiet, merely waving her ahead of him into the bathroom, and Edie was too damn tired to quibble. One at a time, they washed up under the steaming-hot water with the toiletries they'd been given, dried off, got dressed, and prepared for bed— all while the other stood guard outside the bathroom. Because they might have reached an agreement with the counterfeiters, but they weren't fools.

As predicted, Edie still giggled on occasion the entire way back to Pottery Barn. That occasion being whenever she glanced at Max's fresh clothing.

The pants were a glorious, shiny paean to eighties fashion, of course, but the tunic—the *tunic*! It was fricking *amazing*. All gleaming leather and peekaboo skin, like high-necked, boobless chaps. If she didn't think Max would find a way to murder her with the sheer force of his fiery glare, she'd totally boop him on a pebbled rosy nipple. Or tickle his shadowy navel.

Her continued hilarity stemmed from genuine amusement, but also sheer punch-drunk exhaustion. By the time they returned to the counterfeiters' infamous napping couch, she was staggering with fatigue against Max's supportive arm.

As soon as they entered the back room, he closed the door behind them and did something to the handle. She didn't know what. Didn't care.

"Bedtime." Striding ahead of her to the couch, he smoothed a tablecloth over the bottom cushions, then straightened the other makeshift blankets and gestured for her to crawl beneath the pile. "Did you set your alarm for tomorrow?"

When she nodded, he climbed in after her and maneuvered them back into a spooning position, since it was the only way they'd both fit on the sofa. After he carefully tucked the tablecloths underneath her, the warm, soft fabric and his cool embrace encompassed her in a secure cocoon. His arm curved beneath her neck, his chest braced her aching back, and his chin rested atop her head. A slight, pleasant tug against her scalp told her he was fiddling with her damp hair. Maybe de-knotting all the tangles, since she hadn't wasted any energy combing it. Again, she didn't care. It felt good.

Sagging into the couch, more relaxed than she'd been in hours, she rubbed her cheek against his biceps. "What did you think of our dinner?"

"Decent sushi." Each of his deep, slow breaths rocked her

slightly, and it was soothing as heck. "And I'm glad you didn't have to dig into your emergency supplies. Whatever horrors your can of non-falafel might encompass, I cannot imagine. Nor do I wish to."

With a sleepy snort, she wiggled back farther into the cradle of his body, only to feel his hard dick digging into her ass cheek. Still, he didn't meet her inadvertent caress with his own, didn't press forward and grind against her. Didn't make the embrace sexual.

"Max?" she whispered.

"You need to sleep." He might be aroused, but apparently he was content not to act upon that arousal. "It's fine."

Yeah. She liked him. More than she should, given how clearly he'd warned her that vampires didn't care much for anyone, even other vampires.

His hand stilled in her hair, and when he spoke again, his words were uncharacteristically hesitant. "Speaking of horrors and sleep."

She'd been wondering all evening whether Max would push for answers. Over the years, whenever she'd scratched a sexual itch, she'd done so outside the Zone, and she'd never spent the night. No one had ever been present for one of her increasingly infrequent nightmares, so no one had asked about them. Until now.

The two of them had been interrupted earlier, at the moment when most lovers would have naturally posed questions—out of morbid curiosity, if for no other reason. She'd hoped he might forget what had happened. Might let it go, even if he did remember.

"Max." This time his name wasn't a question. It was a protest. "I don't . . ."

I don't talk about this. Ever. I don't want to talk about this, and I especially don't want to talk about your unexpected appearance in a dream that hadn't altered in two decades.

"Please," he said, the word halting and rusty, an abandoned cogwheel kicked into motion after centuries of neglect. "Tell me."

Most people mistook her friendliness for openness. Never even realized she didn't share what she was thinking or feeling. And if they didn't care enough to notice, she certainly wasn't going to expose the raw expanse of her heart to them.

But his tone conveyed far more than idle nosiness, despite all those warnings about his callous nature. And when she didn't answer immediately, he waited patiently, his fingers sifting through her hair, until she surrendered.

"My parents died in the First Breach, when I was eighteen. In our home. My home." The moisture behind her closed lids soothed her stinging eyes, and she tried very hard not to let the familiar, terrible images play out against those lids. "They sent me to safety and held off the creatures long enough for me to escape. I didn't see the end, but I saw enough. I heard enough."

Her mouth clamped shut.

There. Done.

If he didn't intend to make her one of his rare *exceptions* and openly care about her in a more lasting way, that was all he'd get. Facts and basic context. The bare outlines of a picture he could fill in at his leisure with her thoughts and emotions, because she wasn't going to do it for him.

He hummed an acknowledgment and kept stroking her hair.

Slowly, as she realized he wasn't going to press for more, her thoughts began to unravel into slumber.

Then he spoke again. Right against her ear, so quietly it felt like vibration more than sound. "The fae are powerful beyond description and nearly impossible to kill, but they're mortal."

Well, that was random. But it was also a truth for a truth, shared in the silent darkness of a crumbling edifice.

She sucked in a breath. "Really? I thought they were immortal."

"Their natural longevity is close to yours." His body had turned taut behind hers, his forearm like iron beneath her fingers. "The only way for them to increase it is to feed on the lifespan of humans."

Holy fuck.

"No one knows exactly how they do it," he continued. "There are rumors that a particularly powerful witch gave them the ability in an ill-fated bargain, only to perish with their hands on her neck as they exercised their new power for the first time."

Any sleepiness had now vanished. Her eyes were wide open, staring blankly into the shadows surrounding them.

"They can consume anywhere from a day to an entire human lifetime with each feeding, and their victims age that full amount of time within seconds. A single human year only goes so far, though. I'm not sure exactly *how* far—the fae are a particularly secretive species—but perhaps a week of extra life. Maybe more, maybe less. Since only the Fates know our destined lifespans, the fae also can't predict exactly how much time is available for consumption before choosing their targets." To his credit, his tone matched the grimness of his revelations. "Before Supernaturals and the Enhanced revealed themselves to the common human world, the greediest fae, those pursuing immortality at all costs, played the odds. They didn't exercise patience or try to mitigate the impact of their actions. They didn't discreetly consume a few months at a time or only target the elderly. Any vulnerable human would do. And the younger the victim, the more years available for consumption, so the fae stole children and gulped entire lifetimes. No one from your world knew of their existence, so no one suspected their involvement."

That quickly, she was cold again. As if she'd leapt back into that murky moat and let the water envelop her whole.

His breath rattled a bit in his lungs. "Most other Supernaturals don't know about that particular fae ability either. My parents didn't know. As a child, I didn't know."

Her lips pressed together, and she braced herself.

This wasn't simply useful information. This was personal, and whatever story he was telling wouldn't end well.

"We were making our way home from a festival. It was past midnight, but we cut through grimy alleyways and dark, wooded areas, because we had nothing to fear. We were predators, not prey, even though my parents insisted we show respect and mercy to those we fed upon." The bitterness in his tone stung her ears. "I was proud of that. Eleven years old and convinced that strength allied with righteousness would inevitably prevail."

Her breath hitched. *Eleven years old.* Whatever horror he was about to recount, he'd suffered through much too early.

The story rolled on, inexorable. "Only a minute from our home, under the branches of a willow tree, we spotted movement. A human couple attacking a drunken man as he staggered home from an inn. They'd pinned him to the tree trunk and were choking the life out of him as he twitched helplessly beneath their hands. My parents intervened."

Squeezing her eyes shut, she nodded to herself. "But the couple wasn't human."

"Glamoured fae. They dropped the man to the grass and—" He inhaled sharply. "It happened so quickly. Branches encircled my parents' wrists and ankles, holding them in place long enough for another branch to pierce their hearts. A makeshift stake. They were dead before the human took his final breath."

Which meant he'd been right there. Close enough to see his parents' bloodied, lifeless bodies. Close enough to check on the man and feel his heart laboring to a halt.

Somehow, she knew he'd done that. She knew he'd tried to assist the human victim and found himself as helpless to save the stranger as he'd been to save his parents.

And—did he just say the fae could commit cold-blooded murder with a fucking *tree*?

How the hells had he survived? "Did they not see you? Were you hiding?"

"Oh, they saw me. But my death wouldn't feed them, and I wasn't a threat. We vampires had no community to take vengeance for us, no friends, no authorities to intervene, and I was far too young to prove an entertaining foe in combat." Despite his bored tone, infinitesimal tremors racked his entire body. He was vibrating like a tuning fork with anger and grief and heartbreak. "They laughed at my attempts to avenge my family. When I tried to follow them, roots erupted from beneath the grass and barred my path."

Her heart squeezing in her chest, she pressed back against him and reached for his hand. "Max—"

"No," he said firmly. "I don't require pity. It happened a long time ago."

It wasn't pity she'd hoped to offer, but that didn't matter. She wouldn't force her acknowledgment of his grief upon him or offer comfort for emotions he wanted to deny.

There were certain memories too dangerous to touch without some kind of self-protection. Make unguarded contact, and the third rail of your past could incinerate you.

She knew that better than most.

Better to focus on facts than feelings, then. "Do some of the fae still . . ."

Suck away years of human life like an evil Roomba? Murder with impunity?

"I don't know. Probably." Slowly, the rigid tension in his body began to soften. "They'd have to be more subtle, though, now that we're out in the open. Maybe take a year or two at a time and feed more frequently instead of snatching a human's entire lifespan."

"Since that would draw too much attention from either human or SERC authorities."

"Precisely."

Maybe she shouldn't ask, but—"You found the fae couple, didn't you? Later."

"It took me over a century," he said, sounding exactly like the vicious creature of darkness humans had once imagined vampires to be. "In the end, they learned to suffer."

By hunting down his parents' killers, he'd transformed

himself from prey into predator once again. And perhaps his utter ruthlessness and towering determination in doing so—a *century*, dear gods—or the cold, sneering satisfaction in his tone when he spoke of the fae couple's fate should frighten her.

They didn't. She couldn't seem to drum up much sympathy for the prey in question.

"Why didn't you kiss me good night?"

Oh, for fuck's sake. At some point in the last several minutes, her brain-to-mouth filter had apparently flicked a two-finger farewell salute and hitched a ride to parts unknown.

He sounded impatient. "I told you. You need sleep."

"A two-second kiss would hardly delay my—"

"I wouldn't stop after two seconds, Edie." His voice was a near snarl, the press of his erection against her ass steely. "You know that."

"You'd fuck me." Not a question. A statement.

"I'd fuck you." His grip on her hip held her in place as he rolled his own hips, the grinding motion liquid. Sinuous. Taunting. "If you said yes, my Edie, I'd fuck you until you couldn't remember how it felt without ma bite inside you."

Her thighs squeezed together, and it only made matters worse. "I'd say yes."

"I *know*," he snapped. "Which is why I'm not kissing you good night."

After a minute of fraught silence, she said, "I assume *ma bite* means your dick."

"You assume correctly."

She thought back to earlier that day, fighting the urge to slide a hand—hers, his; either was fine—between her legs. "What does *ma puce* mean?"

"'My flea.'" When she twisted her neck to scowl at him, he petted her upper arm soothingly. "It's a term of endearment."

"Sure it is." She flopped her head back onto his left biceps. "As opposed to an intimation that I'm an irritating pest."

"Can't it be both?" His laughter shook them both, and she bit back her own smile. "We vampires have an affinity for bloodsuckers, sweet Edie. And either way, you must be under my skin, no?"

Her exaggerated *harrumph* made him laugh again. As she'd hoped it might.

She hadn't meant to bicker with him about kissing, fucking, or fleas, but the discussion had served them well. All the anger and lingering grief had drained from his voice. His body no longer resembled a granite monolith at her back, and he wasn't vibrating with tension anymore.

As he kept leisurely stroking her arm, she relaxed too, letting his hold and the cushions support her full weight. The ache of unsatisfied desire gradually diminished, and she sighed against the muscled curve of his satiny skin and snuggled closer.

"Do you have nightmares too?" she asked quietly. "About your parents?"

"Not about them." His exhalation tickled her scalp. "Not anymore."

That wording . . . it implied he did have nightmares, at least on occasion. But if those terrible dreams didn't feature his parents, what were they about? What in the world could possibly be more traumatic than watching the murder of your family?

Her mouth opened to ask. Then closed again, slowly.

She didn't have the heart to pry any further tonight. Not after he'd already shared so much of himself and such a painful part of his past with her.

When she remained silent, he gathered her closer. His right hand slowly slid to her chest, as it had earlier that day. His palm came to rest over her heart, his fingertips light and cool on the swell of her breast.

He couldn't surround her completely. She was too generously proportioned for that. But he'd curled himself around her like armor, and at the first sign of trouble, he'd leap in front of her. Exactly as he'd done earlier that day.

She hadn't even thanked him.

"I thought we were going to die today," she whispered. "More than once. Thank you for making sure that didn't happen."

The tablecloths surrounding them rustled as he shrugged. "I could say the same to you."

She sighed and let her eyelids slip shut. "I'm so glad to be alive."

And not only because she was eager to learn whether rumors of vampiric stamina and dicking-related talent had their basis in fact. Although that didn't hurt.

"I am too," he murmured, then kissed the crown of her head. "Strange, that."

13

Max's voice bristled with outrage. "You're not a subscriber?"

"No." With a tap of her finger, Edie selected the next download to watch. "The only *Better Than You* videos I've seen in their entirety are the ones Brad and Tonya referenced on their channel. Which is probably why I didn't immediately connect Mr. Macramé Undies with Chad, even after spotting you in that sheepskin thong two nights ago."

"So you've watched *several* of my videos and actually downloaded snippets of my content *onto your phone*, but you've still chosen not to subscribe?"

Fashion and beauty weren't really her thing, so . . . "I think I clicked the thumbs-up button for one of them?"

That hand-knotted underwear might not have tempted her to subscribe, but she'd wanted to salute his wedgie-inducing efforts—not to mention his ass—in some fashion. He'd earned her thumbs-up, even before she'd known about the Testicular Strangulation Incident.

Her attempt at consolation only offended him further. "Only *one?*"

"Poor Gaston." She patted his forearm, tensed from holding the phone in front of them. "Never fear. You remain a bethonged inspiration to the rest of the villagers."

"Hmph."

The aggrievement in the sound was exaggerated, and they both knew why. Didn't matter. It worked. She buried her snicker in his upper arm, finally relaxing into the couch's cushions and his embrace once more.

Over an hour before her alarm had been due to sound that morning, she'd woken in the painful grips of another nightmare and the cool, careful hold of Max. To calm herself and provide her brain with pleasanter images, she'd grabbed her phone and tapped her downloads folder. At some point, he'd woken up too, and they'd begun to watch together.

In the current snippet, he was somehow transforming mime makeup into cutting-edge beauty, then admiring his reflection.

Which reminded her: "You can see yourself in a mirror, then?"

"Evidently." His sarcasm was thick enough to choke her, and okay. Yes, that was a stupid question, but really, was *none* of the accepted information about vampires correct?

"Then how did that even become a thing?"

"What impressive wordsmiths you humans are," he murmured, then yelped when she kicked his shin with the heel of her bare foot. "Before the Battle for Containment, mirrors made discreet feeding more difficult, so we either avoided them or ensured we moved too quickly to be spotted in their reflections. The fewer witnesses, the better."

Which was a very diplomatic way of saying, *The fewer murders, the better.*

Instead of pursuing that disturbing conversational tangent any further, she gestured to the phone and asked, "Why do this? If you simply want to be left alone, as you keep telling me, why make videos of yourself for worldwide public consumption?"

She had her theories, but she was curious how he'd justify his contradictory behavior. What he told himself in lieu of admitting to loneliness and a need for connection to others, however limited and one-sided. What he'd say to avoid acknowledging both a genuine interest in fashion and a healthy dose of justifiable vanity.

"Unlike many of my brethren, I refuse to exist as a sentient anachronism." To his credit, he answered her question without hesitation. "I won't hold on to a past that can't be recaptured, and I'll deal with the world as it is, not as it was. Which means employing modern technology and means of communication."

Ah, there it was again. The inimitable scent of bullshit wafting through the chilly mall air. "You can do all that without modeling furry thongs on YouTube, dude. Try again."

He paused this time, but only briefly. "When I inspire humans to put on the clothing and makeup I've modeled for them, they look like the fools they are. It's very satisfying."

That answer had the ring of partial truth. And since he wasn't pushing her to share emotions she'd rather keep hidden, she'd grant him the same favor.

"Hmmm." With a sigh, she reached out to swipe her cell's screen and close the downloads folder. "Dawn isn't too long from now. We should eat before we go. Did any of your blood packs make it? Or did they all fall into the moat?" A thought occurred to her. "Or maybe vampires don't need to eat every day?"

"We don't." He devoted unusual attention to placing her phone atop her bag. "In theory."

Uh-oh. "What about reality?"

"If I went too long between meals, I'd eventually lack the strength to protect us both." His chest swelled against her back with his deep inhalation. "And at some point, basic biology would take over."

That . . . did not sound promising. "Explain."

"I'd go feral." When she twisted her neck to frown at him, he clarified, "Lose conscious awareness of my actions and take what I needed to survive."

In other words, *Wave bye-bye to your throat, human.*

New life goal: continuing to have a life. By, say, making sure Max never, ever went feral in her vicinity. "Would that be a permanent state, or would you regain control once you'd had enough to drink?"

"It's unpredictable. But if my feral state became perpetual, SERC would eventually resolve the issue. Dispatch one of their licensed hunters."

A stake through the heart, then. He seemed entirely too matter-of-fact about that possibility, especially given his current lack of bagged blood.

She scowled into the predawn darkness of the Pottery Barn staff room. "And there's no way to prevent turning feral other than feeding regularly?"

His shoulder shifted in a shrug. "Eliminating oneself before it's too late. Which I'd prefer over devolving into a mindless animal."

Neither of those horrifying outcomes would happen. Not on her watch, anyway.

"How soon would that happen? How long can you go between meals if necessary?" Because as much as she hated the thought of losing more time and driving back over that damn bridge, they could return to his home for more blood packs. Or . . . there was another option, of course.

It frightened her, but she couldn't say it didn't tempt her too.

"I don't know. Testing that boundary isn't a risk I've either needed or wanted to take." His exhalation ruffled the hair at the crown of her head. "Edie, don't concern yourself. I'm sure I can come to an agreement with one of the counterfeiters."

No doubt about that.

Edie could see it. Max, his lips moving softly over Belinda's wrist. His mouth pressed against her neck as she arched against him. Or if not Belinda—because Austin might have something to say about that—one of the other counterfeiters who'd watched Max with as much hunger on their faces as any Hollywood vampire.

"Yeah." She swallowed against a sudden surge of nausea. "What about the person who feeds you? Are there any . . . lasting effects for them?"

He shifted against her, uncharacteristically restless. "If the right amount is taken, none. The bite heals within moments, and the feeding confers a temporary immunity to most illnesses. If the donor doesn't eat or drink properly afterward, they may become dizzy. Otherwise, they remain exactly as they were."

How does it feel for them? was what she meant to ask next. A disinterested inquiry. A matter of academic curiosity, or perhaps simple pragmatism.

"How would it feel?" came out of her mouth instead, and that question contained entirely different implications. Revealing ones.

His biceps drew taut beneath her neck. "Edie . . ."

"How would it feel?" she repeated. Because she needed to know. Now.

"However I wanted it to feel."

"What . . ." She blinked. "What does that mean?"

"I could numb the bite. I could make it hurt." His forefinger lightly traced a line from the inside of her elbow to the raised, vulnerable veins at her wrist. "Or I could turn it into pleasure, my Edie. Pleasure and heat and lust."

She pressed her thighs together. Just a little bit. "And you could confuse my memory afterward?"

"Yes." His fingertip stilled on her pulse. "Would you want me to?"

"*No.*" Gods, no.

Max's steady grip ensured she didn't topple off the couch as she fought against the twisted confines of their tablecloth burrito and turned in his arms. The lack of light meant she couldn't truly meet his eyes. Still, she needed to say this face-to-face, because losing some blood didn't scare her. The possibility of pain didn't scare her. But forgetting a fleeting moment of intimacy with Max, however bloody and fraught it might become?

Yeah. *That* scared her.

She'd remained a single barrier wall away from fucking *zombies* for twenty years to preserve her memories, however painful. Those memories were the framework of her existence. The inalterable, rock-solid foundation of the life she'd built for herself. The walls she leaned against when she needed support and hid behind when she felt too exposed. The true home she'd inhabited for the last two decades.

So she wanted to ensure she retained every detail about what came next. Especially since he hadn't promised her new memories after this breach had been reported.

He might dissolve into a lost past too. Even if he remained her neighbor.

"Promise me you won't do that." She braced her palms against his shoulders. "Promise me, Max."

"I promise." His lips rested against her forehead. "But . . . Edie, I keep telling you. You'd be foolish to trust the promises of others. Particularly the promises of a predator."

"Fuck everyone else." When she poked his chest gently, there was no give there. Only hard muscle and coiling tension. "What about *your* promises? Can I trust them?"

For all the chill of his flesh, his heart thumped strongly against her palm. Quickly. And maybe he didn't say yes, but he wasn't telling her no either. Not anymore.

It wasn't such an insignificant shift. And she'd rather take a risk than let someone else give him what he needed or experience that kind of intimacy with him.

Fine, then. "Bite me."

He didn't react. Didn't move. Didn't speak. Unlike her, though, he could see in the dark, and she knew those sharp eyes were trained on her face. She could feel them, as hot as the summer sun on bare, tender skin.

He wouldn't spot hesitation in her expression. Wouldn't locate even a whisper of unease.

"Feed from me." Her doubts had been vanquished, leaving only desire and demand. "Make it feel good, and make sure I remember how good it felt."

A rough sound from deep in his chest rumbled through her. She basked in the sensation, arching and rubbing her body against his, until his hands caught her and held her in place.

"You need to be certain." His mouth swept to her temple and pressed there hard enough to emphasize the firmness of his teeth behind his soft lips. "Are you?"

She cupped the back of his skull and pressed him even closer, until those tempting lips parted and his incisors became an insistent, sharp prickle against her skin. A featherweight more force, and she'd draw her own blood.

"Don't you dare leave me hanging, Euro Chad," she whispered against his jaw, then licked its jutting edge. "If I'm satisfying you, you'd better satisfy me too."

He didn't move. "Is that a yes?"

"Yes," she said, and nipped that arc of bone.

In an eyeblink, before she was aware of moving or being moved, she was upright and straddling him, perched atop his lap with her knees indenting the sofa cushions on either side of his hips. To sleep, she'd stripped down to a clean tank and a fresh pair of panties, and the velour of his boxers swept against the insides of her thighs in a soft caress. His broad, strong hands gripped her ass and pressed her down firmly, grinding her clit against the solid ridge of his dick through two layers of fabric.

She gasped and involuntarily spread her legs wider, dropping deeper, rubbing harder. The rhythm he set with his sinuous hips was unrelenting and carnal and voluptuously slow, and she followed his lead. She chased the drag of his hard cock between her legs and the jolt of heat and electricity with each rock of her own hips, each scrape of her fingernails against his satiny skin. She clutched his shoulders and used his immoveable strength for leverage. For her own pleasure.

"Such a hot little chatte." His breath dusted her earlobe before he bit down. Hard enough to pinch deliciously, but not hard enough to draw blood. Yet. "When I finally get inside you, you'll burn me alive, my Edie."

"And you'll thank me for it." With the next sway of her hips, the perfect pressure and friction, white fireworks burst behind her eyelids. "Won't you?"

He didn't respond in words. One hand remained on her ass cheek, pressing and squeezing and urging her on. The other circled her wrist and guided her arm above her head, twisting it slightly, until the knob of her elbow pointed away from him. His fingers slid through hers and twined. They were holding hands up in the air. *He* was holding *her* hand. Tenderly. Loosely enough to offer little resistance if she tugged away from him.

It felt as intimate as his fingertips slipping through her vulva had the previous day.

Then he ducked his head, his lips teasing the sensitive skin inside her raised upper arm and sliding toward her inner elbow. He nipped there, forcing a needy sound from her throat, and began slowly lowering their interlaced fingers as his mouth dragged over her prickling flesh. He drew a trail of heat along her inner forearm with his tongue, her nerves firing to life inch by inch.

At her wrist, that agile tongue traced precise, branching lines. Her veins, she dimly realized, and shivered. He was mapping her veins in the darkness, leaning his forehead against the knot of their hands and nuzzling against her with his nose.

His mouth sealed over her pulse point and sucked, his tongue swirling. She moaned aloud for the first time, long and low, arching back to grind harder against his cock. Desire had transformed from a tease to a fiery ache between her legs, hunger and emptiness and *need*.

He stopped moving, stopped rocking and licking and squeezing her ass.

In that stillness, two sharp, needlelike spots of near pain became recognizable. His fangs. Her inner wrist. His final, silent demand for consent before he bit down and swallowed.

Her grip of his shoulder eased, and she slid her palm toward his nape, cradling the back of his skull. She held him there for a heartbeat, still and quiet. Suspended in the moment.

Then she used her hold on his head to press him forward, tighter and harder, until his teeth broke her skin. Until her blood flooded his mouth.

"Yes," she said, and slid her tongue over the rim of his ear.

The faint sting of penetration was her last moment of discomfort. After he bit into her wrist, there was only the sweep of his own soft tongue and the way each suck and swallow felt like he was drawing directly on her clit. There was only dizzy heat and the glide of a knowing hand up her spine and their fingers clasped tightly together.

He was everywhere, and he was everything. The fire that scalded her flesh and the chill soothing her burn. The pitiless, grinding rhythm pushing her toward pleasure and the slide of gentle fingers in her hair. The smell of copper, the tang of sex, and the waft of lavender from the shampoo they'd both used. Quiet suckling and his sharp, loud inhalation against her skin when she cupped her own breast and pinched her nipple and made a lost, raw sound deep in her throat. Salt on her tongue as she licked his neck and the sweetness of his hand in hers.

It didn't take long. The glow of heat between her legs expanded and exploded, and she rubbed her clit against his dick frantically, shamelessly, gasping as the tension and need fractured into shuddering hitches of pleasure.

His hand was on her ass again, still sliding her against his cock, while she panted and twitched and trembled. Her head tipped back, and she basked in all the pleasure he brought her, all the pleasure she'd claimed for herself.

When the pulses slowed at last, she slumped on his lap, damp with sweat.

"Holy gods and goddesses," she rasped.

With one final lick, he raised his mouth from her wrist. The two small wounds left by his teeth didn't even bleed, as far as she could tell. He brought their clasped hands to his lips and kissed her knuckles, and she could feel his smile against her fingers.

"Thank you," he said quietly.

His dick was a steel bar between her legs, which couldn't be comfortable for him. Despite her boneless state, she maneuvered herself a few crucial inches to the side, reached down into his boxers, and gripped him in her free hand, squeezing tightly. He grunted at her first stroke and groaned after her second and orgasmed with her third.

His body formed a gorgeous arch beneath hers, and he came with every muscle locked into place, trembling and taut. He didn't seem to breathe for a few seconds, before he began dragging in desperate gasps of air like someone who'd been deprived of oxygen for far too long.

After a long while, he sagged against the sofa cushions. Then, lurching forward, he sealed their mouths together. She swallowed down the purr of his lingering pleasure and licked her own blood from his tongue. Did it taste metallic to him too? Or was it salty? Sweet?

His release was slick and cool against her fingers, almost silky, and when he cupped her between her legs and stroked gently over the cotton, her body contracted in pleasure one final time.

He made a sort of pleased hum, his thumb passing lightly over her clit.

She wished she could see his expression through the darkness. Wished she could read his mind and know whether this *intensity* was normal during his feedings and sexual encounters. Whether it was about his being a vampire, or about . . . them. Max and Edie. The two of them, specifically, rather than a predator who'd learned to please his prey and enjoy himself in the process.

After a minute, she broke their kiss and wiped her palm on his underwear, because silkiness was rapidly becoming stickiness.

There was a meditative silence, and she could almost feel his eyes on her again. After a few moments, he let go of her hand, and she heard the faint pop of lips against skin.

She felt nothing. So whom or what was he kissing?

Befuddled, she squinted in the darkness, trying to figure out what in the world he was doing. Then he lightly pressed a fingertip against her wrist, on the exact spot where she'd urged his teeth into her veins. His movement was deliberate and precise, his touch whisper-soft.

Suddenly, she understood.

Using that fingertip, he was kissing her wound and making it better. Just as her mother always had. Just as Edie had once done for him.

Her eyes prickled, and she exhaled shakily as he interlaced his fingers through hers once more. After a moment, he slid his palm from between her legs and claimed her other hand too.

"You made me come in my velour boxers." He sighed. "It's not especially comfortable."

She snorted. "If you're waiting for an apology—"

"No, no. Merely requesting that the next time you make me lose control, you do so while ma bite is inside you, entirely uncovered, or at least encased in a breathable fabric."

Her laugh echoed in the near-empty space, and she squeezed his hands, suddenly inspired. "No . . . one . . . comes like Gaston—"

"Human. This is neither the time nor the—"

"—spurts on bums like Gaston. In his—"

"I did *not* spurt on my own ass. Just because some of it ended up back there—"

"—boxer shorts, no one—"

"Godsdammit, Edie."

AFTER EDIE AND Max each took another speedy shower and dressed—Doug had cheerfully offered to wash their dirty clothing overnight, and they found the pile of clean, dry laundry just outside Pottery Barn's back room—she hastily gnawed on some Pizza Jerky from her bag. Max asked whether the plasticky-looking foodstuff contained meat, and she enjoyed his look of horror when she told him she didn't actually know. And then, right on time, they gathered their belongings to leave just as the sun rose.

"Max..." She frowned, settling her cross-body bag into place. "The siren still hasn't sounded. How is that even possible? The government has camera footage of the compound. Wouldn't they have noticed the zombies leaving? And even if the cameras were disabled, wouldn't there be telltale satellite images of the area?"

"I assume whoever tampered with the bridges also tampered with all electronic surveillance measures. Somehow." Arms akimbo, he tipped his head as he considered the matter. "Do you want us to visit the breach site ourselves before we leave the Zone so we can pass along firsthand information about the scene?"

Her head was shaking before he even finished speaking. "No. Our priority has to be reporting the incident and getting help as soon as possible. Investigating why and how the breach happened can wait until no one is dying."

He inclined his head, and they turned for the store's back entrance. On their way out, she patted the top of the couch lovingly.

He shot her a questioning look, and for some reason she was willing to tell him. Maybe even *wanted* to tell him.

"A couple years before the First Breach, my parents went shopping for a new couch. They'd intended to get something cheaper, but there was this one sofa in Pottery Barn we all loved. It was just so comfortable, and Dad argued that the slipcovers made it a practical choice, despite the expense, so..." She smiled slightly. "It took three separate trips to this mall, to this store, but they finally ordered the couch in gray velvet."

"This couch." His broad hand skated over the sofa's rolled arm. "This design."

She nodded. "We had it in our living room until..."

Until it became ripped and blood-soaked and unsalvageable,

slipcovers or no slipcovers. A reminder of everything she wanted to remember and everything she needed to forget.

He didn't push her to finish her sentence. Instead, he studied the piece of furniture, a line drawn between his brows, then nodded and took her elbow as they left the store.

A rosy predawn glow brightened the winter sky. Belinda, Austin, and Doug were waiting by the dumpsters, their weapons sheathed. Austin handed Edie the measuring spoons, which she tucked into her duffel, and Doug passed her a white bakery bag filled with something that smelled like cinnamon and sugar and deliciousness.

When she hugged him, he gave her a gentle squeeze. "Be careful, friend. Email me when you're free to troubleshoot my cupcake soap."

"I will. Thank you for all your help and the amazing tour." She stepped back. "As soon as we leave, go inside and secure the door, okay?"

Doug's smile crinkled his eyes. "Will do."

"Just as a reminder . . ." Belinda's eyes narrowed on Max, and not in appreciation this time. "I know who you are. If you fuck us over in any way, I'll—"

"Murder us both in the grisliest possible fashion," he finished impatiently. "Yes, we know."

She smirked. "Good."

"Good." Max turned back to Edie. "Ready?"

"Yes. Just . . ." The counterfeiters knew what to do. But she had to say it anyway. "Please stay on guard. You should continue the zombie patrols until you get an all clear from the government. And remember, the creatures aren't the only threat you need to worry about. Whoever set them loose on us . . ."

She shook her head, too angry and disgusted for words. Whoever set them loose had unleashed destruction and violence, knowing innocents would die. The zombies couldn't help their condition, but the unknown saboteurs had chosen to do harm with conscious intent.

They were the true monsters.

"Of course." Austin shook her hand firmly. "Good luck."

"Don't worry, Edie." Doug's sweet smile widened then, turning sharp and pitiless, and the machete he unsheathed from somewhere in his clothing gleamed. "We're prepared to kill anyone or anything we need to. Gladly."

"Okay." Holy gods and goddesses, why was that even more unsettling than Belinda's threat to murder her and Max? "That's . . . good. Right. Um, Max? You're ready to go too?"

"Yes," he said, his palm firm on her lower back, and he didn't need to tell her twice.

14

After Max duct-taped the holes in the windows, the SUV's temperature stayed relatively comfortable. By the time they turned onto the main access road and Edie polished off her first warm cinnamon roll, she was feeling pretty good, considering the circumstances.

As she ate the second roll, she pretended to wipe her sticky hands on his leather seats and hummed the Gaston song between bites just to fuck with Max, and his offended mutterings made her feel even better.

"About ten more minutes until the drawbridge into Zone C." Digging a wet towelette out of her bag, she cleaned her icing-covered fingers. "Do you think that one will be down too? If so, what's our strategy?"

The memory of yesterday's terrifying, zombie-swarmed jump into dark water flashed through her thoughts, and she shivered.

With a flick of his forefinger, he set the temperature in the vehicle even higher. "Scout out the situation ahead of time as best we can. Wait and hide if we see the pack nearby. If we don't—"

"Drive like hells for the other side," she finished for him.

"Exactly." His hands tightened on the steering wheel. "I'll stay on the shoulder, as close to the guardrail as possible. Which is what I should have done last time."

"Max." She reached over to rub his bunched shoulder muscles. "Please be patient with yourself. Neither one of us knows what we're—*Stop!*"

When he stomped on the brake pedal, cursing, the smell of burning rubber filled the SUV. She wrinkled her nose but kept her eyes trained on the roadside.

A dozen tween girls in green uniforms stood in a loose cluster near a stretch of forest. They were sitting ducks. Shit.

As soon as the car juddered to a halt, she flung open the door and ran.

"Edie!" Max shouted behind her, sounding deeply unhappy. "Wait for—"

"All of you need to find immediate shelter," she called as she approached the group. "There's been another breach, and we haven't been able to sound the alarm! The zombies could be anywhere!"

No screaming. No scattering. For fuck's sake, why weren't the kids even *reacting*?

One of the taller girls, her hair arranged in neat box braids and twisted into a bun, moved smoothly in front of the others. Her expression calm, she watched Edie approach without any noticeable surprise or alarm at the news of the breach.

"We'll be fine." She offered a serene smile. "The zombies are already over the bridge and inside Zone C."

Presumably because everyone in Zones A and B was either

dead or holed up somewhere out of reach and the creatures had moved on in search of fresh food. Even so—

"There could be stragglers." Edie skidded to a stop in front of the girls and frantically scanned the area. "We need to locate a house or some other sturdy structure nearby. Preferably one with access to food and water so you'll *stay* fine until this clusterf—" After considering her audience, she rephrased. "This cluster of . . . unfortunateness . . . is over."

Climbing into the trees would serve as a temporary solution, but eventually—

"Woman, you can't just run off." Max had reached her side, and he was eyeing the humans before them in suspicion and obvious disfavor. "Not without waiting for backup."

"Clearly, I can."

Now that she was closer, she recognized the distinctive uniforms. These young women were Girl Explorers, complete with badge-studded vests, and the taller girl must be a troop spokesperson of some sort.

"We're attempting to get word of the breach to authorities outside the Zone, since our internet and cell coverage is down," Edie told her, then frowned. "I assumed that was true here too, but maybe it's not. Have you been able to—"

"We have no way of contacting anyone outside the Zone either. We've been trying since this morning, when the first zombies arrived," the leader said, answering Edie's question-in-progress. "I'm told the door through Wall Four is closed, at least for now. Since the sirens haven't sounded, we figure it hasn't been breached yet, and the creatures are still contained within the Zone."

Edie nodded. "We think that too."

"I'm Riley, Lead Explorer for Troop 3874." The girl stepped forward and offered Edie a firm, confident handshake. "We appreciate your concern for our safety, even though it's unnecessary."

Nearly twitching with anxious impatience and biting back the urge to argue—because really, the Girl Explorers *should* be finding shelter, *pronto*—Edie played along instead. Perhaps a little friendly persuasion could save the girls, even though their instinct for self-preservation had entirely failed them.

"I'm Edie." When she laid her hand on Max's forearm, his muscles there flexed distractingly. "And this is—"

"A vampire," the troop leader said. "Interesting."

Edie sucked in a shocked breath. How in the world could Riley have figured that out upon first meeting him? Three years as his neighbor, and Edie had never even considered the possibility. And oddly enough, the remaining players in their little tableau barely reacted to Riley's statement. The other Girl Explorers simply nodded, as if she'd merely confirmed what they already suspected.

Was there some telltale sign of vampirism Edie should have known about from the start?

Apparently Max had similar questions, because his stare narrowed slightly as he studied Riley. "You're human. How did you know that?"

There was a moment of utter silence.

"Dude." A girl with a high blond ponytail edged in front of Riley. "Look at you. Look at your outfit. Someone *that* hot in all black? Vampire."

He glanced down. "I could be an incredibly handsome goth."

As one, all the girls rolled their eyes.

"No visible piercings." The blonde ticked observations off on her fingers. "No makeup. No black hair. I bet you don't even listen to the Cure."

Edie couldn't resist, despite the urgency of the situation. "Also, you have resting murder face. RMF, if you will."

"Exactly." The girl nodded. "You look like you'd rather maim someone than wallow in unbearable ennui."

His neutral expression became an affronted scowl. "I can maim and wallow at the same time, young woman. I multitask very effectively."

The dregs of Edie's patience abruptly emptied. The girls would find shelter—she hoped to goodness they did—or they wouldn't. Either way, Edie and Max needed to go.

"Which is why he's such a useful companion on our mission," she interjected smoothly. "Speaking of which . . ."

"Enough, Delia." Riley sliced a hand through the air, and her compatriot fell back into the crowd. "You two are trying to get word of the breach to authorities?"

Edie nodded. "Yes. Do you have any additional information we should pass along?"

After considering them for another moment, the troop leader nodded.

"My next-door neighbor is a witch. After the first zombie appeared in our neighborhood, she scried with water to find out what had happened and check the status of all four Zone walls." She spoke slowly, her brow furrowed. "She saw the site where the initial breach occurred. Afterward, she said she couldn't tell for certain, but . . . she believed demons were involved."

Demons. Fucking *demons*. Wow. This *cluster of unfortunateness* kept becoming even more unfortunate by the minute, didn't it?

Max had stiffened beside her. "What's your neighbor's name?"

Why did that matter? Confused, Edie swung to face him, but his face told her nothing. His features might have been carved from granite.

Riley's stare turned distrustful. "Why do you want to know?"

"In case we need to find her and ask for more details," he said, sounding bored. "Obviously."

Well, that was rude.

Sorry, she mouthed to Riley, who merely lifted a shoulder in response.

"If you need to find her, find me first." The troop leader smirked. "You're a vampire. I know you can track my scent from here, as required."

Max inclined his head in acknowledgment, still stone-faced. "Very well."

Edie hadn't realized vampires possessed such a keen sense of smell. It certainly wasn't common knowledge. So how did Riley know? Did she have a vampire friend, or . . . ?

Didn't matter. They had no more time to waste.

"Thank you for sharing your information." She offered the girl a smile of gratitude. "Is there anything else we should know before we get back on the road?"

Riley shook her head, her braids shining in the sun. "That's everything."

The girls still needed to find shelter. Maybe if Edie made one final plea, they might—

"You shouldn't remain out in the open like this," Max said to Riley. "Before we go, we can help you locate a place to hide, if you'll accept our assistance." When Edie stared up at him, pleased surprise at his offer warming her from the inside out, he met her eyes and shrugged in that casual, infuriating, extremely French way he had. "If they died, you'd be sad."

"And . . ." she prompted, hoping for something along the lines of *and I'd rather not have the grisly deaths of a dozen tweens on my conscience either.*

He raised a brow. "And . . . your sadness isn't enjoyable to me."

Her brief beam of approbation turned into a glare, which he confronted without any obvious remorse. There was no good way to determine whether he harbored any real concern of his own for the girls, but she supposed that didn't matter right now either.

Sighing silently, she removed her hand from his arm and ignored his small grunt of protest. When his own hand came to rest on her lower back, though, she didn't shake it off.

"Thank you for your kind concern." Lips twitching in amusement, Riley raised a brow at Max. "But we'll be fine, and we need to warn anyone still outdoors to find secure shelter. Otherwise, our Community Helper badges mean nothing."

At the thought of leaving them behind, every instinct within Edie revolted. Surely there had to be *some* argument that would convince the girls—

"Very well." Max looked down at Edie. "I know their decision distresses you, ma puce. But we can't force them to find shelter, and we need to get back on the road. The sooner we alert the authorities, the sooner *everyone* will be safe."

"Riley . . ." She drew a hitching breath and tried not to picture the entire troop of Girl Explorers sprawled lifeless and bloody across a shadow-soaked forest. "Please."

"Don't worry, Edie. We really will be fine. I promise you." Riley stepped forward, and her hug was quick but warm.

"Besides, we all have our hiking and tracking badges. We'll catch up with you soon enough."

"We have a *car*," Edie said slowly. "So . . ."

How exactly were the girls supposed to catch up with *that*?

Riley and the rest of her troop simply smiled, and before Edie could protest further, they headed into the woods. As soon as they vanished behind the trees, Max's hand on Edie's back urged her toward the SUV.

When he opened the door for her, Edie sighed and boosted herself into the passenger seat. As she situated herself comfortably, he lingered, with one hand braced on the SUV's frame, one hand on the door itself. He was forcing her to stay within the vehicle, an outside observer might conclude. Eliminating her means of escape, like the canny predator he was.

But Edie knew better. Although he was probably tempted to handcuff her to his SUV after her impromptu roadside dash, this wasn't about keeping her inside. This was about making sure any and all threats to her well-being remained safely *outside*.

Unable to resist, she planted a fond kiss on his nose before buckling up. "Thank you for offering to help the girls."

"You were going to volunteer my assistance anyway. I just saved you the trouble." Her door closed with a quiet *thunk*. Then, before she could even blink, he'd sprinted around the hood, boosted himself into the driver's seat, closed his own door, and hit the lock button. "Before we get going, we need to consider what we just heard. If Riley's unnamed witch is correct and the door through Wall Four is closed, we may not be able to leave the Zone."

"And we've now identified the culprits responsible for the breach. Demons." She hesitated. "Assuming we can trust what we were told."

Max's lips thinned. "We don't know anything about this very informative witch. Including whether she or Riley might have an agenda different from ours."

"Yeah." She slumped in her seat. "I hate that we can't take anything at face value. You're right, though. We don't know either of them. They could have some kind of vendetta against demons."

His forefinger tapped against the steering wheel. "Or Supernaturals in general."

"If we manage to get past Wall Four and alert the authorities, whoever caused the breach will be in deep, deep shit. Like, Mariana Trench deep." Her lip stung as she bit it slightly too hard. "I don't want to point the finger at demons if they might not be at fault."

"There would be government payback." He swept an alert glance around their surroundings before speaking again. "Probably vigilante violence against demons by common humans too. Anti-Supernatural bigots have been looking for an excuse for over two decades."

If something she told the government led to that kind of indiscriminate violence, she wasn't certain she could live with herself. "We could simply fail to mention the possibility of demon involvement. Let officials discover it for themselves."

"That might not be possible." His eyes met hers, blue and solemn. "The perpetrators have had ample time to clean up any tangible evidence at the breach site. Scent evidence may be the sole remaining indicator of demonic involvement. And while there's still no good way to erase an olfactory signature, despite the efforts of various Supernatural species, it fades rapidly."

Fuck. "There might not be any traces left by the time authorities arrive."

"Correct." He exhaled slowly. "Even if the human government coordinates with SERC immediately and recruits the urgent assistance of an extremely high-level vampire to gather olfactory clues. We're the only ones who can determine a species' designation from scents too faint for even werewolves to detect."

"And the government may not contact SERC right away." Bowing her head, she dug her fingertips into her temples. "Either because of bureaucratic delays or simple mistrust of their ostensible allies."

"Correct again." His strong fingers massaged the taut muscles of her neck. "I apologize, Edie. I didn't consider scent evidence when we discussed inspecting the site this morning."

Her poor brain was spinning. "You're a high-level vampire. Right?"

He simply looked at her.

"Of course you are. Show-off." She dismissed that question with a wave of her hand. "So you can gather that kind of evidence?"

He raised a single, judgmental brow. "Yes. Obviously."

"Given your previous involvement with SERC, would any testimony you offered be considered reliable evidence?" Because if authorities wouldn't trust his findings, there was no point wasting precious minutes or hours gathering clues at the breach location.

At that, he paused. "Probably. I left under"—another hesitation—"fraught circumstances, but my honesty was never in doubt. And like I said before, I still have a few contacts there."

Her curiosity pricked at her, but there was no time to discuss what, precisely, *fraught circumstances* entailed. They had an immediate decision to make.

Further delays to their alert-the-authorities mission would

only hone her impatience to a killing edge, but … dammit. "I was wrong. We do need to inspect the breach ourselves and gather any remaining scent evidence there. It'll cost us time we don't have, but at least the main zombie pack has already crossed into Zone C. We should be able to get to the site and back relatively quickly."

"Agreed," he said.

His big, cool hand dropped from her nape and gently squeezed her knee. Then he reached for the gearshift, faced forward, and executed a quick U-turn on the access road. Soon enough, they were zipping back toward Wall Two while she devoured another cinnamon roll from her white bakery bag.

The SUV hurtled through the wall and onto the bridge just as she swallowed her last sticky-sweet bite. The water below was more a blur than anything else, and the low barricade between the vehicle and the moat wasn't even visible through her window, not from only a handsbreadth away. He was driving absurdly fast, absurdly close to the concrete barrier.

That should probably make her nervous, shouldn't it? Somehow, though, she just couldn't seem to get there. At this point, only a fool would believe he didn't care about her survival, no matter what edgelord nonsense he spouted. He wouldn't willingly endanger her. In fact, when it came to Max, she had another, much more salient concern jockeying for her attention: namely, what he might risk to keep her safe.

His own safety, definitely. His stupid sword-swinging stunt on the zombie-covered bridge had proven that. Would he risk his immortal life too?

Now, *that* possibility did scare her. More and more with every passing hour.

She didn't want him in danger, and if he landed there anyway, she wanted to help him escape unscathed. But if she didn't understand his capabilities and vulnerabilities, didn't grasp how his species functioned, she couldn't assist or protect him as she needed to. For her to become an asset rather than a liability as his companion, she required far, far more information.

Luckily, she knew just where to start digging. "I'm surprised that Riley was able to identify you as a vampire so quickly, black clothes or no black clothes. How did she know? What signs am I missing?"

With a slight jolt, the SUV cleared the bridge and reentered the main access road through Zone A. Max immediately eased the vehicle closer to the center of their lane and slowed slightly, his brow furrowed in seeming concentration.

"I was surprised too," he said slowly. "Like most vampires, I am, of course, spectacularly hot—"

Edie feigned an enormous yawn.

"—and as a species, we do traditionally wear black clothing, due to countless centuries spent hiding our existence in darkness. But there are quite a few good-looking humans who wear black as well. Not *as* good-looking, clearly, but . . ."

This time, she regaled him with a loud retching noise, which he ignored as he contemplated her question.

"Supernaturals and Enhanced humans can reliably identify one another if given a few moments for study and consideration," he finally said. "The exact mechanism still isn't clear. It might involve pheromones or sensory capacities not yet discovered by researchers. But for whatever reason, almost all of us can do it. The means of identification and level of specificity differ among various groups, though."

Unable to locate any unused wet towelettes, she wiped her sugar-crusted fingers on her coveralls. "What does that mean?"

"As I mentioned earlier, vampires can usually recognize every Supernatural species by scent, but most of us can't be quite so specific with the Enhanced." His sideways glance lingered on her new stain before he shook his head and returned his attention to the road. "When it comes to witches and oracles and so on, the average vampire can only say with certainty what they're not. I.e., common humans or Supernaturals."

"But you're not an average vampire."

He scoffed. "As should be more than evident by now."

"So if Riley were either a Supernatural or Enhanced, you'd have known, and you'd have been able to pinpoint her exact designation by smell alone."

"Correct." Apparently unable to help himself, he reached into his console and plucked out a pristine wet-wipe packet, which he tossed in her lap. "Different species have different identification mechanisms. Elves, for example, primarily recognize other Supernaturals and the Enhanced by appearance. They can typically see through glamours and distinguish visual differences that are too subtle for even vampires to detect."

"Huh." Edie cleaned her fingers and contemplated the new information. "That wet wipe was hiding from me, by the way."

"Sure it was."

In retaliation, she hummed the opening bars of the Gaston song, enjoying his pained expression and faint groan. Once she felt he'd suffered enough, though, she returned to the matter at hand.

"Okay. I get everything you're saying." Shifting in her seat, she angled her legs toward him. "But that still doesn't explain how

Riley identified you at first sight, and it doesn't explain what happened with the other girls."

His brows drew together. "What about the other girls?"

"Weren't they common humans, like me?"

He answered without hesitation. "Yes."

"Then why didn't they look surprised when Riley announced you were a vampire?"

His mouth opened, then closed and stayed that way for a long while. By the time he finally responded, they weren't too far away from their neighborhood and Cloverleaf Drive, where they'd begun their journey.

"I don't know," he said at last, each word emerging slowly. "But that's an excellent question, Edie."

15

After the First Breach, the government had built an extra line of defense between the zombies' underground compound and the settlements in Zone A. As Edie recalled, patching Wall One had taken the assigned workers only a few days, but digging the new wide, deep moat between the wall and those settlements had required weeks of noisy construction. Filling the finished barrier with sufficient water had demanded even more effort from the workers.

Numb and cold and lost, she'd walked over to watch them labor every morning.

One particular task hadn't taken them any time at all, though: building a bridge. Because there wasn't one. No one and nothing was meant to cross that moat. Not troops or officials, not tourists, and certainly not zombies.

And yet. Here Edie and Max were, staring at the moat. Staring at a makeshift bridge.

The rickety-looking wooden structure stretched from a ragged hole in that first, crucial wall all the way across the water and to the other side. To Zone A. To the place where they lived.

Someone had built that crossing of destruction, and that someone wasn't a zombie.

Apparently the government did still post a couple of guards to watch for trouble outside the compound, at least occasionally, because she couldn't stop staring at them either. At least, not until Max stepped between her and their butchered, headless bodies, cupped her face, and turned it his way.

His voice was soft and tender. "Why don't you stay in the SUV, ma puce?"

Blinking hard, she shook her head.

"I already know you're brave to the point of foolishness." His thumbs stroked her cheeks. "You have nothing to prove, my Edie. Nothing to gain by upsetting yourself."

"I might notice something you don't." Suddenly exhausted beyond belief, she waved a hand as Max began to reply. "Yes, yes, I know all about your *inherent superiority* to humans and our paltry sensory capabilities, but I'm just as smart as you are, and I'm observant. I might see a clue you'd overlook on your own or think of a crucial bit of evidence to check."

She wasn't wrong. He knew it. She knew he knew it.

His jaw worked. "Very well."

Mouth drawn into a grim line, he released her face, stepped aside, and let her study the scene however she wanted.

It wasn't the worst thing she'd ever witnessed. But it would probably still live in her nightmares for months or years to come.

"I don't understand." Before speaking again, she had to swallow down the sour taste rising in the back of her throat. "I scout this area at least once a week, so I'd know if there were guards stationed at Wall One all the time. Did they make their rounds here so infrequently that I just didn't notice them?"

Sharp eyes still scanning the scene, he lifted one hand and gently rubbed the back of her neck again. "Since I moved to Cloverleaf Drive, I've seen no evidence of guards posted at this site. My sources haven't mentioned any regular presence at Wall One either."

"Why were they here, then?" Without dislodging his hand, she turned her head to look at him. "Did the government hear rumors of a possible breach attempt and send these people to keep watch?"

"I don't know." For a moment, the burden of untold centuries seemed to engrave itself upon his features, and he no longer looked smug or even confident. Simply . . . tired. "I also don't comprehend how a swarm of officials didn't descend on this spot long before now, immediately after they lost contact with the guards."

Reaching up, she caught his hand in hers, tugged it down from her neck, and entwined their fingers. "I'd think their families would have reported them missing too. Or maybe their shifts normally lasted several days, and they weren't expected home yet?"

Somehow, the thought of the guards' families going about their daily lives, happily unaware that their loved ones had already died days ago, broke her heart into yet more pieces.

Her next inhalation hitched, and his grip on her fingers tightened. His thumb stroked over the back of her hand slowly. Soothingly.

"I don't know," he repeated, the exhaustion in his tone hardening to stony determination. "But I intend to find out."

She allowed that resolve, that self-assured conviction, to soak into her bones. To draw her shoulders straighter and stiffen her spine. "*We* intend to find out."

His denim-blue eyes, now rimmed with black, met hers. "Study the scene, then. Find out what you can. And if you need to stop, just rest in the SUV until I'm done."

He squeezed her hand, pressed a hard kiss to her temple, then let her go and headed for the narrow makeshift bridge. She left him to it, because she had no desire to test either her balance or the jerry-rigged structure's sturdiness.

Swallowing back bile, she slowly walked over to the guards, who'd managed to flee as far as the tree line before succumbing to the onslaught. Maybe if they'd been younger, they'd have made it, but apparently the government hadn't felt the need to assign prime agents to a spot that hadn't seen any disturbance for over two decades. These men couldn't have been far from retirement.

Not a single wedding band between them. Statistically, that seemed a little odd. Or were they not allowed to wear rings on duty?

Their heads had been clawed and chewed from their necks, their empty, white-haired skulls cleaved in two. Classic zombie injuries.

Only . . . what was that mark on the nearest guard's arm?

"Max," she called out. "Come look at this."

After a minute, he reappeared at her side. "Both the hole in the wall and the bridge show distinct tool marks, so the creatures clearly didn't break out on their own. Which we already knew, but it was worth confirming."

"Hmmm." Crouching by the corpse, she pointed a trembling finger at a small blistered spot on the guard's elbow. "Is that a burn?"

He hunkered down beside her. "Yes."

Something smelled . . . odd. The Edie of last week would

never, ever have even imagined what she intended to do next, but that didn't matter. Squeamishness wouldn't get in the way of her survival, or possibly the survival of all humans on this continent.

Bending lower, she sniffed the charred wound. "Rotten eggs. Sulfur?"

"Brimstone. Still remarkably strong, given how long these guards have been dead." He exhaled slowly. "I caught whiffs of it by the wall and on the bridge too. It's the olfactory marker of demonic violence. Under most circumstances, they smell pleasantly smoky, but when they kill . . ."

She crawled to the other body. "This guard has a burn near his ear. It's tiny, but it's there."

"Demons prefer to kill by turning their victims inside out." His thumbnail scratched over his chin as he thought. "It's their signature move. But whoever murdered these guards didn't do that, so this scene could easily be mistaken for pure zombie violence, if common human authorities didn't look closely or recognize the significance of the burn marks. Even the telltale brimstone smell should've dissipated hours before now and become detectable only to the strongest vampires, only for a very brief time longer."

Her brows pinched in thought. "You're certain the guards were killed at the time of the breach?"

"Yes. They've been dead two days." In response to her skeptical glance, he sighed faintly. "I've seen enough corpses to know. Do you want me to explain the signs?"

"*No*," she said quickly. "Okay. So if they died two days ago, why is the sulfur smell still strong enough for a normal human nose to detect?"

She wrinkled hers in emphasis, because the rotten-egg reek wasn't subtle.

His shoulder lifted in that inimitable Gallic shrug. "The demons were dealing with a horde of ravenous zombies they'd just released from captivity. Perhaps the stress heightened their scent. I'm not certain."

"So you think the witch was right." When crouching became uncomfortable, she knelt on the dirt instead. Her coveralls were already stained anyway. "Demons loosed the zombies."

"Maybe." He was silent for a moment. "If so, surveillance footage should clearly indicate their involvement, unless they bought and wore glamours. The zombies escaped before the power and internet went out."

"Or the demons could've broken the cameras before the breach—without getting caught—or altered the feed somehow." Her poor brain. It was attempting, with limited success, to wrap around all the possible scenarios that could explain everything they'd seen. "Could they survive entering the compound with the zombies still inside?"

"It would be highly unpleasant for them. Not fatal."

Something was niggling at the edge of her thoughts, and she couldn't quite grab hold of whatever it might be . . . until . . . yes. That was it.

"If demons did this . . ." A swing of her arm indicated the death and destruction around them. "They were careless. Even if they glamoured themselves or tampered with the footage from inside the compound, there are burns on the victims. Common human authorities should be able to detect the abnormally strong smell of sulfur. And if they somehow couldn't, those authorities would typically cooperate with SERC investigators, who would *definitely* detect it."

She didn't buy that scenario. It didn't smell right, brimstone be damned. "Are demons known for being reckless and sloppy?"

"No. Quite the opposite." Max's fingertip lightly tapped her forehead. "What are you thinking, my Edie?"

"We're missing something." She bent over the bodies again, swallowing against renewed nausea. "Give me a minute. I don't want to disturb the evidence, but . . ."

She forced herself to study the two guards from head to toe. Or, rather, from neck to toe, with the head inspected separately. Max did the same. And just as she was about to give up and concede that demons had probably caused the breach, all her doubts notwithstanding, she finally noticed the creases. Rings of wrinkles in the fabric covering the victims' wrists and ankles, as if they'd been bound in those spots.

"Max." Her hair had swung in front of her eyes, and she tucked it behind her ears. "Can you uncover their wrists and ankles without destroying any evidence?"

From somewhere in his hoodie, he produced the spiky metallic tool he used to open his blood packs and gingerly raised the edge of the nearest guard's cuff with it. Ducking so low her head brushed the ground, she inspected the man's wrist.

The faintest tinge of blue. Bruises. A ring of them.

She tipped her chin, a mute invitation to Max, and he studied the marks too. Sniffed them, his brows snapping together. Then they repeated the process with the bottom of the guard's pants leg. Another ring of bruises. More sniffing.

All four wrists. All four ankles.

"I assume the smell of brimstone can be created without demon involvement." Her hesitance and misgivings now had some rational justification, which was a relief . . . until she considered the further implications. "And burns can be inflicted in a variety of ways."

"You assume correctly."

Sitting back on his heels, Max shifted his attention from the guards and studied their surroundings. The grassy edge of the moat and the sparkling dark water below and the splintered wood of the bridge. The dirt and pine needles underfoot, the ground's surface uneven and furrowed in several spots by a mole or some other burrowing creature. The graceful, arching branches of the trees above. Loblolly pines, red maples, and other species she couldn't identify.

A few branches hung lower than the others. As if a significant weight had dragged them down, and they hadn't yet sprung back to their original positions. A well-fed squirrel, possibly, or a heavy vulture sighting nearby carrion.

Or . . . something else entirely.

"As I said earlier, demons smell like smoke or brimstone. Vampires smell sharp and either piney or metallic. Trolls smell like the earth. And the fae . . ." Max spoke quietly, using his metal spike to lift the guard's wrist cuff again and indicate the near-imperceptible bracelet of bruises underneath. "Roses. Usually fresh ones, but when they feed or turn violent . . . the dead-roses scent is unmistakable. Sweet rot."

For all his surface calm, strong emotion had scored austere lines into Max's aristocratic face once more. If she'd first met him at that moment, she wouldn't have guessed he was in his twenties. She'd have wondered whether those haunted, ancient eyes had witnessed the birth of continents or foreseen the death of all civilization.

"You smelled dead roses on the guards' wrists and ankles." It wasn't a question.

His jaw twitched. "The faintest trace. Another hour, and even the strongest surviving vampire wouldn't be able to detect it."

She could picture what had happened in far-too-vivid detail. Roots erupting from the ground and twining around the guards' ankles. Branches descending from above, circling the men's wrists.

The *elderly* men's wrists. Shit.

Those guards probably hadn't been anywhere near retirement. They just *looked* old.

Newfound certainty settled in her bones, as heavy as lead. "The fae fed on and killed the guards. Then they built the bridge, freed the zombies, let the creatures attack the guards' bodies, and planted signs of demonic involvement to avoid blame."

"Yes." He sounded grim but sure. "I believe so."

"Which means zombies didn't cut our power. The fae did." Suddenly, that odd hotline conversation in Max's house, their lack of cell and internet coverage, and the missing sirens made a lot more sense. "They somehow took over the emergency hotline, waited for the first report of a zombie sighting to confirm their plan was in motion, then disabled our means of communication so we couldn't get word to either authorities or other Zone inhabitants."

He inclined his head, a silent affirmation. "I would guess they've been tampering with whatever information the government and media are receiving about the Zone as well. If officials had received footage of the zombies' escape, no matter the cause, troops would be here already. And if the fae spread word that the Zone's entry door, internet, and phone lines were simply malfunctioning again, and the problem was getting addressed but might take a while to resolve—"

"Then family members and friends wouldn't have any reason to question that story. They'd believe it." Dammit, she needed more ibuprofen. Her head was throbbing. From tension and exhaustion, but also suppressed tears. "They'd continue believing it until Wall Four fell too. At which point, the real slaughter would begin."

Those revelations were important pieces of this horrible puzzle, but she was still missing the overall picture. Still unable to understand the scope of the danger they faced.

"Why would the fae do this?" Her hands fisted on her thighs, hard enough that her ragged fingernails bit into her palms. "Why set a pack of zombies loose on their only source of immortality?"

"I don't know." Blowing out a breath, he stood and glanced around them. "And I don't want you out in the open like this. There could be stragglers. Come on."

She let him take her hand, help her to her feet, and urge her toward the SUV.

Her heart might ache for those two lost guards. Her eyes might prickle. Her fingers might itch to right their bodies, close their eyes, and allow them some dignity after their violent, terrifying deaths. But there was nothing she could do for them right now. Not without disturbing crucial evidence.

As soon as Max had both of them safely settled in the locked vehicle, he clasped her hand again and played idly with her fingers.

"Within SERC, rumors of fae revolutionaries have circulated for years." His words emerged slowly, as if he was thinking through their implications even as he spoke. "There's a significant fae faction that resents working with humans or even cooperating with other Supernaturals. Members of that faction consider all of us their inferiors, and they want out from under the thumb of SERC. They're tired of not using what they see as their full potential or having free rein to do whatever they want."

She frowned, confused. "And how would releasing the zombies and killing humans help them get that power?"

"I don't know," he said again, dragging his free hand through his rumpled hair. "Maybe they really are smarter than everyone else, because I genuinely have no idea what their goal is here. Sowing discord and taking advantage of the resulting chaos, possibly?"

That sounded too nebulous to her. Too slapdash to match the effort and planning that must have gone into this act of destruction and sabotage.

"The zombies can slaughter any common human they encounter. Any Enhanced human too?" When she raised her brows in question, he nodded. "What about Supernaturals?"

"The creatures can and will kill vampires. Shifters." He thought for a moment. "Trolls too, I believe. Demons, elves, and the fae can be injured by zombies, but not slain. I'm not certain about the other species."

With that information, a terrible new possibility stole her breath.

"They . . . they could . . ." Bile rose in her throat once more, bitter and choking, but she forced herself to continue. To explain her theory clearly and quickly. "The fae could use the creatures to wipe out humanity, other than a few common humans kept alive for feeding and breeding purposes, all while pretending to be our allies. Any Supernatural species vulnerable to zombies would die too, and so would the demons, because they'd be blamed for the carnage and murdered in retaliation. And then the fae could slaughter the zombies, along with any other surviving Supernaturals." Despite the heated leather seat cradling her, she shivered. "Do you think that's their plan?"

His fingers stilled against hers. "Maybe. The revolutionaries despise all other species. Perhaps to the point where they wouldn't even want to rule over us, but would rather just have us dead—and they're certainly arrogant enough to believe they could crush any Supernaturals who survived the zombies."

He considered her idea plausible, then, and she wasn't even the slightest bit pleased. In this particular instance, she didn't want to be correct.

"If we went to common human authorities with that theory, would there be sufficient evidence to convince them?" Because she and Max might be right, but if they couldn't prove it, their warning would have no impact. "Based on what you've told me, the dead-rose scent would be long gone by the time they arrived. The burn marks would remain, though, and there would be enough lingering brimstone smell for a Supernatural ally to detect."

His leg jiggled, the movement uncharacteristically restless. "The bruises could be blamed on demons too."

In other words: no. No, there wouldn't be sufficient evidence. No, the authorities wouldn't believe them or suspect fae involvement.

Finding a best-case scenario took some effort, but she persevered. "If we manage to spread word of the breach quickly enough, maybe the government-SERC alliance can drive back the zombies again before it's too late. Like in the Battle for Containment. And while they fight, you can contact your old SERC buddies as soon as possible and persuade them to listen to us."

"Some of my SERC contacts may owe me favors, but they're not my buddies, and they're not going to make enemies of the fae without incontrovertible evidence of wrongdoing." His expressionless tone belied the tension in his shoulders and his near-painful grip of her hand. "As to whether the government-SERC alliance can drive the zombies back into the compound again: By the time the creatures leave the Containment Zone and face organized resistance, they'll be fully fed and at peak strength."

"If the fae truly have left Wall Four impregnable for now, ensuring that strength could be the reason why," she said slowly. "The delay allows the zombies sufficient time to bulk up."

He nodded. "Since they no longer have to eat their young for sustenance, their population will swell rapidly too. And unlike the last battle, they'll have at least some of the fae supporting them. Once they leave the Zone, I don't know whether they can be stopped this time."

They'd filled in enough of the puzzle pieces now. The full, terrifying scope of the disaster was finally becoming clear.

"Here's the thing, Max." She took one deep breath, and then another. They didn't help. "Even if the government believed us, even if the alliance somehow managed to beat back the zombies, large swaths of the human population would want vengeance against Supernaturals as soon as word of the incident spread. It wouldn't matter whether the fae or demons or fucking *sprites* were actually responsible for the breach. All of you would be hunted down and slaughtered. There would be open warfare between humans and Supernaturals."

After a few seconds of eyebrow-furrowing contemplation,

his leg stopped jiggling. "You're right. Which makes this whole matter very simple, my Edie."

She clung to his hand and stared at him, confused as all hells.

"Wall Four hasn't been breached yet. If it were, we'd know." His brow cleared, and his blue eyes met hers with renewed confidence. "There are too many people living just outside the barrier to keep that a secret. Even if the sirens didn't sound, we'd hear helicopters and see other signs of a government response."

"I'm guessing the zombies haven't even gotten close yet," she agreed. "Zone C is by far the largest, and the creatures are on foot. Assuming they followed the most direct path and stayed on the access road, it'd still take them a while."

"And Zone C is far more densely populated than Zones A and B. The zombies will be . . ." He paused, seeming to choose his words carefully. "Preoccupied. They'll . . . have reason to stray from the access road."

Translation: They were too busy slaughtering her Zone neighbors to move quickly.

When he studied her expression, he winced. "I know it's horrifying, my Edie, but it means—"

"We still have one shot to prevent a fucking apocalypse," she finished for him.

She saw what he meant now. The way forward might not be easy or even survivable, but it was relatively straightforward.

"We can't let the zombies leave the Containment Zone." The statement was matter-of-fact, and he even managed to offer her a faint smile. "We have to stop them while they're still contained and before the government finds out what's happening. Then we'll use my SERC contacts to meet with someone discreet on the Council. Someone who won't overreact and can point us toward an equally discreet human government official who *also* won't overreact."

"Because if word of the breach's origin spreads, we're all fucked."

"Correct."

"So that's our plan." She snorted, giddy with dread and gallows humor. "Easy-peasy."

His smile broadened, turning unmistakably fond as he regarded her.

"We'll need help." The logistics were arranging themselves in her brain, forming an orderly to-do list. It was surely missing a few elements, but at least it gave them a place to start. "Every resident of the Containment Zone we can get."

The curve of his lips abruptly flattened into a thin line, and his grip on her hand tightened. But after a long pause, he inclined his head in agreement. "I suppose we will. Unfortunately."

He looked grumpy as hells at the prospect.

"Sorry. I know you're not exactly a group project enthusiast. Or an other-sentient-beings-in-your-vicinity enthusiast." She tipped her head in thought. "Mostly, you seem to like sex and impractical, testicle-entrapping underwear." After another moment of consideration, she concluded, "That's about it."

"I like *you*." The admission sounded aggrieved.

"I'm very likable." She grinned at him, pleased. "But we need more help than just me, and I'm not sure where to start looking for volunteers. Should we go back to the mall and talk to Doug and his merry band of counterfeiters?"

His shoulders rose and fell on a silent sigh. "I doubt they want to announce their presence to a crowd of neighbors. We can ask, but I think we should start elsewhere."

"Where?" She had no other ideas, sadly enough. Max wasn't the only resident of Cloverleaf Drive who needed to get out more.

"Riley mentioned living beside a witch. One powerful enough to scry." His jaw worked. "I may know who that witch is. If I'm correct, she's headed various community advocacy and safety initiatives. She'd know most of her neighbors and their capabilities, and her wife is a strong telepath."

"So between the two of them, they'd make recruiting a zombie-killing team much easier." Which was great news, for all his evident crankiness. Still, she couldn't help but wonder . . . "How in the world do you know her? Your time on SERC?"

Edie was pretty sure he hadn't been hitting any neighborhood block parties in recent years. Mostly because there hadn't been any, but also because he'd rather stake himself than socialize.

"Something like that." A vein in his temple pulsed. "To be clear, I don't know her. I know *of* her. And I hope she knows absolutely nothing about me."

Because he prized his privacy? Because she objected to vampires for some reason?

Given his apparent bad mood and the urgency of their mission, those questions would have to wait.

"Oooooh-kay," she said slowly. "But it's all right to ask for her help?"

"We don't have a choice." His brusque response was the closing of a conversational door. "As soon as I grab a few blood packs from my house, we'll head her way."

Edie frowned, confused. "We don't have her address."

"If we return to the spot on the roadside where we met Riley, I should be able to follow her scent, as she suggested earlier. Hopefully straight back to her home." Seeming to shake off his earlier grouchiness, he raised a smug brow at her. "My tracking ability is just one of my many areas of sensory superiority."

"I see." She scratched the tip of her nose with her middle finger. "So, basically, you're like one of those sniffer dogs. Floppy ears. Wiggling butt as you waddle along."

His gasp of feigned outrage was a thing of beauty.

"How dare you?" Straightening in his seat, he lifted his chin high and *harrumph*ed dramatically. "I do not waddle. I *stride*. Manfully, with the grace of a sexy gazelle."

She tipped her head. "You find gazelles sexy?"

"Perhaps I do." The lofty outrage in his expression fractured a tad, and his mouth twitched. "You, a non-vampire, could not even begin to understand the intricacies of my agile brain and my complex desires."

"If those intricacies include humping a gazelle, I'm okay with not understanding."

He laughed, the remaining tension in his expression falling away.

"You win." His face lit with mirth as he dropped his Pretentious Asshole Vamp shtick and planted a kiss on her cheek. "Buckle up, my Edie. Let's go."

As she clicked her belt into place, she grinned back at him. "No . . . one—"

"Absolutely not."

"—fucks like Gaston—"

"Human."

"—dicks down bucks like Gaston," she sang out as they swung onto the road once again. "With an antelope cock—"

"Neither male nor female gazelles are called bucks. They are in fact antelopes, but—"

"—nobody sucks like Gaston!"

"Vampires are pansexual. Thus, I am quite accomplished in the dick-sucking arts." He paused. "I do draw the line at bestiality, however. I want that made clear."

"In your grassland clime he'll be *forn*-i-cating—"

In the end, shutting her up required another quick stop on the roadside shoulder and a hard kiss.

When they got going again, they might have been headed to their doom. Didn't matter. They were both smiling.

16

At some point, they must have let their guard down. Maybe because they hadn't spotted a zombie for nearly a full day, and they knew—or thought they knew—that the pack remained within Zone C, fully occupied by inflicting grisly violence on helpless residents there.

Still, Edie had no good explanation for how they could fail to anticipate or notice a stray zombie lurking in the most obvious place imaginable: just inside Max's home, hidden behind the front door, which was half hanging from its hinges.

Despite their evident distraction, he insisted—as he always did whenever he thought there was even a slim possibility of danger ahead—on entering the house before her. Given his height and the bottleneck created by the doorway, she couldn't see around him. Couldn't try to intervene before it was far too late.

A shuffling noise, immediately followed by a triumphant, guttural howl and a spray of cool blood across her cheek, was her first warning that something had gone terribly wrong.

She shouted his name, and his hand reached below his nape

to unsheathe his sword, the movement so quick it was little more than a blur. He didn't answer her. Couldn't answer her. Not when he was engaged in full-scale battle with a zombie while—judging from the growing pool of Merlot-red blood at his ever-shifting, agile feet—bleeding heavily.

Very heavily.

Hands shaking with adrenaline, she unzipped her cross-body bag and unearthed her cleaver. She gripped it so tightly her knuckles ached, waiting for the moment when Max would edge forward and allow her to enter the doorway and support him in the fight.

The seconds ticked past. She kept waiting. And waiting.

It took her unforgivably long to realize what he was doing.

As long as he blocked the doorway, she remained safe. Even if it meant he couldn't drive the zombie backward into the hall, where he would have more room to maneuver. By protecting her, he'd put himself in a position where he couldn't pursue an advantage and advance on the creature, and he couldn't easily dodge the creature's tearing claws—or, worse, its ragged, needlelike teeth.

Another few endless moments crawled by, punctuated by rage-soaked growls and grunts of effort and pain.

More blood. Wet ripping noises that indicated tearing flesh. Max's flesh.

Assuming the zombie didn't do the job for her, she was going to *murder him*.

"Fucking *move*, asshole!" she shouted.

No response. He wasn't going to let her inside, the stubborn jackhole, and pushing him forward could destabilize him and might very well lead to his death.

Fine, then. This godsdamn house had more than one entrance, and all of them were currently busted wide open. Turning on her heel, she leapt down from his front porch and raced for the patio around back, whose door—if she remembered the house's layout correctly—would give her a pretty straight shot at the zombie's rear flank. Skidding around the corner of the garage, she slipped and fell heavily to the muddy, brittle grass but immediately heaved herself back upright and kept running.

The patio door hung askew, its window panes' remaining shards of glass tipped with dried yellow blood. She batted the door aside and finally got a clear view of the zombie and the stupid fucking vampire she was going to kill as soon as she saved his stupid fucking life.

The war cry tore from deep in her chest. It rang in her ears and shredded her throat.

"Over here, fucker!" she bellowed, and brandished her cleaver with her feet firmly planted.

Max's startled jerk unbalanced him. In a moment of uncharacteristic awkwardness, he slipped in his own slick blood and fell to one knee, and if she'd wondered how badly he was injured, that answered the question.

Very. Very badly.

Even as he slipped, though, the feral intruder snarled and swung around to confront her. Disaster averted, if only for a few seconds longer.

The creature's red-rimmed eyes narrowed on her, agleam with animal cunning. For a heartbeat, she and the zombie simply studied each other, sizing up their new opponent.

The intonation vibrating in its throat sounded remarkably like a raspy *bonjour*.

Max had come very, very close to cutting out its heart. The gash wept yolky blood but was placed slightly too far to one side. The zombie's neck also gaped wide from a neat slice that hadn't gone quite deep enough. Other glancing wounds dribbled miserly amounts of viscous fluid, but clearly none of them were sufficient to end the battle.

The same couldn't be said for Max's injuries. She had no idea how he was still scrambling upright or even breathing after suffering that kind of damage. While she'd been running around to the back of his home, he'd obviously taken another claw swipe to his own neck, one that tore his flesh there into raw meat, with ivory bone visible in several places and blood pouring in a ceaseless stream down his torso. Other sets of ragged, parallel furrows marked his upper body, the creature's claws biting hard enough to rip through muscle and cause the average human to bleed out within minutes.

As he'd so often reminded her, he wasn't human. But he wasn't made of stone either. Even though he was immortal, he could still fucking *die*, and that outcome seemed entirely plausible in this moment.

And then there was the issue of whether he'd been bitten. Whether a fluid exchange had occurred. Whether a vampire might transform after a bite, as a human would, within ten minutes.

If he'd received a bite, the clock had already started counting down.

But that was a problem for later. Right now, she had a zombie to kill.

Max's eyes burned into hers as she tore up her throat with another battle cry—the better to distract the creature and draw it away from her half-dead vampire. Even through all the blood, his scowl should have turned her to stone.

"Edie!" he roared, and actually had the nerve to sound angry at *her*. "Get out!"

Instead, she charged forward, his lost blood a red haze clouding her thoughts. The zombie that was bounding toward her—while grunting something that could have been *magnifique*—had hurt Max. *Max*. When she was done with that gray-skinned fucker, it wouldn't have an ounce of that yellow fucking blood left in its misbegotten fucking—

With a sudden fierce lunge from behind, Max chopped off the creature's head. Spraying fluid, it landed with a *thump* and a *squish* on the faded, curling linoleum, swiftly followed by the louder *thud* of the zombie's body collapsing in a heap maybe two feet in front of her.

Max staggered to the nearest wall and braced himself with a heavily bleeding arm while he used his other hand to keep his gushing neck attached to his shoulders. He sagged there, bent over at the waist as he gasped for breath and glared up at her through his lashes.

His skin had turned as pale as any Hollywood vampire, and it scared the hells out of her. When she rushed toward him, though, he held up a staying hand.

"Max—" she began, stopping a step away from him.

"Wasn't bitten." His voice was rough and low, his tone urgent. "Couldn't avoid claws, but kept its teeth away. I think. Can't be sure. If I'm wrong, stake me. Right through my heart. Or cut off my head." To her shock, he managed a thin huff of laughter. "Job's already half-done. Easy . . . peasy, right?"

Her brain promptly supplied the image. The gleam of her

knife raised high. The crunch of cleaving bone. Weak spurts of Merlot-hued blood. His head rolling away, his eyes open and sightless. His chest stilled forever.

She twisted away from him, jackknifed forward, and dryheaved violently. Her eyes watered at the force of it, her breath coming in choked sobs between every jolting retch. Max tried to push off the wall to get to her, but he was too weak to stand without assistance.

"Edie." He sounded desolate now. "Don't."

She shook her head, unable to speak. He gave her a few moments to calm herself, then issued more orders she wasn't certain she could follow. Even if it might save her life.

"Elevator," he rasped, one hand still clamped to his neck. "Get us belowground. Check for bites. If you find one, do it. Put me down. Promise."

"I'm . . ." Raising her head, she gagged anew and swallowed back bitter saliva. "I'm not sure I can promise that, Max."

A similar promise had nearly destroyed her once. She wasn't putting herself in the same position again.

"Either promise or . . ." By leaning his shoulder against the wall, he was able to free a hand to delve into his hoodie pocket. When he looked up a moment later, he had a smooth, viciously sharp wooden stake clutched in his red-stained grip. "Won't risk you. I'll do it myself, right now. Bite or no bite."

Oh fuck. He would. She knew he would. Other than her promise, the only thing that could stop him might be a physical confrontation.

When her eyes fell to his shaky grip, he gritted out, "Still strong enough, human. Don't test me. *Promise*."

Her retching had stopped, but her tears hadn't. She sheathed her cleaver, slapped the moisture away from her cheeks, and made herself say it. "I promise."

Uttering the words felt like issuing her own death sentence. Part of her—the softer, more hopeful bits—wouldn't survive keeping that vow. Not this time.

She'd honor it, though. Even if it killed her as surely as it did him.

"Thank you, ma puce." The terrible tension in his face and body eased a fraction. "Down now. Safer."

When she took a cautious step toward him, he didn't ward her off again. Instead, he muttered instructions, directing her supportive hold around his hips as his less-injured arm settled heavily over her shoulders. He leaned much of his weight on her, trusting her to keep them both steady while they moved down the hall toward the discreetly hidden elevator.

Once he told her the trick, the door opened. She haltingly hauled them both within the tight confines of the lavish cab, trying to be as gentle with him as possible. Some of her burden eased as he sagged against the wall, and she exhaled quietly in relief.

The entrance slid shut. The long descent began.

"Strip me." When she stared up at him in shock, mouth dropping open, he actually rolled his eyes. "Check for bite marks."

She'd been hoping to delay that task as long as possible. Depending on what she saw, she might be forced to act on her promise, and she'd do almost anything to avoid that. Anything except letting him preemptively kill himself on her behalf. Which the asshole would actually do if she didn't inspect him for bites, so . . .

Godsdammit.

With his limited help and the judicious use of a knife—getting both arms out of his sleeves when he had one hand wrapped around his neck wound required a few strategic cuts—she managed to bare his upper body. But it was impossible to tell whether he'd been bitten under all that blood.

"I won't know until I clean you off some." Locating one of his few patches of intact flesh, she stroked his inner forearm soothingly, the pressure of her fingertips featherlight. "I'll do that when we arrive. No point in taking off anything else before then."

Legitimate excuses for avoiding potential murder and heartbreak were the *best* excuses.

He side-eyed her a bit. But after a glance down at his chest, which was simultaneously crusted with old blood and wet with fresh blood, he silently conceded the point. Carefully angling himself lower, his breath hitching in pain, he kissed the top of her head. Which only made her want to cry again. She gave his waist the gentlest possible squeeze in response, and his soft sigh ruffled her hair.

After another few seconds of their descent, her fingers began to twitch with impatience. Even though she didn't want to proceed with her inspection, she *did* want to treat and bind his wounds, and she couldn't do that until they actually *reached their destination.*

"Oh my gods and goddesses," she said when she couldn't stand it anymore. "Is this fancy-ass elevator as old as you are? Because the ride may be smooth, but the speed is *geriatric.*"

She didn't expect a response to her complaint. Based on his wheezing inhalations, she figured he should conserve his remaining strength for the last bit of their journey. Besides, he had to know she was only taunting him to distract them both from his pain, her anxiety, and whatever horrors might lie ahead.

To her surprise, however, he did speak. Not about the elevator or even his undisclosed age. About her. About *them*.

"I wanted . . ." When he shifted, he gasped a little. "I wanted to be alone. Three years ago. I came . . . to Zone A . . . to be alone. Was going to buy a house down the road. Far away from neighbors." His nose nudged her temple. "I saw you walking. Scouting, holding your . . . cleaver. You smiled. Waved at . . . at a total stranger."

Upon ransacking her memory, she found . . . nothing. She hadn't marked that moment in her mind. Didn't recall the first time she'd ever encountered Max.

Exhaling deeply, she tried to set aside her bitter regret. "I don't remember. I'm so sorry."

"You wouldn't." He nuzzled into her hair, the gesture playful and affectionate. "It was . . . automatic. Just who you are."

Her heart swelled, even as it twisted in her chest. "Honey, you should save your—"

"You . . . wore stained coveralls and boots. Hadn't brushed your hair . . . in days, looked like. Tangled. Always tangled. But such a shiny brown. Such a . . . pretty face. Such a pretty woman. So . . . soft everywhere. Doe eyes, big and bright." He raised his head then. His gaze locked on hers, his own eyes as warm and unguarded as she'd ever seen them. "Smile like the sun."

She was frozen in place. Speechless. Because of his words and the emotion in them. Because of his expression as he spoke.

The elevator door opened, and he didn't budge. "Moved next

door. You were so . . . patient. Kind. Even with . . . fucking *Chad*. Brought brownies. Delicious. First power outage, you gave me . . . candles. Didn't know I . . . had a generator."

"Max." As hungry as she was for his memories, his revelations, she needed to treat his wounds. "We should—"

"Two nights ago . . . didn't offer shelter . . . out of obligation. Wanted . . . *needed* you safe. If you got hurt . . . couldn't stand it." His voice grew louder, steadier, as he forced whatever strength he had left into his words. "Remember that. No matter what happens next. Whatever you have to do, ma puce."

When she hiccupped, blinded by tears, he dropped his forehead to hers.

"No guilt, sweet Edie. I . . ." He listed to the side, and suddenly she was bearing as much of his weight as she could handle. "I'd die . . . grateful. Knowing . . . you were safe. Seeing your face. I'd see it even with . . . eyes closed."

Before she could muster a response other than continued weeping, he used her support to take one halting step out of the elevator. Two.

Then he collapsed on the floor of the hidden library, cried out in pain, and fainted.

BY THE TIME Edie returned from her frantic supply run, Max's fingers had begun to twitch. Setting down her armful, she dropped to his side and laid her hand gently over his, but he didn't open his eyes or respond to his name. After a minute or two, he began mumbling indecipherably. A woman's name—Jackie? Jacquelyn?—and something about . . . Yanni?

Maybe Max harbored surprisingly intense feelings about New Age music?

Edie couldn't quite make out everything, but his increasing agitation was clear. His spasms of movement were becoming more violent, his words more guttural. A snarl of rage twisted his features one moment, followed by a flinch of unspeakable agony.

Whether that pain primarily came from his unsettled dreams or his battered and torn body, she couldn't have said. But his flailing was exacerbating his injuries, so once she got the gash in his neck clean and bound, calming him became her top priority.

She wasn't strong enough to restrain him, so she'd have to take a different tack.

He didn't have many unmarred stretches of skin, but she found them. Stroked them, murmuring words of comfort. And slowly, bit by bit, his distress and tension waned. His jerky movements stilled once she began gently carding through his hair. When she traced his cheekbones, his disturbed muttering subsided into an occasional murmur, and he turned his face into her open hand, nuzzling her palm.

Eventually he calmed for good, and she could address his other lacerations.

He didn't stay unconscious much longer. Which relieved at least some of her anxiety, because she hadn't been certain when or if he'd wake up again. It was a real shame for him, though, since she was still wrestling him out of his remaining clothing, cleaning blood from his too-pale skin, and bandaging his open wounds, and the whole process must hurt like fuck.

As he returned to his unfortunate senses, he was lying prostrate on a gorgeously thick, silky rug of rapidly depreciating value, wearing nothing but his boxer briefs. After her desperate search for necessary supplies, she'd filled a decorative bronze bowl with warm water and was gently soaking and sweeping away the crusted blood from his spine with the softest hand towel she could find. The red-tinted runoff soaked into the priceless textile beneath them, and she was trying her best not to notice the ever-spreading stains.

Unable to find bandages of sufficient size in his first aid kit, she'd ripped up some of his designer shirts to bind his wounds. Tearing apart fancy shit had been oddly satisfying, she had to admit. Even though her fingers shook with dread the entire time.

His hand flexed, then reached tentatively toward his neck and encountered multiple blood-soaked strips of very smooth cotton holding that whole region of his body together.

"Is that . . ." He paused, and his voice was a little stronger when he started again. "Did you use my micro-striped Trecapi cotton button-down as a bandage?"

She couldn't see his frown, but she could hear it. "Hard to say."

"Why . . ." His muscles jumped under her light touch as she moved to a fresh patch of carnage on his shoulder. "Why is it hard to say? Either you irreparably ravaged my favorite shirt or you didn't, human."

"Trecapi. *Trecapi*." She tested the unfamiliar word on her tongue, hoping it would chase away the metallic taste of fear. Tried rolling the *r* and failed utterly. "Does that involve orange juice somehow?"

His head turned slightly, the movement drawing a groan from deep in his chest. "What the . . . hells are you talking about?"

"Wait." The current clump of dried blood was particularly

stubborn, so she dipped the hand towel back into the bowl and tried again. "I was probably thinking of Tropicana. Sorry."

Could they do this forever? Maybe if they bantered long enough, he'd never remember the crucial issue at hand. Literally, right beneath her hand.

Where she'd just spotted teeth marks.

He actually snorted. "Edie. You're killing me."

With that ill-chosen turn of phrase, his fingers curled into a fist, his shoulder turned to granite beneath her fingertips, and any hint of levity between them disappeared.

She sniffled, loudly.

He waited, and they both knew what for.

"Tell me," he said after a moment. "Now."

Not a suggestion, but a firm imperative. And he had the right to know. She understood that. It was just . . .

Her hand stilled, and she bowed her head. "I haven't had time to look everywhere, but . . . there are scratches here. Where I'm touching you. They don't look like claw marks."

"Teeth?"

"Maybe." Almost definitely. "The skin isn't broken, Max, so let's not assume—"

"I'm a vampire. The wound could have partially healed already."

The stake rested on the gleaming wood of the library floor, right next to the rug where he lay. Within easy reach. One blurred movement, and he had it gripped tightly in his hand.

She'd thought about moving it far away while he remained unconscious. Hiding it until he was either healed or undeniably transformed. But she'd never forgive anyone who stole her ability to decide the terms of her own life and death, so she'd forced herself to leave it near him, hoping like hells he'd bide his time and not do anything rash. Especially since they didn't yet have definitive proof of his eventual fate.

"Yes. You're a vampire. Which means we don't actually know what would happen if you *were* bitten deeply enough for a fluid exchange," she rushed to point out. "And let me emphasize this again: Whether that even occurred is something *else* we don't know."

She laid her palm over the scratches as an Enhanced healer would, begging all the gods and goddesses for their intercession. For an entirely unprecedented flow of energy through her body and into his. For a bearable future, however long that future might be.

Nothing happened, of course. She wasn't a conduit for the divinities, and she contained within her no real power, other than hope and determination.

"How . . ." He grunted, shifting uncomfortably on the floor. "How long has it been?"

Although he didn't sound convinced by her argument, he didn't stake himself either, and she considered that a victory. As she fumbled for her cell, she smeared his diluted blood across her bag and her screen. Only to recall that she hadn't checked the time at any point between their zombie encounter and now, so she had no good answer for him.

"You were out for maybe five minutes?" It was her best guess. "And it took us at least another five minutes to get down here after I confronted the zombie. So that's ten minutes, Max. Ten minutes and no zombification. I think you're good." She paused. "Well, still horribly injured. I meant *good* in a relative, yay-I'm-not-turning-into-a-brain-slurper sense."

"Transformation . . ." His speech had begun slurring a bit. Slowing down. "Might take longer . . . for vampires."

Even as he spoke, the tension in his body seemed to drain away, leaving him limp against the floor once more. Dipping the hand towel back into the warm water, she slowly swept it up his relatively undamaged spine, then back down, encouraging his relaxation. Urging him without words to rest.

"It could. Or maybe there was no fluid exchange."

"Hmmm." He gingerly turned his head again, meeting her eyes for the first time since his collapse. His lids were heavy, the blue of his irises hazy, but his next words turned sharp again. "Sleep will speed my healing. I need it. But if anything happens, my Edie, if you see any signs that I'm—"

"Yes, yes. I *know*. If you go all chompy, I'll take care of it, *dude*. I already promised." Gods, did they need to discuss this for the millionth time? Glaring at him even as her sinuses prickled and filled, she mimed a karate chop near his jugular. "Cleaver. Neck. Hack hack."

For good measure, she added a gargling death sound at the end.

And that seemed to be what he needed, bizarrely enough, because he let those half-lidded eyes close entirely then. His mouth even curved a little in what might have been an actual smile. "Good. Thank you, ma puce."

"Thank yourself," she muttered sourly. "Jerkface."

"Don't mind if I do. Thanks, me."

Yes, that was definitely a smile, and if he weren't so injured, she would have been tempted to smack it right off him. But he *was* terribly injured, so she took his hand instead and cradled it between both of hers. Tears slid down her cheeks, and she didn't try to stop them. Didn't bother blinking them away.

"While you sleep, I'll take care of you. No matter what it t-takes," she told him, her voice cracking. "You can trust me."

His other hand lifted off the floor. In a slow, deliberate movement, he uncurled his fingers. The stake dropped soundlessly to the carpet, and he nudged it a few inches away.

"I know," he said, and fell asleep.

17

Other than some surprisingly vigorous snoring—Edie would have to mock Max for that later—and a lot of healing, nothing much happened as he slept. No agitated thrashing. No transformation. No decapitation. No additional trauma.

Minute by minute, though, his bleeding waned as the rents in his flesh turned shallow and slowly knit together. The less egregious injuries disappeared entirely within a couple of hours, and while the gaping wound at his neck required longer to mend, at some point his eventual recovery became a factual prediction rather than wild conjecture or the panic-stricken hope of a desperate woman.

He would live. Probably wouldn't even have scars to show for his troubles.

When she knew that for certain, when she was absolutely sure he'd be fine sooner rather than later and wouldn't require the neck-rending services of her cleaver, she tucked a pillow beneath his head, covered him with a thick, down-filled duvet, rose up from her stiff, sore knees, and stumbled to his bedroom. To his en suite shower, where she washed his blood off her numb limbs with trembling hands. To his bed, where she huddled naked beneath the covers and finally allowed herself a much-needed, much-delayed breakdown.

For a while, she was too busy shaking and crying to think much, other than a brief moment of wondering whether she'd gotten snot on his very nice sheets.

Spoiler alert! Of course she had.

But once she'd calmed enough to gather her thoughts, she couldn't avoid the obvious any longer: She cared about Max. A lot. Like, *a lot* a lot.

She'd like to believe that witnessing anyone's near-fatal battle with a zombie would distress and panic her, as would promising to personally cleave someone's neck before they fully transformed into a violent, brain-gulping creature.

But Max wasn't just *anyone* or *someone* to her. Not anymore.

Mere *distress* and *panic* couldn't describe her emotional response, not unless she redefined the words. Not unless they encompassed a riptide of gut-wrenching terror, twisting and yanking at her as she flailed helplessly, sucking her deep where she couldn't breathe, couldn't think, couldn't do anything but drown in her own fear and devastation.

She hadn't experienced anything even remotely comparable in a long, long time. Twenty years, to be exact. And no amount of denial could fully hide the significance of that, despite how inconvenient her emotions were or how ill-fated her connection to him might be.

The unbroken stretches of her heart were no longer entirely her own.

Her instincts told her to run like hells. She even had a great excuse for leaving: The sooner someone alerted the witch and began putting together a zombie-containment force of Zone inhabitants, the better, right? And Edie could definitely find her, even without a trail-sniffing vampire or the internet. Almost certainly. Somehow.

So she could take her car and drive away right now. She could force a rupture in the ever-strengthening tether that connected the two of them. She could leave Max to his healing and pretend she was being noble and mission-focused.

But she couldn't lie to herself. Fleeing wouldn't be noble. It would be cowardly. The act of a woman unwilling to risk further agony and grief. And honestly, leaving wasn't even a real possibility, because he was unconscious and vulnerable, and when he woke up, he might need her. He might be too weak to reach his blood packs, given how much of his own blood he'd lost. He might go feral or starve in her absence. If she were confronted by another stray zombie and died, who would help him? Who would even know he was down here, much less understand how to breach his security measures and reach him in time?

He trusted her. *Her.* A human woman with tangled, rarely brushed hair, stained coveralls, and a weakness for preservative-laden foodstuffs.

How could she just abandon him?

She couldn't. She wouldn't.

While he slept, she'd take a brief nap of her own. She'd get her shit together. She'd muster the courage she needed for the fight ahead and a future she could no longer predict.

When he woke up, she'd help him and let him help her. That

tether between them would probably keep strengthening, and if it broke, she wouldn't be the reason why.

Come what may, she'd stay by his side. From now until . . .

Well, she hoped the end wouldn't be bitter. But if it was, so be it. Some things were important enough to justify any risk.

Even a mere human could see that.

ACCORDING TO MAXI'S security cameras, the sun had just dipped below the horizon when he woke again. From her comfortable little blanket-wrapped nest on his library sofa, she watched him blink in sleepy confusion for a few seconds before his gaze sharpened. Prodding at his neck, he gave a small, pleased nod.

Other than his continuing paleness, he looked good. Alert. Strong. Gratifyingly non-perforated. She let herself appreciate the sight in silence as she chewed.

Abruptly, his look of satisfaction darkened into a ferocious scowl. He sat up in a single swift motion, and the duvet she'd draped over him fell to his waist. He impatiently shoved it aside and leapt to his feet, his narrow-eyed gaze searching the room.

Then he spotted her. Her mouth still full, she raised her free hand and wiggled her fingers in a welcoming wave.

Letting out a relieved breath, he thumped back onto the rug. "There you are, human."

"Here I am," she confirmed after swallowing.

He scrubbed his palms over his face. "I thought you might have gone up to the surface to get your duffel. If you'd met another stray while you were alone . . ." His throat shifted as he swallowed hard. "Anyway. You were wise to wait. I can accompany you."

Discreetly, she tucked the can by her hip beneath the blanket, along with her fork. "Yep. Super wise. That's me."

"What time is it?"

He began testing the recovery of his various muscle groups. His broad shoulders bunched and released, swiftly followed by his biceps and triceps, then his pecs, and her mouth promptly went drier than even a meal of not-falafel could explain.

"Right about dusk." Dammit, she was thirsty. But if she got out her juice box—

"So it's too late to find the witch tonight." He rotated his neck, his mouth pinched into a thin line. "Fuck."

Now. Now was her chance, with his face pointed the other way.

With an unobtrusive swipe of her wrist across her mouth, a telltale crumb went flying. "How are you feeling?"

Because *she* was feeling pretty hopeful about his overall recovery. Also pleased with her exemplary level of sneakiness and subtlety.

"Hungry." One shoulder, gleaming in the lamplight, lifted in a shrug. "Otherwise fine."

Hmmm. "Even your neck?"

"Still stings a little." He flipped a dismissive hand. "Some blood and another hour or two will take care of it."

"Let me have a look." She began untangling herself from her cocoon of blankets, tossing them aside carelessly. "If it's closed up enough, we can take off the—"

Her can clanged as it hit the wooden floorboards. Her fork landed somewhere near his knee. One piece of not-falafel rolled gently until it hit the side of the rug.

"Um." Her gaze surveyed the room, studiously avoiding the rug and anyone who might happen to be sitting atop said rug, but she could still sense his eyes on her. The heat of his glare should have singed her skin. "Maybe I should wash my hands before touching your wounds. I'll just—"

"Edie." His voice was a furious, gravelly rasp. "What the *fuck*."

Turned out, her shit was decidedly *not together*, despite her earlier attempt at gathering it into a neat, manageable pile. At the anger in his voice, his chiding tone, all her repressed emotion broke over her head like a wave, filling her lungs until she couldn't seem to catch a breath.

She threw her hands in the air, her sinuses afire. "I was *starving*, asshole! It was an exhausting, shitty day, and you were unconscious from having your godsdamn neck nearly *clawed the fuck off*, and I didn't have any internet to distract me, and I was painfully hungry, okay? So sue me for not waiting when I had no idea how long you'd be out, dickwad!"

"Edie," he repeated, much more softly.

"And you know what makes a human woman *especially fucking hungry*?" she spat out. "When she's forced to watch someone she cares about fighting a fucking *zombie* without letting her fucking *help*. Risking his life to protect her, even though that's *the last fucking thing she wants happening ever again*. And then, when he's *bleeding the fuck out* before her very eyes, *then* she gets to spend an hour or two with a fucking cleaver clutched in her sweaty fucking hand, bracing herself for the possibility that he might turn into a fucking *brain slurper* and she might have to fucking *murder* him, even though she l—"

Cutting herself off just in time, she gave a frustrated growl and slapped the moisture from her cheeks. "I checked the security footage before going anywhere and brought my fucking knife, asswipe. I was fucking *vigilant*. I've been taking care of myself for years, and I'm not a godsdamn moron. So fuck you, fucking *Gaston*. Don't you *dare* yell at me, you Beast-tormenting French jackass!"

Snarling and muttering to herself, she bent down to reclaim her can and her fork and stabbed at her missing sphere of not-falafel on the floor. After shoving it in her mouth, she plopped back onto the couch and chewed belligerently, all while glaring directly into his eyes. Even though she couldn't see him that clearly through her angry tears.

The good news: The salt from those tears added a necessary bit of extra seasoning to the starchy not-falafel. The bad news: More salt seemed to be arriving by the moment, and she was going to choke to death if she kept hiccupping as she chewed.

Silently, he handed her the pomegranate-lime juice box, which had apparently fallen to the floor with everything else. While she coughed and sputtered and tried to wash down her mouthful of food, he cautiously perched beside her on the sofa and circled a soothing hand between her shoulder blades.

She was too exhausted and dispirited to jerk away from him. Besides, the Beast-tormenting French jackass gave a good back rub.

After another minute, he scooted closer, then closer again, until he was pressed tightly to her side. His arm wrapped around her shoulders. Then his other arm encircled her too, gently turning her to face him. And then her can and fork were neatly set aside on a nearby table, she was on his lap, and he was tucking her against his chest, one broad palm stroking up and down her spine while the other cradled her head and urged her face into his bandaged neck.

"I'm sorry," he murmured. "I'm sorry, my Edie."

She sniffled and wiped her wet nose on his shoulder. "I didn't do anything wrong."

"I know you didn't." He paused. "Other than using my skin as your tissue just now."

"You deserved that." For good measure, she did it again.

"I suppose I did." He kissed her hair. "Although, and I feel this must be noted—"

"No, it mustn't. You can shove that note right up your be-thonged ass."

"—there are torn strips of exquisitely woven cotton literally an arm's length away. Ones you could have used as a handker-chief. Both times."

"Your fancy shirts can go fuck themselves for all I care," she grumbled.

"That's fair. Not to mention logically possible."

Try as she might, she couldn't entirely stifle her amused huff. His shoulders lowered a fraction at the sound of it, and—his mission achieved—he let the conversation end there.

He began carding his fingers sweetly through her hair, detan-gling it strand by strand. Her scalp tingled with each tiny, pain-less tug. She sniffled loudly at the tenderness of his touch, its patience and consideration, and he rocked her a little in response.

Eventually, she managed to stop crying again. Which was when he spoke quietly into her ear, as humble and solemn as she'd ever heard him.

"I was angry at myself, ma puce, not you." Even once her hair slipped smoothly through his fingers, he kept playing with it. "When we entered my house, I was inattentive and careless with our safety. Because of that carelessness, I put you in a position where you had to relive your worst memories and watch me get injured, and I put myself in a position where I had to extract a terrible promise from you. Thereby upsetting you to the point where your sweet face got blotchy and swollen and your pretty eyes turned red from crying. Then, to top it all off, I found out I was incapacitated when you needed food and protection, entirely due to my own stupidity."

If he was trying to earn her forgiveness, the sincerity and self-deprecation and compliments were definitely helping. The reference to her tear-ravaged face? Not so much.

"And now I've upset you again," he unwisely added. "So you're even more blotchy and swollen, and you have full-on albino rabbit eyes."

When she lifted her head to glower blearily at him, he backtracked. "You're as lovely as ever, obviously. Albeit somewhat damper than usual."

"*Hmph.*" Another swipe of her runny nose against his neck relieved her feelings considerably. "Asswipe."

His voice turned coaxing. "Albino rabbits are adorable, are they not?"

Yes. "Maybe."

"Not so much because of the eyes, I must admit, but—"

"Oh my gods." She began laughing helplessly. "Please tell me you're doing this on purpose, *dude*, because if you aren't . . ."

He didn't actually need to tell her, though. She knew. In part because she was beginning to understand how he dealt with emotion, both hers and his own. But mostly because his entire body relaxed against hers when she laughed, all the terrible tension keeping his muscles taut and his posture stiff simply . . . vanishing. In an instant.

For such a condescending, infuriating vampire, he was really kind of a sweetheart.

Outside his house, the last traces of light would have already vanished from the horizon. They weren't going anywhere until morning, so there was no need to hurry. In the wake of her emotional outburst and his uncharacteristic openness, they could hold each other until they both fully calmed, or as long as they damn well wanted.

Apparently *as long as they damn well wanted* meant *a really fucking long time.*

After countless minutes of cuddling, he murmured, "Edie, love, I don't know how to ensure you survive this . . ." He sighed, somehow gathering her closer. "This cluster of unfortunateness."

"Ensuring my survival isn't your responsibility, Max." She poked him in the shoulder. "Even if it were, there are no guarantees. Not ever. Not for anyone. Even immortals like you."

He continued as if she hadn't spoken. "Despite what your human stories told you, I can't turn you into a vampire with a simple bite. If I could, I would've already done it. Without hesitation."

It was a noble sentiment, she supposed, as well as an unmistakable marker of how deeply he actually cared for her. But also arrogant as hells, because—

"Who said I want to be a vampire?" she demanded with a frown.

He laughed at her. Actually *laughed.* With a sweeping gesture, he drew her attention to his impressive body and undeniably gorgeous face, then their luxurious surroundings.

"Oh, sweet Edie." His expression mingled amusement with total incredulity. "Who *wouldn't* want to be a vampire?"

She leaned back a few inches so he could watch her eyes roll to the ceiling, with all its ornate plaster medallions. "Do we need to move out into your living room? I'm worried you don't have sufficient room in here for your ego. It must be feeling cramped."

"Your concern is noted and appreciated, human," he declared loftily, "but my ego is fine. Exemplary, in fact. The envy of all. Much like the rest of me."

"Of course." A mere two-word response couldn't hold a sufficient amount of sarcasm, but she shoved as much in there as possible. With impressive results, if she did say so herself.

"Thank you for that entirely sincere and heartfelt acknowledgment." His smirk slowly faded from his face, revealing the concern hidden underneath. "Since I can't turn you into a vampire, I keep searching for some other way to make you harder to kill. Another means to keep you alive. Through our upcoming battle, but also indefinitely. Forever, if at all possible."

"Sounds exhausting." Or so she'd keep telling herself, since immortality wasn't something she could achieve.

His face changed then, his brow crinkling in thought. "Huh."

"What?" When he didn't answer, she repeated, "*What?*"

He failed to explain himself. Instead, he simply rested his lips against her forehead—and when they curved into a slow smile, she could feel it.

"Well, this isn't alarming. Not at all," she muttered, and he only laughed again.

Sheesh. What a jerkface.

It was a real shame she was falling in love with said jerkface. Luckily, she probably wouldn't survive long enough to suffer the consequences.

Hooray?

18

Eventually, Edie wiggled free of Max's embrace long enough to reclaim her dinner, while he took the world's briefest shower and donned some silky-looking lounge pants.

As soon as he returned, she crawled back into his lap, forked up another bite, and tried not to think about how close the zombies might be to the final containment wall or whether they might breach that wall too before morning.

Traveling at night with a pack on the loose and strays roving nearby was a death sentence. Her untimely demise would help no one. Not Max. Not her Zone neighbors. Not all the hapless humans and Supernaturals unaware of the threat gathering only one stone wall away. All of which she kept telling herself, again and again, in hopes of relieving some of the crushing guilt currently roiling her stomach.

Max watched her chew with horrified fascination. "I'm going to regret this, but I have to know. Does I Can't Believe It's Not Falafel taste like falafel?"

"Nope." She swallowed with difficulty. "Not at all."

"Chickpeas?"

"Not even a little."

His brow creased further. "Fava beans?"

"I don't think so?" After a swig of pomegranate-lime juice and another bite, she was able to confirm, "No. No hint of fava beans."

"Herbs? Spices?"

She shook her head, chewing industriously.

His lips formed a disapproving line. "Preservatives and fillers moistened sufficiently to form glutinous brown clumps?"

"Huh." Her brows rose as she considered the description. "Yeah. Yeah, that's it."

"*Edie.*"

She raised a shoulder. "Still not seeing the gourmet feast your cook prepared for us, dude. A woman has needs."

"As do we all, human." His mouth softened, and his gaze drifted over her tank top and panties before lingering at the crook of her neck. "As do we all."

That look had become familiar to her over the last two days. Familiar and welcome.

Swallowing the last bite of not-falafel required sucking back her final sip of juice. Before she could even ask where to put the empty containers and her fork, Max gathered them and set them aside.

He resettled her atop his lap, astride his hips, his broad hands gently but firmly positioning her exactly as he intended. Her own hands gripped his satiny shoulders for balance, and she arched back. Offered herself to him.

She'd sat exactly like this once before. Felt the give of couch cushions beneath her knees, the rise of his cock between her legs, the delicious pressure against her cotton-covered clit, the taut tension in his muscled thighs as he flexed and lifted his body for their mutual pleasure.

A repeat of that experience would be more than welcome right now.

With a light sweep of his thumb, he stroked the line of her collarbone, then slowly traced the deep scoop of her neckline, his eyes pinned to his task. The texture of her skin seemed to absorb his full attention. The way it slid smoothly under the pad of his finger, then prickled into gooseflesh as soon as her nerves registered the contact, rising in bumps to greet him.

His lips curved faintly. "Do you want me, ma puce?"

That light, taunting thumb trailed over the ribbed cotton of her tank and rode the curve of her breast downward. When he reached her hardening nipple, he rubbed it softly. Sweetly. It shouldn't have been enough to make her gasp and clench deep inside, but it was. It did.

"No," she said.

His hand immediately stilled, then lifted entirely away from her.

"No?" To his credit, he didn't sound angry. Simply curious.

"This isn't simple *want* anymore. I'm well past that point." Reaching for the tucked-in edge of his makeshift bandage, she unwound it carefully from around his neck. "I *need* you."

Her need wasn't just physical, and it wasn't just about distraction. But he didn't need to know that. Not yet. Maybe not ever.

As he'd slept, she'd periodically checked his various wounds and removed the bloodstained strips of shirt covering them as soon as he'd healed. The gash in his neck—the most serious of his injuries by far—wasn't quite gone yet. It remained red and painful-looking. But it was now entirely closed and in no danger of reopening. He was done bleeding for the night, assuming her ragged nails didn't bite too deeply into his skin when she came.

Ducking her head, she brushed a kiss over that angry red line.

"Sweet Edie." He sighed and moved his hands to her hips. Massaged there lightly. Pressed down until her clit rubbed against his dick. "Let me give you what you need. What we both need. Let me fuck you, love."

"Mmmm." Lazily, she ground down against him and gloried in his hitched breath. "You made me a promise, Max. About what would happen when we had enough time."

"I did. I said I'll—" When she rolled her hips again, his head tipped back, digging into the sofa's cushioned edge, and he inhaled sharply through his nose. "I'll fuck you so long, you'll feel empty without my dick stretching your hot little chatte. So hard, you'll feel me in your throat. And you'll come for me until you cry."

She had to close her eyes at that, if only for a moment. "You took some paraphrasing liberties there, but I'm prepared to accept your amendments to our agreement."

"Generous of you." Deliberately, he took her hand, squeezed it between their bodies, and curved her palm around his thick cock. "Ma bite is going to be your new best friend, sweet Edie. Use it for your pleasure."

She smiled, her stare holding his as she scooted backward on his lap. Far enough that she could drag his lounge pants lower in front and ease his erection free from the fabric.

Gripping him firmly, she rubbed the head of his cock over her clit. Shit, it felt amazing, even through her panties. So amazing she couldn't help squirming in his lap and moaning.

"Just like that," he whispered hoarsely. "Just like that."

"So good." Unable to hold back, she sped up her movements. Rubbed harder. Faster. Her lids slipped shut, and stars began to burst behind her lids, white-hot and blinding-bright. "You make me feel so fucking *good*, Max."

"Edie." He gripped her shoulders. "Edie. Stop."

She released his dick with a plaintive sound, dazed and so damn close to an orgasm she wanted to weep. When she tried to slide off his lap, though, he held her in place.

"When you come, I want you naked and spread out on my bed, not half-clothed on a couch," he told her. "And before we go any further, you need to tell me whether you want my bite."

She'd thought the answer to that question was obvious. "Max, we're about to fuck. Of course you'll drink from me."

"One source of pleasure doesn't necessitate another, ma puce." He kissed her nose. "You can tell me no. You can *always* tell me no."

Her delayed-orgasm crankiness receded at that kiss, at that declaration, and she offered him a small, genuine smile.

"If you don't want my bite, I should open a blood bag and feed now, before getting my mouth on your skin. The way you taste, the way you feel . . ." He shook his head, his thumb teasing the base of her neck. "It's too good. Too much. It'll muddle my thoughts and intentions, and I might instinctively bite you. Even if we've decided I shouldn't."

Her head tipped, and she studied him curiously. "I imagine fresh blood tastes better."

"Usually. Not always. Yours, sweet Edie, is . . ." His gaze clouding over, he ran his tongue over his incisor. "Spectacular."

Pleased by that, she wiggled a bit. "Does blood straight from the tap help with healing or strength, over and above what the packaged stuff can do?"

"Marginally." His hand flicked in a dismissive gesture. "But I'm mostly healed already, so a bag or two will give me sufficient strength for whatever needs doing."

"Or whoever," she pointed out, unable to resist.

A corner of his mouth tipped upward in a tiny, sexy smirk. "Correct."

"That would be me."

"That would be you." Shaking his head at her, he nuzzled a kiss into the corner of her wide grin. "This is no longer an emergency situation, Edie. I don't want you to agree to feed me out of obligation, or to be nice, or because you want me to heal faster, or for any reason other than the right one. The *only* right one."

"Which is?"

His grip on her shoulders tightened, and the warmth in his gaze turned molten, his irises darkening to obsidian. "Because you want it too. Because you need me inside you in every way possible, and my bite makes you come so hard you think you're dying."

The zombies might have been a million miles away. They might never have existed at all. There was only Max, only pleasure and lust, only the long night they'd burn through together.

"So many promises, vampire boy." Slowly, she rose up in his lap, leaned forward, and sank her teeth into his lower lip. When she spoke, every word brushed her mouth against his. "Bite me. Fuck me. Start keeping them."

He didn't respond in words. Instead, with a smile as sharp and hot as a newly forged blade, he took her hand and led her to his bedroom.

* * *

IN THE GOLDEN glow of a corner lamp, Edie spread her legs for him.

The silky sheets rustled beneath her, a pillow raised her ass high, and Max's hands urged her even wider, until another scant inch would strain her muscles. He knelt between her thighs, naked, cupping the backs of her knees. Lifting and bending them. Exposing her to his heavy, dark stare.

She was naked too. Entirely bare to him, all fading bruises and eager lust.

His forefinger slid down through her curls, then traced the seam of her body, parting her vulva. Opening her further to him. Cool air swept over damp, private flesh, and she shivered.

"Next time," he murmured. "Next time, my Edie, you'll sit on my face and fuck it. I don't require much oxygen. You can force-feed me this delicious chatte until you're all I can see or taste or breathe. Put my mouth and nose exactly where you want them, grind down, and take everything you need."

Distantly, she wondered why, exactly, they weren't doing that right now. Because it sounded really, really fun.

"So pretty here. So pretty everywhere." His thumb slowly circled her entrance, then dipped inside in a shallow, fleeting tease as his forefinger lightly petted the hood over her swelling clit. "I want it, ma puce. All this beauty is mine."

With every touch, her breath hitched.

"Next time, you can take me." He dropped to his belly then. Stretched out. Slid his strong arms beneath her thighs and laid heavy hands on her hips. Held her in place, every steady breath ruffling her pubic hair. "Tonight, I take you."

She couldn't see him anymore. Not over the swell of her own belly. But there was no missing what she felt, what he was making her feel, and every other sense was swamped in him too. The mint lingering on her tongue from his ravenous open-mouthed kisses on the way to his bedroom. The sharp eucalyptus scent filling her lungs with every ragged inhalation. The faint growl rumbling in his throat as he held himself perfectly still and studied her for an endless fever-bright minute.

The stream of air he blew over her vulva wasn't even a little hot. It still burned.

She moaned and shifted restlessly, and he smiled. She couldn't watch him do it, but she knew it was happening, knew how it would look. She could re-create its infuriating, glorious arrogance in precise detail.

"I'm hungry, darling." His lips skimmed over the very tip of her clit. "I'll eat, and you'll give me what I need. You'll beg to give me more."

Okay, enough. It was time to justify that towering ego.

"Dude." Reaching down, she laced her fingers through that dark gold hair, took a good grip, and yanked. "Less tongue talking. More tongue fucking."

When he laughed, he did so against her increasingly slick flesh, and she gasped at the vibration. Then he licked away all that slickness like a spill of honey, his tongue agile and soft and relentless. It swept over her clit and along her folds, turned firm and slipped inside her for a shallow, slick, twisting thrust. His nose nudged, and his teeth scraped faintly, and the hungry sounds he made hummed over her nerve endings like her very favorite sex toy.

His fingertips teased her entrance, circling and rubbing as he settled in for a long, slow, luxurious suck of her clit. Delirious, panting, eyes squeezed closed, she untangled one hand from his hair and cupped her own breast. Pinched her stiff nipple until the jolt of pleasure connected her tit to the playful swirl of his tongue and draw of his mouth between her thighs.

When her hips hitched higher, seeking more pressure, he shoved them right back down and held her in place, forcing her to take only what he gave her.

White heat built deep in her belly, and her legs began to tremble. She twitched against his tongue, the tension in her body growing with each lick, each hum, each leisurely suck, and this time she could actually *feel* his self-satisfied smile against her flesh.

"Not yet, sweet Edie," he crooned, the words an open taunt. "Patience."

Then his lips and tongue slid off to the side, and she tugged viciously at his stupidly thick hair and groaned in disbelief, because where the *fuck* was he going?

His open mouth trailed over her labia and dragged through her curls. Pushing her right knee to the mattress with one hand, he nuzzled his face between her heaving belly and the top of her thigh. He fastened his mouth there and sucked hard enough to bruise, blood rushing to the surface of her skin as her nerves prickled. The pressure increased in two distinct spots, rising almost to the point of pain.

His other palm slid between her legs and squeezed until she moaned.

"Yes?" he grated out, and it took her a few seconds to grasp what he was asking.

Her femoral artery. His fangs. Her hunger and his, satisfied in one bite.

"Oh gods, please." The bastard still wouldn't let her lift her hips, and she squirmed against his inexorable hold, her nails digging into his scalp. "*Max*."

His fangs pierced her flesh at the same moment he sank three fingers inside her and thumbed her clit, and the strangled noise echoing in her ears might as well have come from a stranger, because she didn't recognize it.

His long fingers fucked and twisted inside her as she tugged sharply at her nipple. And each pull from his mouth on her thigh, every swallow of her blood, felt like slow, relentless suction on the same spot where his thumb rubbed and stroked and pressed.

Splayed helplessly beneath him, she came within moments, pulsing against his hand in voluptuous wet spasms with each racking wave of pleasure. A long, drawn-out moan from deep in her throat vibrated with the sound of his name.

He kept working her body relentlessly, kept swallowing her blood and teasing her clit, as she shook and gasped. When the clench of her body around his fingers began to weaken at last, he finally raised his head, and she could feel the slide of warm liquid over her thigh. Blood welling from his bite.

"So sweet, my Edie." He pressed a soft kiss on her clit, still fucking her steadily with his tireless, twisting fingers. "Again."

His eager tongue lapped up the trail of blood, and then his fangs slid into her flesh once more. His mouth sealed over the bite as he sucked and swallowed and made starbursts appear behind her eyelids, and she threw her head back with a cry.

Delirious with pleasure, she eventually orgasmed again, and

probably a third time too. By that point, her thoughts were more than a bit hazy, and she didn't consciously pay attention to much of anything until he was crawling up her body and telling her how gorgeously she came for him. Gripping his hard cock, he knelt between her limp legs and pumped himself a couple of times before sliding a condom down the thick length of his erection.

Dazed, quivering and empty without him inside her anywhere, she blinked up at him when he pushed her knees high and wide again. He interlaced their fingers, stretched her arms above her head, and lowered himself atop her trembling body, pressing their knotted hands deep into the mattress as he nudged against her entrance.

"Need to have you, my Edie. Sink my dick inside that slick chatte," he rasped, a small smear of blood staining the corner of his mouth. "Bite your neck."

Then he waited, those soft lips curled into a snarl, his incisors long and red-tipped, his eyes black as pitch and inferno-hot.

When her fingers flexed in his, he bore down with more of his weight, a silent rejoinder. She wasn't going anywhere. Not until he allowed it.

Only . . . he was still waiting for the words. For consent.

If she told him no, he'd climb off her right now, his cock still stiff and needy. All his forcefulness, all the fierce demand in his claim, was for her. Because it turned her on, and he knew it. Had probably smelled her arousal and seen her pupils blow wide every time he took control and made promises he was clearly able to keep.

So she wrapped her legs around his hips, a silent claim of her own. Arched her back and rubbed her slick vulva along his throbbing dick now that she could move her lower body again.

His snarl deepened, a growl vibrating in his throat, but he continued waiting for her verdict. Continued justifying the trust she'd placed in him and the lust she felt for him.

He'd waited long enough. They both had.

"Fuck me." Lifting her head, she brushed a light, tender kiss over his swollen lower lip. "Drink from me. Now."

His fingers tightened, pressing their hands even deeper into the mattress, but his mouth was soft against hers, the press of his lips a sweet caress. When he ended the languid, exploring kiss, he nuzzled the tip of his nose against hers, the gesture unmistakably fond.

He smelled like her. Tasted like her. In such a close embrace, she'd fill his entire field of vision. He'd see nothing but her, just as she saw nothing but him.

She smiled up at him, and his breath hitched.

Then he finally, finally notched the head of his cock exactly where she wanted it.

Holding her stare, he pushed inside her for the first time. She was already oversensitive from coming repeatedly, and he penetrated her inch by deliberate inch, making her feel every bit of it, the stretch and pressure of his dick splitting her open in slow motion. The endless slide was glorious, slick and leisurely, her every nerve firing with pleasure as he sank deeper and deeper.

When her eyelids slipped shut, his hips stilled. His chin nudged hers.

"Let me see those pretty brown eyes." When she bit her lip, he freed the pinched flesh with a sweep of his tongue. "Don't hide, ma puce. I want all of you."

She was desperately afraid he already *had* all of her. Terrified he might see it in her eyes. But she couldn't deny him, and she wouldn't deny herself either. With her eyes closed, she couldn't watch his pleasure. Couldn't bask in the sight of him drunk on her blood and her body.

As soon as her eyes opened, he kissed her again. "There you are. Thank you, darling."

His hips snapped forward, and he ground into her, making her take the last inch of his cock. The avid hunger in those dark, dark eyes flared hotter as she exhaled in a long moan, and she couldn't have looked away again, even if she'd wanted to.

He reared up over her then, using their entwined hands as leverage, and began to fuck her. Hard enough to snatch her breath and white out her brain, so smoothly she could have cried with the joy of having Max—confident, knowledgeable, attentive Max—inside her at last. Max, who brought her nothing but pleasure even as his fangs scraped down her throat.

Her body jolted each time he bottomed out, and when he rotated his hips and rubbed right where she needed pressure and friction, she squirmed beneath him. A fuse lit within her, desire turning to desperation, and she hitched her legs higher on his back and spread her thighs wider.

"That's—" He grunted into her neck as he sank even deeper. "That's right, Edie. Give me what's mine."

The heat between her legs flickered brighter with each heavy thrust, and she laughed, the sound a joyful challenge. "Give it? Thought you—*ah*—were gonna—*fuck*—take it. *Chad*."

He snorted breathlessly and raised his head. "Apologies. Let me—rectify—"

"Gods," she moaned.

"—the situation—"

"*Yes*." Her mouth fell open as he slowly pulled out of her. "Wait, where are you—"

"—immediately."

Then he spread her open again with his dick, shoving it deep and grinding hard, even as he lunged for her throat. His fangs sank into her flesh, the sting distinct and sharp, as if he was too fuck-addled to remember all his usual expertise.

Somehow, even that pain arrowed directly to the spot where his cock stretched her wide.

Then, abruptly, the pinch was gone, leaving only the drugging caresses of his soft lips against her throat and long pulls of his open, wet mouth. The pleasure echoed everywhere, sparking to life in every nerve, every secret reach of flesh. He could have been pulling her nipples taut with his teeth, tonguing the backs of her knees, drawing the sensitive bend of her inner elbow into his mouth until he left bruises, a reminder of where he'd been and what he'd done to her. He might have been tongue fucking her or sucking her clit into his ravenous mouth.

He should have been a mere dream. A fantasy of fangs and lust and devotion.

"Edie," he groaned into her neck, and let go of her hand so he could reach down between them and feel their connection, trace her stretched, aching entrance as she took everything he had, again and again, before he finally—finally—gave her needy clit a firm little slap.

She had no breath to scream when she came. The orgasm obliterated everything.

Her nails clawed into his shoulders, his arms, as she scrabbled closer and spread her legs wider and clamped down on his dick over and over, seeing nothing despite her wide-open eyes, hearing nothing even as her voice shredded in her throat, feeling nothing but—

Oh gods, ecstasy. Not just pleasure. Actual godsdamn *ecstasy*.

He's going to be absolutely insufferable after this, she thought dimly a long time later, once a few synapses began firing again.

Somehow, she was still climaxing. Still twitching around his cock, albeit less violently. At least until he rubbed roughly at her clit and his mouth drew hard on her throat and she was full-on coming once more with a sharp cry, shaking apart beneath him with each spasm.

"Yes." His tongue dragged over her throat, closing the wounds he'd inflicted, and she sobbed as he kept fucking her deep into his mattress, faster and even harder. "*Mine*."

"I'm yours," she agreed, her voice thin and hoarse, because there was no point denying it now. "And you're—oh *fuck*—mine."

A ragged sound ripped from his heaving chest, and his hands dug beneath her and clamped on her ass and held her steady as he planted his dick as far inside her as he could. His bloodstained fangs gleamed in the lamplight when his body arched above hers, and he jerked against her in a powerful, racking orgasm, throat-tearing groans and gravelly, incoherent words pouring from his gaping mouth.

"Shit—so fucking *good*—never like this . . ." He moaned, his hips bucking powerfully enough to shove them both farther up the mattress. "Beautiful—my Edie—yours . . . *gods*."

Somehow, she came again with his final thrusts. Not as hard, but ... yeah. Definitely a climax. She kind of hoped he didn't notice, what with his own climactic ecstasy to process, because the known universe wouldn't be enormous enough to contain his ego if he realized exactly how many orgasms he'd wrung out of her.

That was when she started to laugh, because everything was so ridiculous. *He* was so ridiculous, but also so amazing and undeniably gifted in the dicking arts.

Then again, she'd clearly given him a good time too. When he finally collapsed on top of her, he was actually *warm*. Sweaty, even, with heavy-lidded, pleasure-dazed eyes the color of faded denim. She took real pride in that.

He was also heavy. Very, very heavy. She stopped laughing then, largely because she couldn't breathe all that well.

After a few uncomfortable moments, he must have noticed all the wheezing and rib poking, because he rolled to the side. After disposing of the condom, goodness knew where, he dragged her back into his arms, hugged her fiercely, and planted a hard, lingering kiss on the crown of her head.

Reality filtered back into her consciousness, which was a damn shame.

Because this entire situation was a true heartbreaker, wasn't it? The two of them couldn't simply hole up together, shut out the world, fuck for a few weeks. The sirens might sound at any moment, indicating that zombies had already escaped the Zone and started tearing through the helpless population awaiting them outside, and a Supernatural-versus-human war was about to erupt. If the sirens *didn't* sound, she and Max had to leave with the sunrise, muster a zombie-fighting force, battle the aforementioned zombies, and somehow make various important officials believe their cockamamie-yet-accurate story.

One or both of them probably wouldn't even *survive*.

Their timing was absolute shit. But it was kind of hard to feel much dread or sadness after such a ludicrous number of climaxes, so . . . that was a plus, right?

"I said you'd come until you cried," he murmured into her hair, "because I didn't know coming until you laughed was an option. But I consider that an even greater achievement."

She cleared her throat, deciding to try for nonchalance. "Yeah. Your bites have . . . quite an effect."

"Bites alone wouldn't make you orgasm like that, human." Benevolent superiority saturated every smug word. "Trust me."

Okay, he sounded entirely too satisfied with himself. "I assume you used other vampire sex tricks or your Supernatural powers, then."

"No tricks or powers necessary," he told her breezily. "Unless you consider my incredible stamina, my total dedication to your pleasure, and my vast quantity of natural fucking-related talent to be *tricks*. And while I am, obviously, a creature of great and ineffable power, I didn't require its usage to make you come like a godsdamn freight train. Five times."

Oh good. He'd missed one of them.

"No, wait." At which point, the jerkface made a big production of counting it out. "Three times with my mouth and hands, then four . . . five . . . six. Six times in total. A full half dozen."

He let her go and edged back a few inches, all so she could more clearly see his smirk and watch him hold up one hand, palm out, along with his other thumb.

"*Six*," he emphasized.

In response, she held up one finger. A single, very expressive finger. And when his obnoxious beam only became brighter and cockier, she realized her mistake.

"Oh, darling," he said condescendingly. "You already did."

She feigned a heavy sigh. "I knew you'd rub this in."

He mimed fingering her. "And so I did. Quite spectacularly."

"*Dammit*, Chad."

This time, when she laughed, he laughed too.

19

Far too early the next morning, Edie and Max showered, donned fresh clothing, and discussed anything other than what awaited them that day.

"Chad thinks a clitoris is related to a rhinoceros," she said as she checked her knives, sheathed them, and tucked them away. "Or maybe a hippopotamus. Every time he hears that old song, he wants one for Christmas."

Max snorted. "No, he thinks they're fictional. Like unicorns, or remunerative work."

"He thinks a clitoris is a new hybrid car model." She filled a fluted wineglass with tap water. "And he's not a fan of models found outside the pages of *Sports Illustrated*'s annual Swimsuit Issue."

"Because a clitoris has a hood, he thinks it's shy and he shouldn't bother it." When she choked on her water, he rubbed her back until she could talk again.

Clearing her throat, she pretended to push a button repeatedly. "The first time a hookup pointed out her clitoris, he kept booping it and waiting for candy to emerge from her vagina."

That did the trick. The tension darkening Max's irises and stiffening his frame abruptly disappeared as he began laughing.

"God, Edie." His chin dipped to his chest, and his shoulders quaked. "You win."

"What's that?" She cupped a hand around her ear. "What did you say? I couldn't quite hear you. Please say it again, much more loudly."

Raising his head and a cocky brow, he held up six fingers again, like he'd been doing all morning. Only this time she actually believed that annoyingly supercilious smile.

"I faked it," she told him. "Every time. Mentally, I was compiling a grocery list."

His grin broadened. "Unless your grocery list makes you squirt, I think not."

"So crude." She rubbed her hands over her face so he couldn't see her snicker. "You'd think someone your age would have more class. That age being . . . what?"

Silence.

"Was Pangaea still a thing? Or had the continents drifted apart already?"

When she uncovered her face, he was shaking his head at her. Still grinning. And gods, she hated to return their attention to more serious matters, but time was slipping through their fingers. They didn't have much left, not if they wanted to leave at dawn.

"Speaking of groceries . . ." Zipping her coveralls up to her neck, she looked over at him regretfully. "I need to get some from my house before we leave. I'll change out these bloody sneakers for boots there too."

The boots would serve her better in battle. Besides, she didn't need to see a reminder of Max's near-fatal injuries every time she looked down, even if his body no longer had so much as a scratch on it.

He inclined his head in acknowledgment, his smile fading to nothing. "I'm still satisfied from yesterday's feeding. I won't eat again until tonight."

"Are you sure?" Her brow crinkled. "You could just drink from me. We wouldn't have to do . . . uh, anything else."

Surely he could be quicker about it than he'd been the previous night. Treat her like a human Go-Gurt rather than his three-course dinner at the world's sexiest, nakedest restaurant.

"If I took any more, I'd weaken you for today's exertions, my Edie. I'd rather starve." When she began to protest, he raised a hand. "But I won't need to, as I remain full and will have blood packs available to me should that change."

He'd produced a new, sturdy-looking backpack from somewhere, and it now held a half dozen blood packs squirreled away in various pockets, as well as a couple of openers.

"Fine. Should I . . ." She thought back to her last blood drive donation as she slung her bag across her body and gathered up her duffel. "Do I need to drink orange juice or have cookies or whatever? To ensure I don't become faint today?"

"No. I was careful, and you had one of your . . ." A pained expression drew his features taut. "One of your *juice boxes* afterward, as well as some"—he shuddered—"*Pizza Jerky*. You'll suffer no ill effects from the feeding."

She'd been intending to munch on cheese cubes and granola bars and other less objectionable foodstuffs from her home today, but . . . nah. Not after he'd made *that* face. Eating her weirdest nonperishable shit in front of him would be *way* more fun.

His thumbnail scraped over his chin, and he looked contemplative for a moment. "That said, I should start stocking human food in my refrigerator. *Fresh* human food. Whose ingredients don't necessitate a chemistry degree to pronounce correctly."

Well. That was a statement right there.

Slowly, her lips curved as she gazed at him from across the enormous kitchen island.

He anticipated her future presence in his home—and he hadn't made it sound like a short-term exigency, something that might occur only until the danger fully passed.

He'd made it sound like he *wanted* her here. Indefinitely.

His back angled away from her, and he moved something small and silvery from the cut-up, blood-soaked remains of his old black leather hoodie into . . . his *new* black leather hoodie.

"Wow, Max. You're a vampiric stereotype." She rounded the island, suddenly itchy to leave. The sooner they took care of the zombie menace once and for all, the sooner she could hang out with him in his lair without a godsdamn clock ticking. "Do you even own any clothing that's not either black or the result of an X-rated arts and crafts project?"

For the rest of her—possibly very short—life, those macramé undies would continue to bring her untold amounts of joy. Whatever visionary had first thought of entrusting testicles to a latticework of knotted fibers? Chef's kiss to them.

"You wouldn't recognize high fashion if it reared up and bit you, human." He sniffed and secured a final zipper, turning to her. "Which I know for a fact, since it *did* rear up and bite you. Pleasurably so, for all parties involved."

"High fashion?" Her gaze rose to the starkly modern light fixture overhead. "You were naked, dude."

"I'm high fashion made flesh, *dude*." After donning his backpack, he took her hand and led her toward the open door of his little library. "Its very personification and exemplar, whether I choose to grace clothing with my superlative beauty or remain gloriously nude."

She patted her free palm over a wide, feigned yawn. "And, as always, high fashion left me entirely unimpressed."

He dropped her hand and held up six fingers. She pinched his ass and ignored them.

But by the time they wedged themselves into his tiny, luxurious elevator and rose to meet their fates, they were holding hands again. Kissing too. Because Max might not be the embodiment of fashion, but his tongue?

Yeah. What he could do with that was indeed a thing of *superlative beauty*.

MAX'S SUV DIDN'T start.

No zombie encounters had yet occurred, so that was a real plus. But since yesterday's abuse had apparently sapped his vehicle's will to live, and they didn't have time to troubleshoot whatever the issue might be, they were now stuck driving her compact sedan instead. Which—to their mutual, if unspoken, consternation—featured neither bulletproof glass nor fancy tires that could handle a horde of climbing, jumping zombies without popping.

Nor—to Max's solitary, decidedly spoken, and annoyingly *loud* consternation—did her car boast fine leather seats that turned toasty-warm with the flick of a switch.

"The vents are still blowing cold air," he complained as they backed out of the driveway.

"At least my windshield doesn't have duct-taped holes in it. Those weren't exactly warm either, Max. And bulletproof glass only helps if it isn't already smashed in various places."

"My lips will get chapped." His tone implied that such an occurrence would rival the tragedy of the *Hindenburg*. Oh, the vampire-manity.

"Gods and goddesses, Max," she told him, checking her rearview mirror. "You are *such* a little bitch."

"Take that back, woman." In pursuit of more legroom, he adjusted his seat for the third time. "I'm not little *anything*. Which you can now confirm from firsthand experience."

She put the car into Drive. "Fine. You're an *enormous* bitch."

"Thank you."

"My pleasure."

His fingers drummed on the console as they trundled through their neighborhood. "I'm getting you new tires with actual tread as soon as this shitstorm is over. Dammit, Edie, you must hydroplane whenever the fucking *humidity* gets too high. No rain necessary."

"Are you my goth-vamp sugar daddy now?" she asked interestedly.

"You wish, human." He paused. "But . . . maybe. If that title made you accept new tires."

"Nice try. But no."

Her bank account could absorb the hit. She simply hadn't taken the time to deal with the issue, and there hadn't been anyone else in her life who'd have noticed her bald tires. Noticed and cared enough about them—about her—to raise a fuss. Until now.

Drawing himself upright, he raised a peremptory finger. "To be clear: If I *were* your sugar daddy, I'd excel at the role. You'd be the envy of ... uh ..."

She waited at a red traffic light as he searched for the right phrasing.

"You'd be the envy of all recipients of sugar daddy services—"

"Sugar babies, Max," she supplied. "They're called sugar babies."

"You'd be the envy of every *sugar baby* worldwide."

"Of course I would." Her forefinger pushed the appropriate button, and her window opened several freezing-cold inches. When he looked at her incredulously, she explained, "I'm allowing a little extra room for your ego."

The red light turned green, and she took a left onto the main access road. When she'd accelerated enough to reach the speed limit, she raised the window again, steadied the steering wheel with her elbows, and ripped open her huge bag of neon-orange puffed ... things.

Some sort of grain had been part of the manufacturing process. Probably.

"Fucking hells, Edie," he groaned, and she aimed a satisfied smile at the windshield.

By the time they made it to the roadside spot where they'd last seen Riley and the other Girl Explorers, she was full of both preservatives and glee at Max's discomfiture. Unfortunately, however, the latter faded as soon as she concentrated on the tasks ahead.

Before leaving her car, they scanned their surroundings and

ensured their weapons remained in easy reach, because neither wanted a repeat of the previous day's debacle. Then, without a word, she let him lead her into the woods as he tracked Riley's scent trail.

While they walked along, Max's nostrils flaring every so often, she kept watch and rested a hand on her sheathed cleaver. If, from time to time, she also whispered a bit of encouragement—"What's that, Lassie? Timmy fell into the well? Good boy!"—that was only to be expected.

He couldn't divert enough of his attention for an effective glare in response, but she wasn't hurt. It was the murderous thought that counted.

Ten minutes later, they stood in front of a small brick duplex.

He nodded toward the left door. "Riley's residence."

After taking good whiffs of the buildings on either side, he shook his head, then approached the duplex's right door.

Immediately, his shoulders stiffened. "A witch and a telepath live here."

Edie strode forward to ring the bell. There were footsteps and rustling noises behind the door—the homeowner checking the peephole, no doubt—before the wooden barrier swung open.

A twentysomething woman with coppery brown skin, a long ponytail, and a knife strapped to her thigh stood framed in the doorway, her dark eyes sharp with suspicion, her feet braced in a battle-ready stance.

"Hi!" Edie waved. "I'm so sorry to bother you, but we couldn't afford to wait. I'm—"

"Edie. Riley warned me you might show up sooner or later. I'm Sabrina." The other woman offered her a tight smile before turning to Max. "Vampire."

"Witch," he responded with silky cordiality.

There were far more important matters at hand, Edie knew. Given the circumstances, this encounter had already taken far too long, but . . . yeah. She had to say it.

"Sabrina?" Edie tried very, very hard not to snort. "You're a witch named . . . Sabrina?"

"My parents had a weakness for nineties sitcoms," Sabrina the Twentysomething Witch muttered. "Just ask my brother Urkel."

Edie turned away and coughed. Loudly.

"Sorry," she choked out. "Swallowed wrong."

Max thumped her back, his own stern expression cracking a little at the edges.

The witch rapidly regained both her composure and her wary scowl. "I want your name, vamp. Then I want to know why I should let a blood-hungry, far-too-powerful creature of violence past my wards and into my home."

Yikes. The creation of the Supernatural and Enhanced Ruling Council must have been *fun*.

He took his time replying, and when he finally spoke, he sounded bored. "All our lives are at stake. And if I'd intended harm to you, you'd know by now."

"*Max*." Edie elbowed him in the ribs. Hard. "That wasn't reassuring. Like, at all."

If they hoped to coax Sabrina into helping them, the three of them needed to reach at least a tentative truce. Which meant Max should let Edie take the lead and shut his very attractive mouth.

"No, it wasn't. But the fact that you're human and apparently unharmed, and you seem to trust him . . ." Sabrina's chest rose and fell on a sigh. "*That's* reassuring. I suppose. Although you could just be an idiot."

Max stiffened again. "Edie is highly intelligent, witch."

His voice had turned sharp, his accent slightly French, and Edie wound her arms around his waist and pressed up against his side in an effort to distract him with her boobs.

"Hmmm." Sabrina eyed them both balefully.

Max's mouth opened, most likely in preparation to say something offensive or inflammatory. Edie reached up and gently but firmly sealed her palm over his lips. In retaliation, he lightly scraped an incisor over the pad of flesh below her thumb. As she shivered in response, he somehow managed to radiate smug satisfaction without uttering a single word.

Sabrina's coffee-brown stare focused on Edie. "He sniffed out Riley's trail, didn't he? Like an overgrown, leather-clad bloodhound."

When he didn't attempt to protest that description, Edie dropped her hand, although she left it free for emergency-silencing purposes. "Or Lassie. That was my go-to reference."

"Nice." Sabrina's brief grin flickered, and then she sighed again. "Give me five minutes. My wife is gravely ill, and I need to take care of her before dealing with you two."

She shut the door in their faces.

"Such gracious hospitality," Max said loudly enough to be heard through the paneled wood, and Edie's elbow found his ribs once again.

"I hate that Sabrina's wife is so sick." She hung her head. "Now I feel even worse about asking her to risk her life."

He tugged gently at a lock of her hair. "You had no way of knowing and no choice but to ask."

"Maybe once our cluster of unfortunateness is less . . . uh, unfortunate, I can get to know them better and help out somehow."

His voice was as dry as her dehumidified garage. "Much like a reality television contestant in the early 2000s, I'm pretty sure Sabrina isn't here to make friends."

"Then it'll be a delightful surprise for her when she makes friends anyway. I've broken the will of greater cynics than Sabrina." Like, say, the vampire currently stroking a thumb down her bent neck. "I intend to make her my cream cheese–swirl brownies. Resistance is futile, albeit delicious."

"I might hold back on the Borg comparisons, at least until she's been fully assimilated." He sounded like he was smiling. "But if anyone can turn a suspicious witch into an ally, it's probably you."

The sound of rapid footsteps drifted through the closed door, and then Sabrina swung it open again and impatiently waved them inside. Once they were standing in the narrow entry hall, the door safely locked behind them, Edie didn't waste more time on pleasantries or even a brief, nosy study of the home's interior.

Instead, she turned to Sabrina and launched into an explanation. "Did Riley tell you what we were trying to do?"

The witch gave a brief nod. "She said you wanted to get word of the breach to authorities outside the Zone."

"We didn't succeed." Edie blew out a breath. "As you've probably guessed by now."

"Since we didn't hear any sirens or helicopters, we thought you might have gotten stuck at Wall Four. Or, more likely, that you'd encountered the pack on your way out, and—well." Sabrina's lips pressed together, and her voice softened. "I'm glad we were wrong about what happened to you."

Edie smiled at her. "Thank you. Anyway, after Riley told us what you saw while scrying, we decided to visit the site of the breach, because we wanted to gather any remaining scent evidence. We also didn't want to mention possible demon involvement to authorities without confirming it for ourselves." Which was hopefully the nicest possible way to say *We weren't sure we could trust you.* "You need to know what we saw and smelled there, Sabrina."

The witch's brow creased. "Tell me."

While Edie explained everything, Max stood silently at her back, offering support and an occasional grunt of affirmation. Sabrina listened without interrupting, apart from a few clarifying questions.

"We intended to find you immediately and ask for your help in gathering allies," Edie concluded once she'd shared all the pertinent information, "but we ran into a stray zombie at a moment when we weren't paying sufficient attention, and . . . uh . . ."

The words wouldn't come. She couldn't skim over Max's injuries as if they were simply another event in their series of terrible misadventures. As if seeing him near death hadn't traumatized her and underscored how deeply she actually cared for him.

Max's hands clasped her shoulders from behind, kneading her taut muscles gently. "I needed Edie's help, a few hours, and a safe place to heal. By the time I regained consciousness and full mobility, the sun had set."

"And with a pack on the loose, it was too late to find me," Sabrina deduced.

"Yes. Exactly." Edie spread her hands and stared pleadingly at the other woman. "Sabrina, we can't let the zombies out of the Zone. They have to stay within the final wall. If they escape, countless people and Supernaturals will die. And even if the government and SERC were able to drive the creatures back again, as soon as officials studied the breach site, word would spread that Supernaturals were involved, and then—"

"Full-on slaughter. Apocalyptic violence." Sabrina pinched the bridge of her nose between her thumb and forefinger. "So the government can't be part of our containment efforts, and afterward, we can't tell just any random official about the breach and its probable cause. We have to find someone who's open-minded, strategic, and able to keep secrets for the greater good."

Edie's newly massaged shoulders slumped in relief.

That *we* meant the witch would help them. Thank heavens.

"Also someone not connected or beholden to the fae in any capacity," Max added.

"But first . . ." Edie chewed on her lower lip, her brief respite from worry over in an eyeblink. "We have to either kill the zombies or get them back to their compound and keep them there. All of them."

Gods and goddesses, this entire plan sounded impossible. Like a fool's errand. But they had no other choice, did they?

"Agreed." Sabrina's hand lowered to her side. "And at least one of us has to survive long enough to find our strategically minded, secretive official. Luckily, I think I can help with that bit. Or, more accurately, my wife can."

Swiveling to address the shadowed loft area toward the back of the home, she called out, "Starla! Did you hear all that, sweetheart?"

"Of course." The voice drifting down from the loft was soft and sweet. "I can start contacting our neighbors and telling them to gather here, if that's what you need, Sabby."

Something about that phrasing—"Your internet is working? Or your phone?"

"Everything's still down, unfortunately." A lovely Black woman appeared behind the loft railing, with a shy smile and a bare, gleaming head. "And I'm mostly stuck here in bed, so I won't be able to fight or recruit help in person, but I'm a telepath. I can communicate with anyone I've recently seen, as long as they aren't too far away or blocked by something solid. Like a huge, thick stone wall, for example."

Max had been right, then. Starla was an Enhanced human, like her wife.

"Star, you have limited energy right now, and you already wore yourself out contacting our neighbors and warning them to find shelter yesterday." Sabrina's fists were planted on her hips, and the glare she directed up at the loft was full of pained love. "If you don't rest today—"

"If I don't rest today, maybe you can recruit enough people to save us all. Including me." The telepath shook her head, lips pursed. "Sabby, if there's a war, do you really think common humans will let the Enhanced live? We've cooperated with Supernaturals too many times and far too closely. An enraged gun-toting mob won't consider us innocent bystanders. They'll call us their enemies and slaughter every last one of us."

A mutinous expression creased Sabrina's face, but she didn't argue. Her wife was correct, and they all knew it.

"I need to help," Starla said. "And if the worst happens, I'll somehow find a trustworthy official and tell them everything. But that won't be necessary, because you're going to survive this, babe. We all are." Her narrow, intelligent face brightened with a small smile. "Honestly, most everyone we know is gone for the holidays, so I won't have much work to do. I'll need to take a car ride over the bridges to Zones A and C, though, so I can contact our friends who live there without a wall blocking my thoughts."

"Starla, sweetheart . . ." Sabrina rubbed her forehead. "I'm not sure I can carry you to the car. Maybe we can—"

"I'll get her into the car," Max interrupted. "You know how strong I am, witch. I won't jostle or hurt her in any way."

A long, tense silence stretched between them.

When she finally replied, her voice had turned chilly once more. "Swear on her life, vampire." She tipped her head toward Edie, fear and suspicion pulling her delicate features taut. "Because if you harm my wife, your sweet companion will pay the price."

Max's fingers bit into Edie's shoulders, and when she looked back at him, his irises had darkened to the cold, deep blue of a fathomless ocean.

"Do it, Max," she demanded in a low whisper. "We need their help. And we both know you won't harm her wife, so your promise changes nothing for me."

He made a sort of growly sound deep in his throat as he scowled down at her, but he eventually turned back to Sabrina.

"I will not inflict intentional harm on Starla or act carelessly in regard to her safety and comfort," he told the witch, reluctance in every syllable. "I can't promise she won't come to harm due to chance or someone else's actions—"

"Let him finish, Sabby," Starla gently ordered when Sabrina began to protest.

"—but if I can prevent that harm, I will. That much I'll willingly . . ." He paused, his skin an odd shade of pale. Almost greenish. "I'll willingly swear on Edie's life."

"That works for me." Starla curled a trembling hand around

the loft railing. "Baby, his thoughts indicate he's telling the truth, and I shouldn't be wasting my energy on this conversation. Stand down, please."

"Fine." Eyes still narrowed on Max, the witch extended a hand to him. "I accept your promise."

"Good," he said pleasantly enough, and shook briefly. "Glad we're in agreement."

Sabrina offered him a curt nod, and Edie let out a relieved breath.

"Also . . ." An unsettling smile spread across Max's face. "Please know that if you willingly harm or allow harm to befall Edie, I won't kill your wife." He bared his teeth, displaying lengthened, needle-sharp fangs. "I'll kill *you*, witch."

"All righty, then," Edie quickly said, taking Max's arm and yanking him farther away from their openly seething host. "Let's move on from the threat-issuing portion of this morning's schedule, shall we?"

"Seconded," came Starla's gentle voice from upstairs, right before her face disappeared into the shadows once more.

Her wife grunted. "Fine."

"Fine," Max sneered.

And then—gods and goddesses help them—they all got to work.

20

Over the course of a long day, the others arrived.

There weren't many possible helpers, as it turned out. Most people Starla and Sabrina knew had traveled outside the Zone for the holidays, so the telepath couldn't reach them. Those who'd stayed behind were often either homebound—like Starla—or elderly. Others simply refused to venture outdoors with a horde of ravening zombies nearby or battle said horde of ravening zombies, and despite the high stakes, Edie had a hard time blaming them for that.

At first there was only one addition to their small battalion. No one showed up while Max and Starla took their road trip, but by midmorning, a white redhead named Gwen, round and short and roughly Edie's age, knocked on the door. She appeared nervous and didn't say much. After nodding in greeting to Sabrina, Edie, and Max, she immediately went upstairs for a quiet conversation with Starla and came back down looking even more concerned.

She seemed human, but who knew, really? Not Edie.

Around lunchtime, when Edie and Max traveled back to the

mall and warned the counterfeiters about the upcoming battle, Belinda said they appreciated the heads-up but couldn't join the fight.

"Too dangerous," Belinda told Edie, ignoring Doug's pleading look. "We've pared our group down to essential personnel only. If we lose even a single person, the entire enterprise falls apart."

Austin's head tipped in thought. "But we can offer you weapons."

"And a pan of homemade lasagna." Doug smiled apologetically at them. "I made the pasta from scratch. Oh, and don't forget the tiramisu!"

So Max and Edie returned to Sabrina's home with plenty of weapons and tasty provisions in tow, but no new recruits. None had arrived in their absence either, sadly.

Only a minute or so later, though, two more people— beings?—arrived at the witch's front door. And . . . *whoa*.

Edie had never seen trolls up close before. As it turned out, movies and television shows didn't do their size justice. These particular trolls were almost eight feet tall, according to Edie's best guesstimate, with sturdy builds and thick, ridiculously long limbs.

They didn't just stand in the entry hallway. They *loomed*.

Lorraine and Kip were cousins, Edie soon learned. Very attractive, very large cousins. Lorraine's candy apple–red bob and blunt bangs glowed against her pale skin and wide white smile, while Kip's dark waves almost brushed his bespectacled brown eyes and curled around the warm golden skin of his muscled neck.

For beings who reportedly lived underground among tree roots, their rumpled clothing remained remarkably clean. And while both of them did in fact smell like the earth, it was in the best possible way. They smelled like . . . living things. Green grass and fertile, newly turned soil and the sun.

They were also extremely friendly. Perhaps a bit *too* friendly.

"You're a vamp! Hey there! Nice to meet you!" Lorraine exclaimed, then offered Max a high-five that—hilariously—almost knocked him over. "Sorry! Sometimes I forget my own strength!"

Looking wary, Max visibly braced himself before Kip clapped his back in welcome, and it helped. It really did. Max barely even swayed at the audible impact, although he did begin coughing.

Ah yes. Edie had read about that particular quirk. Although trolls were widely considered the most easygoing and loyal of all Supernatural species, they were famously clumsy as well—and that clumsiness could injure or even kill those who weren't alert and prepared.

Max rotated his shoulder, grimacing faintly. Good thing he was a vampire instead of a human and able to absorb that kind of hit, because otherwise . . . yeesh.

The handshakes Lorraine and Kip offered Edie were much gentler. Possibly because they'd learned from their recent error or possibly because Max was overseeing their introductions to her with a certain amount of murderous intensity.

"Edie's such a pretty name!" Lorraine beamed down—far, far down—at Edie. "And it's always fun to get to know another Zone neighbor!"

"Wonderful to meet you, Edie-my-love!" Kip grinned toothily, then turned toward Sabrina. "I smell snacks, little witch! Excellent! Can't battle zombies while we're starving, right? Right!"

"We have a pan each of lasagna and tiramisu." Squatting by their mall haul, Edie surveyed the other resealable plastic containers Doug had pressed into her hands. "This is some sort of vegetable gratin . . ."

"I smell Gruyère. The good stuff, direct from Switzerland." Kip closed his eyes, sniffing blissfully. "Oh yes."

"Here's a grain salad. Is that . . ." Edie's knowledge of grains was somewhat limited, sadly. "Quinoa, maybe?"

"Farro. Which, when cooked properly, is a bit toothsome and utterly delightful," Lorraine declared as soon as Edie cracked the lid. "With fresh goat cheese, pine nuts, and a lemon-based vinai-grette. Some dill too. Green onions. Oh, and garlic-sauteed Gulf shrimp!"

Edie blinked at the cousins, somewhat startled. Which wasn't really fair, upon further reflection. Just because someone lived among tree roots didn't mean they couldn't recognize and appre-ciate imported cheeses and whole grains, right?

"Hey, Starla!" Lorraine directed her shout at the loft. "Want me to bring up some food for you? I'll be there in a jiffy, as soon as we fill up the tank down here!"

"Yes, please," came the tired-sounding answer. "A little bit of everything?"

Lorraine's brows drew together, her gaze at the loft turning worried. "Can do, dearest!"

"Get your share while you can," Sabrina murmured to Edie. "This entire spread is a mere amuse-bouche to Kip and Lorraine."

There were more containers of food at their feet. Ones Edie hadn't even mentioned yet. Large ones. She nudged the pile with the tip of her boot. "Even including these?"

"I've seen them at a fancy brunch buffet, Edie. Halfway through their fourth helping, all the crab puffs, truffled potatoes, and freshly carved prime rib were gone, and the manager began weeping." Sabrina's lips curved slightly. "Although, to be fair, they left a gargantuan tip and paid extra on the bill as an apology, and when she saw the amount, she began crying again. With joy. She tried to hug them and nearly gave Kip an inadvertent blowjob. That woman was *tiny*."

"Later that night, it wasn't *nearly* and it wasn't inadvertent," Kip said as he strode by. "And before she left the next morning, she cried more happy tears."

"Gross," Lorraine muttered loudly.

Another knock reverberated against the front door.

When Max checked the peephole, his expression tightened, but he didn't hesitate to open the door and step aside. "Riley. What are you doing here?"

Her box braids still twisted in a pristine bun, the young woman swept past him and into the entry hall, followed by the other Girl Explorers. "Starla told us what was happening."

"It was a warning, Riley, not an invitation." The telepath's quiet rejoinder drifted down from the loft. "I told you and your troop to hunker down at home and stay put."

"I paid less attention to that part. Sorry, Star." The troop leader smiled confidently. "We're here to help. Tell us what needs doing."

No, that wasn't happening. Edie wouldn't *let* it happen.

"We can't put children in jeopardy." Agitated, she raked her hand roughly through her hair, ignoring the pinches of pain as she ripped out tangles. "Sabrina, tell them."

The witch stood in the juncture between her hallway and kitchen, massaged her temples with her fingertips, and said nothing. Behind her, clattering noises rang through the home as Kip and Lorraine each grabbed a plate and utensils and began dishing up their meal.

No help there either, apparently.

Edie turned a beseeching look on Max, who sighed resignedly.

"We're not using you in battle," he said, the statement definitive. "If I allowed it and you wound up headless, Edie would never forgive me. But we can use your assistance as we prepare and find a noncombat role for you during the confrontation."

Riley dipped her chin. "I think that's a compromise we can accept."

"*Max*." Edie's jaw ached from all the teeth-grinding. "Those girls are—"

Max raised his brows, entirely unrepentant. "Those girls are going nowhere. I recognize their expression, my Edie. It's the same one you wear when you stubbornly refuse to see reason. We can harness that stubbornness for our own ends and do so as safely as possible, or we can discover what a dozen young humans eager to prove their worth in battle will do when left unsupervised. My prediction: get in our way, then die. Within moments."

The logic in his argument infuriated her. Mostly because he was right, and she knew it.

"Alarmingly enough, I agree with the vampire." Sabrina waved a tired-looking hand. "You can help with preparations and tactics, but there'll be no hand-to-claw combat against zombies, Riley. Not for any of you girls."

"Understood." Riley met the gazes of her troop. "All those in favor?"

After the loud chorus of *ayes*, Edie had to close her eyes for a minute.

"They'll be fine, love." Max's fingers gently combed through the patches of hair she'd recently abused, coaxing the remaining knots loose. "I'll make certain of it."

"That's a big promise, Max." When the pad of his thumb flicked her earlobe, she shivered. "And the only reason you're making it is . . ."

"I don't want you upset or angry at me," he supplied immediately.

"Yes. That's what you said." Tipping her head, she nudged against his hand. "If it weren't for me, you'd be perfectly fine watching a dozen tweens die in the grisliest possible manner due to a decision you'd made. Correct?"

A lengthy silence fell between them.

"Like I said." His jaw worked. "You wouldn't forgive me."

A nonanswer. Which was, in its own backward way, her answer.

Holding his gaze, she whispered, "No . . . one . . ."

"I swear to all the gods and goddesses, Edie, I'll kill those girls myself if you—"

". . . cares like Gaston, strokes through hair like Gaston," she singsonged below her breath, distantly noting the house's sudden silence. "In a zombie scare no one shares lairs like Gaston!"

"He has a lair?" someone said, their voice hushed. "Is he Batman or just really emo?"

Lorraine's fork scraped against her platter. "Are you sure he's a vamp? Because caring and sharing aren't exactly hallmarks of the species, to be frank."

Well, if everyone could hear Edie's song anyway, she might as well belt it out, right? "As a vampire man, yes, he's so *ag-gra-va*-ting—"

Max held up six fingers, and Edie kicked him lightly in the shin.

"But my, how he tries, that Gaston!" she finished grandly, then swept a bow in response to the resulting applause. "Thank you. Thank you very much. For an encore, I'd like to introduce a different, macramé-related version of the song, one I think you'll find edifying in a variety of *mmphmmm*—"

With his palm firmly but painlessly covering her lips, Max marched her toward the kitchen, where Kip and Lorraine had plowed through half the food already and were still going strong.

"Use that mouth of yours for eating instead of singing," he murmured in her ear, "or I'll find a different way to fill it."

"Don't threaten me with a good time, vampire boy," she said, then grabbed a plate and a large square of the lasagna, because woman couldn't live on vampire dick alone.

AS IT TURNED out, Gwen was an Enhanced human. An oracle, to be precise.

When Sabrina's attempts at further scrying proved unhelpful, she'd asked her friend to provide prophetic guidance. And for some reason, Gwen's face had twisted into a pained wince at the request, even as she'd agreed to it.

"You know I'm not . . ." After pursing her lips for a moment, the redhead squared her shoulders. "Okay. Okay. I'll do it."

The oracle now sat at the kitchen table, everyone else arrayed around her in concentric circles. The athame she produced from her backpack gleamed by candlelight, its edge wickedly sharp. With a single deft gesture, she sliced downward across her palm, and the cut welled up with blood immediately. The oracle didn't react in any way, although Edie had to suppress a sympathetic cringe.

That must hurt. Even for an oracle. Even the thousandth time she did it.

Slowly, Gwen's eyes went blank, her face expressionless. She gasped once, then fell silent once more. Her palms lifted from the round kitchen table, hovering above the surface, before slapping back down again viciously fast and hard in a concussion that made everyone—even Max—jump. When she raised them again, her blood was smeared across the wood, mute evidence of what she suffered on their behalf, and the cut on her palm had turned black, as if cauterized.

"What are our possible futures, oracle?" Sabrina's tone was quiet. Respectful. "We beg for your assistance and will heed whatever information you're able to offer."

Fascinated and unsettled, Edie awaited Gwen's pronouncements. Held her breath in anticipation of the visions their resident prophet might share with all of them.

"The troll . . . Kip . . ." she eventually intoned, her voice cold and deep and inhuman. "He will fall."

A chorus of gasps rose, and Lorraine's eyes grew tear-bright. "He's . . . is he going to die?"

Oh fuck, I'm not sure I want to know, Edie thought frantically as Max wrapped an arm around her shoulders and tugged her against his side. *I can't—*

"These are only possible futures, remember," Kip reassured his cousin. "Don't worry, Lorrie. I'll be careful."

"He will fall," the oracle repeated. "He will stub his toe on a root in the dark, and he will fall."

Edie's wringing hands stilled. Okay, some clarification was needed. Pronto.

"*Fall* as in *die*?" Edie asked tentatively. "Or *fall* as in—"

Gwen didn't blink. "He will lose his balance and hit the ground."

"Oh. You mean he'll *literally* fall." Lorraine's thick brows drew together as she sniffed back more tears. "Does he injure his head? Or maybe the accident leaves him vulnerable to attack—"

"He will trip and fall." The oracle's voice remained expressionless. "The Power offers no insights as to Kip's fate afterward."

"Wow." Kip frowned, scratching his head. "Not to be rude, but that was kind of a useless—"

But the oracle had already turned her attention elsewhere. "Eden. Human. Creator of beauty from harsh, unforgiving matter."

"Are you talking about lye?" Because she'd never personally found olive or jojoba oil all that unforgiving, to be honest. "I mean, that's a flattering description of my job, but—"

"Your essential oil has been gravely contaminated."

Huh. She had her oils safely capped and stored off the garage floor, and she kept her doors locked at all times. How could anyone or anything have possibly—

"Deliberately?" Max's tone turned steely, and he pulled her tighter against him. "If someone attempts to poison Edie, I'll find them. Find them and rip out their—"

"The blackberry-sage oil is too old. It has spoiled." Gwen's eyes . . . they weren't a soft green anymore, but a chilly shade of steel gray. "The next time you use it, you will have a cold. You will not be able to detect the scent of rot. Your batch of Berry Beauty soap . . ."

Edie leaned forward. Gods, what the fuck did that soap *do*? Was it so spoiled that it caused some sort of horrible transmissible disease? Had she made herself or her customers ill?

"Your batch of Berry Beauty soap . . . according to the emails you'll receive . . . will . . ."

Everyone else around the table leaned forward too.

"It will *smell like butt*," Gwen finished. "That is a direct quote."

Riley failed to turn a snort into a convincing cough, and a soft giggle drifted down from the loft.

"Refunds will be issued." The oracle wasn't quite done yet. "Apologies will be made. Regrets will be had."

"Oh." Yeah, Edie could only imagine. "That's really helpful, actually. I'll replace my blackberry-sage oil as soon as I can. Thanks."

"Don't you have any other information about Edie's fate, oracle?" A weird grinding sound emanated from the vicinity of Max's teeth. "Something involving our upcoming battle with fucking *zombies*?"

Edie elbowed him. "*Max.* There are children here. And be nice."

"No." Gwen—or, rather, whoever or whatever she was channeling—didn't sound offended. Didn't sound . . . *anything*, really, other than dispassionate and inexorable. "But the Power has a warning for you as well, Gaston Maxime Boucher."

For some reason, Sabrina gasped at that.

"His name really is Gaston?" A blond tween snickered behind them. "That's . . . unfortunate."

Edie couldn't even take any pleasure from the mockery. Not with Max's fate at stake. "What can you tell us, Gwen? Will he be okay?"

The other woman's palms rested lightly on the table, her hands completely steady. "There will be a spill of red, Gaston. All over you. So much red."

Edie gasped and clung to Max's waist. That had to be blood. Max's? Someone else's? Zombies bled a sickly yellow, so—

"You will . . ." The oracle spoke slowly, then paused before continuing. "You will . . . spill red glitter on yourself during your next recording session."

Giddy with relief, Edie rubbed a hand over her lower face and tried not to audibly giggle.

"Recording session? Red glitter?" Lorraine glanced at Sabrina, dark brows raised high. "Dude might be a mini-vamp, but he's a hot one. If *Gaston* has an OnlyFans account, you'd best be sharing the link, girlie."

Max was muttering to himself. "I was going to use red glitter in an upcoming video. How did she know? Did someone hack into my—"

"She's an oracle, bro," Kip said before Edie could gather the right words. "Duh."

"The spill will prove disastrous," Gwen told Max.

His mouth snapped shut, and he scowled at the oracle. "How?"

"For weeks afterward . . ." Gwen's fingertips twitched for the first time as she prophesized, and her lips did the same. "You will resemble a sunburned Edward Cullen."

Kip choked on a bite of tiramisu and doubled over coughing. In fact, a great number of odd-sounding coughs occurred after that pronouncement, Edie's among them.

"We should have stayed in my lair, human," Max grumbled under his breath, pitilessly tickling a sensitive spot on her ribs. "Wait, not my *lair*. My *home*. Dammit, Edie—"

Sabrina's hand raised in a peremptory gesture, demanding silence. "Do you have prophecies for anyone else in this group, oracle?"

"I do not."

Sighs of disappointment swept through the room.

"Aw, man," a nearby Girl Explorer mumbled. "I wanted to know weird crap about the other troll too."

"The Power—" Gwen began.

Then her entire body jerked, and her hands lifted from the table. Her face contorted and her eyes scrunched shut, her rosy cheeks turning paler by the moment.

The witch came over and laid a gentle hand on her shoulder. "Hey, are you—"

"The Power has extinguished." When Gwen's eyes opened, they were back to their previous soft green. Still looking pained, she visibly swallowed, sweat beading along her hairline. "Your possible futures lie in wait, subject to will and chance both. It is done."

At the reminder of what their immediate futures held, silence descended over the room. Gwen slumped into her chair, and Sabrina poured her a fresh glass of ice water.

Eventually, Lorraine spoke again. "Hey, if all that stuff happens—Edie with her soap and Max with his glitter—at least that means they'll survive what's coming, right?" Her smile's wattage had dimmed significantly, but she did her best. "That's something."

Gwen bit her lip, swallowing convulsively. "The visions . . . they aren't certain. They're only possible futures, contingent on variables and choices that aren't yet set in stone."

"In other words, we may not actually survive," Edie said.

"I don't know. I'm so sorry." Her eyes shone with tears as she glanced around the table, and her hand hovered near her mouth. "The only prophecy that felt relatively certain was Kip's. He'll almost definitely stub his toe on a root in the dark and fall to the ground. What happens after that, I can't say."

"Yeah." Kip grimaced. "Okay. Thanks anyway for trying."

"I know my predictions aren't the most . . . useful. I, um . . ." Gwen clamped that waiting hand over her mouth and gulped before lowering it again. "I told Sabrina and Starla I'd try, but it's not . . . not really under my . . ."

Another gulp. Two. Then she lurched to her feet, stumbled, and almost fell as she tried to push through the crowd of Girl Explorers surrounding her, her face pasty and green-tinged.

Suddenly, Max's arm vanished from around Edie and appeared at the oracle's elbow. He half carried the other woman toward the hallway and into the nearest bathroom, where the two of them disappeared. The sound of miserable, repeated retching filled the house, then grew muffled as someone—probably Max—kicked the door shut behind them.

"I've got you," Edie heard him say, his voice muffled but gentle. "It's all right, little oracle."

It wasn't the same tone he used with her. There was no intimacy there. No heat. Just . . . kindness. Patience. Simple goodwill toward a woman who'd tried to help them and was evidently suffering for it.

That was the vampire who'd been poised to serve his community on SERC. *That* was the neighbor who'd watched out for her safety from the very beginning.

That was the real Gaston Maxime Boucher. Or at least the Gaston Maxime Boucher he could be when he wasn't so intent on distancing himself from the world.

Something anxious in Edie's heart settled and warmed. She rubbed absently at her chest, welcoming her new certainty. Basking in the intensity and depth of her feelings for her impossible, irresistible vampire of a neighbor.

He could protest and deflect all he wanted from now on. He wouldn't be able to convince her—even for a moment—that he truly meant her or anyone else harm, unless he considered that harm fully justified. Which was, obviously, a somewhat subjective determination. They'd have to tease out precisely what he considered just provocation, sooner rather than later.

But no matter what, she now believed his sense of right and wrong matched hers much more closely than she'd once imagined. Much more closely than he'd willingly admit. And if that was true, she didn't need to fight falling in love with him. She didn't need to fret. She could simply fling herself into the joyous maelstrom, headfirst and heedless.

After a brief pause and the sound of running water, poor Gwen's gagging began anew. In the kitchen, there was a collective wince of sympathy.

"Does that always happen?" Lorraine asked Sabrina. "Every time she prophesizes?"

But the witch, staring at the closed bathroom door with a furrowed brow, didn't answer.

21

Gwen eventually emerged from the bathroom, supported by Max's steadying arm, pale but composed. After sipping at her water for a few minutes, she declared herself recovered, and they began making plans as a group.

Max slipped back to Edie's side as soon as he could. "Everything okay?"

She simply smiled at him, then got up on tiptoe and kissed his cheek. His brows rose in silent question, but she pointed toward Lorraine, who'd just begun outlining the troll cousins' capabilities and vulnerabilities in battle.

We need to listen, Edie mouthed.

His eyes rolled to the ceiling in response, but he didn't insist on further conversation. They stood side by side for a few minutes, her hand cradled in his, while everyone discussed what they were and weren't capable of doing. And as soon as she began shifting on her feet, he left the room, only to return a minute later with an armless chair. He wedged it into the only free spot around the table, waited for her to sit, and stood at her back, a protective vampiric wall.

That chair turned out to be a lifesaver. For endless hours, they talked tactics and brainstormed strategies. Divvied up responsibilities and assigned tasks to be accomplished either before or during the battle. Gamed out possible tricks they could use to lure the zombies back toward the compound and either trap them behind a repaired wall or kill them.

The latter would be their preference. Not only because it was simpler, but also because—unlike the government—they had no desire to preserve the creatures for potential further use. Especially since the cynics within the group had various unpleasant theories as to what that official usage might entail.

Occasional stomping occurred, along with some shouting and sullen pouting. But by the time night fell, they had a rough plan in place for the coming day, assuming the zombies didn't breach the final wall standing between them and the rest of humanity in the meantime.

"My guess? There's a fifty-fifty chance we'll be too late." Lorraine pursed her lips, her broad brow creased. "But we have no choice. There's no way we can get everything in place tonight, and we need the advantage of darkness when we fight."

"Agreed." Sabrina rose to her feet and began preparing something at the stove. "Let's relax for the rest of the evening and get as much rest as possible. I'll make us Starla's famous spiced apple cider, then get a fire started."

"I can help with the cider." Kip ambled in her direction. "It's nonalcoholic, right? Ripping off zombie heads would probably be less fun with a hangover."

"No alcohol," she confirmed. "No hangovers."

"Good." Lorraine rose—and kept rising—to her feet too. "I'll take care of the fire."

"And I'll keep Starla company for a while," Gwen said.

"We'll figure out the sleeping situation, if you'd like?" When Sabrina nodded, Edie turned to the Girl Explorers. "Once Max and I have a plan, all of you can divvy up the blankets and pillows, okay?"

Together, she and Max went in search of bedrooms and possible linen closets. But as soon as they rounded a corner and found themselves alone in a dim, cool hallway, he propped himself against the wall and gathered her into his arms.

"How are you, ma puce?" he asked quietly. "Did you get enough to eat?"

"Yep. I'm good." Leaning forward, she rested her head on his shoulder and allowed him to support her weight. "I'll feed you later tonight, once we have a bit of privacy, if that's all right with you."

"Of course." His fingers sifted through her hair, the gesture already familiar. "Edie, I'm not . . ."

When he didn't finish his thought, she raised her head to look at him. "What?"

"Given our resources, I think we've formulated the best plan possible." His gusty exhalation tickled her forehead. "I'm not sure it's good enough."

"Yeah." She couldn't say that thought hadn't occurred to her. "I know."

His eyes bored into hers, intent and pleading. "If I promise to stay and fight to the absolute best of my ability, how would you feel about returning to my—"

"Nope. Not happening." When she sagged forward again and nuzzled her face into his neck, his throat rumbled with a growly sound. "I'm not going anywhere, except into battle by your side."

His fingers closed on a handful of her hair, gripping it near her nape.

"If you were hurt . . ." His voice had turned hoarse. Rough. "I don't know what I'd do. Edie, you have to keep yourself safe. Promise me. *Promise*."

"As safe as I can. I promise." Soothingly, she stroked her palms up and down the tension-taut curve of his lower back. "Honey, there's no point in agonizing over what might happen tomorrow. We've made our plans. We'll execute them soon enough. But we still have tonight, and we still have each other."

Slowly, his body softened against hers. The rhythm of his breathing slowed, and he lowered his head until his cheek rested against her crown.

"Let's drink our cider and warm ourselves by the fire." She pressed a tender kiss against his cool neck. "Then we'll find a bed and some time alone before we have to face whatever comes next. Okay?"

His shoulders slumped, and she rubbed them soothingly. "Okay."

"Okay." *A spill of red. All over you.* If she scrunched her eyelids tightly enough, fireworks appeared behind them and erased the vision of Max soaked in blood, still and silent. "Promise you'll keep yourself safe too. Please."

"As safe as I can," he echoed, then paused. "I'm not sure I trust the witch enough to drink something she's prepared for me. Fuck knows what she might have done to that cider."

Were all vampires such drama queens? Or was that just a Max thing?

"Don't be so cynical." Her teeth gave his throat an admonishing nip. "It'll be fine."

* * *

EVERYONE DRANK SABRINA'S cider. Even cynical, mistrustful Max.

It was fucking delicious. Sweet and tart and cinnamony. Kip and Lorraine, their resident gourmands, gave the beverage four enthusiastic thumbs up and nearly broke a lamp and a ceiling fan in the process.

And approximately ten minutes after they all took their first sips, the effects of the spell the witch had cast upon the beverage became unmistakably evident. In retrospect.

Neither Edie nor anyone else recognized those effects at first. No, she was too busy enjoying an unexpected and unusual sense of well-being to notice anything amiss. Sprawled back on the comfy sofa, belly warmed by the cider and the prospect of another night spent in Max's embrace, she looked around at their compatriots and smiled happily.

Gods, she missed having neighbors. She missed *people*. Or . . . whatever word encompassed all the different amazing species that existed. So many species! And some of them were really, really hot!

She wasn't an introvert. Like, at all. What the fuck was she doing, living in the most sparsely populated part of the Containment Zone? Sheesh, what a dork.

"Max. Hey, Max." Laughing a little, she leaned over on the couch and whispered into his ear, "Your penis is awesome. The best ever. I didn't fake *shit* last night."

She held up six fingers, then wiggled them in happy emphasis.

"I know, love." He laughed too, rubbing the tip of his nose affectionately against hers. "That was the best sex of my life. Bar none. And I've had a lot of sex over the centuries. You honestly would not *believe* how much sex I've had. Gods, I think the first time was back in—"

"Hey, Riley." Sabrina's elbow rested on the mantel above the fireplace, and she surveyed everyone sprawled around the room with careful attention. "When you first met Max, how did you figure out he was a vampire? Because I'm guessing he didn't intend to tell you."

"What a great question!" Edie poked Max's thigh. "We wondered that too!"

"Oh, we knew right away. Determining species is an automatic thing, since we're all half-fae." Riley propped herself up on her elbows and yawned widely. "Glamoured for privacy, obviously. Our troop is sort of special that way."

Oh. For some reason that Edie couldn't quite grasp, Riley's revelation was . . . troubling. But honestly, what a lovely young woman—half-fae, whatever—Riley seemed to be. Good for her. Good for all of them!

"Huh," Max said under his breath. "Guess I can't detect glamoured half-fae. Good to know. Gooooood to know."

"We couldn't detect them either!" Spreading her hands wide, Lorraine met Max's eyes and shrugged expressively. "Or so it seems!"

"I see." The witch stared down at Riley, her eyes sharp. "Zombies can't kill full fae. What about half-fae?"

Riley's shoulders lifted in a desultory shrug. "Not sure. Maybe yes, maybe no. Hey, are you certain there isn't anything weird in this—"

"I'm certain." The intensity in Sabrina's voice ratcheted higher.

"Whatever's going on here, do you have any part in it? Did you come to sabotage our efforts?"

"Nope." Idly, the half-fae crossed one leg over the other, then swung her foot. "The exact opposite. We had a feeling that stupid splinter group of fae might be involved, and we wanted to help clean up the mess they made. Not all fae are jerkwads, you know. Even the full fae." She scrunched up her nose. "Although, to be fair, a lot of them kind of are."

"Yuuuuuuup," Max muttered. "Got the trauma to prove it."

Edie patted his arm.

"A *lot* of them," said the blond Girl Explorer with feeling. "But even most of the jerkwads aren't megalomaniacal murderers. That's honestly pretty rare."

Happy again, Edie grinned at everyone. Yay for the non-jerkwad, non-homicidal fae! And their wonderful half-fae kids! And all the whole-fae kids too!

Sabrina did not appear to be similarly pleased. "Do you know anything about the breach or what the splinter group's larger ambitions might be?"

"Uh-uh." Riley flopped back down on the carpet. "No clue. It's probably horrible, though." She tittered nervously. "Really, really horrible. Those fae are *evil*."

Max raised a hand. "Seconded. The motion passes!" As he lowered his arm, he studied his palm. "Wow. Hands. They do a lot, huh?"

"Yours certainly do!" Edie tried to wink, but it felt more like a whole-face scrunch. "I'm talking about sex stuff, by the way."

As one, the Girl Explorers all straightened and scooted a little closer.

"Yeah, you are," he said, and they high-fived before he suddenly frowned and angled himself toward Sabrina. "Wait a minute. Witch, I feel—"

"Don't worry, Max." Their host offered him a toothy smile. "You're fine. Everyone's fine."

"That's so cool. Not the murdery part, the glamour part. You're lucky you can disguise yourselves like that." From where he hung half off the love seat beside his cousin, Kip pointed at Riley. "Lorrie and I can't. Glamours just aren't a troll thing. That's why we had to hide in the woods for so long, until stupid common humans—" He looked apologetically at Edie. "Sorry. Until *certain* stupid common humans encroached on our territory, found our cabins and cottages, and forced us out in the open."

"No worries." Edie tipped her head in consideration. "You don't live among the tree roots, then?"

Kip snorted. "We live in a condo, bro."

"That's awesome!" No wonder their clothing looked so clean!

"It has a heated pool out back," he announced proudly. "Booyah!"

"Dumbass Kip's forgetting the Battle for Containment. Our"—Lorraine hiccupped ear-splittingly—"honor as trolls compelled us to fight for the protection of innocents. That's the main reason we went public when we did. But it probably would have happened sooner or later anyway because of the whole stupid-common-humans-and-diminishing-territory thing."

Kip's head lolled on his neck, and he smiled at the ceiling. "We fought for our own survival too, obvs. Those scary-ass zombies can't reach our brains when we're standing, but they can sure as hells force us down on the ground and kill us *there*."

"Yikes. I can't even imagine how many trolls must have died in that battle." Edie cringed. "I mean, given how . . . you know . . . physical things aren't really your . . ."

Using gestures, she did her best to mime their disastrous lack of agility and grace. Her elbow whacked Max in the head, and he grunted but accepted her sincere apologies.

"Yeah. About that." Lorraine clapped a hand over her mouth, chortling. "We're not actually klutzes. All those people we kill through our"—she crooked the index and middle fingers of both hands—"*clumsiness*? Pretty much all of them are our—"

"*Eeeeeen-e-miiiiies*," Kip sang out. "If we hurt you, it's no accident. Generally. We all have our off moments, am I right?"

"Wait." Max's brow creased again. "Earlier. When you said hello and hit me so hard in the shoulder, did that mean you . . ."

Lorraine spread her hands and grinned at him. "Vamps, bro. You're basically all dicks."

"He's *not* a dick! Not really." Edie's brief spurt of outrage faded, and she began giggling. "But—oh my gods and goddesses, his actual dick is *amazing*. You would not even believe—" A thought occurred to her, and she gasped. "Hold on. All this time, you've been *trolling* us?"

Trolls. Trolling. Like trolls would. Ha! So clever!

"It's not exactly subtle. I mean, it's in our actual *name*, right?" Lorraine's eyes danced with mirth. "As a species, we're kind of incredulous no one has caught on before now, Edie-my-love. Edes. Edes-a-lot. Beware the Edes of March!"

"Also, we know we come across a little dim at times, but . . ." Kip swayed forward and raised an authoritative finger. "That's on purpose too. Do you know which Supernatural species has never been trapped in a fae bargain? *This* one, bitches! Woot-woot!"

When he and Lorraine leapt to their feet and chest-bumped each other, the chandelier swayed at the impact.

"So don't worry about us, Sabby," Lorraine told Sabrina, sitting back down. "We'll kill those freaking zombies. Lots of them. Lots and lots and lots!"

Something about that punctured Edie's happy bubble, and she found herself frowning.

Leaning to the side, she burrowed against Max. "I'll kill as many as I can. Don't get me wrong. But . . . am I the only one who doesn't feel great about . . . like, *luring* them to their deaths, when they aren't actually trying to murder us first?"

"Oh, my softhearted Edie." He pressed a tender kiss to her forehead. "Yes, darling. You're the only one. The rest of us want to kill those fuckers. Super dead."

Lorraine patted her head fondly. "They'd slurp our brains, bro."

"Everyone else's brains too," Sabrina pointed out. "Without hesitation or remorse."

"I get that, but don't you wonder about their . . . their *humanity*?" Before everyone opening their mouths could protest, Edie raised a hand. "I know they're not human. They *are* sentient beings, though. Sentient and intelligent enough to . . . and maybe I'm hallucinating this part . . . speak a little bit of . . . French, possibly?"

"Huh." Kip scratched his chin. "I thought I'd imagined that. Because it was beyond freaky to hear a zombie say *bonjour* when it spotted me."

Starla spoke from the mattress Kip had carried downstairs and arranged on the living room floor. "I've wondered too, Edie. When the pack passed within sight of our house two days ago, I even tried to read their minds to gauge how sophisticated their thinking actually is."

"*Star.* You didn't tell me you did that." Sabrina's hands settled on her hips as she stared down at her wife. "No wonder you were so tired that day. You overexerted yourself, sweetheart."

Fascinated, Edie leaned forward on the couch. "How much were you able to read, Starla?"

"Not a lot, frankly." The telepath's lips compressed. "Usually, with complete strangers located at that distance, I wouldn't be able to get everything, but I would sense quite a bit. The thoughts at the forefront of their minds would be clear to me. With the zombies, though . . ."

All other conversations had ceased. Everyone was listening to the telepath now.

"I got next to nothing." When she shook her head, Starla's smooth scalp gleamed in the firelight. "Their minds aren't . . . whole, Edie. It's all hunger. Terrible, insatiable hunger. Except . . ."

"Except?" Max prompted.

"One of them had faint, staticky thoughts about . . . maps, I think? Maps and, um"—her brow crinkled—"*mimes*, oddly enough. And I caught a momentary flash of the interior of the compound. The creatures were all standing in front of a television, and a minder in a uniform turned it on for them before leaving."

Sabrina's expression turned contemplative. "The zombie was recalling things from before the Battle for Containment, then. Before that final serum. When they were . . ." She bit her lip for a moment. "Different. Less . . . mindless."

Maps. Mimes. Television. *Bon appétit. Bonjour. Magnifique.*

There was only one possible explanation that encompassed

everything, and Edie was the godsdamn genius who'd found that explanation. This truly was the awesomest evening *ever*.

Edie thrust her hand in the air and waved it with all the enthusiasm of a teacher's pet in the classroom's front row. "Starla, the part involving mimes. Was it something like 'Mimer, no miming'?"

"Maybe." The telepath thought for a few seconds. "Yes. I think that could be it."

"Then I know what's happening with all the French!" Edie shouted delightedly. "Their guards must have let them watch *Enora the Explorer* sometimes! Before the scientists tinkered with things once too often and everyone got murdered horribly!"

Slowly, the entire living room full of people turned to look at her.

"*Enora the Explorer*? The children's television show?" Kip appeared dubious. "The one where they try to teach kids French?"

Kip could doubt all he wanted, but she was ten million percent sure she'd solved this particular puzzle. Suck on that, troll-boy!

"When I was fourteen, our neighbor was a single mom, and I babysat her kids. They were allowed to watch two episodes of *Enora the Explorer* every night," Edie informed him. "Anyway, the show had an anthropomorphized map and a malicious, trouble-making mime and—"

"Whoa. I always suspected mimes were dicks." Lorraine blinked at Edie, then turned to Max. "Hey! Are you a mime, bro?"

"That's . . . very odd and somewhat interesting, I suppose," Sabrina cut in, "but also of limited relevance. Let's talk about—"

"Did you ever babysit an actual baby, Edie?" Gwen, who'd

been sitting slumped in her armchair all evening, suddenly perked up. "What did—"

"Good gods, this is like herding kittens." Sabrina rubbed her forehead. "Again, we're veering off topic. Before time runs out, I need to ask Max about—"

"The passage of time feels different when you're my age, witch." Max idly scratched the growing stubble on his cheek. "I mean, I've been around since—"

"Hey. Wait just a freaking minute, Sabby." The oracle's chin sat at a stubborn angle. "Babies are *not* off topic. I need to know about them, okay? The sooner the better."

"Oh." Starla's eyes went wide. "*Oh.*"

Edie tugged on Max's sleeve until he lowered his head and she could whisper in his ear. "Does Gwen want to start babysitting too? Like, for extra cash? Because I could give her tips if she'd like. Tip number one: Put something over a baby's penis when you change his diaper, because he can and will urinate directly into your face. Like a cherub in a really gross fountain!"

"No," he said slowly. "I think maybe—"

"I told you I threw up after prophesizing because the upcoming battle made me anxious, but I was a lying liar-pants who lies lyingly." Gwen got to her feet and drew herself up straight. "I wasn't anxious. Well, I was. I am. But I am also pregnant AF. Or as I prefer to call it, *preggers*. Because that sounds like more fun than being pregnant, am I right?"

Edie considered the matter, then nodded in agreement.

Sabrina's voice was shrill. "You're *pregnant*?"

"Yep." Gwen swirled a hand in front of her belly. "Eating for two. Knocked up. My oven has hereby been bunned."

Kip's brow crinkled. "Someone brought buns? Are they fresh-baked?"

"No, Kip. Gods." Gwen's eyes flicked heavenward. "Anyway, now you know. Also, I have no idea how to fight. Like, at all. So my bun and the entire kitchen setup surrounding its oven will probably get slaughtered two point three seconds after the mano a mano—woman-o a zombie-o?—part of our plan begins. Just FYI."

The hazy blue of Max's eyes had sharpened. "We'll teach you some self-defense moves tomorrow. And since you're not comfortable fighting, we'll keep you out of the actual physical battle as long as we can. That's a promise, little oracle."

"Agreed," Kip, Lorraine, and Edie said in unison.

Gwen grinned, relief evident in her expression. "Oh. Thank you. I appreciate that."

With a thump, she dropped back into her armchair.

"Gods and goddesses." Sabrina's palms scrubbed over her face. "Why didn't you tell me, Gwen? I'd never have . . ."

The witch trailed off, her chest rising and falling on a deep sigh.

"I said this wasn't a great idea, Sabby." Starla shook her head. "Did you use anything that could harm either of them?"

"No." Her hands dropped to her sides. "I'm almost entirely sure."

"What are you two talking about?" Riley asked, her dark eyebrows gathering into a single line. "What's going on?"

Murmurs of agreement and confusion rose from the room at large.

"I'll explain shortly. But first . . ." Sabrina eyed the Girl Explorers on her living room floor. "Riley, I need you and the rest of the troop to give us a few minutes of privacy."

Despite identical disgruntled expressions, the girls shuffled out of the room. As soon as they shut themselves into the main bedroom, Sabrina swiveled toward the sofa.

"Now, Gaston Maxime Boucher, I have a question for you," she said.

"I thought you might." Max's body seemed stiffer against Edie's now, his posture more upright. "Ask away, witch."

"My mother's college roommate was Jacquette Mounier." Sabrina laid heavy emphasis on the name, as if he ought to recognize it.

Since he didn't ask for clarification, evidently he did. "That wasn't a question."

The unexpected intensity of the confrontation had silenced everyone else in the room. Wherever this was going...it wouldn't be pleasant. Edie knew that much already, and so did Gwen, Starla, Kip, and Lorraine.

The telepath was casting a worried glance upward at her wife from the mattress on the floor while the oracle shrank back in her chair. The troll cousins, in contrast, had scooted forward, until they were sitting on the edge of their love seat cushions. They were watching the tense conversation like a tennis match, their heads swinging in tandem toward each speaker, their expressions avid. If they could have purchased a bucket of popcorn to share, Edie was certain they would've already done so. Several buckets, in fact.

And beside her, Max had gone so still and tense she might have been cuddling a concrete pillar. His hand cupping her shoulder squeezed tighter, until she could feel each individual fingertip pressing into her flesh. Then, with a detached-sounding apology, he let her go entirely and dropped his arm to his side.

"Jacquette Mounier, your longtime lover," the witch elaborated, dragging out the words syllable by syllable. "The Enhanced human you fucked and fed from for over a decade. The woman last seen disappearing into your luxury DC condo shortly after the Battle for Containment, never to return. Mom told me all about her. Even years after they graduated, they stayed in touch."

At that, Edie twitched. He spared her a quick glance, his mouth thinning, before turning back to their host.

"Again." He sounded bored. "Still waiting for a question."

Sabrina's eyes were cold and dark as they studied him. "Did you kill her?"

"Yes," Max said without hesitation.

22

Blood rushed deafeningly in Edie's ears, muffling whatever reaction the others might have had to Max's admission, and she struggled to think. To reason through what was happening and what he'd just admitted. Because the Max she knew—the Max she'd decided not to doubt, even for a moment, ever again—wouldn't murder anyone, much less a longtime lover, in cold blood.

Well, his blood was always cold. That was kind of a fundamental thing about vampires. So yeah, okay, if he killed, he'd definitely do so in cold blood. But he wouldn't kill an innocent or someone who didn't force his hand through their own actions.

She believed that. Down to her marrow.

Looping an arm through his, she pressed closer to Max's side. He exhaled slowly, and the thigh muscles that had bunched beneath her palm relaxed a tad.

"So you admit your guilt." Judgment dripped from every sneering syllable of Sabrina's next question, and she stood tall, fists braced on her hips. "Do you feel any remorse for murdering a woman so much weaker than you?"

"None at all," he told her with a smile.

Gwen inhaled sharply and curled up into a fetal position in her armchair, while the trolls' eyebrows rose in unison. Starla continued to watch Sabrina, concern cutting deep creases across her forehead.

And Max . . .

Not that he would willingly reveal any vulnerability to the witch currently interrogating him, but—Edie couldn't spot any falseness in his expression. More . . . genuine amusement.

What had this Jacquette woman *done* to him?

"And then, after you pitilessly murdered your human lover, you disappeared, seemingly into thin air"—Sabrina's fingers flicked outward in a sort of *poof* gesture—"and managed to entirely escape punishment for taking the life of an innocent person."

Now Edie sat forward too, because they were finally coming to the crucial bit. The context. The part of the story Sabrina had gotten wrong, which would explain what he'd done and why.

"Innocent?" Max actually laughed, long and hard. "Yes. Of course. Poor, innocent Jacquette, slain by her cruel vampire lover despite her utter blamelessness."

"Are you—" Sabrina's nostrils flared, her cheeks darkening with her enraged flush. "Are you smearing the reputation of a woman you *murdered*, vamp?"

"I'd explain more, but . . ." He waved a dismissive hand. "My apologies. I can see you rendered your verdict long ago, witch. I'd only waste your time by arguing my case now."

The thought of Sabrina—of everyone in this room—believing such a terrible thing of Max for even one more minute . . .

No. They needed to hear the truth. The *entire* truth. Because it would absolve him of blame, and they needed to believe in his fundamental trustworthiness before entering battle with him tomorrow. Otherwise, the only one who'd have his back would be Edie, and she couldn't be everywhere at once. She didn't have the strength of a troll, or the potential power of witches and oracles and telepaths, or . . .

Or whatever the half-fae Girl Explorers had. Other than badges. And delicious cookies.

"I want to hear it, Max." Remembering his half-delirious confession the previous night, Edie immediately commenced Operation Doe Eyes, tugging on his arm until he had no choice but to look down at her and confront her wide, pleading stare. "Tell me what happened. Please."

As he met her gaze, she might have fluttered her lashes once or twice. Then one of those lashes must have detached and fallen onto her freaking eyeball, because suddenly she was squinting and blinking involuntarily, her right eye watering. Dammit.

"My coveralls-clad femme fatale," he murmured, and brushed away the moisture from the crest of her cheek. "I think it's out now, darling. Better?"

After she nodded, he spoke to her. Only to her, albeit at full volume.

"Feeding directly from a human is a vulnerable act for everyone involved, my Edie." He took her hand in his and laced their fingers together. "We can easily kill our blood source, of course."

"Of course," said Sabrina with bitter sarcasm.

He ignored her. "But drinking fresh blood is an intimate, pleasurable process for vampires, with or without sex. It's such a powerful relief of hunger, it naturally engenders goodwill and trust toward our human suppliers. Whether or not they deserve that trust. And the more often you feed on the same person, the easier it gets to become attached and . . . careless. Particularly if sex *is* part of the experience."

"Basically, you catch feelings," Edie said. "Even if the relationship is meant to be entirely transactional, but especially if it's not."

She was trying her best not to envision Max holding other lovers' hands over the centuries. Combing through other lovers' hair with gentle fingers. Watching other lovers with soft denim-blue eyes.

But she wouldn't have wanted him to be alone all that time, would she? And those previous men and women had helped him develop the dicking-related skills he'd displayed last night, so . . . maybe she wasn't jealous of all those exes after all. Maybe she was grateful to them.

Other than this Jacquette fucker. Without even knowing the full story, Edie already hated her for betraying Max. For forcing him into violence and turning him even more cynical. For driving him into total isolation.

"So you trusted . . . Jacquette." The other woman's name tasted bitter on Edie's tongue. "And then you got careless."

His thumb skimmed over the back of her hand. "After the Battle for Containment, I was tapped to become a SERC representative. I was reluctant to get so deeply involved in political wrangling among and within various species—"

Edie snorted. "I bet."

Max wouldn't have been known for his tactful diplomacy and goodwill toward all, even back then. Not after centuries of bloodshed and infighting and hiding from those who'd gladly eradicate his kind, and *especially* not after what happened to his parents. Edie would lay good money on *that*.

"—but my mentor, my late mother's truest friend, convinced me the Council needed a vampire presence, especially one with my longevity and power. So I agreed to serve. Jacquette supported me in that decision."

The only sound in the room came from a shadowy corner, where a clock perched on a bookshelf ticked away their remaining hours. Otherwise there was utter silence.

"There are very few Enhanced humans with two separate, distinct talents." The muscles in Max's jaw jumped. "I knew Jacquette was a necromancer, but she didn't tell me about her second ability. Pyrokinesis."

Gwen's palm rested protectively over her belly. "She could set fires with her mind?"

A stake through my heart will kill me, he'd once told Edie. *So will removing my head or . . . burning me alive.*

His voice had gone a bit funny at that last part, if she remembered correctly. And he'd swallowed hard enough that she'd noted his discomfort.

Oh shit.

"Yes," Max said tersely. "As I discovered firsthand, at the same time I confronted her *other* vampire lover. Janos, an ally of many centuries who wanted the SERC seat for himself. He arrived at my home fresh from slaying my mentor, and Jacquette let him inside as I slept."

Eyes wide, Kip ripped open a bag of truffle-flecked potato chips he'd unearthed from somewhere. "Daaaaaaamn."

"That's some *Jerry Springer* shit right there," Lorraine agreed, and grabbed a handful.

Max's attention didn't stray from Edie. "To her credit, Jacquette had no interest in political power. She desired my wealth. At the time, she was the main beneficiary in my will."

Only complete trust would have prompted him to change his will for her. And then—

"After feeding and other ... activities with Jacquette, I'd dozed off." Max's hand tightened on hers, and she squeezed back as hard as she could. "I woke in flames."

Her breath hitched, and she had to close her eyes for a moment because ... dear gods and goddesses. She couldn't imagine it. She didn't *want* to imagine it.

Starla gasped. A choked sound came from Gwen's chair, where she had a hand clamped over her mouth, her stare tear-bright and horrified. Sabrina's fists fell from her hips.

Kip and Lorraine made big eyes at each other, then each took another mouthful of chips.

The question stuck in Edie's throat, too terrible to utter in full. "Janos ... what did he ..."

Her hands were trembling, and Max chafed them. As if she were merely cold and not aghast and sickened and roiling with too many emotions to name.

"He held me in place." When she furrowed her brow in silent confusion, he somehow interpreted the look correctly. "Protective gear, sweet Edie. He came prepared. For the fire, anyway."

His lips twisted into a small smile then. It wasn't pretty.

"If that's what actually happened," Sabrina said, her voice gruff but less hostile than before, "how the hells did you survive?"

Max's shoulder lifted in that signature Gallic shrug. "I'd always been mindful of Jacquette's relative fragility. She didn't have any conception of how strong I truly was. And Janos might have been an old, powerful vampire, but I was older. More powerful. More than capable of ripping out one betrayer's throat and removing another's head. Even as I burned."

"Holy fuck," Edie whispered. "Max, you must have been in agony."

He inclined his head. "Yes. That."

She could only make a pained noise in response.

Her nose was running. She couldn't see him or anything clearly anymore, and then something soft brushed against her wet face. A handkerchief, which he'd apparently kept tucked away in his hoodie's pocket. Tenderly, Max blotted her eyes and cheeks before pressing the cloth into her free hand.

"Since I know you'll doubt my version of events . . ." After a final, light kiss to Edie's temple, he turned back to Sabrina. "Once the inaugural SERC representatives took office, they sent authorities to investigate the incident. I'd called one of the other reps-to-be myself as soon as I was capable of crawling to the nearest phone. The records are sealed, however, because the Council was new and fragile back then. Reps were worried a story about violent infighting would damage their reputation and bring bad press to all Supernaturals and Enhanced humans."

The witch pursed her lips, her fingers uncurling. "Convenient."

"At the moment? Not especially." The words were surprisingly wry. "After communications are back online, I'll have the documents made available to everyone in this room. With one caveat."

Kip and Lorraine froze mid-chew when that awful smile stretched across Max's face again.

"If you disclose the incident to anyone else," he told them, cold eyes sweeping across the living room and all its inhabitants, "you won't live long enough to regret it."

When his gaze met Edie's, he shook his head.

I don't mean you, he mouthed. *You wouldn't tell anyone.*

Her lips curved, and she nudged his knee with hers.

Kip spoke through a mouthful of potato chips. "Did SERC ask you to drop out of sight? So they could keep things quiet?"

"Yes. But I was preparing to disappear even before they made their request. Janos and Jacquette each had their defenders, who might wish to avenge them. And my desire to interact with anyone of any species was . . ." He thought for a moment. "Minimal, shall we say."

Everything he'd just told her—told them all—explained so much about the man she'd met three years ago, and even more about the vampire she'd met only that week.

The wrist cuff of his hoodie had folded over on itself, and she smoothed it back in place. "You've passed for human ever since?"

"The day I left DC, Chad was born"—he flashed her a brief, bright grin at the mention of his beer-bro persona—"and Gaston Maxime Boucher disappeared. Not even the Council knows exactly where I live now or what I'm doing, despite their repeated requests for that information. Any communication with my remaining SERC contacts occurs via secure encrypted messages so they can't let anything slip either."

Had she been the first person to learn his true name in two decades?

He turned toward the others and waited until everyone was looking at him. "Let me be clear once more: If the Council discovers my current identity or whereabouts because of someone in this room, I will find out." He paused for emphasis, his voice subarctic. "And you will suffer before you die."

"Take it down a few thousand notches, bro." Lorraine munched on a cheese-topped cracker. From whence that cracker had arrived or by what means, Edie couldn't have said. "No one here's narcing on you to the dipshits at SERC."

Despite Lorraine's comment, Edie didn't imagine anyone in the room had missed the primary target of Max's challenging stare. Sabrina herself certainly hadn't.

"Why did you do that, vampire?" The witch was rubbing her forehead again, the dark shadows beneath her eyes mute evidence of her exhaustion. "If you're such a secretive recluse, why share so much private information with an entire roomful of strangers?"

"You're the one who tampered with our cider, witch," he said flatly. "Seems like you should know the answer to that question."

Gwen's mouth dropped open as she straightened in her chair. She directed an incredulous glare at Sabrina, even as a dozen Girl Explorers—whose auditory capabilities were apparently quite impressive—burst from the main bedroom and marched back into the fray.

"What did you do to the cider, Sabrina?" Riley demanded. "Tell us. *Now.*"

The glamour disguising Riley's true features flickered for a split second, revealing the unearthly glow of her skin and the soft points of her ear tips. Her fingers lengthened, then shrank back to tween girl size before Edie could blink.

Their host sighed. "It's a simple truth-telling spell. Even if you drank your whole mug of cider, it should be wearing off by now. There are no permanent effects. And it shouldn't have done any harm whatsoever to your baby, Gwen, so please stop looking at me like that."

"You didn't trust me?" Kip set aside a platter of blinis and caviar, genuine hurt in his warm brown eyes. "Or Lorrie? After all these years?"

"I knew you two were hiding something, Kip. Hells, even Riley and the godsdamn Girl Explorers were keeping secrets. How could I trust you with my life, and possibly Starla's too, if I didn't know what those secrets were?" The weary sadness in Sabrina's expression vanished as she turned her attention back to Max. "You haven't answered my question, vampire. Yeah, I cast a spell on the cider, but we both know you metabolized its effects more quickly than anyone else here—"

"Because you're suuuper old," Edie said under her breath.

"—so telling us everything was a choice you made. Not a magical compulsion."

For the first time all night, even Max seemed tired too. "Edie needs to survive tomorrow's battle. I'm the one who can best ensure her safety, so I need to survive too. We require allies who trust us and will help watch out for us, and your accusations undercut our credibility. I had to repair the damage you inflicted, witch. If that meant telling my sad tale of flesh-melting, throat-ripping woe and jettisoning over two decades of secrecy, so be it."

"The story sounded genuine," the witch said. "But since you told it *after* the spell wore off, I have no way of confirming its truth before the battle."

His smile displayed a large number of teeth. "I guess you'll just have to trust me."

"Fuck." Sabrina turned to her wife. "Star? I know you're exhausted already, but . . ."

Starla slumped down onto the mattress and shook her head. "I can't. Not if you want my help with communications tomorrow night."

Max pointed at the telepath, his smile softening. "That reminds me—we haven't heard *your* secrets yet, have we, Starla?" The words should have sounded like a challenge, but Max's teasing tone stripped them of any real aggression. "Do you have something you'd like to tell us?"

"As a matter of fact, I do." She offered him a cheeky grin. "You should know better than to drink something a witch offers you. Even if that witch is my incredibly hot wife, whose motivations are both admirable and benign." The relentless *tick-tick-tick* of the clock filled her brief pause. "*Relatively* benign."

Lorraine *harrumph*ed, shoving her blunt bangs away from her eyes so as to glower more effectively at Sabrina. "Even if you could tell we were keeping secrets, you should have had faith that they weren't dangerous. Not to you, anyway."

The witch dropped down onto the mattress beside her wife. Her ponytail, disheveled and limp at the end of a long day, flopped against her slim back, and the telepath smoothed it with a shaky hand.

"I can't die tomorrow. I can't. I have to get back to Starla." Carefully, Sabrina settled an arm around her wife's shoulders and eased her closer. "I needed to know tonight whether I could count on you to have my back in battle tomorrow or whether you might betray me."

Max made a very rude, very emphatic noise. "How do we know we can trust *you*? You just tricked every single one of us without compunction or apology."

"Mini-vamp's not wrong." Lorraine raised a dark brow and eyed their host with disfavor. "You might be hiding something too, *friend-o.*"

Sabrina winced at the sarcasm in the troll's voice.

"So here you are, witch. Your own credibility damaged by your attempt to determine ours." A slow smirk spread across Max's face. "And you want us to have your back tomorrow?"

"Yes," Sabrina said, clearly biting back the urge to add *asshole.* "As I just said. In almost those exact words."

"Then I have some good news for you." Max's cup rested on the floor by his feet, and he reached down to reclaim it. "After I poured out most of my own cider, I transferred half of Edie's into my mug when she wasn't looking, just in case you'd deceived us. Which you did."

Standing, Max loomed over the Enhanced couple and pushed his mug into Sabrina's hand.

His smile curdled into a sneer. "Drink it, witch."

No one in the room objected. Even Sabrina's longtime friends.

"Hey, vamp bro." Kip was craning his neck to check the couch and its surroundings. "Where'd you pour your cider? There's not, like, a potted plant near you or anything."

Max never took his eyes off Sabrina. "Consider that a delightful mystery for you to solve, Kip. Later. Once our interrogator gets a literal taste of her own medicine."

"Fine." Expressionless, she tipped the mug and swallowed the remnants of Edie's drink. "Now what?"

Lorraine crunched on a burrata-topped bruschetta of mysterious provenance. "Now we wait roughly, uh"—she glanced at her cousin, who held up ten fingers, since his mouth was full of bruschetta goodness too—"ten minutes? Ten minutes. And then we start asking questions."

So they waited, steeping in awkward silence all the while. But at least Gwen was no longer shrinking away from Max whenever he glanced in her direction, and Kip and Lorraine had stopped studying him with fascinated horror, like visitors at a zoo's tarantula exhibit. The Girl Explorers appeared entirely indifferent and unconcerned with his presence, as they always had.

Getting a handle on Starla's state of mind proved more difficult, because the telepath had focused her entire attention on Sabrina. The women were deep in conversation, murmuring to each other while the witch gently rubbed circles on her wife's back. Which was, in fact, the exact same thing Max's hand was currently doing between Edie's own shoulder blades.

She had to wonder whether either Max or Sabrina had caught the irony yet. Whether they'd recognized how closely they mirrored each other in what they were doing and their reasons for doing it. Probably not.

Starla's gaze flicked in Edie's direction. When their eyes met, the telepath tipped her head toward her wife, then toward Max, and winked. Edie bit back an answering grin, whereupon the other woman resumed her conversation with Sabrina.

Before this cluster of unfortunateness ended, Edie intended to get Starla's number and email address. Clearly, the two of them had *a lot* to discuss.

Lorraine pounced as soon as the ten minutes were up.

"So, Sabby . . ." Sitting back in the love seat, the troll swallowed her final bite of fig and chevre pizza. "Before we go into battle with you, what should we know that you haven't told us?"

After glancing down to where Starla's hand was squeezing her knee, the witch exhaled slowly. "I'm usually stronger than this, magically speaking, but I'm devoting a good chunk of my energy toward Starla's health right now."

"I'm not sure I fully understand how energy expenditure works when it comes to magic." Gwen's forehead crinkled. "What exactly do you mean?"

"Minor enchantments, like the one I cast over the cider, only require a bit of memorization and a limited burst of strength. Major spells, though . . ." Sabrina rolled her neck on her shoulders, stretching out any kinks there. "They demand a far higher cost. To invoke that much power without draining your own resources, you need vast amounts of inherent talent, a near-eidetic memory, and a background of lengthy, intensive study of the Magical Arts."

"Okay." Gwen seemed fascinated. "But what if you don't have the opportunity for that kind of study or you don't have quite enough talent?"

"In other words, what if you're a witch like me?" Sabrina's laugh held a bitter, sharp edge. "If you're insufficient in any area, those sorts of spells—serious healing spells, for example—can leave you essentially powerless for days or weeks. And even for the most gifted practitioners imaginable, saving a life that's already been assigned to the reapers exacts a greater and greater cost over time."

The witch didn't look at her wife. She didn't have to.

Lorraine's voice had gentled. "What happens when you can't pay that cost anymore? When you have nothing left to give?"

"You can give up. Let the reapers take their due. Or if you know the right rituals . . ." Sabrina shifted uneasily on the mattress. "You can offer another life in exchange."

If that witch was thinking what Edie *thought* she was thinking, she could think again.

The witch, that was. Sabrina. Not Edie.

Anyway. Antecedents be damned, if that magical motherfucker tried to sacrifice Max, even for such a heartrending, understandable cause, Edie and her cleaver would intervene. Violently.

Kip inclined his head. "Blood magic."

"Blood isn't necessary. Only a human or Supernatural life." Sabrina smiled wryly at that. "I would gladly relinquish mine, but Starla would never forgive me."

Her eyes fell on Max. "Once I heard your full name and figured out who you were, I thought about offering your life instead. But as weak as I am right now, I wasn't sure I could get the drop on you. Also, my stubborn wife vetoed that option."

"I believe your story," Starla told Max. "Even though I can't read your mind at the moment."

Discreetly, Edie slipped her cleaver back into her crossbody bag.

"My wife is far more trusting than I am. Until I see some definitive evidence, I'm not declaring you innocent of that woman's murder." The suspicion on Sabrina's face softened into resignation. "I'll say this much, though: After talking to Starla, I do trust you at my back in battle tomorrow. Not because of your inherent goodness or because I know you're not a conscienceless killer, but because of how you look at Edie."

Starla nodded, then murmured her gratitude when Sabrina readjusted the pillows supporting her upper body. "Like you'd tear apart the world with your bare hands if she got so much as a splinter."

Did he truly look at her like that?

Edie twisted her head to study his expression. Met his fierce blue gaze.

Yeah. Yeah, he kinda did. Wow.

"Saving Edie will be your primary objective tomorrow. Saving yourself will be your secondary goal. The rest of us are tertiary concerns for you at best," Sabrina told Max, ticking off his priorities on her fingers. "But to keep Edie happy, you'll do your best to save us too. She'd mourn our deaths, and if you blithely let us fall when you could have prevented our grisly demises, she wouldn't forgive you."

Still looking down at Edie, he pursed his lips and shook his head.

"It's true." His forefinger skimmed over a particularly ticklish spot near her ribs. "She's a real pain in the ass. Sadly, however, she's *my* pain in the ass."

She opened her mouth to say something about the endless ass-based pain she'd been experiencing since the day they'd first met. Then she considered the possible anal sex implications, noted their rapt audience of Girl Explorers, and chose a different response.

"How dare you." Smacking away his hand, she feigned outrage. "I'm a godsdamn *delight*."

"It's true!" Lorraine said. "I can tell already. We're going to be bro besties!"

Riley frowned at the troll. "Earlier, you said I would be your bestie."

"Bestie connections know no limits." Lorraine flicked a wrist. "You can *both* be my new besties! Gwen too!"

"I'm not certain you entirely understand the word *best*," Riley told her. "Or *bro*."

Sabrina ignored the side chatter and continued addressing Max. "You'll help us tomorrow. I believe that, and I'm genuinely grateful for it." Her chest rose and dropped on a deep, deep sigh. "My wife and I don't have much power left. We'll need all the help we can get."

In her overstuffed armchair, Gwen was looking a little greenish again.

Not that the Fates had ever interceded on Edie's behalf before, but she sent them a mental entreaty anyway. *Please let us kill all the creatures before we have to actually battle them face-to-face. Otherwise, our merry band of zombie fighters is fucking toast.*

No answer. Stupid unresponsive Fates.

"I've now told you all my relevant secrets." Without rising from the mattress, the witch extended a hand toward Max. "Truce?"

When Edie kicked him in the leg, he grunted.

"Truce." He shook Sabrina's hand. "I'll do my best to keep you and everyone else alive, witch."

"For Edie's sake." Starla's lips twitched. "No other reason."

Yeah. The telepath was definitely onto his bullshit too. She and Edie really did need to talk at some point in the near future.

"Correct," he said.

Thank goodness they'd only be battling zombies tomorrow instead of the zombies *and* one another. Knowing that everyone involved could be trusted was really—

Edie's brows snapped together. "Wait a minute."

"Oh gods." Sabrina groaned. "What now?"

Starla didn't seem surprised when Edie looked to her. "Question, Star. Are witches affected by their own spells?"

Because if not, if Sabrina's enchantments didn't influence her, she could have lied to Max and Edie and everyone else about everything she'd just told them. And they'd have no way to verify the truth before tomorrow.

Much like Max's story.

The two of them had probably been twins in a past life. Annoying-as-fuck drama-queen twins who'd tried to eat each other in the womb.

Pressing her forefinger and thumb together, Starla mimed zipping her curved lips.

"Dammit, woman," Max—who'd apparently worked out the implications too—complained, and Starla giggled.

"So sorry, vampire." The witch's voice was saccharine-sweet. "I guess you'll just have to trust me."

He *harrumph*ed at the echo of his own words but didn't bother arguing. At least, not after Edie pressed her breast against his side in a particularly persuasive way.

Gwen levered herself up from her chair and trudged toward the kitchen. As she passed by them, Edie smiled up at her. "Thank you again for your warning about my blackberry-sage oil."

The oracle stopped, and her loose red braid swished along her back as she shook her head. "I appreciate your kindness, but we both know my prophesies were next to useless. They always are."

"I'm not just being nice." She truly wasn't. "You saved me a bunch of time and money and hassle, and I'm genuinely grateful."

Max shifted beside her. "As am I. Once spilled, glitter is a relentless adversary."

"Then why use it?" Edie asked him, befuddled. "No one's forcing you to."

"Because my sculpted features deserve to be highlighted in every way possible." His elegant nostrils flared as he sniffed. "Obviously."

Of course. She should have known.

Gwen's amused snort sounded a little damp. "If I helped you, I'm glad. But I still owe everyone in this house an apology. Our lives are at stake tomorrow. I can't fight worth a damn. And even though I'm a freaking oracle, my most helpful prophetic guidance tonight involved wayward craft supplies. For all our sakes, I wish to goodness I were much more Enhanced than I am."

Edie's heart ached for her. Before she could find the right words to comfort Gwen, though, Max spoke quietly.

"You made my life easier, little oracle." There wasn't a hint of sarcasm or glib charm in his words. Only truth and compassion. "In my centuries upon this Earth, very few others have done the same. That's not such a small thing."

"Thank you." Gwen inclined her head in acknowledgment, green eyes shining a little too brightly, then offered them both a small but genuine-looking smile before beelining toward the snacks.

"Hey. Vamp bro." Kip shuffled over to their couch on his knees. "You must have been worried about Sabby tampering with our food too, right? Did you squirrel away anything else? Because I'd gladly take leftovers off your . . ."

His face scrunched up, and he halted abruptly. Stretching an absurdly long leg out before him, he considered the wet spot on the knee of his jeans.

"Good news!" he called out, twisting around to address everyone in the room. "I solved the mystery of the missing cider! And Sabby, your new carpet is super great at hiding stains, as I now realize! Good call on the color!"

"It was Starla's choice." Sabrina's head tilted. "And . . . congratulations?"

The troll beamed. "Thanks, bro!"

"No leftovers," Max told him, then added a patently insincere "Apologies."

"That's disappointing. However . . ." Kip eyed the compact love seat where he and his cousin had been sitting, then the more expansive dimensions of the sofa directly in front of him. "Maxime. My good buddy."

Max raised an eyebrow.

"Someone's gonna have to sleep on the floor." The troll's sweeping gesture indicated the patch of sodden carpet. "And he who makes the wet spot takes the wet spot, so . . ."

Max's tone conveyed polite confusion. "Is that your ill-chosen way of asking us to move off the couch? So you can sleep here tonight?"

Kip's shoulders slumped. "It's not happening, is it?"

"Nope." Max leaned forward and gave him a hearty thump on the back, much like the one the troll had given him upon their introduction. So hearty, in fact, that Kip was basically flung face-first into the sofa. "Nice try, though."

"I suppose I deserved that," Kip wheezed when he got back to his knees. "But you're still an enormous dick, bro. And I don't mean the size of your penis, so please don't start talking about that again, Edie-my-love. *Please.*"

"Thank you," Max said placidly, tugging her closer to his side. Together, they watched Kip crawl off in search of more food. "I try."

23

At some point, everyone else drifted to other parts of the house, and Edie and Max finally had enough privacy to talk.

Well, semiprivacy. In the loft above, the trolls were ranking their evening's refreshments as they noisily crunched on yet another snack. But it was the most solitude Edie and her favorite vampire had managed all evening, and the most they might have until after the battle. And even this limited isolation wouldn't last long. Some of the Girl Explorers would need to make a bed on the living room floor, sooner rather than later.

She had so many things to say and no time to waste.

"Shit, Max," she whispered, as soon as they were alone. "I'm so sorry."

His voice was quiet too, and very, very warm. "Why? You've done nothing wrong, my Edie."

Gods and goddesses above, where to begin? She could apologize for the remainder of the night, and it wouldn't be enough.

Kissing her fingertips, she pressed them over his heart and took a deep breath.

"I'm sorry you were forced to reveal your secrets so publicly when you'd have preferred to keep silent. I'm sorry you had to re-live such an awful moment in your life. I'm sorry you were betrayed and terribly hurt on every possible level by your ally and your lover." Her breath hitched. "And I'm sorry my decisions brought you here, to a place where you don't trust anyone. I'm sorry you're about to risk your life to protect me—to protect all of us—instead of hunkering down safely and comfortably in your basement."

One broad hand rose to cover hers on his chest while the other cradled her nape.

"You know," he said thoughtfully, "I think I prefer *lair* to *basement*. It sounds classier. More archvillain, less *guy who lives with his mom and works part-time at Foot Locker*."

She huffed out a laugh. "Less Chad, you mean."

"Precisely." His fingertip smoothed a strand of hair behind her ear. "Darling, I don't think you understand what was happening to me down in my lair. Without your intervention, I might have been safe in the moment, but not for much longer."

Did he think the zombies could potentially reach him down there? Despite the ladder and the freaking water pit? "You're right. I don't understand."

"I was detaching." The words were stark, his eyes certain. "Some days, even drinking a blood pack felt like too much effort."

Was he telling her he'd eventually have starved himself? Compared to the alternative form of detachment he'd mentioned—a blood-drenched killing spree—it was certainly the preferable option, but . . . there would have been no more Gaston/Max/Chad in the world? Anywhere?

The thought of it squeezed her heart like a vicious fist.

His forehead came to rest against hers, underlining the intimacy of his confession. "The only living being who truly interested me anymore was my human neighbor. The only duty I still cared about was keeping her safe, even as I kept her at a distance. The only bright moments in my endless days were my encounters with her, when she'd ring my doorbell and patiently suffer through another conversation with fucking *Chad*."

"But . . ." That couldn't be true. "What about your videos?"

"They helped, but not enough to keep me tethered to my life." He lifted his hand from hers, and his fingers tunneled through her hair, working out the tangles in slow, gentle tugs. "I'm grateful to care deeply about anything at all, sweet Edie. And I'm beyond lucky to care deeply about *you*."

Her sinuses had begun to prickle. "I don't . . ."

I don't think anyone's valued me this much in over two decades. I don't know what I'll do if you die tomorrow. I don't care what anyone else believes about you, or about us as a couple, as long as I know the truth of who and what you are.

"You're worth every risk I'm taking. You deserve everything I have to offer." The tip of his nose glided along the side of hers, the tenderness in the gesture matching the open adoration in his words. "I don't want your apologies, ma puce. I want to thank you."

A declaration that nakedly heartfelt from such an embittered and suspicious vampire would have melted the knees of even the most hardened soul. Edie was many things, but not hard.

She sniffled. Loudly. Then ducked her head for a moment.

"Did you . . ." He paused. "Did you just wipe your nose on my hoodie? Again?"

Yes. Because her system simply couldn't handle more sincere emotion right now, and if he kept being so sweet, she'd be tempted to jump him despite the presence of nearby trolls. Who would most likely peer over the loft railing and watch, snacking happily all the while.

She wasn't shy. Dabbling in a little exhibitionism might be worth it.

No, she had to remember the Girl Explorers. They could walk in at any moment, dammit.

"Who's to say?" she said breezily. "Maybe I did smear leaky mucus on you. Maybe I didn't."

His gusty exhalation caressed her face. "You did. Even though I have a handkerchief. You *know* I have a handkerchief. I used it on you earlier tonight."

"But it's not clean anymore. I don't want a dirty handkerchief."

"Yes." Lifting his head, he glanced down at the glistening patch on his shoulder. "How awful that would be."

"Thank you for your very sincere agreement." She eased back an inch or two. "I know you don't want me to apologize, but I still wish I hadn't brought you to the home of someone who doesn't trust your good intentions."

He gave the back of her neck a comforting squeeze. "Prior to SERC's formation, Supernaturals and Enhanced humans preyed on common humans and one another without consequence, other than occasional vigilante justice. When her mother's friend died in my company, the first SERC reps hadn't taken office. No one knew about their investigation of the incident. No one knew about Jacquette's perfidy. Of course the witch suspected me of murder." His shoulders lifted in a tiny shrug. "I wasn't sure whether her mother had shared the story, but if so, I knew I'd be the villain of the piece. Which was part of the reason I kept track of her whereabouts over the years, and why I was reluctant to come here today. But we had no real choice. I took a calculated risk and lost."

And he'd taken that risk trying to do the right thing. For her, but also for the world at large. It wasn't, as he'd said to Gwen earlier, such a small thing.

"The witch's suspicions might annoy me," he added, "but they don't offend me, and they certainly don't hurt me. If we hadn't needed allies tomorrow, I wouldn't have even bothered rebutting her accusations, except to you. In private."

Honestly? That was an awfully tolerant view of Sabrina's interrogation. Especially given the abject horribleness of the events he'd been prodded into recounting and the crowd of strangers who'd also borne witness to his unwilling confession.

"I'd rather have heard the story under other circumstances, but I understand your cynicism better now." Using the sleeve of her coveralls, she swiped at the moisture on his hoodie. "And I understand why it might take a while to trust me with all your secrets. I won't badger you. Not even to find out your true age."

His grin brightened the dim living room. "We both know that's a lie."

"Yes." She raised a finger in emphasis. "But one told with the best of intentions, as well as a sincere desire for it to be true. So it basically *is* the truth in all important respects."

"That's also a lie."

"According to certain faulty definitions of the term."

He snorted, then steered them out of their conversational detour. "Jacquette was the last human who fed me directly, mouth to skin. Also my last lover. I didn't intend to put myself in such a vulnerable position ever again, and I didn't need to. Bagged blood had become widely available for the first time, and I'm more than capable of taking care of my own sexual needs. So there was no more biting. No more lovemaking."

Pinning her in place with a meaningful stare, he waited for her to say it.

"Until me," she whispered.

"Until you." Lightly, he tugged a fistful of her hair in emphasis. "That's my point. Despite all your unconvincing, easily disproven lies, I *do* trust you. If I didn't, I wouldn't feed from you. I wouldn't fuck you. My Edie, I don't require more time to allay my doubts, because I no longer have any."

For a secretive, jaded vampire like Max, a statement like that was . . .

It was a declaration of love. Full stop.

Edie couldn't breathe. Couldn't speak. Couldn't do anything but cling to his hoodie with one hand, his shoulder with the other, and bask in the warmth that filled her chest and coursed through her veins.

"If I hadn't worried about frightening you, I would have told you about Jacquette after our first night together. But I did worry." His brow creased. "If I'd confessed to killing my last human lover and you'd flinched away from me . . ."

Not long ago, she would have. Even yesterday might have been too soon. But since then, she'd seen him soaked in blood, absorbing wound after life-threatening wound in his own front doorway, determined to spare her even the slightest injury. She'd watched him carefully assist a nauseated human he didn't even know. She'd heard the gentleness in his voice whenever he spoke to a very, very ill woman he'd only met earlier in the day.

This evening, when he'd admitted to killing his former human lover, she'd been confused. Concerned. But not afraid of him, even for a moment.

"If you'd turned away or fled . . ." His throat bobbed in a hard swallow. "I thought it might break something inside me. Irrevocably."

She still had no words, so she kissed him instead. Hard.

He seemed more than happy with her nonverbal response.

LATER THAT NIGHT, as Max and Edie lay spooning beneath a quilt on the couch, various Girl Explorers snoring on the floor below, he quietly asked if she still dreaded the prospect of killing zombies who hadn't attacked her first.

After wriggling deeper into the curve of his body, she searched for an honest answer.

"I think of them standing in a sunless underground compound, watching a television," Edie finally whispered, gathering her words in small handfuls. "Groomed to kill and be killed from their first breath. Disposable. Unloved."

He made a sort of humming sound. Acknowledgment of what she'd said and encouragement to continue speaking.

"It hurts my heart, Max." Her breath hitched, and his arms closed more tightly around her. "But whatever they used to be in that moment . . . it's gone. Starla told us as much. They have no conscience. No drive except hunger. They murdered my parents, they would gladly kill everyone in this house and on this continent, and they won't stop until they're dead."

"True," he said neutrally.

"I'd be figuring out ways to capture them alive so scientists could fix whatever went wrong in them, but I read the documents you sent me." When she shook her head, her hair rubbed against the couch cushion serving as her pillow. "The government already tried all that. The few zombies they managed to lure outside the compound and whisk away to yet another secret underground laboratory failed to respond to any known or experimental treatment. Whatever snapped in them ..."

He kissed the top of her head. "It stayed broken."

"Yes. And without fail, scientists and researchers died in the process of reaching that conclusion." Restlessly, she picked at the seam of the cushion. "We both know the government has no interest in the creatures as sentient beings. At best, they'd become cannon fodder. Weapons to use against anyone deemed too dangerous to live. At worst ..."

His hand came to rest atop hers, stilling her anxious fidgeting, and he interlaced their fingers. "At worst?"

She skimmed her thumb over his. "At worst, we'd find ourselves in the exact same place we are now. Hunkering down in our homes with mindless, bloodthirsty zombies on the loose, wondering how far they'll get and how many they'll slaughter before they're stopped again. *If* they're stopped again."

She wished they had more privacy. Whenever they lay skin to skin, their barriers of clothing tossed aside, the coolness of his embrace calmed her agitated thoughts.

As did the very enjoyable orgasms he gave her while naked. Alas.

She sighed. "So . . . to answer your original question, I'm not exactly thrilled to kill creatures who haven't tried to kill us first, but I don't see another livable choice."

"If tomorrow's encounter devolves into a physical battle, don't wait for them to attack before you do." His biceps bunched beneath her neck, steely with tension. "You can't hesitate, my Edie. If you hesitate, you're lost. And I am too."

"I understand." Ducking her head, she rubbed her cheek against that bulge of flexed muscle. "Is that something you'll have to remember too? Are you worried you'll hesitate to kill them without immediate provocation?"

Silence.

Then his hands curled into fists, and his cold, quiet words emerged in neat lines, like ice blocks chopped from a glacial lake.

"They took your parents from you. You had to listen to your family die." The statements radiated so much chilly menace she actually shivered. "Almost every inch of your fragile body is bruised. You nearly drowned. You became hypothermic. Your ankle is injured."

Now that he mentioned it, she probably should have popped some ibuprofen in preparation for tomorrow's exertions. Running for her life would have been easier in her twenties, that was for certain.

"They've stalked you in my presence. Treated you like common prey. Savored the anticipation of your death." The subarctic precision of his voice raised goose bumps on her arms. "If they could, they'd rip out your throat and snatch you from me."

She winced, but he wasn't quite done.

"I intend to scour them from this earth," he said calmly.

It was a simple declaration of fact, so cold and emotionless it sounded dead. The verbal equivalent of absolute zero, and she hoped never to hear its like again.

For a while, they continued cuddling in renewed silence.

She cleared her throat. "I'll take that as a no."

"That was a no," he confirmed.

24

Edie couldn't decide which of Max's hands she appreciated more: the one idly playing with her clit or the one clamped over her mouth, stifling her moans as he fucked her slowly from behind.

On the one hand—ha-ha—this predawn rendezvous only remained private because of their absolute silence. They'd crept out of the living room and down the hall without waking a single Girl Explorer or restless troll. They'd shut and locked the bathroom door behind them without even a single incriminating click or creak. He'd bent her over the vanity and slid inside her, and she'd bit her lip against the gorgeous stretch without so much as a whimper. At a certain point in the proceedings, though, her own efforts hadn't been sufficient, and he'd offered to help muffle the desperate sounds vibrating in her throat.

In short, his left hand was doing good, necessary work.

On the literal other hand, dude was also fingering her clit. With a great deal of know-how, manual dexterity, and commitment.

Yeah. She couldn't even lie to herself. Clit hand won, hands down.

Like, down between her thighs. Where he was currently working her toward a second orgasm, because apparently the drop from six climaxes to one during a single sexual encounter would bring shame upon him and the entire Boucher lineage. At least, that was what she thought he'd muttered. She'd been too busy coming around his cock and keening into his palm with incredulous pleasure to listen all that closely.

The vanity mirror reflected the fierce lust in his gaze as he watched himself sink into her each time, watched his fingers stroking and teasing and circling, watched her clutch desperately at the sink's countertop as her legs shook and threatened to collapse beneath her.

He paused, waiting until her eyes met his in the steam-edged reflection. Then he sank his fangs into the side of her neck, the penetration as leisurely as his endless, deliberate pushes inside her. The heat between her legs flared and bloomed everywhere. His bite was a firm pinch of her nipples, the heel of his hand against her clit, a flick of his tongue against her earlobe, the glide of fingertips up her inner thighs, and a wet mouth dragged down her throat.

And she was done. Done.

His rhythm didn't falter when she came. As she clamped down on his dick and spasmed against his knowing hand, he kept his palm sealed over her open, gasping mouth and the guttural moans she couldn't bite back, and he held on to his control.

Once she'd gone limp beneath him, though, he yanked the hand towel free of its hook.

"Bite on this," he told her, the order sharp but quiet, as blood dripped from the punctures in her neck.

Once she obeyed, he ducked his head to lick the carmine trail clean, gripped both her hips, and held her in place as he bit down once more and fucked her to oblivion. Again.

The tight leash over his control had slipped, and only his mouth against her throat muffled his grunts as he pumped inside her. Her final orgasm followed his by a split second, spurred on by how perfectly he ground into her, the way each swallow of her blood might have been a slow, sweet suck of her clit.

When they'd both begun to recover and he'd taken care of the condom, he tongued the small wounds he'd made and studied her flushed face and pleasure-hazed eyes in the mirror.

His own expression relaxed and happy, he smiled at her as he lifted his head. His faded-denim eyes were soft and bright, the curve of his lips fond. He looked young in that moment. Care-free, for all the horror that awaited them later in the day. More Chad than Max.

"You know," she rasped in a thread of sound. "Ridiculous as Chad was, he was still uber-hot. I didn't want to, but . . . sometimes I thought about him when I touched myself."

"Is that so?" His murmured response against her ear, full of salacious interest, touched off another small, electric aftershock.

She nodded.

"Show me."

And somehow, she ended up with the hand towel back in her mouth, her fingers swirling around her swollen, sensitive clit while his own fingers rubbed insistently inside her.

So that was orgasm number four, otherwise known as the

orgasm that would make Max unbearably smug as soon as she stopped coming. Which would be infuriating, but not nearly as infuriating as it would have been prior to four orgasms.

Afterward, she had to wash her hands, then run water into her cupped palms and drink several times before her parched throat could produce more words. Silently, he gestured toward the stack of disposable cups beside the sink. Silently, she encouraged him to mind his own beeswax via an upraised middle finger.

He grinned and drew an invisible check mark in the air. Then he pointed to her, held up four fingers, indicated himself, and lifted a single pointer finger. In retaliation, she flicked her wet hands to spray his face with water, then counted out six of her own fingers and spread her hands in confused dismay, doing her best to radiate sexual disappointment.

His nostrils flared in a silent snort.

Spoiled, he mouthed.

Well, she couldn't argue with that. Instead of trying, she simply shuffled over to the shower on jellylike legs and got the water running. As soon as it was lukewarm, she stepped into the stall and began soaping away the sticky evidence of their early-morning activities.

He stripped down and joined her shortly thereafter. A lot of people—beings?—were going to need hot water soon, so when his hands began to wander again, she smacked them away. Despite his aggrieved groan, he kept things speedy and non-lascivious after that.

When they finished up and stepped out, the obvious occurred to her: There wouldn't be enough full-size towels for everyone, so . . . okay. The saliva-spotted hand towel would suffice for her water-removal efforts. After all, it wasn't as if she could simply hang it back on its hook and figure no one would notice freaking *teeth marks*.

"I need you to be honest with me, ma puce." He plucked the undersized cloth from her loose grasp and knelt to blot her legs. "Do you truly wish to keep living in the Zone after everything that's happened this week? Or would you prefer to move?"

It was a fair question. Too bad she didn't know what to tell him.

When she didn't answer right away, he clarified, "Money isn't an issue, darling. Don't let financial considerations sway your decision."

"That's not the problem." And since the two of them might not live through the day, any argument over whether she'd let him support her monetarily could happen at a later date. "It's just..."

She wasn't certain she'd ever tried to put her feelings about her home into words before. Even to herself. And to make things still *more* confusing, those feelings were changing. Rapidly. Because of Max, the vampire kneeling at her feet and scanning her expression with a frown of concern.

"I've stayed so long because..." Hesitantly, she explained as best she could. "My house on Cloverleaf Drive is almost all I have left of my parents. Most of our furniture and possessions got broken or"—she swallowed hard—"stained. I had to get rid of them. But I still owned the house itself, and it's where I had my last truly happy memories with them. My last truly happy memories in general, I suppose."

The hand towel paused on her thigh, and he pressed a light kiss to her knee.

Her mouth twisted as she fought for composure. "Besides, no one was going to buy an old brick split-level from the 1960s in Zone A. If I left, the house would simply stay empty and rot. Like all the other places on our block."

If she left her parents' house behind, what she abandoned would shortly cease to exist.

Exactly as they had when she'd left them behind.

But even that reasoning—which was faulty; she knew it was, but knowing hadn't changed how she felt—didn't fully explain why she hadn't left her childhood home. Why she hadn't gone away to college. Why she hadn't moved to be near friends and neighbors once more.

"I wanted to pay forward what they did for me too. I thought . . . if I stayed in the area, I could call for help as soon as another breach occurred and get the alarm going immediately. I'd be in a good position to help others. And if I managed to save a neighbor, I could . . ." When he stood to dry her back, she braced herself on the vanity and watched him in the mirror. "I don't know. Give my parents' deaths more meaning, I guess."

So many people had died that day. Her parents had simply been two more names on a long, tragic list. Two more bodies for the funeral pyre, since local mortuaries lacked sufficient capacity to process the victims one by one.

His eyes met hers in the reflection.

"They saved you, my Edie. Their beautiful sunbeam of a child." His voice was very, very soft. "There is nothing in this world that could give their sacrifice more meaning. *Nothing.*"

She turned to face him, and her fingers trembled as she nudged a wet swath of hair off his forehead. "I know they'd agree with you. Much as it pains me to admit that."

"Darling." The towel dropped to the mat as his arms wrapped around her. "You don't have to move. You never have to move. You can stay in that house forever if you want."

He rocked her back and forth a little, his hold gentle but secure.

She buried her face in his neck. Because she wouldn't let her tears fall, they were dripping down her throat instead, and swallowing hurt. When she said so in a whispered complaint, he got her a cup of water from the sink. She gulped it down gratefully and handed the cup back, and he refilled it without a word.

"In all my life . . ." She drained the water again. "I think Mom and Dad are the only people who ever loved me that much. That fiercely and wholeheartedly. If I truly let them go, it felt like—I don't know. What could ever replace them, really? How could whatever came next possibly make up for their loss?"

The ache in her throat had eased, and she set the paper cup on the counter.

He hummed a little and gathered her close again, his fingertips drifting through her dripping hair. Working out her tangles one by one, the routine increasingly familiar. Each tug noticeable but not painful.

"But here's the thing, Max." Her forehead dropped to his chest, and she sighed. "Because they loved me that much, they wouldn't like what I've done. It would hurt them to know I never went to William and Mary or saw the Alps. They'd hate that I'm still only a single stone wall away from the same threat that ended their lives, and they'd tell me they never wanted me to make myself a living, breathing memorial to their love and their sacrifice."

His talented hands weren't so much detangling anymore.

More . . . caressing. Cradling her head against his shoulder and massaging her nape and stroking her hair.

"I know all that. I've always known all that." Burying her nose in his neck, she inhaled deeply. When had his piney scent become such a comfort to her? "Until now, I just chose to ignore it, because sure, they would hate the decisions I've made, but they're gone, and I have to find a bearable way to live without them."

"Ma puce, it's okay." The warmth in his voice trickled through her like syrup. "I'm not asking you to—"

"Maybe, though . . ." Squeezing her eyes shut, she took the leap. "Maybe if I had a new family. New memories. Someone who loves me as much as they did."

His fingers stilled in her hair.

"Maybe then I wouldn't need to cling so tightly to the physical reminders of what I've lost," she finished, and now he knew. What she wanted from him. The future she was beginning to envision, with him by her side and at her back. Always. From this moment until her last breath.

When he spoke again, he didn't sound scared or disdainful. He didn't sound like he found her presumptuous or overly needy or foolishly impetuous.

Instead, he sounded . . . settled. As content and steady as she'd ever heard him. "If you decide to stay, I'll stay too. But I would also relocate for you as needed. And even if we did move, my Edie, we could keep the house. Maintain it."

We. The most beautiful word in the world.

Gaston Maxime Boucher, committed recluse and cynic, was committing himself to her. More than that—committing to rejoin the world at large and mingle with *actual people* again if that was what she wanted. Even knowing she'd bring plates of cream cheese–swirl brownies to all their new neighbors' homes and invite them over for coffee or lunch.

Yep. He definitely, definitely loved her.

Most likely, he would also discover urgent business in his former lair that required his immediate attention shortly before their neighbors' arrival, but so be it. The offer was still incredibly sweet.

"Yeah, but . . ." She'd leapt, and he'd caught her with ease. Gods, she loved him right back. "That would be a terrible waste of money."

"What did I say about money?"

As she smiled against his neck, she deliberately tickled his throat with her lashes. "That you have far too much of it, and you've chosen to spend it on an enormous underground lair, apparently in preparation to become Superman's next archnemesis?"

"Ingrate." His retaliatory tickling targeted her ribs, and he had to cover her mouth again when she squeaked in helpless laughter. "Listen to me, human. I'm not asking you to leave your home, and I'm not asking you to abandon all tangible mementos of your lost family. If I did, I'd be an utter hypocrite."

"You don't care if you're a hypocrite," she pointed out, lifting her head.

He grinned down at her. "True. But in this instance, I don't qualify anyway."

"You have mementos of your family? Where . . ." Those ubermodern rooms in his lair hadn't contained a single sentimental item. She'd swear to that. Which meant—"Your library. Your family's possessions are in your library."

That warm, cozy nook with honeyed wood and a thick, silky,

now-stained rug. The small private space he'd initially kept locked away from her.

Because, she now understood, it revealed the softness of his heart, its reluctant vulnerability, beneath all that cold, harsh armor.

"I didn't keep much. But the things I had, I wanted displayed in a suitable location. A room my parents would have found comfortable and welcoming." After one last stroke of her now-smooth hair, he crouched to search the pockets of his hoodie where it lay on the floor. "And there's one memento I always bring with me. Here."

Rising, he flipped over her hand and placed something in her palm.

Metallic. Round. Cool.

Instinctively, her fingers curled around the silver sphere to protect it from falling, and she lifted it for closer scrutiny. A band of the shiny metal ringed the middle of the ball, splitting the item into two clear hemispheres, both finely pierced and engraved with birds, leaves, and delicate flowers. At the top, a small suspension ring—also silver—attached to nothing.

The piece was gorgeous. Clearly very old. And she had no idea what it was.

When she looked up at him questioningly, he touched a reverent fingertip to one of the tiny birds. "My mother's pomander. A long-ago gift from my father. At one time she wore it everywhere, either hanging from her neck chain or attached to her girdle."

Somehow, she didn't think he meant midcentury shapewear. "It's beautiful."

He didn't offer any further explanation. Just watched her study his offering.

Apparently he thought the average twenty-first-century human would know precisely what a pomander did besides look pretty and—evidently—dangle from an outfit. So . . . okay, maybe she could figure it out on her own. Challenge accepted.

As she bent down to study the gorgeous openwork, a whiff of something delightfully citrusy made her crinkle her nose in thought. "Was a pomander . . . something she wore and sniffed whenever things smelled bad?"

"Her human friends would roll together various perfumes in a net—ambergris, cinnamon, musk, civet, and so forth—and put the ball inside their pomanders. They thought it would protect against infection during times of pestilence."

Pestilence? That was an awfully archaic term. And the reliance on a spa-scented silver ball for continued health instead of, say, antibiotics or vaccines kind of implied . . .

"You're talking about the Plague, aren't you? Like, Black Death." Holy shit. "Oh my gods, you are so fucking *old*."

He merely rolled his eyes. "Since vampires don't get sick, Mom wore it to help combat foul odors instead, as you suggested. But she also paid a witch to create a recovery charm that would fit inside, with orange peel, clove, oils, and a golden ribbon."

"Is that what I'm smelling?" She gave the sphere another sniff. "Because the scent is yummy, but it's also remarkably strong for something that incredibly, unbelievably *ancient*."

It was also very . . . familiar? And she had no idea why.

He didn't bother responding to her gibe. Instead, his eyes narrowed on the pomander in her palm, and he did something subtle to the band circling its center. "Here. Look inside."

The top and bottom of the gorgeous silver sphere opened like a book, and—

"You stole one of my soaps?" One of her shaped soaps, to be exact. Custom-ordered, scented with orange and clove, and made to resemble the iconic citrus fruit for a farmer's market in California. "Do I need to hire security guards for my garage to prevent shoplifting, or should I simply bill you?"

Despite her tart tone, she smiled down at her own handiwork.

He'd wanted that little orange badly enough to snatch it secretly, while—if she remembered correctly—distracting her with some stupid software question, and then he'd transferred the purloined soap from outfit to outfit every time he'd changed clothing.

He prized it enough to store within his mother's gorgeous pomander. Which she'd carried with her everywhere. Which he now carried with *him* everywhere.

"I think I can afford your fee," he said dryly.

"Calm down, Scrooge McDuck. I already know you bathe in gold ducats." When Edie glanced up, he wasn't looking at the soap. He was looking at her. "Does the scent remind you of your mother?"

Edie liked the thought of that, of something she'd created bringing him comfort. A product of her own hands helping him remember the parent who'd loved him and whom he'd loved back with such fierce, bloody devotion.

"It reminds me of both of you." His tone strongly implied she was a moron, even as his eyes crinkled in an affectionate smile. "Obviously."

Oh. Oh, that was even better.

The melting sensation in her belly . . . that couldn't be healthy, right?

Slowly, the curve of his mouth flattened. "She didn't bring it to the festival that night. The suspension ring had detached, so she'd left both pieces with the silversmith. By the time I remembered to reclaim her pomander, the charm inside was gone. But as I said, the witch's concoction had orange. Clove."

"Like the soap."

He inclined his head, then surrounded her hand with his, closing her fingers around the sphere as tightly as possible. "I want you to carry this today, Edie."

Poised to argue—because like hells she'd be carrying his lucky pomander while he fought fucking *zombies*—she opened her mouth, only to shut it again when a firm knock rattled the bathroom door.

Kip called out, "I don't want to know what you two are doing in there—"

"I want to know!" Lorraine sounded wide-awake. Also very curious.

"—but your time is up. Cease canoodling at once, mini-vamp! Forthwith!"

Max sighed, kissed Edie on the forehead, and spoke to the door. "This is because I didn't let you have the couch, isn't it?"

"Sure is!" Kip loudly hummed the *Jeopardy!* theme music until they'd dressed and left the bathroom. "Did you appreciate the old-timey language? You know, since you probably, like, hung out with Plato or whoever?"

Max grunted.

"I appreciated it, Kip." Edie smiled at him, patting the coveralls pocket where she'd tucked the pomander. For now. "Did you sleep okay?"

His lower lip poked out a tad. "No. And I think we both know why."

With deeply sardonic courtesy, Max bowed and swept a hand toward the empty bathroom. "Happy now?"

"Yep." The troll strolled inside, and his grin lit the dim hallway. "Revenge is a dish best served whilst coldly cockblocking vampires."

The sound Max made in response to that wasn't quite a growl. But it wasn't quite not a growl either.

Edie patted his arm consolingly. "Today's going to be super fun. I can already tell."

That time, it was definitely a growl.

25

As soon as night fell, Sabrina set off a few flares, and Edie lit the house two doors down from hers on fire.

Biting her lip, she watched flames lick up the sides of Mr. and Mrs. Buchwald's crumbling wood-sided rancher and tried not to question the group's plan. After decades of closeting herself indoors after sunset, this kind of exposure jangled her nerves. But as the more strategically minded among them had argued the previous evening, they needed to attract every single zombie to their various boobytraps, and during daylight hours there was simply no way to do so without also drawing the attention of outsiders. The flicker of flames in darkness, though— from a distance, it would be silent yet unmissable to the creatures. An inescapable lure.

The sirens hadn't yet sounded, so the group assumed that the zombie pack still lingered within the Containment Zone and fae trickery had left government officials still unaware of the perilous situation. So far, so good. But this was a calculated risk, nevertheless, without much room for error. The inferno had to be large enough, the flares high enough, to capture the creatures' attention and lure them back toward the compound—but not large or high enough to be seen above Wall Four, thus bringing the authorities or other unwanted visitors to the Zone.

The outermost Containment Zone wall was the tallest by far, and hopefully darkness would obscure the smoke already billowing thickly into the sky, but . . . yeah. A lot could go wrong. Even if everything ostensibly went *right* and the entire pack of zombies headed their way en masse without inviting external scrutiny to what was happening on Cloverleaf Drive.

Because then their not-so-merry band would have to incapacitate those zombies. Either via the boobytraps the group had spent all day creating, or via hand-to-hand combat. The latter was an unsettling prospect, given their number of actual fighters.

Five. Five fighters. Max, Edie, Sabrina, Kip, and Lorraine. Against an unknown number of zombies, all of whom were strong, fast, ruthless, single-mindedly committed to brain slurpage, and very, very difficult to kill.

Panic wouldn't help anyone. Breathing deeply, Edie tried to slow her racing heart and still her shaking hands.

"Those oils really helped with flammability." Lorraine stood beside her, fists braced on her solid hips. "Thanks, Edes-a-lot."

As Edie had pointed out the previous night, oils bought in bulk for soapmaking purposes could be used for alternative projects. Such as arson. But now that it was actually happening, seeing such expensive supplies—gods, she'd *just* invested in new containers of tamanu oil and evening primrose seed oil, hadn't she?—going up in flames sort of nauseated her.

Max had promised to reimburse her for her losses. She hadn't even argued. She'd simply quacked at him, savored the moment he'd recognized the Scrooge McDuck reference, and let it go.

Somewhere just inside the tree line, he and Kip were sharpening everyone's knives and checking the final preparations while Sabrina spent a few private moments alone with her wife. Gwen, who was still struggling with nausea, had curled up on a cot nearby for a final bit of rest.

With her booted toe, Edie scuffed the brittle brown grass beneath their feet. "How confident are you in the firebreak?"

"As confident as I can be under the circumstances," Lorraine said, which wasn't really an answer, but it was exactly what Edie would have said in response too.

The Girl Explorers had put both their fae heritage and their nature know-how to hard work that day, and prepping the area around the Buchwalds' home had been their first task. To stop the fire from spreading, they'd cleared fallen leaves and all other vegetation in a wide ring around the abandoned residence, down to the bare soil. Some of them had used shovels or rakes, but most had simply used their fae powers.

In the end, the firebreak looked convincingly pristine and professional.

"We didn't earn that Wildfire Prevention badge for nothing," Riley had told Edie before she and the other girls moved on to their next task.

"How long do you think it'll take for the creatures to come?" Lorraine's broad brow creased. "*If* they come, obviously."

Their best plan depended on the zombies being drawn to the fire and flares. If Edie and the others had to track down and confront the pack in Zone C instead . . . well, everyone would still fight. But their likelihood of preventing disaster or surviving the encounter would be minimal at best.

They'd decided to wait three hours for the creatures' arrival before moving on to their backup contingencies. But truly, it shouldn't take very long, although Sabrina and Max had vigorously disagreed on the exact timing.

Edie had kept her mouth shut for that discussion, because both had made good points, but only one of them had made her come four times that morning.

"The pack is pretty far out, but the access road gives them a straight shot. The bridges are down, the doors are open, and they're fast and fed, so . . . two hours, possibly? Maybe less if they were close to the access road to begin with. And there could be strays nearer to us, of course." The glow of a cell screen high up in the trees caught her attention. "As soon as they spot anything, Riley and the other girls will give us the signal."

Apparently the Girl Explorers found lounging among the treetops quite comfortable, so as soon as the fire had been set and they'd finished their other assigned duties, they'd climbed up into the branches and settled down for an indefinite wait.

Lorraine hummed in acknowledgment and fell silent.

"If there are strays, they could be here any minute. You should eat while you can." Edie mustered a smile for her new friend. "Can't fight on an empty stomach, Lorrie."

"You're as smart as you are short." Lorraine's hair glowed in the firelight. "I'll save you a turkey sandwich, Edes. Maybe some cookies too if I can spare any."

"Thanks," said Edie, and the troll flicked her a salute before walking toward their supply hub in the woods.

Mesmerized by the flickering flames, Edie watched the fire spread. Steadily at first, then in sudden leaps of incandescent flame. The crackling had turned into a growing roar, with occasional crashes as the structure collapsed further, and it didn't smell like a campfire or a cozy fireplace blaze. When the breeze changed direction, acrid smoke filled her lungs and tasted like melted plastic on the back of her tongue.

She coughed, shifting until she found a viewing spot with cleaner air.

An untold amount of time later, Max's cool arms slid around her from behind, and she relaxed into his increasingly familiar embrace.

"You need to eat something, my Edie," he murmured into her ear, then set his chin on top of her head. "Before the godsdamn trolls vacuum up the final crumbs."

She nodded but didn't move, and he didn't push. He simply held her.

"I hope to heaven I don't see any of my neighbors in the pack." It was a whispered confession, too soft for anyone but him to hear. "If they lived through an attack, only to be transformed . . . I'd kill them, because I'd have to." She swallowed, her throat thick. "But it would break a few more pieces of my heart."

Easing forward, he surrounded her even more securely.

"If it helps, I doubt that will happen." His chin rubbed her crown, his stubble catching on her hair. "If they were caught unawares by a zombie pack intent on feeding, the likelihood that anyone survived longer than a few seconds is minimal."

Her attempt at a smile failed. "It's a terrible sort of silver lining, I suppose."

"Who lived in this house?" His voice was gentle. "You must have known them."

"The Buchwalds. An older couple, originally from Canada. No kids." Mrs. Buchwald's hair had gone completely white soon before the Breach, and she'd been using a blue rinse to deal with yellowing from sun exposure. A bit too much blue rinse, as it turned out, because her hair had acquired a distinct but pretty cerulean undertone the last few months of her life. "They used to babysit me sometimes when both my parents had to work in the store. I was sort of their . . ."

She took a moment. Cleared her throat.

"They called me their surrogate daughter." And she'd just set fire to their fucking home. "They died in the First Breach. No one could locate any living relatives, and no one wanted to buy their home from the bank."

The house-proud Buchwalds' retirement paradise had turned overgrown and mildewy. The roof sagged, and the glass windowpanes were cracked. When Edie had gone on her scouting walks, she'd occasionally looked through their windows and seen dust. Insects. The encroachment of nature, as all the couple had built slowly rotted and turned to dust.

"No one will miss this house"—except her—"so it seemed a safe bet for burning."

The conflagration had cast an orange glow over the other homes on the street. Max's, which had once contained Bruce, Christian, and their adopted infant son. The two-story colonial positioned between the Brandstrup residence and the Buchwalds' house, which had been bought by a defense contractor couple during Edie's first year of high school.

Her own home, which had encompassed her entire world.

Every house had held life and now only held memories. Sad ones she carried like lit candles at a shrine, as if the remembrance were her privilege but also her duty.

It *wasn't* her duty, though, and the privilege felt an awful lot like a burden most days.

Besides, remembrance didn't require a shrine.

"I want to move," she told Max. Told the flaming remnants of a wonderful couple's former home. Told the Buchwalds. Told her parents, wherever they were. "Even if we kill every fucking zombie on this planet, I want to move."

He hesitated before answering, his arms tightening around her. "Okay."

"I carry their memories with me wherever I go. I'm a living, breathing reminder of their lives and their love for me, and I'm still alive even though they aren't, so I can go. I should go." She tipped her head in the direction of her childhood home. "I don't need the house."

"You don't have to make that decision now, darling," he said gently.

"I know. But I did." Leaning back, she let him support her full weight, and he didn't falter. Not even for a moment. "You'd better gird those awesome loins of yours, vampire boy. Soon enough, you'll be making small talk with strangers who are *mere humans*, and if you're a condescending jackass to our new neighbors, I'll withhold sex."

His snort ruffled her hair. "No, you won't."

"No, I won't." Even she wasn't that stubborn and self-defeating. "But I'll eat nothing but processed food in front of you for days at a time, *dude*. Endless cans of I Can't Believe It's Not Falafel and various jerkies of mysterious provenance, washed down by weird green-tinged sodas containing absurd amounts of caffeine and chemicals as yet unexplained by science."

"You wouldn't." His forefinger lightly flicked her earlobe. "You'd miss your pomegranate juice."

Insinuating herself further into the cradle of his body, she rubbed her ass against his hardening dick. "Anything in the name of revenge."

"Short of denying yourself orgasms," he said, voice as dry as the kindling they'd used to light the Buchwalds' home on fire.

"Exactly."

"I'll make small talk. If it means I have you." He rubbed his hands up and down her arms, even though the house fire was throwing off an enormous amount of heat. "If you want to move, ma puce, we'll move. If you don't, we won't. Simple as that."

She twisted her head to kiss him, and he met her halfway. Afterward, still wrapped up in each other, they stood and bore silent witness to the final destruction of the Buchwalds' home for a long, long time.

And then . . . something changed. The Girl Explorers hadn't given a signal, and Edie hadn't heard or seen anything unexpected. But somehow she had a feeling.

Time was running short.

If she died tonight, she wouldn't do so regretting what she hadn't said.

"I'm falling in love with you." The declaration wasn't tentative or nervous, but a firm statement of fact. "You need to keep yourself safe for me, Max."

He squeezed her so tightly she squeaked. Although he didn't respond in words, he pressed a fierce kiss to the top of her head, then her temple, her cheek, and her ear.

"I don't need you to say it back." She figured he hadn't offered his love to anyone for a long, long time. Maybe not since his parents' death. "It's okay. I just . . . you had to know."

"You're mine," he finally said, his voice hoarse and low. "I swear I'll keep you safe, no matter the cost."

She didn't want that. She'd never wanted that.

But she didn't argue. Instead, she silently made the same promise to him in the privacy of her thoughts. When she turned in his arms, the flick of her tongue against his lips distracted him even more effectively than she'd hoped. He had no attention to spare for the discreet movements of her right hand or the faint purr of his hoodie pocket's zipper opening, then closing again.

Before he noticed his pomander's return, the signal came.

The Girl Explorers had spread out, so they were barely within hearing distance of one another and covering as much ground as possible. Once the first girl sighted a zombie in the distance, she'd make a sharp, distinctive owl hoot, which the next girl would pass along the chain. In the end, the telltale sound would reach Riley and a few other especially powerful half-fae Explorers where they sat perched far above the central battleground.

That moment had arrived.

From now on, all subtlety was abandoned. They wanted the zombies to know precisely where they were gathered. Right here, right now.

"Take your positions," Riley shouted. "Two strays up front, and the pack not far behind! A mile ahead at most!"

The Explorers lifted Starla and Gwen high up into the trees as well, using the branches as a sort of escalator, while Sabrina, Kip, Lorraine, Max, and Edie ran to their assigned places.

Kip called out a final reminder. "Eliminate or incapacitate as many as possible, and if all else fails, drive them back into the compound! Once we're done, we feast!"

"You've been feasting for the last hour and a half, troll," Max muttered. "I know what happened to that huge pot of saffron-shellfish risotto."

"Understood!" everyone else yelled in response.

Four minutes later, the first snarl echoed through the forest, and Sabrina set off a final flare.

Edie brandished her cleaver just as the first zombies leapt into sight, jaws wide open.

THERE WAS NO missing their small group of fighters. Not when they remained so close to the blazing house and so easily visible through the trees, their exact position highlighted by a torch's flickering light and a small campfire.

There was only one obvious route leading to them, and the two strays took it. The creatures raced along the side of the burning home, on the path cleared by the Girl Explorers, and into the backyard abutting the woods. The fence lining that backyard had long ago begun to sag. In one spot, a substantial section of the fencing had collapsed entirely, leaving a straight shot into the forest, toward all five waiting figures.

Edie tightened her grip and held her breath, invoking the names of all the gods and goddesses she could remember in an urgent request for assistance. Just in case it turned out she was Enhanced and simply hadn't noticed for the past thirty-eight years.

"Come and get it," Sabrina called out, the words a brazen taunt.

Suddenly, this entire plan seemed like a terrible, *terrible* idea. Like, *worst ever*.

When the strays spotted the stretch of collapsed fencing, their determined lope sped into a starved sprint. Their lean gray-pale bodies jolted with every bounding leap forward, saliva dripped from their slavering jaws, and the creature in the lead rasped something that sounded like *bonjour* as it raced past a few dilapidated wooden pickets, through the fence's gap, and up a small incline.

Only to disappear from sight mid-growl as the underbrush and dead leaves beneath its feet gave way to a deep, wide pit. Too deep to jump out of, too wide to leap across. A pit the Girl Explorers had dug after creating the firebreak, using whatever fae powers they could still muster.

Less than a heartbeat later, the second zombie dropped and vanished too.

Stepping forward, Kip peered down into the pit and offered the creatures a cheerful wave. "Bonjour!"

More growls and hisses erupted from the depths of the hole, but as Edie and everyone else had fervently hoped, the zombies seemed unable to climb out of their makeshift enclosure.

Edie glanced around, her heartbeat slowly steadying. Under her breath, she whispered, "If I'm an Enhanced who can now commune with deities, please give me a sign."

Nothing. She waited a few seconds more, though, just to be sure. When she shifted her feet, she stepped onto what appeared to be a fossilized remnant of dog poop from the Buchwalds' boisterous little terrier.

Okay. Fair enough. No unexpected powers for her.

"Next wave, coming right up!" Riley hollered. "The main pack this time! Girl Explorers, collapse in toward the center as soon as you safely can!"

The zombies burst into view from around the side of the house, their appearance wavy and distorted in the intense heat emanating from the blaze. And Edie had to believe that most or all of the strays must have found their brethren and joined the main group at some point, because *holy shit*. It was paralyzing, the way the pack seemed to roar endlessly forward like water from a collapsed dam, the creatures so innumerable and tightly spaced that they could have been a single, enormous entity, with a single, inexorable intention: death.

Tearing, clawing, throat-ripping, head-removing, brain-slurping death.

The leading edge of the apocalyptic river reached the back-yard. Ribs heaving, gray eyes glowing with an eerie, intent light, the zombies raced through the fencing gap and . . . toppled into the canyon awaiting them. Gone in an instant. Gone, gone, gone and raging in their thwarted frustration at top volume, mostly in rumbling howls and keens of rage, but also at least one furious, garbled order for the mimer to stop miming.

The flow ceased, and all the zombies were contained.

Lorraine cracked her knuckles. "This might be easier than we thought. Who's in the mood for a buffet tonight? Your treat, mini-vamp."

"Dammit, Lorrie," Sabrina complained. "Have you truly never heard of jinxing—"

"There are more!" Riley's panicked voice was shredding. "This wave is bigger!"

Kip reached over and smacked the back of his cousin's head.

Lorraine's nose crinkled. "Sorry. That's on me."

The second part of the pack arrived then, and shit, that compound must have been *fucking enormous*, because there was no end. The creatures leapt into the unseen pit by threes and fours, pure rage and hunger in their creepy fucking eyes, and they just *kept coming*.

The zombies on the bridge must have been a group of strays. Not the main pack, by any means, which meant—

"We're in trouble," Max muttered. "Edie, it won't be long until—"

The zombies filled the pit.

They *filled it*, forming a living bridge over top of the gap, and those who arrived afterward didn't even miss a single stride as they crossed the barrier.

"*Fuck*." Sabrina's voice shook as she assumed her fighting stance.

"That's the last of them!" The troop leader sounded close to tears, but she was still screaming out information with all her might. "Girl Explorers, get ready!"

The creatures' howls turned exultant. Expectant. They sprinted closer and closer yet, until the bloodstains circling their muzzles and the chunks of gore in their bared teeth became much more visible than Edie would have preferred.

In an oddly beautiful wave of motion, the creatures at the front launched themselves onto their hind feet in unison, preparing for the kill ahead, and they grunted with each lengthy stride as they reached out with red-smeared claws. Their speed only increased with the proximity of prey—and they'd almost reached their midnight snack when the first zombie's body dropped to the forest floor, decapitated.

Edie stared blankly at the rolling head.

It'd worked.

Her idea had *worked*.

It was eerily noiseless too. She didn't know if she'd expected a sucking noise or a tearing sound or . . . something else.

But as more zombies lurched onto two feet and leapt forward at full speed—directly into the razor-sharp wire Edie used to cut her soaps, strung tightly between the trees at the height of a zombie's neck—their deaths were virtually silent.

"Human. We both know what happens next." Max's face was stone, his stance aggressive, his words rushed and fierce. "You do not risk yourself for anyone else. Understand?"

Yeah. She knew what was barreling toward them. But she couldn't give him what he wanted, because her potential last words to him couldn't be a lie.

Edie raised the cleaver in her right hand and the other knife in her left. "Here we go, vampire boy. Be careful."

The whimpers and grunts from the creatures nearly drowned out Max's rage-filled growl. This close to the zombies, the smell of blood and unwashed bodies merged with the choking smoke still billowing from the Buchwalds' home, and the stench only worsened as more of them leapt toward their prey and into the wires.

She couldn't smell pine anymore. Not from the trees, not from Max.

Her lungs were full of death.

"Edie, *do you understand*?" Max bellowed, helpless fury in every syllable.

She would pat his arm in consolation, but she didn't want to accidentally stab him, so she simply cast him one last, split-second glance. Stamped him indelibly into her memory, strong and whole and nearly unhinged with terrible, terrified love for her.

The howls of the zombies closing in seemed to pierce her eardrums.

"Be careful," she repeated, but she couldn't tell if he heard her over the deafening, knee-weakening sound of last night's plan inexorably heading toward the worst-case scenario.

The razor wire would only work as a temporary measure,

which they'd known ahead of time. It bought them a couple of minutes and removed a few zombies, but that was all.

Far too soon, the stack of bodies under the makeshift garrote became an obstacle, the creatures veered around their fallen comrades, and their speed dropped. Without sufficient momentum, they didn't lop off their own heads when they hit the wires that ringed the fighters. They merely gouged out chunks of flesh and lost sprays of sickly yellow blood, and that wasn't enough to kill or stop them.

It did slow them considerably, though.

"Girl Explorers!" Riley's hoarse shout echoed through the trees. "Troop initiative three-oh-five, Zombie Restraint, begins now!"

Shit. They'd hoped it wouldn't come to this. The girls had already drained so damn much of their power with the firebreak and the pit. They couldn't have much left, but—

"If you die," Max snarled, "I will find you. I don't care if I have to rip out the throat of Death, Edie. I will fucking *find you*, wherever you go, for the sheer joy of *killing you myself.*"

She had to laugh, despite the adrenaline and terror slicking up her palms and shaking her knees. "Love you too, babe."

Branches whipped down from the trees and lashed around some creatures' wrists, while roots erupted from the soil and manacled the ankles of others.

There was no time to panic. Calm settled over her like a cool blanket.

She knew what to do. They all did.

"Now!" Lorraine shouted, and all five of them waded into battle.

26

Hobbled at their wrists or ankles, zombies weren't especially difficult to kill.

Edie didn't let herself think about it. She simply lashed out as hard as she could, cutting through their necks as quickly and cleanly as possible, then moved on to the next creature held in place by the Girl Explorers.

Beside her, Max wielded his sword in graceful, deadly arcs, each one producing a grunt from his chest and a headless zombie corpse at his feet. Not too far away, Sabrina's axe glinted in the firelight as she swung it with a two-handed grip and efficiently took down the creatures nearest to her position. Across the little campfire, Kip and Lorraine were doing . . . something.

"How . . ." Edie paused to decapitate a zombie. "How's . . . it . . . going, Lorrie?"

"Turns out, you can twist off their little heads like a soda cap!" the troll yelled. "It's fun!"

"I'm getting hungry, though!" Kip added. "If my godsdamn cousin hadn't mentioned a freaking buffet—"

"Sue me, bro!" Lorraine gave a pleased exclamation. "I'm really getting the whole motion down now! That one was easy!"

"Shit!" Kip suddenly yelled, all levity gone, and Edie whipped her head his way.

He was falling, hard. He landed on the ground with a wheezing, pained-sounding "*fuck*," even as an unsecured zombie flew over his head, teeth and claws poised for throat-ripping.

In a flash, the troll was back on his feet.

"Good . . . work, Gwen!" He lunged for the creature who'd been trying to de-brain him. "Tripped by a root, just as you predicted!"

"*Edie*," Max hollered, just as Kip clasped the zombie in his huge hands and ripped off its head with a crunching sound and a spray of yolky blood. "Behind you!"

Branches caught the wrists of the creature at Edie's back while it was still mid-leap, and Edie directed a breathless thank-you toward the treetops after she cut off her attacker's head.

Then there was nothing but cutting and blood and bursts of pain as the zombies kicked her with their unbound legs or clawed at her with their free hands while she killed them. It went on and on, terrible and unceasing, until . . . the zombie in front of her broke out of its wrist restraints.

She'd already cut about halfway through its neck, so she was able to finish the job before it lashed out at her, but the near miss was a bad sign. A really, really fucking bad sign.

Sure enough, Riley shouted down to them moments later. "We're almost tapped out up here! Roughly two dozen hostiles left!"

That was far too many to handle if the Girl Explorers couldn't restrain them. The five fighters were going to be overrun. Soon.

"Gwen, you're up! Alert Starla when you're ready!" Sabrina swung her axe with a panting yell. "Riley, one of your girls needs to get her down safely and silently!"

Edie didn't hear Gwen's descent from the tree or see her short journey to a spot deeper in the woods, which was a good thing. If the zombies pinpointed her location, a lone human who knew nothing about fighting wouldn't last long.

The next creature only had one hand loosely bound by a branch, and as Edie began slicing through its neck, its viciously sharp claws raked across her ribs, gouging deeply enough that warm wetness began trickling down her side. The initial lightning flash of agony turned into an intense, throbbing ache. It was her first serious injury, and given the current turn of events, it would be far from her last.

She didn't do more than gasp, but somehow Max knew. Maybe he was able to smell her blood, even through all the effluvia and smoke and body odor.

"*Edie*," he roared.

It was a hoarse demand for information. For the sound of her voice to confirm that she was still alive and mostly okay.

"I'm . . ." Oh shit, breathing hurt now. "I'm good."

The nearest zombie was writhing, twisting its ankle to free itself from a root and just about to succeed. With a cry, she swung at its neck and—missed. Because it wasn't bound by anything at all anymore.

Its thighs bunched for a fatal leap, its snarl rang in her ears, and she stumbled backward on numb legs.

"Now!" Sabrina yelled.

The explosion rang through the night.

It was another of Edie's ideas, using what they had on hand.

Large quantities of lye—*her* lye—in an old abandoned bathtub on the forest floor. A simple wooden trough, swiftly built by Lorraine from scavenged floorboards, perched carefully but precariously on branches high above the tub. The entire setup positioned a safe distance away, with a long, sturdy stick for Gwen to tip the trough, sending water pouring onto all the lye.

And then: *Boom!* Ringing ears. Startled cries and howls.

The extreme heat of the immediate, violent exothermic reaction set some neatly crisscrossed kindling aflame, and every single zombie that remained alive swung toward the site of the explosion and subsequent fire, completely distracted.

Including Edie's current zombie. This time, she managed to remove its head, and everyone else dispatched the creatures closest to them too.

It wasn't enough. There were still a dozen left, maybe, and their attention was beginning to return to their designated prey.

"We need to lure them closer to the compound and keep distracting them." Sabrina sounded grim. "Set the fires, Gwen, and Starla will let you know if we need you back here!"

Edie hoped like hells the oracle was fast and silent in her work. If Gwen moved too slowly, there wouldn't be any fighters left to take advantage of the distraction. Too noisily, and her athame would be her only protection from the predators stalking her.

"We're almost there!" Lorraine yelled. "Let's finish 'em off, bros!"

As another creature swiveled its head back Edie's way, her cleaver felt like an anvil. She swung it anyway, chopping through taut flesh and tough sinew. Not bone.

She'd injured it, which would slow its movements. But she hadn't killed it, and she'd also made it very, very angry.

Fuck. One more kick, and her legs would collapse beneath her. Her arms were shaking, her head swimming from horror and blood loss, and no one could help her now. Max, Sabrina, Lorraine, and Kip had their own battles to wage as they waited for Gwen to light another house on fire, somewhere closer to that gaping hole in Wall One, and set off more flares.

Edie was a sitting duck, and not the kind that swam in pools of gold ducats.

The creature's garbled *magnifique* came from a mouth dripping saliva, and its yellowed teeth shone in the firelight as it stalked the final, necessary step closer. It leapt for her neck, and she slashed her cleaver in its direction, but she closed her eyes too, unable to watch her own death.

Nothing happened.

Her lids flew open, and there was Max, clamping one zombie's jaw shut with a white-knuckled grip, the swing of his sword a graceful arc as he lopped off another zombie's head. *Her* zombie's head.

A third one was sprinting up on him from behind, and the sweet idiot wasn't paying a fucking bit of attention, too concerned about her to do his damned job.

"Max!" she shrieked, thrusting her cleaver in the direction of his would-be killer.

Even as he turned—too late, he was going to be too late—flares shrieked into the night, while climbing flames illuminated in the distance, closer to the breach site. Gwen's work.

And there was Gwen herself. Silhouetted by the flames, clearly visible.

Irresistible temptation, especially since the creatures' current prey had proven troublesome.

The zombie behind Max had pivoted to face the new fire, to face Gwen, and Max managed to remove its head in a single swing, but the rest of the creatures—four now?—were suddenly gone. Loping at top speed toward a human woman with no knowledge of fighting, armed only with a small, sharp knife.

In the group's absolute worst-case scenario—i.e., the scenario they were experiencing right this moment—they'd planned to lure the pack's remnants closer to the compound with fires and flares in hopes they could drive the creatures back through the hole in the wall. Then they'd intended to use Sabrina's small store of remaining power to close that hole and maybe even collapse the compound's structure on top of the zombies. Which—like their fall into the pit—wouldn't kill them outright, but should contain them until the main battle was over and Max and Sabrina could finish the job.

That wasn't going to happen. The situation was too out of control for such tricky maneuvering. Either the last clutch of creatures died now, or they'd kill Gwen.

Even as they bounded toward her, all four—yes, definitely four—zombies kept looking back at the snacks they'd left behind, and it slowed them down a bit. Almost enough for Max to catch up to them, because he was sprinting in an inhuman blur, with everyone else running behind him.

Almost. He wasn't going to make it in time.

And then Gwen cried out loudly enough to echo through the forest and collapsed where she stood. She didn't move or make another sound as the zombies bounded closer and closer. Sixty feet away. Fifty. Forty.

Two more humanoid silhouettes appeared in front of the fire

and scrambled to stand in front of the fallen oracle, weapons at the ready.

Okay. So now those people were going to die too, whoever they were, because they couldn't fight off two zombies apiece and protect a seemingly helpless woman at the same time, and no one else was going to reach them before the attack began. Not even Max.

Each footfall was a stab of fire in her side, but Edie kept running, and as she drew closer, she could actually see what was happening.

Doug stood with his tire iron raised, shoulders square, ponytail flapping in the breeze. Belinda waited at his side, brandishing a wicked-looking knife.

"Hi, friends!" Doug called cheerfully, never taking his eyes off the incoming zombies. "If we live through this, we have fresh doughnuts to share!"

Belinda's voice rang with aggravated tolerance. "Doug made me come!"

Holy shit. The counterfeiters—two of them, anyway—had decided to help. Even if that meant dying in the effort.

At their feet, Gwen occasionally twitched, her face stony and cold. It was the same expression she'd worn while prophesizing. When she'd communed with her oracular power at Sabrina and Starla's kitchen table, though, a stream of livid red blood hadn't poured from her nose, and she hadn't been seconds away from a grisly death.

Last-ditch effort time. A little surprise Edie had considered but hadn't even mentioned to Max, because it seemed too goofy and unlikely to help anyone in any way. But it might help Gwen and Doug and Belinda now, and there was absolutely nothing to lose, was there?

She sucked in the deepest breath possible as she ran through the woods, watched the zombies lurch onto their hind legs as they growled *bon appétit*, and began to scream the dumbest song ever at top volume.

Over and over again, she shouted that she was the map. Like that ridiculous anthropomorphized scroll in *Enora the Explorer*. And to her absolute shock, the zombies whipped their heads her way, their full attention captured by the familiar asinine refrain.

Whereupon Doug killed one with a single, vicious, head-separating swipe of his tire iron, while Belinda decapitated another. Max, coming up from behind, managed the final two.

Ears ringing in the sudden silence, her heartbeat echoing in her skull, Edie slowed and frantically scanned their surroundings. Nothing. Absolutely nothing that shouldn't be there, apart from flaming homes and a catatonic oracle and injured fighters and headless zombie bodies strewn on the forest floor.

"Is that all of 'em?" Kip shouted, and waited for an answer.

None came. At least, nothing audible.

After a minute, Sabrina tipped her head. "Starla says that must be the whole pack. The Girl Explorers don't see any more creatures."

A ragged cheer rose, along with a stifled sob from Sabrina.

Kip and Lorraine sprinted to Gwen's limp body, falling to their knees on either side of her. Sabrina dropped her knife, sagged against a tree trunk, and appeared to be having an intense, tear-soaked conversation entirely within the confines of her thoughts. Doug and Belinda high-fived each other and tucked away their own weapons, then began gathering Tupperware containers in their arms.

Max sheathed his sword and turned to Edie, his exhaustion evident in dark hollows beneath his blue eyes and creases lining his yellow-splattered features. "You're injured, ma puce. Let me see."

He reached for the zipper of her half-shredded coveralls.

A stray zombie burst through the trees behind him, no longer hidden by the shadowed depths of the forest, its hind legs bunched for the killing leap.

There was no time and no choice. Only instinct.

Shouldering Max out of the way with a violent shove—he stumbled to the side, caught by surprise—she dove between him and the zombie and lashed out with the cleaver, pouring all her remaining strength into the strike.

The creature's momentum drove them both into the ground, the impact bone-crushing, and she had no breath to yell. It hurt. Everything hurt. She was taking agonizing claw swipes to her sides and arms and a dozen other places, but she couldn't pinpoint precisely where, not when she was busy slashing and swinging and trying to remove that fucker's head from its motherfucking neck, because *shit*, this needed to be *over*.

Bone cracked with her final blow. Blood sprayed. And at long last—thank *fuck*—the head detached, the zombie's bloodstained teeth still snapping at her.

With a vicious kick, Max launched that head deep into the woods before dropping to her side, his eyes black as coal and hot as a furnace.

"What the *fuck* were you *thinking*?" It was a terrified, enraged bellow, the harshness of his words belying the gentleness of his hands coasting over her limbs, checking her wounds. "My gods, Edie, you're bleeding fucking *everywhere*. If you'd just told me—"

"No time. I was . . . still armed. You . . . weren't." Cautiously, she shifted the slightest bit and had to pant for a minute before she could speak again. "Nothing . . . broken, I . . . don't think. But some . . . of the . . . claws did damage."

Each breath *burned*. Gods, she needed painkillers. The good stuff.

"I know. When I tried to yank the zombie off you, its claws were so deep, they"—he gulped air—"tore . . . things." Raising his head, he shouted for Sabrina, then a first aid kit. "We're going to stabilize you here, then get you to an ER. Hold on, my Edie."

Elbowing Max out of her way, the witch thumped down onto her knees beside Edie. "How bad is it, vamp?"

"Bad." The word was curt. Ice-cold, even as his fingertips tenderly swept Edie's hair back from her forehead. "Do you have enough power for healing? Whatever you want for payment, you can have. Just fucking *fix this*."

"Since I didn't need to repair the wall or collapse an enormous building . . ." Sabrina smiled at Edie. "Time for us to hold hands, hon. Squeeze as tight as you can."

Edie did. It was hard to tell how hard she was squeezing, though, since her fingers were kind of numb. No, her hands. No, her arms.

"This is . . ." She looked up at Sabrina and tried her best to smile. The expression must have looked pretty unconvincing, because the witch actually jerked back a little, her face creased with horror. "Very . . . romantic."

"Try not to fall in love, okay?" The other woman winked as

she moved closer again, but her eyes didn't hold even a smidgen of levity. "I know I'm a better bet than that asshole vampire you've been banging, but I'm spoken for."

"Alas," Edie rasped.

Max made a choked sound. "I can see the wounds closing a bit, witch. Thank you."

Now that he mentioned it, nothing seemed to hurt much anymore. Or at least the pain was drifting farther and farther away every second. That was some first-class witchy healing, all right.

Sabrina's hand patted hers before pulling away.

"Max." It was the first time Sabrina had ever used his actual name. "Look here."

With her eyes closed, Edie couldn't quite tell where the other woman was pointing.

"I see the blood. What are you—" Max's voice cut off. "No."

"She's been bitten," Sabrina said softly. Kindly. "There's been a saliva-blood fluid exchange. We have less than ten minutes."

"Tell me how to save her." When the witch didn't answer, his volume rose, and the order rolled through the forest like thunder. "*Tell me how to save her.*"

With her thoughts so fuzzy, it took Edie a few seconds to put things together. Especially since his slow, gentle strokes through her hair felt so nice.

She was dying.

No, that wasn't quite right.

She might die, but if she didn't, they'd have to kill her. Very, very soon.

If she weren't so addled, she'd probably feel worse about that. At the moment, though, she was more worried about Max.

With an effort, she opened her eyes and made eye contact

with Sabrina. "Don't . . . have him do . . . it. Don't let . . . him see. Maybe . . . Belinda? Very . . . pragmatic."

"No," Max gritted out, his voice shaking. "Edie—"

She redirected her attention his way. "Don't . . . tell me . . . would have been . . . fine . . . this time. I saved . . . your ass."

"I was focused on you and not paying enough fucking attention to my surroundings. Again." Ducking down, he leaned his forehead against hers. "I had no weapon. You saved me. Without you, I'd probably . . ."

His breath hitched, and his words trailed to a halt.

He'd probably be in the same position she was now. Or headless.

"Yay . . . me," she whispered. "You . . . protected. Killed . . . for me. My turn . . . to protect . . . you. Save . . . someone . . . I love. Finally."

Cool wetness dripped down onto her temples, her cheeks. Her chin. She closed her eyes again, savoring her last moments with Max. Because they were out of choices now. There was only one solution to this problem.

"I do . . . love you. So much." Her lips had gone numb too. She hoped she wasn't drooling. "Do it . . . now. Before . . . change."

There was a long pause, as if he were conducting a silent conversation with someone.

A cold, round object pressed into her palm, and he closed her hand around it. "Hold on to this for a minute, my Edie. When you're better, we're going to have a long talk about you giving it back to me against my express orders."

Her eyelids were so heavy, but she raised them. Simply to see the adoration in his faded-denim eyes one final time.

There it was. All the love he couldn't put into words.

Vamp boy looked absolutely terrible. Filthy and terrified and far more ancient than a mere twentysomething. Also beautiful.

So very beautiful.

The faint scent of citrus and warm spice broke through the miasma of death and blood all around her, and a flood of warmth pushed aside some of her numbness. His pomander. He'd given her his mother's good luck charm to hold, filled with Edie's orange-clove soap.

"Don't you dare give up, human." He brushed a kiss she couldn't feel across her mouth, then stood and confronted Sabrina. "Your wife says there's a solution if I'm willing. I am. Do it, witch. Now."

Gods, Edie was getting so hungry. Why the fuck wasn't anyone feeding her? Did she need to go hunt down some sustenance and feed herself? Because honestly, she felt strong enough to do it. Like she could run a fucking *marathon*.

Kip suddenly appeared at her side.

"Forgive me." Squatting down, he tucked a strand of hair behind her ear. Then she felt pressure on her wrists. Her ankles too. "We wouldn't restrain you if we didn't have to, Edes-a-lot. Whatever you're feeling, can you try to push it back? Your mini-vamp would be *hella* grateful."

In her vicinity, other conversations were happening. Doug and Belinda, the former crying as the latter worked her knife on a strop and bit her lower lip until it bled. Max and Sabrina, arguing about . . . something. Steep sacrifices, and a life for a life, and how little time they had left. But it was hard to focus on those other discussions when Edie was doing her best to shove down the weird alien-feeling rage cramping in her belly.

Belinda looked over at Kip, nodded, and began to walk slowly toward Edie.

But—hey. Who was that other woman? The one Edie had never seen before?

She was pretty. Round and soft-looking. Clad in cozy pajamas, with long brown hair pulled into a rumpled ponytail. Gracefully, she sat on her heels and smiled at Edie.

Why did no one else seem to notice the stranger?

"Sorry about the pajamas." Her voice was warm. Sweet. It rang inside Edie's head, which was odd. "It's late, and I was sleeping when I got the call."

"No worries," Edie told her as the rage began to feel more distant. "Those look very comfy. I like the polka dots."

The woman laid a gentle hand on Edie's shoulder. "Thank you. Listen, Edie. I know what Kip just told you, but it's okay. If you don't want to fight anymore, you don't have to."

Wait. Wait a minute.

"Are you a reaper?" Edie blinked up at her. "You aren't a surly European dude in a sheepskin thong?"

"Why would . . ." With a little shake of her head, the woman dismissed that tangent. "Yes. I'm a reaper."

"Hey!" Edie brightened. "If I go with you, will I see my parents again?"

The reaper's hand burned into Edie's shoulder, but in the best possible way. "Maybe. You can't know until you go."

"I want to hug them again. Hear their voices." Edie's nose crinkled as she thought it over. "But I think I want to stay alive more."

"That's fine." The proclamation didn't seem to bother the other woman. "For now."

Wow. The reaper's phrasing . . . "Is that a threat?"

"Of course not." Violet eyes. The woman had actual *violet eyes*, like all those spunky kidnapped virgins in old-school romance novels. "I haven't hurt you, Edie, and I won't. I'm just here to keep you company on your trip. When I said *for now*, I meant you might not have a choice much longer, and neither will I."

Belinda was standing over them, her knife orange-tipped in the firelight.

"It's getting harder to hold her." Kip's voice had turned hoarse. "I don't . . ."

"Move aside. *Move*."

That familiar voice of arrogant command washed over Edie, and she tried to beam happily up at Max as he strode toward her. She wasn't sure her face was listening, though. It seemed to be snarling, not smiling.

Then he was stretching out on the ground next to her, tugging her into his arms, and embracing her so tightly she could feel it even through the odd numbness.

"Forgive me, ma puce," he murmured. "You're going to hate this. But it's what I wanted, and it's far preferable to living without you."

"Skip the sweet nothings," Sabrina snapped, because apparently she was here again too? Interesting. "There's no time. Are you absolutely certain, vamp?"

"I'm certain." He pressed a kiss to Edie's temple. "Your survival gives my death all the meaning it requires, my Edie. If you wallow in guilt or consecrate your life to my memory, I swear I'll figure out how to become a ghost and fucking haunt you. Don't test me, human."

"Max—" Sabrina sounded desperate.

"Do it, witch," he told her, and hitched Edie closer. "Now."

I hope I have the power for this," the witch muttered, and then everything got . . . weird.

Well, weirder.

Against Edie, Max abruptly turned stiff enough to snap a tendon, then jerked convulsively, as if he'd been struck by lightning. But it wasn't even a cloudy night, so that didn't make sense.

As he twitched and spasmed—was he okay?—the rage and clawing hunger in Edie's belly faded, and faded some more, until it was entirely absent. Which was a relief, yes, but also odd and unexplainable.

At long last, Max finally relaxed again, his body limp. Good. He could use some rest after the long evening they'd all had.

Why everyone seemed to be crying, even Sabrina, Edie had absolutely no idea.

The reaper stood, smoothing out her pajamas. "Goodbye, Edie. I've been called to a different job, and I need to leave. I may or may not see you again, but if I do, I hope it's not soon."

And that was another odd thing.

Was Edie not dying anymore? And if she wasn't, why not?

"But . . ." As Edie's thoughts began to clear, sheer horror stopped her breath. "What the hells did he . . ."

No. No, he couldn't have. He couldn't have done this to her.

"Wait." Desperately, she clutched at the hem of the reaper's pajama pants. "Please tell me your next job isn't Max."

The woman's smile was sad. "I can't say. I'm sorry."

Then the reaper vanished, and Edie seemed to be sobbing uncontrollably in Kip's enormous, comforting arms, because she was back to herself again, not a zombie-in-progress or even especially injured, and she knew exactly what had just happened.

The person who loved her most in all the world had saved her. Had died for her.

He'd traded his life for hers, the same way her parents had, and she wasn't certain she could survive it again.

Oh, honey, came Starla's voice in her head, and Edie jerked in surprise. *It's okay.*

But it wasn't. They were doing something to his . . . to his body. Behind her. And she should watch, should help, should hold him one last time, but she couldn't seem to slow the heaving gasps of grief that made her cough and shudder and curl in on herself.

"Don't cry." Sabrina's voice cut through Edie's sobs, its sharp wryness a cruelty. "I know it's disappointing that he's still around, but calm yourself."

Choking on her own tears, Edie pushed away from Kip. "Wh-what?"

The witch rubbed trembling fingertips across her forehead, even as she smiled. "None of us knew this, but apparently giving up immortality is the equivalent of sacrificing a life."

Probably because he gave up infinite mortal lifetimes, Starla murmured, and Edie twitched again at the brain-tickling sensation. *Which is all very dramatic. I imagine he'll get a lot of mileage out of that.*

"Is he . . ." Slowly, hope was pushing back Edie's despair, and she struggled to make sense of what was happening. "Sabrina, is he . . ."

She couldn't look for herself. Not until she knew for certain.

"He's alive but no longer immortal," Sabrina told her, "which means he'll eventually be the first-ever vampire with wrinkles and creaky joints and age spots. I'm really excited to watch that happen."

"Bite your tongue, witch." A pair of strong hands hauled Edie into a crushing embrace, and those were definitely Max's hands. That was definitely Max's face buried in her neck, his self-satisfied voice vibrating into her skin, and his body so hard and fierce and . . . hot? . . . behind hers. "As if I've never heard of retinol and Botox."

He carefully, tenderly turned her in his arms.

Frantic and fumbling, she unzipped his hoodie, shoved his tee out of the way, and scrabbled for bare skin. Her head butted against him as she dived down, searching for inarguable proof that she wasn't imagining this. That he wasn't gone.

Thump-thump. Thump-thump. Thump-thump.

There it was. His heartbeat pounding against her ear.

It was still strong and steady, but significantly faster now. And that wasn't the only change.

"You're warm," she breathed, then sniffled loudly. "And you tried to sacrifice yourself for me, you total asshole."

In revenge, she rubbed her dripping nose back and forth on his skin.

"Technically, I did sacrifice myself for you. Endless lifetimes, gone." His chest rumbled with his words. "I intend to hold this over you forever, darling."

The implications of what he'd done to himself seeped into the puddle of utter joy and relief she'd become, and suddenly her face was crumpling again.

He wasn't dead, thank heavens. But he would be, untold centuries earlier than necessary. Because of her.

"I'm—I'm so s-sorry." She tried to pull away, to raise her knees and hunch her shoulders and become a miserable human ball, but his gentle hands kept patiently uncurling her, and he was still so *strong*. "Max, you shouldn't have—"

"None of that, please." His thumb nudged her chin. "Edie, my darling. I need to see those sweet eyes of yours again. Won't you look at me?"

Sniffing uncontrollably, she mustered her courage, lifted her head, and met his gaze.

Faded denim, without a hint of darkness. Warm. Soft.

There was no anger there. No regret. Nothing but open adoration and a relief all-encompassing enough to match her own.

"There you are," he murmured. "Such pretty brown doe eyes. Good. All that red didn't suit you nearly as well, beloved. Now let's take a look at your neck . . ."

"As if it never happened." Sabrina sighed, then clambered to her feet with a groan. "I am so fucking tired. If I needed to light a godsdamn candle, I don't think I'd have the juice to do it."

After planting a kiss on the spot where Edie had apparently been bitten, he looked up at the witch. "Thank you, Sabrina. I owe you, and I have an excellent idea for how I can repay that debt."

"We'll talk later. Starla told everyone to give you two some privacy, including me." She offered him a faint smile. "Besides, I need some time with my wife too."

"And that's precisely what we'll be discussing," he said, and her smile widened. "Find me when you're ready."

"I'm sorry," Edie repeated as soon as he returned his attention to her. "I can't even—"

His big, warm hands cupped her face. "Sweet Edie, this is nothing. I would have gladly died for you. And here I am, *living* with you, having given up nothing but endless centuries of isolation and an unmourned, detached death. This is an ending happier than any I could have envisioned, and I shouldn't have teased you about it."

For such a cynical vampire, that perspective positively *radiated* optimism.

Naturally, she was suspicious. "Truly?"

"Truly." The tip of his nose nudged hers. "I want nothing more than this. Nothing more than you. You're mine, ma puce. Mine to protect. Mine to keep and cherish as long as I draw breath on this earth, and possibly after that too, if I have my way."

"Hmmm." Tenderly, she kissed the corner of his mouth. "Yours to love?"

She didn't *need* the words, not when his actions spoke so clearly. But hearing it aloud would still be nice.

"It's been centuries, Edie. I don't remember what love feels like." After his thumb slid across her cheek one last time, he stretched to retrieve something from the ground behind him. His mother's pomander, which he pressed into Edie's palm. Then he covered her hand with his, closing her fingers more tightly around the silver sphere. "But all of me is yours. Every atom. Every thought and hope and desire. And if I'm entirely yours, that must include my heart, no?"

Strong emotion had brought out the slightest hint of an accent, and she adored it. Adored him.

She grinned at him. "I'll take that as a yes."

"Also, no one can exist as long as I have without doing the occasional favor. I have several extremely powerful creatures in my debt." He nuzzled her temple as he spoke, sounding very smug. "So fear not, darling. You may yet get to bask in my glory for centuries to come."

"What does *that* mean?" Propping herself up on her elbow sounded like a good idea until she actually did it, promptly became dizzy, and dropped down onto his chest again. "And precisely how long *have* you existed?"

He snorted, stroking a broad palm up and down her back. "Nice try. But I'm not telling you how old I am."

"You're so vain."

"For good reason." His muscles flexed beneath her, because he was a freaking show-off. "I'm perfection made flesh."

Her fake retching sounds were quite convincing, if she did say so herself. And she did.

He added breezily, "I'm getting immortality for both of us, because I have no intention of getting wrinkled and withered, and I need you around to admire me. Forever."

Okay. That was a discussion they could pursue later. Right now, her priority was puncturing that ginormous ego of his.

She kept her voice to a whisper, because their private bubble would pop soon enough. "No . . . one's . . ."

When he covered her mouth with his in a sweetly ravenous kiss, she simply waited him out. As soon as his head lifted and she could think again, the song restarted.

"No one's vain like Gaston—"

"This is not new information, human. In fact, mere moments ago—"

"—lacks all shame like Gaston!"

"Shame requires a sense of wrongdoing, and since I've never done anything wrong—"

"No one brags about how much you came like Gaston!"

Arching his brows, he held up six fingers.

She held up four, doing her damnedest to exude discontent and sexual frustration. "In his hand-knotted briefs he's so—"

"Wait," Kip interjected. "What's this about hand-knotted briefs?"

Max sighed. "Dammit, Edie."

GWEN'S HEAD HURT like a mofo.

Two people were quietly talking nearby—including one with a deep, rumbly voice—and she wished they'd stop, because each word was a vicious spike hammered into her poor beleaguered skull. For that matter, she wished she could open her eyes or move or do anything but lie on . . . whatever she was lying on . . . and involuntarily eavesdrop on what seemed to be a very private discussion.

"We handled the pit, so the entire pack is dead," the woman said flatly. "No more zombies. What's next?"

Mr. Rumbly Voice sounded extremely determined. Also

extremely homicidal. "Next, I'll find whoever's responsible for this clusterfuck—"

"Cluster of *unfortunateness*, as Edie always says," his companion chided. "Remember, the Girl Explorers are nearby."

There was an aggrieved sigh. "Fine, witch. Let me rephrase. Once I find whoever's responsible for nearly killing my Edie, I will track that fucker—"

A vigorous throat-clearing produced no noticeable reaction.

"—down and bring them to you. Alive." When he spoke again, he sounded very pleased with himself. "Temporarily, anyway."

"You're giving me someone to . . ."

That was definitely Sabby speaking to Max. But what in the world were the two of them—

"Sacrifice. Yes. Their life for your wife's. Because they've earned their death, and Starla deserves to live."

Whoa. That was kind of—

"I'm in." Gwen's friend hadn't even hesitated.

"Although the exchange healed Edie, she's still quite weak. But as soon as she regains her strength, I'll begin the hunt." He paused. "I'll also buy her a Pottery Barn couch."

A moment of silence.

"What the hells does Pottery Barn have to do with—" Sabby began, echoing Gwen's own thoughts.

"After we've executed our agreement, I'll be calling in favors on a different matter as well," he continued, ignoring the attempted interruption. "I intend to regain my immortality and offer it to my beloved. Since you saved her life, I would gladly offer the same to you and your wife. As a gesture of my . . ." He cleared his throat. "Heartfelt gratitude."

"Saying that to me hurt you, didn't it?"

"Correct."

"Good." Sabrina made a thoughtful humming noise. "It's an incredibly generous offer, Max, but I'm not sure immortality is something either of us wants. A single healthy lifetime together is enough for me. I'll talk to Starla, though, and find out what she thinks."

He was offering *immortality*. Double whoa.

Clearly, Gwen needed to be hanging out with more vampires. Only, that would involve actually hanging out with vampires. Who were generally terrifying and total dicks, so . . .

"Fair enough," he said. "Let me know."

Leaves rustled in the wintry breeze, and Sabrina's teeth had begun to audibly chatter. "Who are you going to talk to about the breach and the fae?"

The breach. The fae.

Without warning, the memory of her vision exploded to life in Gwen's throbbing brain, replaying behind her eyelids and echoing in her ears. Protectively, she wrapped her arms around her belly and trembled at what she saw and heard and all its terrifying implications.

For more than two decades, she'd wanted to be a different sort of oracle. One whose predictions would hold grave importance and not focus, inevitably, on piddling shit.

But if these were the horrors powerful oracles saw?

More piddling shit, please. Piddling shit *forever*.

By the time Gwen gathered herself again, Max was already answering Sabrina's question. "—been considering my various contacts on SERC and in the human government too. I think—"

"No!" Gwen shouted, pushing herself up on a shaking arm. "You can't—"

"Hey, hey, hey. Gwen, honey, I've healed you as best I can, and as far as I can tell, the baby's fine, but please don't . . ." Sabrina strode over and dropped to her knees beside Gwen. "Let me help you back down until we figure out what happened to you, okay?"

Down apparently meant *onto a very large pile of leaves*, which was serving as a makeshift mattress. The work of the Girl Explorers, Gwen presumed.

Lorraine came racing toward them. "Careful, bro! You were bleeding from your nose, and you passed out for a good while, so you can't just—"

"You have to *listen*. I collapsed because of a vision. A huge one." Gwen looked beseechingly up at Max, who was definitely a terrifying dick vampire but had also been nice to her, and when he came closer, she grabbed both of his hands and shook them for emphasis. "There was a massacre. Endless piles of bodies. Supernaturals. Enhanced humans. All dead. *All* of them."

"Gwennie . . ." Sabby spoke gently. "You've never seen anything like that before in your visions. Are you sure it's not . . . I don't know. A trauma response?"

Gwen shook her head frantically and almost vomited at the jostling agony. "No. I swear to you, it's real. It's a genuine vision, and oh fuck, it's *cataclysmic*."

"We believe you, little oracle." Max freed his hands, squatted beside her leaf pile, and helped support her with a strong arm across her back. "Can telling us about it wait until you've rested more?"

"You need to know now." She swallowed down the acid creeping up the back of her throat. "There's no time to waste."

"Okay." He didn't seem entirely happy with that answer, but he didn't argue. "Did you see what caused the massacre? Was it the fae, or warfare between humans and Supernaturals, or . . . ?"

"It was the fae," Gwen whispered. "But not only the fae."

His brows drew together. "Who else?"

When he handed her a bottle of water, she only managed a single swallow before nausea twisted in her belly. "Common humans in uniform. They were working together with the fae. Using fae powers and military weaponry to slaughter . . . everyone else."

"Holy fuck," Sabrina whispered.

Max's mouth tightened. "Holy *unfortunateness.*"

Sabby kicked his shin, and Gwen couldn't blame her.

"Even if we found someone in the human government who was discreet, strategic, and powerful enough to take action, I don't know how we could possibly trust that person not to be part of whatever conspiracy Gwen witnessed." Lorraine leaned against the nearest tree and rubbed her eyes. "We don't know enough about it to eliminate anyone, and if we went to the wrong official, the information would go nowhere."

Sabby pinched her temples between her thumb and forefinger. "And our lives would be forfeit."

"So that leaves SERC," Max said.

"Yeah." Poor Lorraine. Maybe she hadn't been snacking sufficiently, because even her bright red hair seemed limp and exhausted. "We need a SERC rep who fulfills a *very* long list of requirements."

"A councillor who's discreet, strategic, powerful enough to

take decisive action, unbeholden to the fae *and* the human government, and also willing to believe Gwen's prophecy." Max met her stare, his blue eyes kind but unflinchingly honest. "I imagine that last bit's going to pose a problem, little oracle."

Her breath hitched. "You know what happened? When I was eighteen?"

"Yes."

Her stomach churned harder at the confirmation, even though there'd been no judgment in his tone. "Then you know how hard it'll be to find a councillor fitting that description."

"I don't know of such a paragon." His head tipped to the side as he studied her. "But I get the sense that perhaps you do."

Yes. She did. Unfortunately.

Too bad she'd rather gargle razor blades than ever see him again.

"I know someone," Gwen said, surrendering to the inevitable. "He's all the things you want. If I tell him what I saw, he might even believe me."

Fresh hope dawned in the expressions of everyone but Max, who simply waited patiently for the rest of it.

She sighed. "And he's a real pain in the ass."

"Paragons usually are," Max said, and patted her arm consolingly. "I mean, just look at me."

When she vomited all over his expensive leather hoodie, it was exactly what he deserved.

ACKNOWLEDGMENTS

Drafting this book was absurdly fun, and that's entirely due to the company I kept while writing, so thank you to Kat Latham and Emma Barry, from the bottom of my heart. Both of you also looked over the draft and made very wise suggestions, and I am so grateful for that as well.

My agent extraordinaire, Sarah Younger, deserves enormous credit for a million reasons: her general excellence as an agent and human being; her incredibly hard work on behalf of me and all her authors; the time and care she devoted to this particular project (including while on vacation!); and so much more. But she deserves *extra* credit for the moment she heard me propose writing a zombie romance and promptly told me to do it, without even a moment's hesitation—partly because she knew my brain (*braaaaaaain*) needed a random fun project, but mostly because she believed in me and my work. *Thank you*.

From the moment I met Kate Seaver and Amanda Maurer, I knew I'd love working with them. But I had no idea just how *much* I'd love it! My editors' kindness, thoughtfulness, enthusiasm, humor, and creativity have made the entire publication process a true joy, and I'm thrilled that we're a team on this ongoing project. I am so very grateful to you and for you. ♥

The rest of my team at Berkley has been absolutely amazing as well: supportive, inventive, detail-oriented, and so very smart. Thank you for all your time and work on my behalf, and thank you for always making me feel valued. The book's launch felt like a committed group effort from day one, and I can't tell you how happy that makes me.

I want to specifically acknowledge everyone who was part of that group effort, and this is my best attempt at doing so:

Kate Seaver and Amanda Maurer, editors
Abby Graves, copyeditor
Michele Suchomel-Casey, proofreader
Stacy Edwards, production editor
Jenni Surasky, interior designer
Anika Bates, marketer
Kristin Cipolla, publicist

Thank you, thank you, *thank you* to all of you.

Leni Kauffman slayed this cover like it was a brain-starved zombie, just as she always does. I'm so thrilled to be working with you again, my absurdly talented friend, and I remain amazed at how you manage to create such gorgeous, note-perfect cover illustrations *every single time*.

And finally: My family's pride in my work and love for me fill my heart to bursting. Thank you for all your goofiness and affection, as well as the way you make me feel supported and appreciated, always. I love you so very much.

ZOM ROMCOM

OLIVIA ♥ DADE

READERS GUIDE

EXTREMELY SERIOUS AND IMPORTANT DISCUSSION QUESTIONS

1. Under what circumstances is eating a cold burrito acceptable, even after it's been used to swat a zombie's snout? If you were designing a burrito as a zombie-fighting weapon, what toppings would you choose?

2. What other processed foods of mysterious provenance should Edie eat ostentatiously in front of Max? Which do you think would upset him the most? Does your list include Honey Bunches of Indeterminate Grain-Adjacent Food Pellets? Why or why not?

3. Would you rather wear macramé bikini briefs or a sheepskin thong? Which one would result in the most intractable and chafing wedgie?

4. What other lazy deployments of French stereotypes could Olivia Dade have included when discussing *Enora the Explorer*, in addition to evil mimes? Should Enora have been wearing a beret and carting a baguette with her on her adventures?

Should all her quests have involved adding butter and heavy cream to various sauces? Why or why not?

5. If you were dedicating your own version of the Gaston song to Max, which grassland creature would you have him ostensibly fellating and why?

6. Should Dade have resisted the urge to make an Edward Cullen reference in her vampire romance, despite the vast temptation she was experiencing as she wrote? If so, how? No, really, please tell her how, because she clearly wasn't capable of the feat.

7. If he weren't counterfeiting money in an abandoned mall, what would Doug be doing for a living? Which secrets would he readily share about that job? And whatever work he might choose, how can we protect him at all costs?

8. Is there such a thing as too many orgasms? Why or why not? If someone gave you six orgasms and was unbearably smug about it, would you be willing to acknowledge all of them?

9. At which abandoned store in an old mall would you most like to be given an orgasm? If it isn't the Gap, so you can snicker and say "C'mon, fall into *my* gap" to your partner(s), why not?

Stay tuned for the second book in Olivia Dade's Super-natural Entanglements' series, which throws together a down-on-her-luck oracle named Gwen and a starchy half-demon named Hugh, as they work to unravel a worldwide conspiracy. Their story picks up immediately after *Zomromcom* ends and includes death-defying adventures, steamy romance, and a whole lot of cheese. SO! MUCH! CHEESE!

Lifelong nerd **Olivia Dade** has held various rewarding jobs over the years—librarian, high school teacher, Colonial Williamsburg interpreter—but is thrilled to have finally achieved her ultimate goal of wearing pajamas all day as a hermit-like writer and enthusiastic hag. She currently lives outside Stockholm with her delightful family and their ever-burgeoning collection of books.

Ready to find
your next great read?

Let us help.

Visit prh.com/nextread

Penguin
Random
House